THE GHOST WOODS

C.J. COOKE

HarperCollins*Publishers*

HarperCollins*Publishers* Ltd
1 London Bridge Street,
London SE1 9GF

www.harpercollins.co.uk

HarperCollins*Publishers*
Macken House,
39/40 Mayor Street Upper,
Dublin 1
D01 C9W8

First published by HarperCollins*Publishers* 2022
This edition published 2023
1

A catalogue record for this book is available from the British Library

ISBN: 978-0-00-851594-2

Set in Sabon LT Std by Palimpsest Book Production Ltd,
Falkirk, Stirlingshire

Printed and bound in the UK using 100% Renewable
Electricity by CPI Group (UK) Ltd

This book is produced from independently certified FSC™ paper
to ensure responsible forest management.

For more information visit: www.harpercollins.co.uk/green

For my daughters,
Melody,
Summer,
And Willow

and for all the women and children
who passed through
Scotland's mother and baby homes

In a minute or two the Caterpillar [. . .] crawled away into the grass, merely remarking as it went, 'One side will make you grow taller, and the other side will make you grow shorter.'

'One side of WHAT? The other side of WHAT?' thought Alice to herself.

'Of the mushroom,' said the Caterpillar.

Lewis Carroll, *Alice's Adventures in Wonderland* (1865)

He wha tills the fairies' green
Nah luck again shal hae;
And he wha spills the fairies' ring
Betide him want and wae.

Traditional Scottish Rhyme

'You're going to kill me,' he says with a whimper. 'You want me to burn in the fire.'

His words land like blows. I look over his sweet face, at his soft brown eyes that hold no guile. Why would he say such a thing?

'Do you know why?' I whisper. The words are hard to say.

'Because of what I am.'

I reach out and take his hand in mine. 'I would never, ever hurt you,' I say gently.

A shadow falls across his face.

'But you will.'

Just five years old, filled with such terrible knowledge.

My son.

It is said the daughter of the richest hall in the Scottish Borders liked to read in the ancient wood nearby, where the trees were so old their trunks had whitened and their branches were gnarled and crooked.

One day, the girl fell asleep on the forest floor, and as she slept, she dreamt she was visited by a malign and hideous creature, old as time and twisted as a vine, dripping in thick black slime. This was the witch, Nicnevin, Scotland's Hecate, in one of her many forms.

When the girl woke, she raced home and dared not visit the forest for many months.

Nine moons later the girl delivered a baby, despite swearing she had lain with no man. The doctor who attended took one look at the child and fled. While the child had a cherubic human face, long fibrous roots extended from its fingers, toes, and navel, its ears were budding twigs, and the crown of its head was what appeared to be the spongy cap of a mushroom.

The parents would not allow such a creature to live, and it is said that Nicnevin cast a spell on each of them, possessing their minds until they hated each other, or took their own lives out of confusion and misery. The family was forever cursed for their cruel act.

But the witch would not let the hall go to waste. The hall, Nicnevin decided, would be reclaimed as her kingdom, a palace of rot and ruin.

Hence the name, Lichen Hall.

'The History of Lichen Hall', footnote xi, *The Magical World of Fungi*, A.E. Llewellyn (1937)

Then

Mabel

Dundee, Scotland, May 1959

I have a ghost in my knee. There's a small pocket just behind the kneecap and she's hiding in there, all tucked up in the soft mattress of cartilage. She's very small and terrified, so I'm sitting with that leg slightly straightened so I don't disturb her. I've not said a word about this to anyone. They'd think I'm mad.

'Mabel? Are you listening?'

Ma's eyes are wide, as if she's trying to wake herself up, but her hands tell a different story. She's holding on to the strap of her handbag, knuckles white, as though we're on a fairground ride.

'Did you hear what Dr McCann just said?'

I nod, but I didn't hear, not really. I'm always doing this – sliding off into a daydream. I look over the file on the desk beside us. I can see my name. Mabel Anne Haggith. Date of birth 12 March 1942, ninety-eight pounds, five foot two. Dr McCann peers down his spectacles, his fat red fingers laced together like a sea creature. The air in the room pulses with the sense that I've done something wrong.

'When was the date of your last menstrual period, Miss Haggith?' he asks.

'I'm not sure.' Embarrassment hits me like a slap. Nobody has ever asked me that before. It's a private thing.

'Do try and recall,' he says wearily. Ma nudges me as though I'm being rude.

'My . . . my monthlies have always been irregular,' I stammer.

'I only need to know about one menses, Miss Haggith.' Dr McCann sighs. 'The last one.'

'Just before Christmas,' I say, remembering how the ground seemed to tilt that morning in the bakery when I was putting in the first batch of mince pies. A strong twist in my groin, and I knew what was happening. Unlike now.

Dr McCann scribbles something down before flipping through the calendar on his desk. More scribbling, and muttering. The ghost in my knee gives a cough.

'Five months,' Dr McCann announces suddenly. 'Which suggests a due date around the end of September.' He licks his finger and thumb and plucks a leaflet from a pile on his desk. 'Here,' he says, passing it to Ma. 'I expect you'll wish to make enquiries as soon as you can.'

Ma takes the leaflet with a sob. The ghost is restless, unable to sleep now. I rub my kneecap furiously until Ma pulls my hand away, irritated.

'Who was it?' she snaps, her eyes flashing. 'Was it that awful boy, Jack?'

'Jack?' I say, frowning. 'I don't understand. What's wrong with me? Am I dying?'

'Dying?' Dr McCann starts to laugh. 'Come on, Mabel. You're seventeen. You're not a child.'

'. . . would have thought you'd keep your legs crossed,' Ma hisses, angry tears wobbling in her eyes. 'And that dirty, disgusting boy. I knew it would come to this. I *knew* it.'

It's only when I see the title of the leaflet that it dawns on me, a slow realization like creeping fingers along my neck. *St Luke's mother and baby home*. The front of the leaflet bears a picture of a woman sitting in bed, a man and woman beside her. They're all smiling, and she's handing a baby to them. A subheading reads, *Adoption is the best option for unwed mothers.*

They think I'm expecting a baby. That's what this is.

'I'm not having a baby,' I protest loudly, and I almost go to tell them about the ghosts that sometimes sleep in my lungs or hide in my gums, and that maybe there's a ghost in my womb and they've mistaken it for a baby. But instead, I say, 'I'm a virgin,' which causes Dr McCann to splutter into a laugh. But it's true – I *am* a virgin. I've never had sex, not even the type you do with your hands.

Dr McCann looks at Ma, whose face is tight, lips pursed. A fact I heard once drifts into my mind – the average person tells one or two lies a day, but is lied to up to *two hundred* times a day. I know I've told the truth. So is Dr McCann lying?

My stepdad Richard is waiting for us in the car when we go outside. 'Everything OK?' he asks Ma, and she presses her face into his chest as though we've just fled a war.

He narrows his eyes and looks from her to me. 'What did you do?' he says.

I keep my knee straight for the ghost, but she's moved. I can feel her in my tummy now, dancing.

'It's that Jack,' Ma whispers, stricken. 'He's got Mabel in trouble.'

Jack's my friend from two doors down. We've been seeing each other, but we've never gone further than kissing. 'It's not Jack!' I say, afraid that she's going to pin blame on him when he's innocent.

'Mother of God,' she hisses, crossing herself. 'There's a squadron of potential fathers.'

Richard stares at me, his face darkening. My heart flutters in my chest. I don't know what I've done wrong.

We pull off for home. Our house is a four-storey terrace on Rotten Row. There are nine bedrooms, seven of which are usually occupied by strangers. We've lived there my whole life, but it's only been a guest house since Da died ten years ago. It's how Ma met Richard. He came to stay six years ago and never left.

We stop outside Mr McGregor's butcher's shop. Richard winds down the window and the smell wafting from the shop door is like an open crypt. I scramble for the door handle, certain I'm about to be sick.

Adoption is the best option for unwed mothers.

'You can go for the mince, Mabel,' Ma says, handing me some coins. 'A quarter pound and not half an ounce more, do you hear? On you go.'

I press the lapel of my coat to my nose and walk into the butcher's. An inch of sawdust carpets the floor, plucked chickens are strung up by their necks, and a row of dead pigs hang upside down along the back wall.

Mr McGregor's son Rory is working today. He's a little older than me, and he's deaf. When Rory's working, they use a notepad and a pencil for the customers to write down what they want. Sometimes Rory writes back little messages, like 'nice day for a BBQ!' or 'you're looking well today, Mrs Haggith!'

What was I to order again? A dead chicken? When I reach the top of the queue, Rory has been replaced by an older man I've never seen before. He must work for Mr McGregor because he's wearing a bloodstained striped apron and he's wiping his hands on a towel and staring at me. He has a tattoo on the side of his face. A spider's web.

'What'll it be?' he says. 'Got a great deal on pork sausages today. A pound for ten pence.'

I'm still too deep in my body to speak to him. I pick up the notepad and pencil.

Chicken, was it?

I take a fresh page on the notepad and write, but the words don't make sense. They say:

There's a man in the car with a knife to my ma's neck. He'll kill her if you don't give me everything in the till.

I hand the note to the man with the spider's web tattoo. He looks up at me with a look of wild confusion, and suddenly I'm relieved because he's every bit as green about the gills as I feel after what happened in Dr McCann's office. Why did I write that? One of the ghosts must have written it. I can feel one of them lengthening along the bone of my index finger, fidgeting.

The shop is empty. The man glances again at Richard's car parked outside, and whatever he sees must convince him because he makes a quick dash for the till and starts stuffing handfuls of money into a plastic bag. He hands it to me with a grim nod, the bag full of coins and notes swinging in the foul stench of the dead things. I find my arm lifting, my fingers unfolding from my palm, the bag jangling in my hand, my feet turning and cutting a fresh path through the sawdust. And then I'm outside, and I get into the car and hold on to the bag of money. I'm not sure what's going on.

'Pass me the mince,' Ma says, snapping her fingers at me. 'And the receipt. He better not have overcharged you. Always adding on a few more ounces than I asked for, that McGregor.'

I hand her the bag. She opens it and stares down at the cash. There's a moment of complete silence, when all the ghosts inside me are still and Ma's too bewildered to say anything at all. But it doesn't last. She turns sharply and stares at me in alarm.

'Mabel?' she says.

I

Now

Pearl

Scottish Borders, Scotland, September 1965

1

This place is in the middle of goddam bloody nowhere. It's getting dark, and I swear my bladder is going to explode if I don't pee in the next two minutes.

'Do you think we could pull over?' I ask Mr Peterson. He's the Church of England's Moral Welfare Officer.

'Oh no, is it that time?' he says, tearing his eyes from the road to glance at me with horror. 'Do we need to find you a hospital?'

'What? No!' I say. 'I'm not in labour. I just need to empty my bladder.'

The car wobbles slightly as Mr Peterson decides what to do with this information. He flicks the indicator – a pointless act, given that we're the only car for miles – and slams the brakes on, pulling to the side of the road in a cloud of gravel dust.

I burst out of the car and scramble through the bushes at the roadside, arranging my heavily pregnant body before squatting down with relief. It's only when I'm finished that I realize I'm ankle-deep in a bog, and my attempts to yank my feet free of the sucking mud flicks up enough of it to ruin the expensive dress my mother bought for me to impress the Whitlocks. Fat chance they'll be anything but disgusted now.

'Oh dear. Did you have a fall?' Mr Peterson asks when I return to the car. I had to reach into the bog to retrieve one of my shoes, so am now sleeved and socked in black slime. He produces a handkerchief from his breast pocket, and I use it to scrub off the worst of it, but the smell makes me gag.

'Let's go, shall we?' I say.

'Right.' He clears his throat and turns the radio on before heading back to the road. The Beatles' 'I Want To Hold Your Hand' comes on, and he moves a hand from the wheel to change the station.

'Oh, can you not?' I say. 'I love the Beatles.'

He's miffed, but leaves the radio as it is.

'I went to see them, you know,' I tell him. 'Last April. When they came to Edinburgh.'

'Did they?' he says, and I laugh. As if anyone on the planet didn't know this.

'I signed the original petition to get them to come to Scotland.'

'You must be quite the fan,' he says.

I tell him how Lucy, Sebastian, and I camped out for two nights on Bread Street to get tickets. It was freezing cold, a long row of sleeping bags huddled together on the pavements, but I never laughed so much in my life. And then, the night of the concert, the sight of the four of them on the small stage of the ABC Cinema, all in grey suits. When they played 'I Want To Hold Your Hand', you could barely hear them for the hysteria. Everyone around us immediately burst into tears, even Sebastian. It feels like a hundred years ago that we did that.

'I'm more of a Glen Miller man myself,' Mr Peterson says, and he gives into the urge to flip the station to the eight o'clock BBC News.

I wonder how often he makes this trip, driving knocked-up girls to mother and baby homes – although the place we're headed to *isn't* a mother and baby home, per se. It's a residential home. Lichen Hall, a sprawling sixteenth-century manor house owned by the Whitlock family, who lovingly take in girls like me on occasion to spare them the indignity of entering an institution. I'm grateful for this, really I am. But I'm so anxious I've broken out in hives. Lichen Hall is situated on the Scottish Borders, half an hour from the little fishing village of St Abbs – or, like I said, in the middle of goddam nowhere. What am I going to do all day? I should have asked if they have a record player, or, at the very least, a television. I'm used to being busy, up at five to start my shift at the hospital, then straight out to dinner or a nightclub with friends.

'I don't suppose you know if this place has a television?' I ask Mr Peterson.

'I'm afraid I don't.'

'They'll have a phone, won't they? I'll be able to ring my family?'

'You didn't find that out before you agreed to stay?'

Truth be told, I was too ashamed to do anything other than resign myself to whatever fate my parents planned out for me. Pregnant and unmarried at twenty-two. I'm such a disappointment.

'It's not too late to apply for a place at an institutional mother and baby home,' he says, hearing the fear in my silence. 'They've changed, you know. Not as Dickensian as they used to be.'

I don't believe this for a moment. I visited a mother and baby home last month. It was one of the smaller ones, in a terraced house on Corstorphine Road, run by the Salvation Army. The atmosphere inside chilled me. The matron was charming, but the walls were cold and bare, and from the pale, fearful expressions of the girls there I suspected she ruled the place with an iron fist.

'Mum says she knows the owners of Lichen Hall,' I tell him. 'She says they're my kind of people. Mr Whitlock's retired. He was a scientist. A pioneering microbiologist, if I'm correct.'

'A microbiologist? And they own a mansion?'

'He held professorships at Edinburgh University and Yale. Mrs Whitlock's father bought Lichen Hall, back in the day. I'm sure they'll have a telephone.' I say this more for myself than for Mr Peterson. 'And anyway, how would it look if I cancelled so late in the day?'

He arches an eyebrow. 'Your mother is a friend of the Whitlocks?'

'Well, friends *of* friends.' I try to read his look. 'Why? And don't even think about telling me the place is haunted. My brother's already tried that one.'

Charlie kindly cooked up an elaborate tale last night and decided to regale me with it while I was packing. Something about a fairy queen who took issue with the original owners after they killed a fairy baby. According to my brother, she haunts the place and curses everyone who steps inside it. Such a bastard, is Charlie. He knew full well how anxious I was about coming.

We take a right turn and park outside tall black gates, two gold 'W's pronged at the top. This must be it, though it's quite a concealed entrance for what I imagine to be a large estate, just a wee nook on the bend of the road clutched by trees.

Mr Peterson turns off the car engine and pulls a folded piece of paper from his jacket pocket. 'Instructions for the key,' he says. I watch as he steps out and roots around for a while in the dim light, bending over a bush and then heading back to the gates with what I assume to be the discovered key. He opens the gates and returns to the car to drive us through.

'I think you were about to tell me Lichen Hall is cursed,' I say. 'Or that the Whitlocks are murderers.'

'I'm not at liberty to say . . .'

'Oh, for God's sake, spit it out,' I laugh. 'You can't build me up like that and then clam up.'

'It's just a rumour,' he says, braking too hard at a bend and throwing us both forward in our seats.

'*What's* just a rumour?'

He scratches the bald spot on the crown of his head. 'Well, it was a while ago now. '57 or '58, I can't remember when . . .

An awful car accident just past Berwick. Smoke for miles. Neither of the Whitlocks was involved, but their son was.'

'My God,' I say. 'Their son?'

'Their only son, only *child*. Rumour goes that once word of the crash reached the Whitlocks, they went straight to the morgue and insisted the body be given over to them.'

I wait for him to tell me he's joking, but he doesn't. 'That's . . . unusual.'

'Well, that's not the worst of it. About a week later, their son – his name escapes me – was spotted in the village, right as rain, apparently. No sign of injury.'

I digest that for a moment, then shake it off. Lichen Hall is one of the largest properties in the Scottish Borders. It sounds like they've been the victims of vicious gossip.

'That's all I know,' Mr Peterson says, very serious.

'I'll bear it in mind.'

I won't let him talk me out of this. I'm not going anywhere near an institution, thank you.

The drive to Lichen Hall is a single lane tarmacked road with a wall on one side and tall trees on the other, and I crane my head to spot the house at the end of it. Oh God, there it is, lit up by the car's headlights. Four pointy turrets and dark stone walls laced with red ivy. It looks like Dracula's holiday home.

We drive to the main entrance, marked by pillars, broad stone steps, and a forbidding front door. Mr Peterson suddenly looks nervous.

'I'll leave your bags by the steps,' he says, cutting the engine. He jumps out of the car, and I follow, watching him as he hefts the bags out of the boot and dumps them on the ground.

'Can you at least help me carry them inside?' I ask, annoyed at how carelessly he drops my belongings on to the wet cobblestones. He's already heading back to the front of the car, and I assume he's getting some paperwork, some last detail before handing me over to my hosts.

But then the engine sounds, and with a squeal of tyres he's driving off, the back end of the car fishtailing as he disappears down the driveway.

2

It starts to rain. I look around, too dumbfounded by Mr Peterson's hasty departure to be annoyed about it. The storm doors are shut, no one around. I decide to abandon my luggage and waddle to the side of the house where, to my relief, I see a woman in a doorway, throwing what looks like breadcrumbs across the courtyard. A dozen crows are gathered around, fighting for the food.

'Hello?' I say. 'I'm Pearl, Pearl Gorham. I think you're expecting me?'

'Oh, hello!' the woman says, stepping forward with an outstretched hand. She must be Mrs Whitlock. She has cropped brown hair flecked with silver, hooded grey eyes, crooked teeth. She's dressed in dark trousers and a turtleneck. Her skin is pocked with acne scars, and she has broad, capable hands with short clean nails.

'Yes, we were expecting you,' she says. 'Where's your driver?' She's Scottish, but has very little accent, as though she's lived most of her life in London, or had elocution lessons.

'He had another appointment,' I say hastily.

She calls back inside the house. 'Aretta? Rahmi? Come and help Miss Gorham with her bags.'

Two girls emerge from the darkness and I direct them to the spot where I left my suitcases. They're both about my age. Aretta is tall and lean, brown-skinned, with high cheekbones and full lips. She's impressively strong, as she plucks up the heaviest bag as though it's a box of feathers. Rahmi is small, feline eyes the colour of ochre, long black hair tied up in a loose bun. She has a nose piercing and a no-shit-taking stare. At first, I assume they're here under the same conditions as me, but neither of them is visibly pregnant. Perhaps they're maids.

The rain starts to pelt down, so we gather up the bags hastily – though Mrs Whitlock tells me not to help, given that I'm eight months pregnant – and race inside.

I find myself in an old-fashioned kitchen with chequerboard tiles, mahogany cabinets, a vast, marble-topped kitchen island, and an impossibly high ceiling sliced by wooden beams, the kind a trapeze artist might make good use of.

She looks me up and down. 'Did you have a fall?'

I remember the caked mud on my dress and hands. I look a mess. 'Ah, sorry. No, not a fall. We had to make a pit stop earlier . . .'

'Let's get you cleaned up.'

She leads me briskly along a long hallway towards a set of stairs. I hate stairs, since about two months ago. Stairs and the third trimester are not a good combination. But I try to keep up.

'I'm afraid the east wing is closed off,' Mrs Whitlock says, a few steps ahead of me. 'My husband and I aren't up to that kind of work. Not anymore.' She trails off. 'Anyway, there's enough of the house left to accommodate us all comfortably. We have hot water, but only in the mornings, so you'll do well to rise early. Rahmi prepares breakfast at seven, lunch at twelve and dinner at five.'

'Why is it closed off?' I ask.

She cocks her head. 'I'm afraid I don't follow.'

'You said the east wing was closed off. And that you and your husband weren't able to . . .'

'Ah, I see. Shall I give you a tour?'

I nod, brightening. 'Yes please.'

Her eyes fall on the dried mud streaked across my hands and legs. 'You don't want to wash and change first? I can show you after . . .'

'Now is perfect,' I say, not wanting to explain that fear is oozing out of my every pore, and that the only way I'll be able to sleep tonight is if I familiarize myself with these new surroundings as quickly as possible. I'm a creature who thrives on familiarity.

She gives a little impressed tip of her head. 'Follow me,' she says.

At the end of the corridor, the stairs continue up another floor, and I notice a stairlift bolted to the wall. It looks like a new addition.

Mrs Whitlock leads me to the left, which fans out into a huge room, ballroom-sized, with a row of stained-glass windows sending rainbows all over the thick carpet. 'This is my husband's Micrarium,' she says, and I nod as though I know what a bloody Micrarium is. 'When we first moved here, he bought a metal detector to scope out the grounds for old coins.'

'Old coins?'

She looks surprised. 'Oh, I thought you'd have heard about the grounds of the hall. Yes, quite the site we have here – the old wood about a quarter of a mile east is part of the ancient Caledonian forest. You'll notice the trees have very pale trunks, very ghostly. We call them the ghost woods. My father dug up a horse harness the week after he and my mother moved here. From the Bronze Age, it turns out. Three thousand years old.'

'Wow,' I say. 'That's incredible.'

'Well, yes. We've not found anything quite as significant since. A handful of Jacobite bullets, a redcoat button. Lots of bones, some of which turned out to be human.' A grimace. 'Lots of battles on our grounds, it seems. My husband is more interested in nature than history, anyway.'

'Nature *is* history, isn't it?'

'Quite. His health isn't what it was. You'll have seen the stairlift we had installed.'

I nod, and she smiles sadly. 'We keep the Micrarium in place, just the way he left it.'

She leads me past the tables that are set out along the sides of the room, displaying glass cabinets filled with shells and rusted keys. There are more cabinets on the walls, but with tiny square boxes filled with what look like bits of tree bark and dead insects. I want to stop and explore, but Mrs Whitlock is brisk, no-nonsense – both traits I like, though the room is so strange, so filled with questions, that for a moment I forget the reason why I'm here.

Two hallways greet us at the end, forking left and right. Mrs Whitlock turns to the right, and I follow.

'There's a library, if you're keen on books,' she tells me, opening a door on to a spectacular room with bookcases on every wall. I give a gasp, and she laughs, lightly. 'My father installed it,' she says. 'He was a reader. I'm afraid the rest of us are Philistines.'

'I was wondering,' I say. Then, hoping I don't offend her in the asking: 'I mean, I'm a *huge* fan of reading, but I also love the telly . . .'

She beats dust off a shelf with her hand. 'No television, I'm afraid.'

My heart sinks, but I try not to let my disappointment show. I glance over at the shelves that reach all the way to the wooden ceiling, and the two armchairs by the open fireplace. Thank God for the Whitlocks' library. I'm here for at least three months, maybe four. Hopefully there's more than dictionaries and encyclopaedias on those shelves.

We move along the corridor. There's a door at the end of the hallway that appears to be locked. She pats her pockets for the key. Then, turning it in the lock: '*This* is the east wing.'

The suspense is thrilling. We step out on to the top of a beautiful oak staircase that sweeps up to meet us like something out of *Gone with the Wind*. A crystal chandelier the size of a bloody bathtub sits smack-bang in the centre of a vaulted ceiling.

'Do you enjoy the outdoors?' Mrs Whitlock asks.

'When I get the chance,' I say, looking down into the vestibule below.

'Five hundred acres,' she says. 'That's how big the grounds are. That includes the fields, and part of the beach at the bottom of the cliffs. Many of our guests find that a walk every day through the grounds is good for the spirits.'

I nod. 'I'll bear it in mind.'

The main vestibule spreads out at the bottom of the stairs in a grand riot of chequered tiles. There's a stag's head mounted on one wall, a Grecian statue of a naked woman in a corner. Faces frozen in marble peek out from the corners of the arched doorways like angel-faced gargoyles. As I begin to descend the stairs, Mrs Whitlock touches my arm.

'Best not, in your condition,' she says. 'If you look closely, you'll see the reason we can't use this part of the house at the moment.'

I follow her gaze to an enormous mass of yellow fungus creeping up the side of a wall. What looks like a series of giant ears are bulging from the gap in the doorframe, right down to the floor. As I draw my eye across the length of the vestibule I spot more fungus spewing from cracks in the tiles and the window frames. The vaulted ceiling is sullied by black blooms of mould. Black frills poke out from the wooden steps at my feet. And at the end of the staircase, a plume of honey-gold mushrooms nub out from the newel post, perfectly formed. It makes me feel physically ill.

'What happened?' I ask, burying my mouth in the crook of my arm.

She sighs wearily. 'An infestation of fungus. I still can't quite believe it. This house has been standing for four hundred years. It has withstood bombs, floods, and a bolt of lightning.' She folds her arms, exasperated. 'Fungus can eat through rock, can you believe that?'

'Good God,' I say.

'Worse than mice, apparently. It's even in the foundations, which makes it difficult to eradicate the problem. And of course, there are the spores.' She glances at me. 'Not good for humans to breathe in fungal spores, as I'm sure you're aware.'

'Not good at all.'

'Well, we're all safe,' she says. 'As long as we don't use this wing of the house.'

I take a step back. They might have mentioned that the place was coming down with fungi when offering to care for pregnant women. 'Do you know the cause?' I ask, unable to keep the fear out of my voice.

'Apparently the water table rose and has been marinating the foundations of the hall for decades without our knowledge. And where there is damp, there is, sadly, mould.'

'Can't it be fixed?'

She shakes her head and leads me back through the door, closing it tightly behind us. I feel I can breathe easier, now that we're heading away from the east wing. 'It's not an easy solution, as you can imagine,' she says.

'It hasn't affected the rest of the house?'

She shakes her head, and I feel relieved.

'Though it *has* affected some of our utilities,' she says. 'The telephone works for the most part, but sometimes it doesn't. The lighting is similarly temperamental, so we keep oil lamps handy.'

I nod. 'My parents still use them. They remember the blackouts during the war. They don't like my brother and me to be too dependent on electricity.'

'Jolly good.'

She turns back, and I follow her through to the west side of the house, which seems more modern. If I'm not mistaken, an extension has been added in the last ten years or so. The east wing appeared more old-fashioned, with higher ceilings and fancy coving. Perhaps that's why it's been so badly affected. It's older, so possibly less resilient to this kind of damage.

'How close is the village?' I ask.

'Not close enough, I'm afraid. You'll have everything you need here, I think. The postman comes on Thursdays, so you can leave letters in the hall.'

I try not to show how dejected I am. No telly, no phone, and post once a bloody week. Sonny and Cher are due to be on *Top of the Pops* tomorrow night.

'Anyway,' she sighs. 'I'll show you your room, shall I? And then you can have that bath.'

She leads me up the stairs to the top of the house.

'I hear you're a nurse?' she asks.

'Yes.'

I say this with confidence, but actually I don't know if I'll ever be a nurse again. I thought Sister Clark might make an exception for me, if I kept quiet about my pregnancy, but she didn't seem keen on the idea. 'Everyone was against me being a nurse,' I tell Mrs Whitlock, disclosing more than I should. 'My parents are old-fashioned. They think I should have prioritized marriage and children over a career.'

Mrs Whitlock studies me a little closer, interested by this admission. 'I see. I suspect you're quite the rebel, Miss Gorham.'

'Oh please,' I say, my cheeks burning. 'It's Pearl. Even my patients call me by my first name.'

'So why . . . ?' she asks, and I already know what she's asking. We reach the second floor, and I try to disguise how out of breath I am. But she sees, and pauses before taking the next flight.

'I spent a year in hospital,' I explain. 'I was seven. Meningitis.'

'Oh my,' she says, pressing her fingertips to her mouth. 'A year? You must have been very poorly.'

'I was.'

I think back to those long days in the Royal Infirmary, aching for my mother's smell. My parents weren't allowed to visit, and I was distraught without them. One of the nurses, Nurse Haddon, used to cuddle me when I cried, and I swore that if I ever got out of the place I'd become a nurse and make life a little better for anyone as miserable and homesick as I was. At sixteen I trained as a cadet nurse, earning four pounds a week to scrub the wards and cook for the patients, before entering nursing college. I worked hard to get my job.

'Well, your parents must have sent you to a good school,' she says.

I nod. 'I would say so.'

'The reason I ask is because I'd be very grateful if you would feel able to help Wulfric with his schooling.'

'Wulfric?'

'My grandson.' She sighs sadly. 'He's fourteen. He doesn't attend school anymore. My husband was teaching him until he took ill. I've been doing my best to fill his shoes. But I'm afraid that mixing family with education doesn't always run smoothly.'

I think of what Mr Peterson told me in the car, about the Whitlocks losing their only son. Wulfric must be the child of that son. He must live here with his grandparents, after his father passed. What a tragedy.

'I'll be glad to help.'

A gracious smile. 'I'll let you find your feet in this place first. But perhaps after a week or two, we can commence lessons?'

We take the next flight of stairs, and I feel encouraged by our exchange. There may be no telly, and the place is silent as a grave, but the chance to help Mrs Whitlock's grandson and put my skills to use fills me with hope. It'll give me something to do.

'Here we are,' she says, leading me to a circular room at the top of a final flight of stairs, situated in one of the turrets. The curtains are drawn in a velvet crescent, and a lamp casts a honeyed glow throughout the room. It's lovely – a single brass bed made with crisp white linens, a cast-iron fireplace with a vase of pink roses on the mantelpiece, a wardrobe, and a chest of drawers. And a crib. I try not to look at it. I had almost managed to forget the reason why I'm here.

'It's perfect,' I say, flipping open one of the suitcases that have already been installed at the foot of the bed. Mrs Whitlock tilts her head to inspect the contents.

'Good gracious,' she says. 'My dear, you have enough shoes to sink a ship.'

'I'm a bit of a shoe addict,' I say with a sigh.

'A girl after my own heart,' she says in a confiding tone. I lift out the red pair of Mary Janes, revealing a photograph of Sebastian, grinning straight up at us, and my stomach flips. Too late. She's spotted it.

'Oh, my,' she says, plucking out the photograph and holding it up to the light. 'What a handsome chap.'

'He is,' I say wistfully.

Her grey eyes lift to mine, narrowing. 'This isn't a family member, I'm taking it.'

I shake my head. 'No, this . . . he's called Sebastian.'

'Ah,' she says, in a knowing tone. 'The baby's father, I take it?'

I swallow hard, watching her gaze down at Sebastian's lovely face. 'Yes.'

It's a lie – Sebastian isn't the baby's father. But I can't bring myself to admit this, not to her. Suddenly her presence in the room feels invasive.

'I think I'll have that bath,' I say gently, and she steps back, placing the photograph into the suitcase again, as though she's come out of a spell.

'Of course,' she says. 'On the floor below you'll find your own private bathroom. Fresh towels are in the wardrobe.' A broad smile. I notice that the brooch pinned to her turtleneck is not a poppy, as I'd thought. It's a red toadstool.

'It's so lovely to have you here at Lichen Hall,' she says. 'Do join my husband and me for breakfast tomorrow, if you feel up to it?'

I smile back, all the earlier awkwardness washed away. 'I will.'

3

My own bathroom, with an indoor loo. A lion-claw tub filled to the brim with warm, foamy water. I peel off my filthy dress and step in, sighing with relief as the hot water slips over all the places that hurt. My bump sits above the water, a solid mound that jiggles as the baby moves around. Every now and then a little heel will lift the skin in a triangle, and I pat it to say hello to the baby.

I lean my head back on the lip of the bathtub and force myself not to cry. It's fine, it's all fine, really. I'm in a beautiful mansion instead of a horrible institution. By Christmas, the baby will have been adopted and I can go home and pretend that none of this ever happened.

Just then, there's a noise in the hall, the whine of a floorboard. I open my eyes and glance in the direction of the noise. I've left the door ajar; I should have locked it, but I hate closed doors. There's another sound, another creak.

'Hello?' I call. 'Who's there?'

Someone moves outside. The sound of shuffling feet.

'Hello?' I say, insistent. If it's Mrs Whitlock, or one of the maids I saw earlier, surely she would answer?

I get out of the bath and wrap a towel around me before stepping out into the hallway. It's empty. Old houses like this are always groaning and creaking.

As I turn to go back into the bathroom, something catches

my eye. At the end of the hallway, a clutch of fingers are curled around the corner of the wall, a forehead and a pair of eyes just above them.

I give a start, and the owner of the fingers and eyes darts off towards the stairs. It's a child, a young boy, with a head of bushy locks. Mrs Whitlock's grandson, I think, until I remember she mentioned that Wulfric was fourteen. The child I see racing down the stairs is much younger, a boy of five or six.

I call after him and make for the stairs, eager to assure him that he's not in trouble. But he's vanished, no sign of him, like a thief in the night.

4

I wake the next morning just after seven, which is late for me. It's sunny outside, bright light throbbing through the circular windows. What a view! Thick forest for miles, lime green fields of furze and ridge-and-furrow stretching beyond. I unpack a little, setting my Russian dolls out along the windowsill. They were a gift from my grandmother, a hand-me-down from Sweden, the red and gold paint applied by ancestral hands. They make me feel safe.

I take out my rollers and run a brush through my white-blonde hair. I like it to look like whipped butter. The style nowadays is very much a full-face of make-up, with false eyelashes and heavy eyeliner, but I never have time for that kind of thing. My face is high-boned and pale, so I use pink lipstick both for my lips and to draw colour to my cheeks. A slick of mascara, too, otherwise I look a bit dead – the curse of pale eyelashes. Then I throw on the blue maternity dress Aunt Fenella made me, before heading downstairs to use the loo and find some food.

I'm disoriented, and the house is so goddam enormous, but I retrace my steps and find the kitchen with the dining room next door. There's a basket with some bread rolls on the worktop and I eat one hungrily, then fill myself a large glass of water and drink it over the sink. It feels rude to be helping myself, but Mrs Whitlock said one of the maids would make breakfast at seven so maybe it's OK.

I find the kettle and some tea. While I'm waiting for the water to boil, I explore the dining room next door. A wooden fireplace at the top and an oval table surrounded by uncomfortable-looking chairs. There are columns by the window with marble busts of stern, masculine faces.

This place feels too formal to be someone's home – it's soulless, the kind of house you can easily feel very lonely inside. I think of the little boy I saw last night, racing down the stairs, and Mrs Whitlock's grandson, Wulfric. How do they find this place? It's certainly not a house for children.

I look over the paintings on the wall and the handful of antiques on the mantelpiece, checking all the corners and crevices for any signs of fungus. None are to be found, thank God. Ever since Mrs Whitlock showed me the damage to the east wing I've been checking the walls and the gaps in the floorboards in case I spot more of that awful black fungus. The smell of it makes me gag. I well know about the dangers of fungal spores – the meningitis I contracted at the age of seven was cryptococcal meningitis, a kind that's caused by fungus.

I go into the hallway and take in all the details of the place – the high ceilings sculpted with mouldings that sweep down to cherubs at the corners; the tiled floor that has seen better days, and the wooden panels on the walls that darken the place. It's cold, though the windows are closed and brass radiators shoulder the walls. The wall outside the kitchen is bustling with framed photographs, and I take a closer look.

God, the Whitlocks haven't half travelled. All the famous landmarks make appearances in these photos – the Eiffel Tower, the Pyramids at Giza, Niagara Falls. The photographs show a couple at different ages, posing with their arms linked, then with a baby. The Whitlocks and their son, I'm guessing. I think of how Mr Peterson told me that their son was killed, how the tragedy of it moved them to take his body from the morgue. I wonder if there's any truth in the rumour. It seems bizarre. But already I can see the Whitlocks aren't your average family.

Next to the photographs is a painting of what seems to be a fairy carrying a baby. It's a strange painting, very old, by the looks of it, with a brass plaque at the bottom. The fairy is grotesque, with claws for hands and an elongated body. The face is craven. It looks odd amongst the other paintings. Perhaps it's an heirloom.

Mrs Whitlock doesn't show. It's a clear bright morning, so I get my coat and head outside, keen to see the ancient wood Mrs Whitlock mentioned. One side of the house opens on to a long strip of grass and woodland, but there are gardens on the other side, organized in a series of long rose tunnels and walled gardens. I find stone statues of animals beneath overgrown verges, and a charming gravel pathway cuts through what was likely once an abundant rose garden. A stream trickles through the garden with a stone bridge arching over it. I stand on the bridge, looking out over the trees and bushes. There is a towering willow tree just ahead, its thick boughs spilling down to the grass like green waterfalls.

There's movement in the shadows around the base, something small moving fast. A rabbit. As I step forward to get a better look something catches it, the white of its tail streaking up through the branches. It's caught in a trap.

The rabbit thrashes for a few seconds as it hangs upside down, before falling still.

I clap my hands to my mouth, astonished by what I've just seen. Moving quickly to the rabbit, I catch sight of someone running towards it from the other direction. One of the girls who helped bring in my luggage last night, the one with a serious and slightly lopsided face, black hair pulled into a long ponytail, that same no-shit-taking stare, skin like she's been dipped in gold. She's wearing an old white shirt and black skirt with wellies. As she draws nears she doesn't look at me, but draws a sharp knife from the belt of her trousers and slashes at the rope hoisting the rabbit in the air.

I'm too shocked to say hello. Instead, we stare at each other across the lawn, me with my eyes wide and mouth open, she with a grim determination. Then, slinging the dead rabbit over her shoulder like a dishcloth, she stalks off.

'They eat the vegetables,' a voice says. I turn and find the other maid, Aretta, behind me. A straw hat is pulled down over her head, a black braid of hair snaking over one shoulder. She's dressed in the same masculine, over-sized clothing as Rahmi, her face gleaming with sweat. 'We have to catch them so they don't destroy our food. Want me to show you?'

'Yes please,' though I'm still too struck by the sight of the rabbit being killed to really hear what she asked.

I follow her to the far corner of the garden, past the willow tree and through a gate marked with a rusted sign that reads *Winter Garden*. It's a huge plot cordoned off by high stone walls. Rows of leeks, carrots, cabbages, and potatoes spring up from black soil, peas and tomatoes growing in the glasshouse. There's a scarecrow in the midst of it, and a greenhouse in the far corner, filled with plants.

'I'm Pearl,' I say. 'I arrived last night.'

'Aretta.' She straightens. 'Do you garden?'

I shake my head and give a nervous laugh. 'I've never so much as mowed a lawn. Isn't that awful? Did you do this garden, or . . . ?'

Aretta ignores my question, bending instead to rip out a weed. 'When's your bairn due?'

'October.'

'Did Mrs Whitlock say what your task is?'

'My task?'

'She puts everyone to work.'

I pause at that. Are they maids, or are they here like me? Neither of them seems to be pregnant. 'She mentioned something about helping with her grandson, Wulfric.'

Aretta cocks an eyebrow. 'Good luck with that.' She walks to a row of tomato plants, and I stand, taking that in. I guess she dislikes Mrs Whitlock's grandson. I watch as she pours water from a can over the plants and straightens the stakes.

'I saw a little boy last night,' I say, raising my voice a little. 'Do you know who he might be? I think I might have scared him.'

She eyes me suspiciously. 'A little boy?'

'Yes. He was dressed for bed. About five or six years old.'

She shrugs. 'No five- or six-year-olds around here that I know of.'

'Are you sure?' I say.

'Quite sure,' she says firmly.

I feel like I've touched a nerve. 'Well, that's strange. Perhaps he was a ghost.'

'Perhaps.'

I'm not sure how to take this comment, or Aretta, more generally. She's off-hand with me, acts like she doesn't have time for me. I wait beside her for a few more minutes before taking the hint and leaving the garden.

I walk back to Lichen Hall feeling deflated. I suppose I ought to expect a period of adjustment.

Back inside the house, I spot the telephone on the table outside the kitchen. I glance around to ask if I might make a call, but then I remember Mrs Whitlock saying that the phone line only works occasionally. Gingerly I lift the receiver and hold it to my ear. There's a dial tone. Thank God. Quickly I dial my home number, keeping one eye on the stairwell in case anyone appears.

Mrs McQuade, our housekeeper, answers. My mother is out shopping, she says. She won't be long, and she promises to have her call me. The line goes dead before I say goodbye.

I sit by the telephone waiting for her, even lifting the receiver and pressing it to my ear to check if the line is back. It isn't, but I don't want to leave the spot in case my mother calls. Suddenly I need to hear her voice.

I must fall asleep, because when I look up from the telephone seat it's dark. I hear a noise, the sound of wheels over wood. The dark corridor is suddenly creepy, and I feel my heart race.

'Who's there?' I say, fear in my voice.

The noise gets louder, a high-pitched squeal. I stand up, poised for fight or flight. Suddenly an image forms from the gloom: it's Mrs Whitlock pushing someone in a wheelchair. The squealing is from the wheels. I feel shaky with relief.

'My dear,' Mrs Whitlock says, smiling. 'Are you all right?'

'I'm fine,' I say, laughing at how worked up I was before. 'I was waiting on my mother to call.' I nod at the man and hold out my hand for a handshake. 'Hello. I'm Pearl.'

He raises his head a little but appears unable to shake my hand. He's dressed in a robe and slippers, his head bowed. He has a snowy head of white hair and a grisly beard, and his jaw is slack. I'm not sure he is entirely compos mentis.

'This is my husband, Joseph,' Mrs Whitlock says. 'He tends to sleep during the day, so in the evenings I get him out for some fresh air.'

'I didn't realize . . .' I say, tailing off. I didn't know he was so poorly that he required a wheelchair.

She bends over him and speaks loudly. 'Miss Gorham is a nurse, darling. And she's going to help Wolfie with his schooling.'

He lifts his head then and looks at me, or through me, I'm not sure. But then he reaches forward in one surprisingly stealthy movement, as though he wants my hand. I step forward and take his in mine. His grip is strong, and he starts to mumble.

'What's that, dear?' Mrs Whitlock says. She lowers herself to hear, but can't quite make him out.

'My eye,' he says. 'There's something in my eye.'

I look to Mrs Whitlock for an explanation.

'There's nothing in your eye, darling,' she says.

'I can take a look,' I say. Despite Mrs Whitlock's protests I bend forward, trying to see. He widens his blue eyes and lifts his face meekly to mine, blasting me with foul breath. I can see nothing of concern. 'Is it a hair, perhaps?'

'Behind my eye,' he says, pointing at his right eye with a veined hand. I look again, but the light is poor, and there's no visible injury or inflammation.

'I'll have a look when I take him back to his room,' Mrs Whitlock assures me. 'There's better light there. Probably a reaction to his medication. Have you eaten?'

I shake my head. 'Not since breakfast.'

Her face falls. 'Aretta? Aretta!'

Footsteps sound on the stairs, and Aretta appears. She's changed out of her gardening outfit, back in an old-fashioned black dress, her hair smoothed into place. She's holding a pressed bed sheet, as though she's in the middle of making beds.

'Fetch our guest something to eat, would you?' Mrs Whitlock says.

Aretta nods. 'Yes, ma'am.'

I watch as she turns on her heel, quickly enveloped by the gloom of the hall. Mrs Whitlock touches my arm, and we walk towards the kitchen. Mr Whitlock is quietly snoring in the wheelchair, and Mrs Whitlock lifts a towel from the handle of the wheelchair, rolls it up, and tucks it between his shoulder and head.

'I must apologize for not having breakfast with you this morning,' Mrs Whitlock says. 'As you can see, my husband is unwell. I'm still adjusting to his levels of care.'

'May I ask after his condition?'

'Dementia,' she says sadly. 'He has declined this last year.'

'Can I be of any assistance?'

She gives a polite nod: the response of a woman who isn't used to accepting help. 'Perhaps. But first, you must eat.'

Then

Mabel

Dundee, Scotland, May–July 1959

1

The streets of Dundee are dark and slick with rain. It's long past midnight, all the houses dark.

I walk quickly to keep myself from weakening and turning back. It's cold, too, or maybe I'm just nervous – I can't get my hands to warm up. I press them deep into my pockets and try to keep my chin tucked to my chest so I don't make eye contact with any of the people who lurk in the shadows. Prostitutes peek out from back alleys, a serpentine twist of smoke all that's left of them when they draw back into their hiding places. There are people huddled up in sleeping bags and cardboard boxes, and the low din of loud music thrums off the cobbled stones. The further I walk the more fear seizes me.

Behind I hear footsteps, stopping when I stop, commencing again when I keep going. I daren't look back.

I head up the steep hill past the bingo hall towards the bridge that overlooks the railway line. Here, I think. Here. And I stop, and look down, and in one powerful moment I realize the wish I've harboured for years, now: I want to jump in front of a train. I want this all to be over. Not just because I've got a ghost baby inside me.

Ever since Dad died I've wanted it all to end. I just didn't know how to do it without causing a fuss. A train, though – that's quick.

And so I wait. And wait.

No sign of any train. From the corner of my eye, I see someone on a street corner, watching me. My fear has gone, now. I just want this to be over.

I look down at the tracks. Rats dart from one side to the other. I can hear two men arguing drunkenly beneath the bridge, hurling accusations at each other.

I want to jump, but with a sinking heart, I admit it to myself: the bridge isn't high enough.

If I jumped now, I'd live.

2

I wake to the sound of my alarm. I'm back in my house, in bed. Alive, and heartbroken for it. I curl up under the covers and weep. I can't believe what happened in Dr McCann's office is real. I feel disgusting, like I should be punished. But I know I didn't do anything.

It's five o'clock, still dark outside. I get up, get changed, and scape my hair back off my face. It's raining, and I'll need my coat. The bakery isn't far from here, but I've to start up the ovens on Tuesdays to allow Ginny the chance to take her daughters to school.

I walk lightly on my feet down the three flights of stairs that lead into the kitchen. All the bedroom doors are closed, which means we have a full house. Even downstairs I don't turn on the light so I don't wake the guests.

'Morning, princess.'

I give a jump of fright. Slowly the shadow at the table assumes human form. Richard. What is he doing here, sitting in the dark?

'Where'd you go last night?' he asks, cocking his head.

I stare at the floor. 'Nowhere.'

He tuts. 'Don't tell lies, Mabel. You went out. Where'd you go?'

'I went for a walk.'

'At three in the morning?'

I don't answer.

'Spent a long time at the bridge, didn't you?'

He is smiling, but Richard always smiles, a strange little grin that never reaches his eyes. He never laughs, or says kind things, and so the smile sometimes makes me think he's imagining dark things and taking pleasure in them.

'You weren't thinking of jumping, were you?' he says, folding his arms. 'Because that would be a shame. A real shame.'

What he is saying unfurls in my mind like a dark flame. I think of the figure I spotted last night, standing at a street corner near the bridge – I suspected they were watching me.

It was Richard: he followed me. The realization unfurls in me darkly, making my stomach drop: he watched me at the bridge and never came to me, never said anything.

I could have died, and he was prepared to do nothing.

He takes a step forward, coming into the weak light. I flinch. His blue shirt strains over his little gut, and there are stains on the brown trousers that he wears every day.

'Your mother would be devastated if anything were to happen to you.'

His voice is soft, now. Tears prick my eyes, not because I'm upset about how Ma would feel. I had already envisaged her reaction to the news that I was dead. She'd howl and weep about how she'd lost her only daughter, her child *and* her husband, both dead. But I don't believe she loves me, or Dad. Every word is studded with thorns, designed to wound.

I can feel Richard's eyes tracing me, his breath hot and sour as he thinks of a way to use his knowledge against me. I don't move a muscle, though a ghost sits upright in my ankle, covering her mouth with both hands.

Finally, Richard says, 'You can make it up to me and your mother. Now, get to your room.'

I nod and race off. We have six guests and no washing machine. Everything is done by hand. It takes me two hours, maybe three, to get it done every day. But I'm used to hard work. And I don't care anymore. I don't care about anything.

I get changed, then head to the bakery where I've worked since leaving school last year. I earn four pounds and eighteen shillings a week. I give Mum and Richard three pounds for food and rent. The rest is for clothes, buses, and library fines.

Today it's just me and Ginny. We make the dough, then shovel ball after ball into the oven. Ginny works efficiently alongside me, shouting over the drone of the machines to confirm flour quantities and sale prices. It's not easy to carry out a conversation here, but I want to ask her if you can get pregnant without having sex. She would know, wouldn't she?

'Are you all right?' Ginny asks as I stop to dab my forehead with a cloth. She gestures to her face. 'You're looking a bit peely-wally.'

I nod and try to put it into words. 'Do you know if . . .' A ghost jumps into my mouth, hard, hurting my teeth. One of the ovens makes a noise, and Ginny turns to take out the scones, leaving me with my unspoken words.

The ghosts have always lived inside me, since I was little, but they got more active after my dad died. When I was wee, we lived in a cottage in a harbour village in the East Neuk. The father of every child at my school was a fisherman, including mine. Right up until I was eight, I thought that was the only job people worked at. And then, one day, there was a storm, and Dad's boat didn't come home. He and his crew all drowned.

At closing time, I forget that I arranged to meet Jack. When I spot him outside the bakery, spruced up in a clean white shirt, black sports jacket with beige trousers, clutching a single red rose, and looking so nervous he might be sick, my stomach flips. How am I meant to tell him what Dr McCann said? What will he think of me?

'What's wrong?' he says with a frown. 'Did something happen?'

I shake my head. 'No, no, nothing's wrong . . .'

We walk along in silence, up Market Street past the fishmonger's.

Jack is fidgety and preoccupied. 'Here,' he says suddenly, thrusting the rose at me. 'I forgot to give you this.'

'Thanks,' I say. It's so awkward.

Jack's the same age as me and almost as timid. Scared of his own shadow, Ma always says. He's a good head taller than me and skinny as a drainpipe, and his face is long and covered in acne. His dad rags on him like Ma rags on me, so we understand each other. When we left school, Jack was the one who suggested we make things 'a bit more romantic', though I think it was because his dad teased him for years about not having a girlfriend. I like Jack, but I prefer being friends. I'm not keen on kissing too much, though luckily neither is he.

'I got a bit of good news today,' he says. 'Mr Ballard said my probation has been excellent, and he expects to sign off the paperwork next week.'

'That's exciting,' I say. Jack's been working at the accountancy firm on Inverness Street for the last year. He hasn't been paid yet; Mr Ballard said his training more than compensated for the lack of a salary, but neither of us were convinced by that. 'You've worked hard for it.'

Jack twists his mouth into a shy smile. 'He gave me a bottle of wine. I think it's the same bottle I gave him for Christmas, but that's OK.'

'Maybe we can have some. Wine sounds like the perfect thing for that kind of news.'

'I was thinking we could celebrate with a meal,' he says. 'Not tonight, if you're not feeling up to it. And maybe we could go to the pictures. That new Sherlock Holmes film starts.'

'Which one?'

'*The Hound of the Baskervilles.*'

I hesitate. I love the cinema, and I especially love Sherlock Holmes. But ever since Ma remarried I can't watch anything with Christopher Lee in it. He reminds me too much of Richard.

We reach the park, where we sometimes sit under the big oak tree on dry days.

'You went to the doctor's yesterday,' Jack says. 'Didn't you?'

I can feel a sob coiling in my throat. How can I explain this to him?

He must see the look on my face, because the colour leaves his cheeks. 'What did the doctor say?'

I force myself to look him straight in the eye. 'If I tell you something, do you think you could trust me when I say it's the truth?'

He nods, adamant. 'Yes, anything. You can always trust me.'

So I tell him about Dr McCann and what he said about me having a bun in the oven and that Ma thought Jack had put it there.

He laughs awkwardly at this. We're neither of us very sure what to do when it comes to being intimate. Even holding hands feels weird. Maybe it's because we've been friends for so long.

'I've not slept with anyone, ever.' I resist asking him if there's something I should know about sex, because to be honest I only learned the facts of life from Ettie down the street.

'Are you serious?' he says quietly. 'You're having a bairn? This is . . . real?'

I nod and swallow hard. He narrows his eyes at me.

'How far along are you?'

'Dr McCann said five months.'

His face looks like someone stamped on his foot. 'Five months? We've been dating for *six* months.'

'Dr McCann must have made a mistake,' I say quietly.

'What do you mean, a mistake?' he says, cutting me off. 'He's a doctor.'

'But how can I be having a bairn, when I've never had sex with anyone?'

Jack runs a hand through his hair, perplexed. 'He'll have done tests. He can't have got it wrong.'

'Ma says I've to go into one of the homes for unwed mothers,' I say in a small voice. 'Then the bairn will be adopted.'

He looks restless, suddenly, glancing around the park and shifting his feet. 'And you've no idea whose bairn it is?'

'Not just *whose* bairn,' I say. 'I've no idea *how* this happened.'

I see it then, written in his eyes – he doesn't believe me.

'Is this because I'm not very physical?' Jack says in a pained voice, stumbling over the word 'physical'. I can tell that his father's voice is starting to echo in his head. 'I'd have slept with you, you know. If that was what you wanted.'

'Jack,' I say softly. 'You said you trusted me.'

'I didn't,' he says, his gaze hardening. 'I said *you* could trust *me*.'

'Jack,' I say again, reaching out to him. He looks devastated, his whole body weighed down by something. For a long while he stands before me in silence, his hands deep in his pockets and his face turned away, as though he's thinking of the right thing to say. Finally, it comes. He turns back to me, tears wobbling in his eyes.

'If you wanted to break up with me,' he says, his voice cracking. 'You could have just told me, Mabel. You didn't have to fuck somebody else.'

And he walks away, leaving me in the park.

3

All week I feel like my veins are filled with molten iron. Jack's reaction is a gut-punch. Worse, I have no one else to talk to, no one else to confide in.

Ma tells one of her friends that I am pregnant, supposedly in confidence, but within days the news spreads to every corner in Dundee. A man comes into the bakery and refuses to be served by me. Then Ginny finds out and sacks me. I spend my days pacing the park, not returning until I know Ma and Richard will be asleep.

One afternoon, I see a familiar figure approaching me as I doze under the oak tree. It's Jack, his hands deep in his pockets. I flinch, expecting him to shout at me again.

'I'm sorry,' he says. He waits until I nod, accepting his apology, before he sits down next to me.

He tells me that he overheard Mr Ballard talking about a place on the Scottish Borders that takes in expectant mothers. Lichen Hall, it's called. It's a residential home, a lot better than an institution.

He tells me they only take in girls referred to them by friends. They do it as a kindness, as charity.

'I'd like to contact them on your behalf,' Jack says.

'I can't ask that of you.'

'You're not asking me.'

'Jack, it's too much.'

He shrugs. 'It's the least I can do.'

* * *

I leave for Lichen Hall at the end of July. Ma refuses to have Richard drive me there. 'I don't see why you're going all the way to the Borders,' she said. 'There's a perfectly good mother and baby home right here in Dundee.'

She was suspicious about Jack organizing for me to go to Lichen Hall, even accused him of paying me to go to a baby farmer. In the end, I don't think she cared about anything other than the fact that I was getting out of her hair.

On the day I'm due to leave, Jack's employer calls him in to work. We have only a few moments at my front door to say goodbye.

We stand, awkwardly, not knowing whether we should kiss or shake hands. Everything feels so scary.

I lift my arms for a hug, and he steps forward, holding me tight.

'Write to me, please,' he whispers.

I squeeze him. 'I will.'

As he walks away, I feel tears prick my eyes. I don't know if I'll ever see him again.

4

Jack's uncle Angus agrees to drive me to Lichen Hall. He's a nice, gentle-natured man, very like Jack. He doesn't ask me any questions about the pregnancy, or about the hall, and I'm relieved.

When we pull up outside the house, I'm certain we've arrived at the wrong place. 'This is definitely Lichen Hall,' Angus says, studying the map.

It's like a castle from a fairy tale, with pointy turrets and colourful stained-glass windows. This wasn't what I expected. A ghost shivers in my elbow.

There's a knock on the car window. I look up to see a girl standing there with a big smile. She gives a little wave, and Angus urges me to get out and say hello.

I was expecting her to be pregnant, like me, but she isn't. She's got a pale face covered in orange freckles, and she wears an apron over a gingham dress, her mane of cinnamon-red hair pulled back into a fat ponytail. 'Hello,' she says, extending a skinny hand. 'You must be Mabel Haggith.'

'Yes,' I say quietly. 'Nice to meet you.'

'You don't look very pregnant,' she says, her eyes on my stomach. 'How far along are you?'

I have no idea. I shift my feet awkwardly. 'I'm due in September.'

'Jings a'mighty.' She pats my belly. 'And I bet you pop out a big 'un, too. Skinny girls like you always end up hiding hippos in there. I'm Morven, by the way. Come inside. I'll show you around.'

I thank Angus for driving me and watch him take off down the driveway, headed back to Dundee. I feel a pang of terror. I've never been this far away from home. Only, Dundee isn't really my home. The sudden sensation of rootlessness makes me feel nauseous.

Morven is still talking, remarking on how light my suitcase is, asking me questions. I nod at the spaces in her chatter where I think an answer is needed, but I don't hear a word she says. I'm shutting down again, slipping deep inside my bones.

She takes me inside the house, and I stop in my tracks and stare. If the outside is grand, inside is majestic. The walls are gleaming oak panels and marble cornices. An oak staircase sweeps to the upper floors, the newel post carved in the shape of a horse. The ghosts stop writhing for a minute and sigh, as though they're in awe.

'Dining room's this way, just beside the kitchen,' Morven says, pointing at a room to the left, and I realize we're back where we started. 'I do the cooking. Anything you don't like to eat?'

I shake my head, and she pats my hand. 'Music to my ears. Most of the girls we get are fusspots when it comes to food.'

'Are you . . . the household cook?'

She gives a delighted laugh. 'The household cook? I'm the household everything. Cook, cleaner, plumber, dressmaker, gardener, midwife . . . Why do you think the place is such a mess?'

She laughs again, and I don't know if she's joking or not. Everything seems to be a joke to Morven, but in a good way. I start to feel easier about staying here, if she's who'll be taking care of me. She's hard to place, age-wise – she looks about my age, and yet she said she's a midwife. She's missing a tooth, but it has the effect of making her look cute.

She walks quickly ahead, running a hand over the surface of a sideboard as though to check for dust. 'It's a recent development, this state of things. A doctor always came to do it, or the girls got sent to the hospital. I had a doctor deliver my bairn. But a few months ago, Mrs Whitlock decided she didn't like doctors no more. So now I get food and board in exchange for helping out with the mums.' She turns and throws me a wink. 'Beats the Gorbals any day of the week.'

'What's the Gorbals?'

She looks confused, and I sense I'm meant to know this. 'You never been to Glasgow?'

I shake my head. 'Haven't been out of Dundee for years 'til this morning.'

She grins. 'Bless your heart. Anyway, my folks don't want me back and I don't care to go back. So it works out.'

She takes me to the back of the house, where we find a modest sitting room that Morven says is called the Rose room. Two battered armchairs are turned to a small fireplace, with newspapers laid out on a side table.

A woman looks up from one of the chairs. 'Pardon the interruption, Mrs Whitlock,' Morven says. 'Our new resident's just arrived and I thought you might like to say hello.'

I shrink back as the woman jumps up and makes her way to us. She's dressed casually, a plain navy cardigan, beige slacks. The diamond ring on her wedding finger gives away her wealth – it's the size of a pebble.

'Mrs Whitlock,' she says politely, holding out her hand. 'You must be Mabel Haggith. All the way from Dundee, if I remember correctly. Did you have a pleasant journey?'

I nod, too shy to speak. I think of how Richard proposed to Ma without a ring. She bought her wedding band from a pawn shop and it made her finger go green.

'It's wonderful to have you here,' Mrs Whitlock says. She has kind eyes. 'Morven will show you your room and introduce you to the other girls. And my husband, of course. He's upstairs, playing with his toys.'

She laughs, and I laugh, too, unsure of what she means. A ghost curls up into a ball inside the heel of my foot, hiding.

Mrs Whitlock walks with me slowly towards the door. 'Morven will also explain how things work around here.' She glances at Morven. 'We have a schedule, you see, and some things we ask our girls to do while they stay.'

I nod. 'OK.'

'It's not meant to be unpaid labour, and I hope you don't find it that way,' she says gently. 'Nothing too strenuous, of course.'

'I'm not afraid of doing work.'

She smiles, her eyes twinkling. 'I hear you're a baker.'

I stop myself from telling her that I got fired for being pregnant. 'Yes.'

'I'd love to sample your talents, if you feel able?'

I give a nod.

'Well, if you find yourself in any way uncomfortable, please rest. Work is only effective for the mind so long as the body is agreeable.'

'I will.'

As Morven leads me back along the hallway, she says, 'You're a baker?'

'Yes.'

Her face brightens. 'Thank God for that. I'm rubbish at that kind of thing. Cooking, yes. Baking, no.'

She leads me to another room at the back of the house. It's huge, decorated in rich, warm tones: the walls are a mix of dark wood panels and silk wallpaper in shades of russet and gold, with copper curtains by the windows, and a large fireplace. There's a dining table in the centre and a Welsh dresser at the far end.

Two girls sit at the table. One is heavily pregnant and the other holds a tiny bairn in her arms.

'Everyone, this is Mabel,' Morven says. 'Mabel, this is Elspeth and Julia.'

I stare at the girls, and they stare wordlessly back. I wonder if I'll have to share a bedroom. Julia looks a little older than me, around twenty-one. Elspeth looks like a child, though she holds a bairn in her arms, a small breast peeking out from the side of her brown dress.

'What are you in for?' she asks.

'I don't know what you mean,' I say hesitantly. Laughter ripples throughout the room.

'How'd you get pregnant?' Elspeth says.

'She had sex, obviously,' Julia says.

I blush ferociously but don't correct them.

'I had an affair with a captain,' Morven tells me with a wink. 'Came ashore at the Queen's Dock in Glasgow, having sailed all the way from Australia. Didn't know he left a little something behind in bonny Scotland.'

'You met the parents yet?' Julia asks.

'She means the adoptive parents,' Morven translates. 'The ones who're adopting your bairn.'

With a stab of fear, I wonder if I should have already met the adoptive parents. Was this something else I was supposed to have known?

'Come on,' Morven says, and I see something draws her eye outside. 'There'll be plenty of time to chat with the girls later. There's one more matter I need to draw your attention to.'

She leads me upstairs towards a large window overlooking the gardens. There, she stops and glances down. I follow her gaze to a boy hurling something into the woods.

'That's Wolfie Whitlock,' she says. 'Little shit.'

I watch him, noticing how angry he seems, wheeling stones through the trees. I expect someone else to be with him, given how much he's ranting and how angrily he's hurling the stones aimlessly into the woods, but he seems entirely alone. He continues the throwing until it wears him out, and he sinks down on to the ground.

'He tore my dress the other day in a rage,' she says, glaring down at him. 'Doesn't speak, only yells nonsense.'

'Who is he?'

'The Whitlocks' grandson. Never seen his parents. He rants and raves like that all day.'

'Poor boy,' I say, noticing how he's curled up in a ball now on the wet ground.

She gives me a look that says she doesn't share my sympathy. 'I'd give him a wide berth, if I were you.'

We head back along the corridor to a row of doors.

'This one's your room,' she says, stepping inside the last room. It's old-fashioned but charming, with pale wallpaper featuring a delicate rose pattern and a cast-iron bed made with white linens. There's a Moses basket by the window, and a wardrobe twice the size of the one I have at home. I've only brought three dresses.

'Okey dokey?' Morven says. 'Any questions, I'm in the room two doors down. The one with the blue door. Knock any time, day or night.'

I nod. She makes to leave, then catches herself.

'Jings, I've not told you where the bathroom is. It's just at the end of the hallway, white door.'

'It's not outside?' I ask. Everyone I know has an outdoor toilet.

She winks. 'Nope. No more cold bum for you, my love.'

I try to rally at this, but I'm still so overwhelmed. This is all so new, so different.

'You poor dear,' Morven says, sitting down beside me. 'You look absolutely terrified.'

I take my special cloth out from my pocket and rub it between my fingers. The fabric is shiny from where I've worn the thread down. It makes me feel a little better.

'I was a bit like you when I came into this place,' Morven says reassuringly, though I doubt she was. 'I know you're scared. But you'll be fine, I promise. Six months from now, you'll be back in Dundee and can forget you were ever here.'

5

It's long after midnight, but I can't sleep. The ghosts are all moaning, a low drone thrumming in my ears. I'm oddly homesick for my own space. Ever since Dad died I've thought about little else but leaving home, but now I'd give anything to be back in my room in Dundee. I know all the quirks of my bedroom, the bit where the carpet ran out and they had to cut a new piece, so there is a join in the middle of the floor where the pattern doesn't quite match up. It feels strange at Lichen Hall. I don't belong here.

The sill of the window is wide enough for me to sit on, so I pull my legs up to my chin and look out at the back gardens and the ocean in the far distance. I thought I could outrun the loneliness I felt back in Dundee. But it's followed me here, climbing up on my lap like a cat. I can never leave it behind.

Light seeps through the small gap at the bottom of the door, a slit of brightness. Morven, I think, and I feel relieved. She made me feel better earlier, and I was deflated when she had to go back to her chores.

It looks like she's carrying a torch.

I wait for a knock on the door, but it doesn't come. Quietly I pad across the room and open the door. No one is there – the landing is in darkness. I step out and squint into the gloom.

'Morven?' I whisper.

Instantly the dark is broken by another light that swells near the stairs, and I look hard, expecting to see her there. But there's only a light, and no shape of anyone near.

Someone's playing games, I think with a shiver. One of the girls I met earlier, come to taunt me.

But then, I don't sense the presence of another person, and all the ghosts in my bones grow quiet.

I creep towards the light, but again I find myself in the dark. At the foot of the stairs, another light appears. I follow again, and again it turns dark once I reach the bottom, until another light glimmers at the far end of the corridor.

This time, the light shines by the window. I'm more mystified than scared, a strange game of hide and seek. In an instant, the light blinks out, only to reappear far beyond the window in the gardens outside.

I cup my hands to the glass and look hard, hoping to see the source of the light – a person will appear, surely, with a torch. But there is nothing.

I'm feeling brave, or intrigued, and the prospect of cool night air on my face is enticing – Lichen Hall has a strange smell, like the inside of a potato sack. It makes me feel queasy.

A side door takes me to the gardens, but as soon as I set foot outside the light disappears. I stand for a moment in the doorway, disoriented, wondering if I'm dreaming. Perhaps I'm sleepwalking. I do this sometimes, when I have a blackout. Ma says I'm like something out of a horror film, walking around wordlessly with my arms by my sides.

As my eyes adjust, something glows through the trees ahead, a faint, wavering light, like moonlight on water. I hesitate, nervous at getting into trouble for being outside. The Whitlocks might think I am snooping.

I inch forward until I spot the light again. But as I approach the woods, through the tall trunks I see not one light but hundreds, scattered across the forest floor like fallen stars. It seems to be a different kind of light, too, a luminous green, and as I press through the trees to get a closer look I spot the cause – the light is coming from clusters of mushrooms, glowing dimly in the dark.

I'm astonished. I can make out the shape of them, gathered on the understorey and some on the tree trunks. Suddenly the mystery of the light inside the house doesn't matter – it's a magical event, finding these. I had no idea mushrooms could glow like fireflies.

I move a little deeper into the woods, finding that the mushrooms glow brighter as the darkness thickens, an alkaline light. I can't help myself – I pluck one to see if it holds its light in my hand. It does, but only for a minute or so before the light fades. I set it back amongst its companions.

As I straighten, I spot movement by a large tree, about thirty feet away. I squint into the milky gloom, my senses on high alert. I'm much deeper in the woods than I intended to come, and suddenly I don't feel safe. But then I spot the source of the movement – it's a person, quite tall, moonlight falling on a long cloak. The curve of a hood at their head.

I step back quickly, but my foot presses down on a branch, breaking the silence with a loud *snap*. The figure turns in my direction, alerted to my presence. They've seen me.

My heart jackhammers in my throat.

I watch, frozen with fear, as the figure begins to walk stealthily towards me. I turn and stumble back to the house, branches whipping my face. I fall on my hands, my knee connecting hard with a rock. I turn quickly to look behind me. My pursuer is charging through the trees, gaining speed.

I'm too terrified to scream.

Now

Pearl

Lichen Hall, Scottish Borders, September 1965

1

My second night at Lichen Hall is filled with dreams of Sebastian. I dream we're walking through a meadow, holding hands. It's a sunny day, and when we look down at our shadows, there is an extra one – the shadow of a child standing between us. A little boy, I think.

Other strangeness haunts my dreams, variations on memories of him and me growing up together: cycling along Raeburn Street, playing rounders in Inverleith Park, though this time we're batting my heart instead of a tennis ball, laughing as it spurts blood all over the grass.

I feel wretched and tearful when I wake up. And as if to taunt me, his photograph is lying face-up on the floor. Why did I bother bringing it?

I've lived next door to Sebastian all my life. Our parents were good friends for years. We went to school together, all the way through. I suppose I thought his photograph would comfort me, reminding me of home and good times. Instead, it has opened old wounds. I thought he might have come to say goodbye when I left, but he didn't. It's been nine months since he broke up with me, barely a word exchanged since.

I get dressed and head downstairs, looking out for the boy I saw on the stairs the night before last. He raced off so fast, and I was worried he might have got a fright. But the house is quiet, and there's no sign of anyone, not even Mrs Whitlock. In the kitchen, I find a piece of paper folded up on the kitchen worktop with my name on it.

Pearl – good morning! Freshly baked bread and eggs in the basket. Please help yourself!

Mrs Whitlock

I find the basket on the kitchen island. Six eggs wrapped in linen and a long golden baguette. My stomach rumbles at the thought of fresh eggs, and the smell of the bread is mouth-watering.

Before I can pick up the baguette, someone shuffles into the kitchen. He's a teenager, by the looks of it, fourteen or fifteen – he must be Mrs Whitlock's grandson. What was his name? It sounded like Wolf . . . Wulfric, I think? He's built like a breeze-block, with a thick jaw and a head of wild copper hair. He wipes his nose along the sleeve of his pyjamas, then fixes me in a rather bovine stare. In one quick move he swipes the baguette from the basket and bites the top off.

'Good morning,' I say drily, watching him devour the bread.

He holds me in a gormless stare for such a long time that I wonder if he's gone into a trance.

'Who are you?' he says.

'Pearl, Pearl Gorham,' I say, extending a hand. 'And you are?'

He continues eating and ignores my hand. 'Wulfric.'

'Oh – *Wulfric*,' I say, and he looks surprised, so I explain the reason for my reaction, 'Your grandmother mentioned you.' I don't say that she's asked me to tutor him. 'Nice to put a face to the name.'

'How long you here for?'

'Until I've . . .' I feel my cheeks flush, the embarrassment of my situation nipping me once more. 'A few months.'

A moment of silence. 'My hens laid those,' he says then, nodding at the eggs. 'Best eggs in Scotland.'

'*Your* hens?'

'You know, if you talk to hens, they lay better eggs. That's the secret. You have to tell them little stories and speak to them like they're people.'

I smile. 'I shall bear that in mind.'

'You ever seen a hummingbird egg?' he says.

'A hummingbird egg?' I repeat with a laugh. 'I've never seen a hummingbird, never mind one of its eggs.'

'Smaller than a fingernail. Want to see?'

I blink. This was certainly not how I pictured my morning going. 'Well, yes. I suppose so.'

'Follow me.'

He turns, baguette in hand, and heads through the door, and I follow, my stomach growling as I pass the bread basket. He leads me upstairs to Mr Whitlock's Micrarium on the landing, morning light spiralling rainbows across the red carpet through the long stained-glass windows. Wulfric stuffs the last of the baguette in his mouth before bending down to one of the glass boxes. Then he plucks something out and sets it in his hand.

'Here,' he says through a mouthful of bread. 'See? Tiny.'

I stare down at a tiny little bird's nest in his palm, the size of an egg cup, containing three miniature eggs, white in colour and small as pearls. The delicacy of it is quite beautiful, though it seems a shame that Mr Whitlock thought to steal a nest for his collection. I wonder how long it has sat here, now that Mr Whitlock is so poorly.

'You see this?' Wulfric says, plucking another object out of a box. 'Looks innocent, doesn't it?'

He places it in my hand. A dried mushroom, the sort I might chop up and add to an omelette. A small gold dome with a white stem. 'It's poisonous,' I say, reading the look of glee on the boy's face. 'Isn't it?'

He falls serious, his voice suddenly reverent. 'The most poisonous mushroom in the world. The Death Cap.'

Quickly I drop the mushroom back into the open glass box and wipe my hands furiously on the back of my dress.

'I think I've seen enough mushrooms for one day, thank you,' I say, thinking back to the awful black blooms spreading throughout the east wing of Lichen Hall, a sign of rot and malaise. 'They make me think of death.'

'My dad used to take me foraging,' Wulfric says, setting the glass box gently back into the cabinet.

I remember what Mr Peterson told me about the crash. About Wulfric's father dying. He must have only been about seven – such a young age to face such grief. 'I'm so sorry,' I say gently.

He goes to say more, but something behind me catches his eye and he visibly clams up. I turn to see Rahmi – rabbit woman – marching along the corridor.

'You've a telephone call,' she says.

I brighten. A phone call! Thank God – my mother must have finally been able to get through.

'Thank you for showing me the hummingbird eggs,' I tell Wulfric.

He looks awkward. 'You're welcome.'

I follow Rahmi downstairs to the phone table, then press the receiver to my ear.

'Hello?'

'Hello, gorgeous.'

My heart sinks. It's not my mother.

'Sebastian?' I whisper, and instantly every inch of my flesh is alert, my nerves ringing with the tumult of emotions his very name tends to trigger.

'Surprised to hear from me?' he says.

'How . . . how did you get this number?' I stammer.

'Does it matter?'

I open my mouth to answer but I suddenly can't speak. It is wonderful to hear his voice, so much so that I cling to the receiver with both hands. And at the same time, it is heart-breaking and infuriating. Why is there no 'stop' button on love? Why can't you simply *will* yourself to stop loving someone?

'How are you?' he says. 'You must be bored out of your mind without any patients to look after.'

'Well, I've only just arrived,' I tell him. 'And I'm enjoying the rest, truth be told.'

'"Enjoying the rest"?' he says with a laugh. 'That's not the Pearl I know.'

'Maybe that Pearl is gone.'

'That's a shame,' he says. 'I loved that Pearl.'

Tears prick my eyes. How can he say these things, after what he did?

'I was thinking,' he says. 'Maybe I could come and visit you.'

'Visit? Here?'

'Yeah. Why not? You're not in prison, are you?'

'Well, no . . .'

'I could take Jonathan's car and pick you up. We could go for a day trip to the beach, you and me. How long has it been since we did that?'

My heart is pounding, images of the two of us leaping in the waves flashing inside my mind. How does he do this? I have never met anyone like Sebastian. There is simply no one like him on the face of the planet. He could persuade you that black is white, that the moon is a cream cake, that your own name belongs to someone else.

'No,' I say, the tremble in my voice undercutting the word. 'Sebastian, I . . .'

'Forgive me,' he says. 'I should have waited until you had settled in.'

'It's not that, it's . . .' I close my eyes and try to focus. 'You're seeing someone. Charlie told me.'

'Am I?'

'That's what Charlie said. Mariella Fotheringham.'

'Oh, so Charlie's the authority on me, is he?'

'Well, are you or aren't you?'

'Am I or aren't I what?'

'Seeing Mariella?'

'I can see Edinburgh Castle right now. Though it's a foggy day . . .'

'*Sebastian.*'

'Pearl, you know how I feel about you.'

I hate how he does this. No matter how much he has betrayed me, no matter how much I know I can't trust him, it's always there, this flame that burns for him and only him. I hate this about myself. I hate that he knows it.

'You don't love me, Sebastian,' I say.

He laughs. 'OK, then.'

'You don't.'

'So why am I on the phone to you? Hmm? Why do I want to jump out this window right now and run all the way to where you are?'

'Because you're an idiot.'

Another laugh. 'This is exhaustion talking. That's what this is.'

'No, this is *me* talking.'

'I miss you, Pearl. It's like I've lost an arm without you here.'

'I miss you, too.'

It's true. I miss him the most out of everyone. I miss his face, his wild laugh, his capable hands. I miss the way he makes me roar with laughter, the way I feel I can be completely myself with him. Nobody and nothing has ever made me feel the way he does – like I'm understood, inside and out. And I have the terrifying feeling that nobody ever will.

'Then say you'll see me,' he says. 'Say you'll come spend a day at the beach with me. Just one day. Can you do that?'

I lean my forehead against the wall. 'Fine.'

'What does "fine" mean?'

'It means fine, I'll spend the day at the beach with you.'

'You really mean that? You'll spend the day with me?'

I sigh. He sounds so sincere. What a bastard. What a charming, intelligent, and utterly gorgeous bastard.

'Yes, Sebastian. I'll still spend the day with you.'

'Dammit, I love you. Remember that, Pearl Gorham.'

I bite my lip. I want to say it back. But I won't.

'Bye.'

I hang up the phone, and the baby gives an enormous kick. I wonder if it can feel the emotions that are flooding through me. If a portion of the sadness and turmoil and love I'm feeling affects the baby. I rub the side of my belly where I can feel it moving.

'There, there,' I say quietly. 'I'm sorry to pass on these feelings to you. He doesn't deserve either of us.'

I give a sigh. There's a sketch on the wall directly opposite of Winston Churchill. A charcoal portrait of him sitting in his chair with that famous bow tie at his throat, cigar in hand. How very apt. I conceived this little one on the day Churchill died, back in January. His name was Bobby, and I had previously treated him for a broken leg. A mere fortnight after Sebastian dumped me, I bumped into Bobby at a bar. We ended up in bed. I didn't care whether or not he wore a condom. I didn't care much about anything that night.

Always there is before me an invisible fork in my path, the endless *should haves* that this pregnancy has crystallized. The life I *should* be leading is one where I'm still tending to my patients and earning praise from Sister Clarke for my hard work, going home every evening to a cooked meal with my parents and brother and telling them about my day. The life I should be leading has wedding plans in the near future, my father walking me proudly down the aisle. I'm wearing my mother's wedding dress, the one made by her grandmother, with pearls from Sweden. We're in the same beautiful church in which she married my father, a short walk from our home in Stockbridge. The pew ends are bursting with white posies, and I have two bridesmaids – my cousin, Mirrin, and my best friend, Lucy. My groom is Sebastian. We'll spend a few years working and travelling before we start a family, and then we'll live happily ever after.

That was how my life should have gone.

I'm on the wrong side of the fork, and I wonder if I can ever switch back to the right side.

2

I left my job when I was three months pregnant.

I begged Sister Clarke to keep me on a little longer, or at least allow me to return after the baby was born, but she wasn't having any of it. My illegitimate pregnancy was a stain on the profession, she said, and so I had to remove myself from sight before I started to show. I barely left my room for months. Then, at six months, Mum said I should go to stay at Aunt Margaret's farm in Oban. She said the fresh air would be good for me and the baby, but we both knew the real reason – I was starting to develop a noticeable bump, and she didn't want word to spread that I had fallen pregnant out of wedlock.

So off to Oban I went. My time was spent helping Uncle William with silaging and shearing, from dawn until dusk. I was knackered at the end of every day, but it kept me busy, which is exactly what I like. Aunt Margaret and Uncle William had enough on their hands without the birth of a baby to deal with, so my parents sent me here.

After a week in Lichen Hall, I'm sleeping in until well after nine, which I'd be ashamed about if I didn't have to visit the toilet six times a night. This baby is hell-bent on kicking the shit out of my bladder. And I have the most horrendous gastric reflux. Anything I eat sends rivers of stomach acid whooshing back up my oesophagus, burning the back of my throat and sending a sharp burning sensation around my heart. I feel quite bad for the patients I've treated who complained of this, and I told them simply to sleep with an extra pillow. One extra pillow does sod all, frankly, and I'm miserable with it. Honestly, women who have babies are heroes. I don't think I ever want to do this again. I'm not sure it's worth it.

I've lived like a sloth for the last week, spending my days in the library. I find a book on mushrooms, *The Magical World of Fungi* by Professor Arthur Llewellyn. It makes me think of Wulfric, and the memory he shared with me of his father taking him foraging. I learn that fungi are much more than mere mushrooms and toadstools, and small wonder that the meningitis I had as a child was so severe. According to Professor Llewellyn, the world only exists because of fungi, and indeed the plant kingdom and the entire human race would cease to be if fungi were eradicated. A highly intelligent species, fungi live on and inside the human body, causing both sickness and well-being. Malaria and diabetes are treated with fungal extracts, as is cancer.

Stunning to think such things exist with such complexity amongst us. As a child, I delighted finding fairy rings, and often my uncle would take me foraging for mushrooms, just like Wulfric's father did. I can well appreciate the tenderness of his memories. Uncle Jim and I would bring them home and fry them up with wild garlic and butter. He'd often tell me that the mushrooms were like icebergs – beneath the golden chanterelles a fungal network spread deep within the earth, a labyrinth that was said to span for miles.

I can only read for so long before I crave some adult conversation. I get up and explore the long corridors of the house, trying to find someone to talk to.

Mrs Whitlock is elusive, and I can't shake the feeling that she's avoiding me. She was warm and friendly the day I arrived, and that night we had supper together.

I mentioned the boy I'd spotted on the landing later that night.

'Oh, I don't think so,' she said.

I didn't know what to make of it. 'No ghosts in Lichen Hall, I'm taking it?' I said with a laugh, and she smiled, but I could feel it – the atmosphere had changed. She made her excuses after that. I was left picking over my words, wondering what I'd done wrong.

I've barely seen her since.

Meals are prepared and left in the kitchen buffet-style, and so I help myself and eat alone in the dining room, hoping I'll bump into someone. Rahmi collects the used towels from my bathroom, and sometimes I try to strike up a conversation. But she won't so much as make eye contact.

On my third day, I take a walk through the gardens and see Aretta bending over the vegetable patch.

'Need any help?' I call out.

No answer.

'Lovely day, isn't it?' I say, louder this time, in case she didn't hear. This time, she straightens, looks directly at me, then turns her back to me.

I write a long letter to Lucy, begging her to fill me in on life at the hospital. She rang me every other night when I was in Oban, and I drank up her news, mentally walking along the wards again to greet my patients, feeling the weight of my stethoscope in my hand, feeling *useful*.

On my fourth day, I'm in the library reading, when I hear the distinctive crunch of gravel under tyres at the side of the house. I look out of the window and spy a flashy black car pulling up. Perhaps a friend coming to visit the Whitlocks. I head downstairs, hopeful that the guests will talk to me.

Mrs Whitlock is shaking hands with a man and woman. One of them says 'How do you do' to her. They all look very sombre, too, and the woman carries a framed photograph of a little girl. It looks like a school photograph, a smiling black and white portrait, and the visible knot of a school tie. The woman dabs her eyes, and the man comforts her, before they step into the Wisteria room.

Another child follows behind, clutching a teddy. She's younger than the girl in the photograph, and she looks up at me suddenly, catching my eye.

'Mummy?' she says to the woman. 'Who is that lady on the stairs?'

I shrink back. But too late – Mrs Whitlock steps forward to shut the door, glancing up at me in annoyance as she does.

Later, I find her at the back of the house, smoking and throwing crumbs for the crows. They make the most awful racket.

'Good evening,' she says.

'Good evening.' She turns her gaze back to the birds, her body language suggesting she doesn't want to talk to me. I feel more awkward by the moment. 'I hope I didn't intrude earlier,' I say. 'I saw you had guests. I was just headed to the kitchen . . .'

'We both know that isn't true,' she says, taking a long drag from her cigarette. 'Lunch had just finished.'

My words dry up in my mouth. She's right – it is a lie. I was just snooping. Or rather, I was so bored and lonely that I'd hoped to be introduced to the guests.

'There are certain matters of business at the house that must be kept separate from other matters,' she says, glancing at my bump.

I feel my cheeks flush. She means that a pregnant girl in full view of her guests is an embarrassment.

'Was there anything else?' she says dismissively. All the friendliness of my first evening here has vanished.

'Actually, if I may,' I say. 'I'd like to find out the plans for the delivery.'

She blinks. 'The delivery?'

'Obviously, we're a little far away from a hospital,' I say. Also, there's no sign of a car parked anywhere, either. 'I assume a doctor or midwife will be travelling here. I wondered when I might meet them to make arrangements?'

'Oh,' she says, flicking her cigarette. She glances down at the birds gathering around the crumbs. 'No, no doctor or midwife. Aretta will deliver the baby.'

'I'm sorry,' I say, certain I've misheard. 'Aretta . . . ?'

She nods. 'Aretta will deliver the baby, yes. I'm afraid I don't *do* doctors, Miss Gorham.'

I can't help but stare at her. Is this a joke? 'But . . . Aretta's a maid. Isn't she?'

She makes to turn back into the house. 'Aretta has delivered plenty of babies before.'

'I really . . . I think a qualified midwife is in order,' I stammer, following her. But she walks briskly to another room, locking it behind her before I can say anything more.

I feel wretched all night. Embarrassed, humiliated, and frantic about the thought of Aretta delivering the baby. And angry at her dismissal of what is a reasonable thing to ask. She was so lovely to me when I arrived, and now she's acting like I have no say in this matter. It's absurd, and dangerous. The Whitlocks are charitable enough to offer a place in their home when I would otherwise be forced into an institution, and I certainly don't want to seem ungrateful. But no midwife? No way.

I spot the telephone in the hall and decide to check the dial tone. My hearts leaps to find that there is one. I dial home as quick as I can. Someone answers on the second ring.

'Hello?'

It's my mother's voice. Tears prick my eyes.

'Is that you, Pearl darling?' she says. 'The line is dreadful. Are you there?'

'Yes, I'm here.' I swallow back a sob. I miss her. I miss my room, my job, my *life*. 'Mum, I need to talk to you about something.'

'Oh, I'd love to, but I'm about to pop out . . .'

I tell her quickly about the delivery plan, how Mrs Whitlock wants Aretta to deliver the baby despite her not being a qualified doctor. I mention how Aretta is one of the maids and tends to the gardens. 'Did you speak to Mrs Whitlock about how the baby would be born before booking me in here?'

She sounds distracted, and my heart sinks. 'I can't really recall, darling. I had you at home, and your brother. It's how women have done it for centuries.'

'Aretta's not a midwife,' I say, glancing around in case anyone can hear. 'She's not trained . . .'

'Surely they wouldn't put you in danger? I know you're a nurse, but I'm certain it's all in hand.'

I nod at the phone, suddenly awash with guilt.

'I just thought I'd be going to a hospital, or perhaps a doctor would come out . . .'

'We did look into it.'

'You did?'

There's a long silence on the other end of the phone. 'Given that you're an unmarried mother, there's a degree of reluctance, shall we say, on the part of the doctors to come all the way out to Lichen Hall.'

I try to take this in. It explains so much. Shame stings me into silence.

'When I had you,' she says, 'I was out walking with your father. It was during the war, as you know, and he was on leave from the army. We managed to get to the car, and drove quickly home, and then your father caught you in the hallway.'

She laughs. I've heard this story a million times. It always seemed funny – cosy, even. But now I'm wondering if she wasn't frightened, not to have a qualified doctor to hand. Didn't she worry I might die?

'Anyway, I really must dash. Love you, darling.'

'Love you too.'

I feel crushed when I hang up, swamped with the feeling that

I've failed everyone. Nonetheless, there remains the issue that, regardless of whether Aretta is capable and experienced, she doesn't seem to like me.

And that doesn't exactly bode well when it comes to delivering my baby.

3

I decide to attempt to befriend her. The emphasis here is very much on *attempt*. I'm good at making people like me, generally speaking. Befriending her might also help me find out the extent of Aretta's medical skills. If need be, perhaps I can train her. Three weeks to go. Desperate times, and all that.

But how to befriend her?

I decide to attempt it through the medium of cookery. I'm a decent cook, at least when it comes to three meals: mince and tatties, macaroni cheese, and roast chicken. Aretta and Rahmi are always working, either doing laundry or scrubbing the floors, or out in the vegetable garden, so I have to pick my moment. When I had supper with Mrs Whitlock on my first day, she mentioned that the girls get Sundays off, and that she likes to take a picnic and a book to the meadow to enjoy the mild weather. She takes Mr Whitlock in his wheelchair, creaking across the lawn and through the clearing in the forest, and Wulfric goes too.

So the following Sunday I rise early to prepare. I search the kitchen and find some potatoes and vegetables. In the freezer is minced lamb. Mince and tatties it is. But I need herbs.

I venture outside and head to the gardens, scanning the flowerbeds for anything that might resemble rosemary. The gardens are beautiful, though a little shabby – there are a couple of ponds with koi, and a long, trellised tunnel that would look stunning with clematis or roses, but is covered with dried weeds. I head further towards the vegetable garden, but there are no herbs to be found.

The ocean comes into view, the lovely promise of blue spreading out at the edge of the cliff. There's a tall wall at my left, and I notice a gate. It's hidden by the overgrown grasses and brambles, and at first I think it might be another entrance to the walled garden where I first met Aretta. But when I peek through the bars, I see it's not the same one at all. It's a herb garden, by the looks of it, a long, L-shaped plot with terrariums and raised beds.

I try the gate. It's stiff, but it creaks open, letting me inside. On the stone ground I count fifteen wooden raised beds, the size of snooker tables, filled with leafy green plants. One bed is filled with vibrant green basil, its fragrance filling the air, another filled with rosemary. I tear off a handful, and I should really get going in case I'm not supposed to be here. I don't want to cause any more irritation. But I'm intrigued. An old barrel at the end of the raised beds is filled with mandrakes. I recognize the leaves – Lucy is interested in folk medicine, and she grows mandrakes in her garden. I remember her showing me how the roots looked like strange bodies, with legs and arms. Perhaps Mrs Whitlock is growing it to help with Mr Whitlock's ailments.

Along both sides of the garden are a dozen or so brick beds topped with handmade terrariums – pieces of glass in metal frames that cover the soil. I bend to look inside one and find a handful of vivid blue flowers growing inside. I don't recognize them at all – they're not bluebells, and they don't have petals, only a single cone-shaped stamen. It's only when I've stared for a few moments that I realize – they're not flowers at all. They're *mushrooms*. I almost laugh out loud at the discovery. Mushrooms! Bright blue mushrooms!

I walk to the next glass dome and find a bizarre-looking shrub, like a white net skirt. Again, I realize I'm staring at a mushroom – there's the brown, cone-shaped head, rather penis-like in shape, then the white stem, and an odd lace-like skirt of fungus flowing down around it.

It doesn't take long to realize that each of the terrariums contains a different species of fungus, all of them bizarre and beautiful. No British toadstool or chanterelles here – they're exotic, and grown, it seems, perhaps simply for aesthetic purposes. I think of Mr Whitlock's Micrarium, and how the herb garden seems in keeping with his predilection for curiosities. Or perhaps it's something to do with folk medicine. I search my memories for anything that Lucy mentioned that might indicate why such mushrooms would be cultivated, but I can't recall. Her interest was in plants.

I spot something on the back wall that seems to be neither herb nor mushroom: a wooden trellis holds up what looks like a creeping flower, with leaves like crêpe paper and blowsy purple, shiny black berries. A blackberry bush, I think, except the berries are bigger. Perhaps they're a kind of plum, or rosehip.

I leave the garden with a fistful of rosemary, basil, and coriander, and close the gate carefully behind me. The house is quiet – Mrs Whitlock and Wulfric must already be out.

Back in the kitchen, I boil the potatoes and cook the mince in herb-infused juices with peas, chopped carrots, tomatoes, and a dash of Worcestershire sauce, then add some of the rosemary too.

The mince is steaming hot, and when I bring a tablespoon of it to my lips to taste, I consider eating the whole thing myself. But no, I will carry the meal into the dining room and invite Aretta to join me. It seems rude not to invite Rahmi, too. Then, I set the long wooden dining table, which seems far too big for the three of us, but hey ho.

Something seems amiss. I stand by the table, recalling my mother's dinner parties. What was it she always did when it was a particularly special night? Oh yes – she'd create party favours in the form of pretty gift bags placed on the chairs of her guests.

I race upstairs – well, race is probably an exaggeration, but I move as fast as I can for someone who is eight months pregnant – and fling open my wardrobe doors. I find two silk robes, one black, one cream, that I've not worn in years. They've been dry-cleaned, so I don't feel bad giving them as gifts. Lastly, I find some lace-edged, baby blue pillowcases folded on the bottom of the wardrobe, and slip the gifts inside two of them.

Perfect.

Downstairs, I call out for my guests.

'Aretta? Rahmi? Might you join me in the dining room, please?'

Aretta appears from another room. 'Dining room?' she asks.

'I have made us a *feast*.' I give her a brief smile before ducking back into the kitchen to lift the casserole dish out of the oven.

By the time I carry it through into the dining room, both Aretta and Rahmi are sitting on the chairs looking slightly bewildered.

'Ladies, I give you Pearl Gorham's World-Famous, Legend-of-Legends, Tell-All-The-Poets-To-Sharpen-Their-Pencils, Shepherd's Pie.' I whisk the dishcloth away from the top of the dish like a magician revealing a live rabbit.

'It smells delicious,' Rahmi says, eyeing the food.

Aretta looks a little more cautious. 'Are you going to tell us what this is all about?'

I lift the serving spoon and begin to shovel the mince and tatties on to their plates. 'Well, we must be about the same age, and you've both been so kind in looking after me the last few days. I wanted to get to know both of you.'

They both glance at each other warily, as though I'm asking them to divulge their darkest secrets.

'Shall we start with some introductions?' I say. 'I'm Pearl, Pearl Gorham. I'm twenty-two, I'm a nurse, and I live in Edinburgh. I'm mostly Scottish, though about one eighth Swedish on my mum's side.'

A moment's silence. 'I'm Rahmi Mansouri,' Rahmi says, following my lead. 'I'm twenty-four, I'm a singer, and I'm Algerian and a bit Turkish, though I grew up in Auchtermuchty.'

'I've been to Auchtermuchty,' I say brightly, leaping at the chance to prove we have something in common.

'You poor thing,' she says, and I laugh.

I turn to Aretta, and for a moment it looks as if she's not going to play. With a sigh, she says: 'Aretta Nangobi. Twenty-five. I'm a seamstress, and I'm Xhosa, mostly. My mam's in Monzie.'

I smile, pleased that they've not told me to take a running jump. So far, so good. 'A seamstress and a singer,' I say, impressed. 'How does a seamstress and a singer end up working for the Whitlocks?'

Another shy glance from Rahmi, and Aretta keeps her arms tightly folded and her eyes on the table. I worry that I'm pressing too hard. Perhaps I should have started with small talk instead of delving into personal stuff.

'It's quite a long story,' Rahmi says. 'We both came here to have our babies. And then we never left.'

I'm shocked. 'You both came here . . . just like me?'

'Neither of us were all that keen on our families,' Aretta says, flicking her eyes at Rahmi. 'This is our home, now. We get to stay in exchange for the work we do.'

I nod, not wanting to pry too much more. But it sounds like an unusual arrangement. It sounds like they don't get paid. And yet they work so hard.

Aretta spots the pillowcases on the floor next to the chairs. 'What are these?'

I'd almost forgotten about them. 'Oh, they're gifts. Do you want to open yours?'

She scoops up her pillowcase. When she shakes out the silk robe her face lights up.

'This is for me?' she says, and I nod.

'Do you like it? I wanted to say thank you. I know I'm causing you all extra work . . .'

'It's been a long, long time since I've owned something like this,' Aretta says thoughtfully, admiring the fabric.

'Oh my,' Rahmi says, slipping her robe on. She removes her hair clip, letting her long hair cascade in thick black waves over one shoulder. She's really very pretty. An Algerian Brigitte Bardot. She raises an eyebrow and poses, one shoulder forward. 'How do I look?'

'Delicious,' Aretta says, and there's something in her voice that tells me they're more than workmates. I suspect they're lovers. Maybe that's why they've stayed here at Lichen Hall. My friend Lucy's a lesbian, though she regularly dates men to keep people from asking questions. And a brilliant doctor I worked under lost his job last year when someone told the police that he had a male lover. They arrested him at the hospital on 'moral charges'. They didn't have to do it there – they could have arrested him at home, or once he'd left work. They did it to make a point, to shame him in front of his colleagues, to smear his achievements. All of us were furious. But we could do nothing.

Rahmi notices me looking and moves a little away from Aretta, suddenly self-conscious. I'm more certain now – they're definitely a couple.

'I won't say anything,' I say quickly.

To my relief, she smiles at me. 'Thanks,' she says, glancing at Aretta.

'Can I ask what you both do on your days off?' I say, changing the subject. 'I've noticed there isn't a television or record player here.'

Aretta gives a noise of pain, as though she misses these things every bit as much as I do, and for a moment I want to hug her.

'We didn't have those things at home,' Rahmi says, 'so I didn't really notice.'

I lower my eyes, ashamed. Sometimes I forget that my family is well-off.

'We play cards,' Aretta says. 'Go on walks. We read.'

'Most of the girls who come here leave their things behind,' Rahmi says. 'Like they don't want to remember their time here. We've a whole store cupboard full of stuff. Clothes, shoes, baby stuff, toys, even jewellery. And lots of books. You'll not find any Harper Lee or Ray Bradbury in the library. But you will in the store cupboard.'

I tell them I'll be heading straight to that store cupboard after dinner. 'You don't like to head to the nearest village sometimes?' I say. 'No discos? Pubs?'

'Mrs Whitlock doesn't like us to leave the estate,' Rahmi says with a smile of resignation. 'And we like our life here.'

Mrs Whitlock doesn't like us to leave the estate. I bite back my thoughts on that.

'Mrs Whitlock told me you'll be delivering the baby, Aretta,' I say delicately.

'I've delivered four babies before,' she says. 'Probably not as many as you, given that you're a nurse.'

'I've helped deliver fifty babies,' I say lightly, and she raises her eyebrows.

'You could probably teach me a thing or two,' Aretta says, which doesn't fill me with confidence.

'Perhaps I could,' I say. Then, tactfully: 'Would that be OK?'

She shrugs. 'Whatever you like.'

'In fact, I could even teach you some other tricks of the trade,' I say, trying to keep the tone light. 'It might come in handy.'

'Mrs Whitlock has us working night and day except Sundays,' Rahmi says. 'So we don't get a lot of free time.'

'Speaking of Mrs Whitlock,' I say. 'Do you like her?'

'She's become . . . different,' Aretta says in a low voice. 'The last few years especially. She used to be quite nice. She's got worse since Mr Whitlock took ill.'

'What's wrong with Mr Whitlock?' I ask. 'It's dementia, isn't it?'

'Nothing to do with Mr Whitlock,' Rahmi says. She leans forward, her eyes wide. 'It's the thing in the woods.'

'Oh, here we go,' Aretta says, rolling her eyes.

'Don't listen to her,' Rahmi tells me, nodding at Aretta. 'Just because she's never seen it doesn't mean it isn't real.'

'Seen what?' I say, feeling drawn in.

'You haven't heard of the woman in the woods?' Rahmi says.

I shake my head. 'No. But do tell.'

Rahmi glances again at Aretta, who shakes her head in disbelief. 'So there's a story about a witch who lives in the ghost woods out in the forest.'

'I've heard of that,' I say. 'Mrs Whitlock mentioned it. At least, the ghost woods part. I don't believe she mentioned a witch.'

'Well, I heard about it when I first came here,' Rahmi says, and I see Aretta give her a look, as though to warn her not to say more. Rahmi notices, and bites back whatever she was going to say. 'I've seen her,' she says guardedly.

'Who, the witch?' I say, and she nods. I study her face, expecting her to say 'Boo!' or something, revealing it all as a big joke.

'Well, then,' I say, raising my glass of water as though it is a crisp Chardonnay. 'I shall seek out this witch in the ghost woods. A little bit of spookiness will spice this place up nicely.'

'Don't,' Rahmi says, though I'm not sure how much I should take this at face value. 'It might be the last thing you ever do.'

Then

Mabel

Lichen Hall, Scottish Borders, July 1959

1

I barely sleep, quaking like a leaf under the bedclothes. The light of dawn is the best thing I've ever seen. The shuffling of feet and the yowl of Elspeth's baby downstairs brings relief.

I'm alive.

My arms and legs are bruised and scratched from running through the trees. My belly feels strange, too, all tight. I managed to outrun the figure in the woods, but I feel battered from running so hard.

I throw on my dress quickly and brush my teeth before heading downstairs. I need to find Morven. I search all the rooms, the scale of the place just as dizzying as yesterday. The long windows of the lounge overlook the treeline, and the memory of last night comes thumping back into my bones.

I find Morven in the kitchen, drying dishes and putting them back into cupboards. My heart lifts at the sight of her, and I race to tell her about what happened last night.

'Could I have a word?' I say quickly.

Her face shines with sweat, and there are damp patches at the armpits of her dress. The dishes clatter as she files them quickly into the cupboard, some of them still slick with water.

'I'm a bit busy this morning,' she says, fanning herself. 'Why don't you go get some breakfast?'

'Are you OK?' I ask, noticing how rattled she is.

She gives a sigh and pulls out a tray. 'I've to teach Wulfric,' she says under her breath, her words tight with anger. 'Mrs Whitlock must think I'm a bloody octopus. Thirteen loads of laundry to do and she reckons I have time to teach him his bloody times tables.' She flips a tea towel over a shoulder and wipes her brow on the back of her wrist. 'Truth is, I don't even *know* my bloody times tables. I left school when I was twelve, for God's sake.'

'I'm sorry,' I say, tripping over my words. 'I won't bother you any longer.'

She stops and looks at me for the first time. 'Oh, you're not bothering me. I'll catch up with you later, yeah?'

I watch her scurry up the stairs, the tray in her hands laden with fresh fruit and a pot of tea for Wulfric. I head to the dining room, where the other girls are sitting. Julia wears rollers, holding her hair in a pageboy style, and she and Elspeth are in their nightdresses. There's tea and coffee on the table, and a platter of breads and cooked meats. My stomach growls.

Elspeth and Julia are deep in conversation about Elvis being stationed in Germany, and how Julia thinks he'll be killed by the end of the year.

'Think about it,' she says. 'He's a singer, not a fighter. It's a conspiracy, the whole thing. They want to bump him off.'

'So you're telling me they've drafted Elvis Presley just so they shut down rock and roll?' Elspeth says, turning her baby around against her shoulder.

Julia shrugs. 'It's the devil's music. Look what happened to Buddy Holly and Ritchie Valens.'

I sit at the end of the table, closest to the bread basket, hoping they're too caught up in their conversation to notice me. But, too late – Elspeth notices me, and they turn and stare.

'Hello, New Girl,' Julia says.

'Hi,' I say, shrinking a little into my chair. I feel self-conscious, even though I'm fully dressed and they're both in their nightdresses.

'What's your name, again?' Elspeth says.

'Mabel,' I say.

Her eyes fall over my dress. 'Interesting clothing,' she says. 'Did your mum make that for you?'

I give a meek nod. Ma makes all my clothes, even my socks. It would be fine, but she makes everything the same size, regardless who it's for, so my dress is far too big.

'It looks like a tablecloth,' Julia says, pinching the end of it between her finger and thumb. 'Is that a gravy stain?'

'Where are you from?' Elspeth asks me, and I'm glad of the distraction.

'Dundee,' I say.

'Told you,' Julia says triumphantly. 'I said she's a Dundonian, didn't I? It's the smell. You can tell a mile off.'

Elspeth chucks a napkin at her. 'My grandma's from Dundee,' she says.

My face burns. I want to leave, but I'm ravenous. I reach for the breakfast tray in the centre of the table, but it inches away from me. It takes a few moments for me to realize the cause: Julia is tugging the tray from the other end of the table, moving it slowly out of reach and laughing as my hand travels after it to no avail.

'Not until you tell us all the details,' she sneers.

I look up at her. 'About what?'

'About the father of your baby. Who was he, then? Was he married?'

'It's the rule in this place,' Elspeth snipes, leaning towards me. 'You have to spill the details.'

'I don't have any details,' I manage to say, and Elspeth laughs.

'She thinks she's better than us,' she tells Julia.

The ghost in my knee starts to jump up and down, sending my whole leg aquiver.

'Well, if you're not going to tell us,' Julia says. 'You can't eat with us.'

'Don't be mean, Julia,' Elspeth says. She gives me a nod. 'You can sit here.'

I rise from my chair to sit next to Elspeth, opening my mouth to say thank you for her small act of kindness. But the words are barely past my lips when I feel the chair swiped from behind me, right as I'm already lowering into the chair, my knees bent. I feel the shock of empty space, then the hard floor connecting with my tailbone. Their laughter swirls above me as I fall painfully to the ground, tears pricking my eyes.

'How dare you!' a voice shouts, and I sit upright just as Morven appears above me. She continues yelling at the others.

'You stupid bitch!' she snaps. 'What did you do that for? She could lose the bairn that way!'

'Isn't that what she came here for?' Julia says drily.

Morven helps me to my feet. I feel dazed, and my tailbone throbs. Morven keeps a tight grip on me, guiding me out of the room. 'Morons,' she mutters angrily under her breath.

'Are you all right?' she says once we reach the kitchen. I ease down carefully into a chair, balancing on one buttock to avoid hurting the painful part.

'I'm fine,' I lie.

'What about the bairn?' she says. 'Can you still feel it moving?'

I don't mention about how much I don't like the feel of it kicking inside me. I place a hand on my belly. Something squirms against my palm, and I nod.

'That's a relief,' she says. 'Still, any twinges, any blood in your knickers, you need to tell me. Got it?'

I nod. Morven sets about making me a cup of tea and buttered toast.

'I saw you creep out last night,' she says in a low voice. 'Thought you were running away.'

I look up at her, wary of being told off.

'I thought I saw a light,' I say. 'I followed it outside.'

'Well, you're braver than most,' she says. 'Most girls get a fright out there, in the woods. Especially at night. You've heard the stories, I take it?'

I swallow hard, trying to summon up the words to tell her about what I saw. I barely know how to describe it. 'What stories?'

She passes me the sugar bowl. 'It's a really, *really* old story. According to folklore, a girl who lived in here in Lichen Hall centuries ago had a bairn. But the baby wasn't human. It was part tree, or mushroom, or something. And instead of fessing up that she slept with one of the servants, she said a witch cast a spell on her in the woods.'

I finish my tea, an icy shiver rolling down my spine. 'And then what happened?'

She thinks I'm intrigued by the story, and adopts a stage voice. 'And then the parents killed the bairn, and people say the witch has haunted this place ever since, getting her revenge.' She grins. 'Not a very nice fairy tale. Some of the girls that stay here won't go near the woods when they hear it.'

My mouth runs dry. I think back to the moment when I spotted the hooded figure in the gloom of the woods. How my heart seemed to stop at the menace of it. How the light of the mushrooms pooled in corners of the understorey. How the ghosts in my body fell silent.

'I think I saw something . . .' I start to say, and Morven leans in, watching me closely. But just then, a voice calls from somewhere in the house. 'Morven? Are you there?'

Instantly, Morven jumps to attention, as though she'd forgotten something and has just remembered. 'Coming, Mr Whitlock!' she calls back. Quickly she places the kettle back on the stove.

'I said I'd bring him tea,' she explains.

'I thought you were teaching Wulfric,' I say.

'Aye. *Wulfric*,' she says irritably. 'He threw another tantrum this morning. Says maths hurts his brain.' She rolls her eyes. 'So I got off the hook.'

She pours another cup of tea and finds a saucer in a cupboard. 'Shall I introduce you to Mr Whitlock?' she says, and I nod.

2

She leads me upstairs to a long landing lined with cabinets and tables of glass boxes. An older man stands there, holding something close to his face. He is older than Mrs Whitlock by at least ten years, frothy grey hair brushing his collarbone, a hooked nose and eyebrows that jut out from his face. He is eccentrically dressed – a long blue bathrobe worn over a bright blue shirt and shorts, revealing skinny legs that are fuzzy with white hair. On his feet, he wears dress shoes without socks. The shoes look like they've recently been polished.

Morven sets down the tray nearby. 'Your tea, Mr Whitlock,' she says. He turns sharply, as though he hadn't heard us approach. Morven nods at me. 'This is Mabel, Mr Whitlock. She's staying with us for a little while.'

He surveys me with narrowed eyes, then turns back to the box in his hand. 'My little collection,' he says, nodding at it. 'A history of the world in a thousand objects. That's what I call it.' He hands me the box. 'Flesh of the gods. You ever tried it?'

I shake my head, uncertain.

'Psilocybin mushrooms,' he says. 'Surprised you haven't tried it. All the young folk are doing them these days.'

Inside the box is a handful of old cone-headed mushrooms. They don't look very appealing.

'Young people think they've discovered these, but the Incas were taking them thirteen thousand years ago.'

'It's nice to meet you,' I say, turning to leave, but he looks crestfallen.

'You ought to see this,' he says, and I wait, throwing a nervous glance at Morven, as he lifts another glass box and hands it to me.

'Is that an ant?' I ask, noticing a tiny creature inside the box. It's large for an ant, about the size of a wasp, but without the wings. There's something else that renders it strange – a long growth spurts out of its head, and something on the end that resembles a chrysalis.

'It's actually two things,' Mr Whitlock says, shuffling closer and pointing down at the box with a long fingernail. 'It's a carpenter ant, and something else.' He raises his fuzzy eyebrows. 'Can you guess what the something else is?'

I squint harder at the ant. Maybe it's a kind of chrysalis, or an ant hybrid. A butterfly ant, perhaps, the thing in its head a kind of antennae.

'You see the stem protruding from the body of the ant?' he says, tapping the glass.

I nod.

'*That* is nothing more than a fungus living inside the body of its host. Ophiocordyceps unilateralis, to be exact, from the Cordyceps species. Quite marvellous. Have you heard of it?'

'Fungus?' I say, staring again. It looks nothing like the mushrooms he showed me. It's very much a budding flower.

He smiles for the first time, revealing yellowed teeth. 'Cordyceps has defied us for decades, and will continue to do so, I imagine. This species of fungus gets inside a host and exercises what you might call mind control. In this case, it forces the ant to break away from its colony to climb a tree.' He shakes off his robe and takes a step back, as though to act it out. 'Once it's up there,' he says, mimicking a creature climbing a tree, 'the fungus tells it to bite down on a leaf, then kills it, before sprouting out of its body and shooting its spores from that vast distance all over the forest.' He moves his hands from his chest, demonstrating spores shooting out of his body. 'And where do you think they land?'

I throw a glance at Morven for reassurance, and she smiles, giving it.

'On the ground?' I reply.

He sniffs, disappointed in my answer. 'In the bodies of other ants. And the cycle begins again. More zombified ants, more spores shooting from high places.' He stops for breath, wiping the back of his hand across his mouth. 'Cordyceps is no blunt instrument, either – it coordinates the suicide of its host with precision, positioning it to ensure the spores land exactly where the ant colony thrives.' He turns his little grey eyes from me to Morven. 'Can you believe that?'

'It's gruesome,' I say.

He nods, delighted to have found a captive audience in me. 'Gruesome as a parasite. Intelligent as a virus. More so. Fifty million years of evolution will do that. We still don't understand all it can do.' He looks the ant over carefully before setting it back in place. 'Life will not be stopped. That's what the history of the world has taught me. Ruthless, glorious, murderous *life*.'

He manoeuvres the box back into the row of boxes on the table, but his hand knocks over another box, and it tumbles to the ground.

'Oh dear,' Morven says. She gets down on her hands and knees and searches under the table.

She finds the box, but it's empty. 'Something must have fallen out,' she says, scanning the floor by our feet.

With a groan of frustration, Mr Whitlock doubles over to scoop it up by his feet.

It's a lock of child's hair, a small curl of soft brown hair tied with a navy bow. Mr Whitlock seems moved by it, holding it with his forefinger and thumb, placing it in the palm of his left hand with great care, raising it to his face to observe it closer.

'My son,' he says quietly. 'He was the sweetest boy. Just the sweetest child.'

He seems to pull away from us then, lost in a memory.

'Don't forget about your tea, Mr Whitlock,' Morven says gently, but he's muttering to himself, seemingly blind to us.

Morven gestures me to follow her. 'He's a few cards short of a deck, that's for certain,' she says under her breath as she leads me back downstairs. My tailbone is aching now, and I limp slightly with the pain of it.

'You should rest for today,' Morven says when we reach the kitchen. 'I'm going to give you an ice pack and some pain relief. Stay in your bedroom. I'll bring you your meals, OK?'

I'm stunned by her kindness. I don't think anyone has ever taken care of me like this.

She notices my confusion. 'Are you OK?' she says. 'You're not allergic to paracetamol, are you?'

'No,' I say, shaking my head, and as she passes me the ice pack I feel safe for the first time in years.

3

I spend the next couple of days in bed, rising only to use the bathroom. Morven says it's important that my tailbone heals before I give birth because sometimes it can complicate things, or make the pain worse. She brings my meals as she promises, along with a fresh ice pack.

On Wednesday, I feel better, so I venture downstairs after breakfast to find Morven carrying buckets and a long pole to the door.

'What's this for?' I ask.

'Wednesdays are for washing windows,' she says. 'Don't worry if you're not feeling up to it.'

'I can give it a go,' I say.

She hands me the pole with a cloth tied to the end. 'You do the front windows. Use this to wash the ones you can't reach,' she says. 'And *stop* if you feel sore, OK?'

At the front of the house the long stained-glass windows catch the light in rich pools of colour. The embrasures have plants and toadstools carved into the stonework, though time has eroded them. I hadn't noticed them until I stood this close.

The windows are surprisingly filthy, the colours brightening with each scrub of the cloth against the glass. I suspect the other girls haven't exactly taken to their tasks with enthusiasm. There's a ladder propped up against the wall, and when I find the pole doesn't quite reach the corners, I climb the ladder gingerly to finish the job. It's the least I can do for Morven. She's been so kind.

At the top of the ladder, I hear a noise. A quick glance up reveals two faces at the open window above: Julia and Elspeth.

'Hello, Dundee,' Elspeth says, grinning down.

I go to say hello back, but just then Julia lifts a bucket to the windowsill. I see the liquid sloshing inside, and even when she begins to tip it down I have no way of safely scurrying down the ladder in time. The contents fall, splattering both me and the windows.

I stand, drenched, the horrifying realization hitting me that it's not water – it's a bucket of urine. Somehow I manage not to fall off the ladder, sliding down to retch in the hedgerows, before staggering all the way back to my room to get washed and changed.

4

'You've got to stand up for yourself,' Morven tells me that night after dinner. 'They'll eat you for breakfast, those girls. They can see you're not like them.'

I ponder her comment: *not like them*. I already know I'm not like them, and it makes me sad that I never seem to be like anyone. It's another kind of loneliness, being so different.

'They're rich bitches,' Morven says as she stacks the dirty dishes on the worktop. 'They come from homes where they're waited on hand and foot. They *expect* to be treated like royalty. You and me – we come from nothing.'

You and me. Her words light something in me.

'How do I . . . stand up for myself?' I say, not looking at her.

'You don't take no shit, that's how,' she says. 'You don't let them bully you. They mock you, you mock back. They ask questions you don't want to answer, you tell them straight that it's none of their business. Got it? You don't take *no shit*.'

The dishes stacked, Morven lifts the mop and bucket and heads towards the dining room. I follow her, and spot Elspeth and Julia at the foot of the stairwell, sniggering about something. Elspeth's baby is nowhere to be seen. Julia's bump sticks out from her dress like a planet. They pause on seeing me, scorn etched into their faces.

'Your ma make you that dress, too?' Elspeth says, eyeing my change of clothing. My cheeks burn. I'm wearing an old pair of lilac curtains that Ma made into a dress; even by Ma's standards it's pretty drab. But I've nothing else to wear.

I take a deep breath, walk straight up to Elspeth and Julia, and clench my fists. I think of the face Morven pulled when she spoke to me, and I try to mimic her.

'I don't take no shit,' I say. 'Any of you rich bitches think you're better than me, you can think again.'

The room falls silent, and they stare at me. From the corner of my eye I see Morven in the doorway of the dining room, agog, but I don't turn my eyes away. They need to know I'm serious.

'"Rich bitches"?' Elspeth says.

'Aye. That's you,' I say. 'It's none of your business how I got pregnant. I don't want to answer your questions. Got it?'

I stumble over my words, not sounding terribly convincing. But I keep going.

'Oh, piss off, Tiny Tim,' Julia says. 'You're stinking up the hallway. Don't you wash in Dundee?'

A small chorus of laughter. My face stings with shame. How dare she say that?

I spot a dirty cup and saucer on the side table, abandoned by one of them. Without thinking I reach for it and fling it to the floor with a terrific smash. I glance up at them, relishing the look of shock on Julia's face.

'Got it?' I force myself to shout.

Julia gives a little jump, and I feel a flash of satisfaction. 'Got it.'

5

Later, when all the girls have gone to bed, I tiptoe downstairs to the kitchen to find something to eat. The cupboards are bare, but the sink is stacked with dirty dishes, and I can't help but run a finger across the leftovers, sucking the cold gravy from it with relish.

'There's some bread in the pantry,' a voice says, and I turn to find Mrs Whitlock standing in the doorway. She's smiling, all her pointy teeth on display, her hair pulled back off her face and a long navy dressing gown brushing the floor. A cigarette swirls smoke from her fingers.

'Mabel, isn't it?' she says, and I nod. She takes a drag on her cigarette before opening a cupboard and taking out a bread roll.

'Thank you,' I say as she passes it to me.

'It occurred to me that I haven't had a proper chance to make your acquaintance,' she says through a cloud of smoke. 'Is this your first time staying somewhere like this?'

'Aye. It's my first time staying anywhere.'

She gives a husky laugh. 'Home bird, are you?'

I glance at her, shyly. 'I've just never had the opportunity.'

'I'm a home bird, too,' she says. 'I'm not one for travel, nor leaving this place. The outside world seems a very different place these days.'

She turns to leave the room. With the slightest tilt of her head, I see that she's beckoning me. Curious, I follow. In the hallway, she pauses at one of the big paintings of a man wearing a soldier's uniform.

'This was *my* great-grandfather,' she says. 'Ewan Henry Muir. We know him as Harry. Fought in the Crimean War. Won some medals but lost an arm. *And* his mind, if I'm to believe the stories.'

I nod, not knowing what to say. My great-grandfather was also called Harry. He was a coal miner and died in his thirties, leaving my great-grandmother with nine children. She ended up giving away the four youngest to neighbours and relatives to raise. She had no way of feeding them.

Another painting shows a younger, sombre man, with a long pale face and black hair to his collar. 'This was my grandfather, Rory,' she explains. 'He designed the orangery. And he laid out the gardens, too.'

'That's impressive,' I say.

'Oh, you think so? I think the orangery is hideous, personally. But I suppose the gardens are all right.' Another smile, which I return, awkwardly. I feel completely out of my depth talking to her. 'Speaking of someone who only likes herb gardens – your friend, Jack Wingard,' she says, opening a window to flick her cigarette ash. 'His employer Mr Ballard is an old friend of mine.'

'Is he?' I miss Jack, and I wonder what he is up to back home. I make a mental note to write him a long letter in the morning.

She closes the window and moves further along the corridor towards the long stained-glass windows by the Micrarium.

'Forgive me for saying so,' she says, 'but Mr Ballard spoke highly of Jack. He didn't think Jack was the sort of boy to get a girl in trouble.'

It takes me a moment to understand what she means. 'Oh,' I say, putting a hand to my stomach. 'No. Jack isn't the father.'

'Of course not.'

'We're friends,' I say. 'But . . .' I fall silent. I can hardly tell her I'm pregnant with a ghost baby.

'You know, you can be honest with me,' she says, facing me. She's smiling, but there is something behind her eyes that unnerves me. A hardness that is chilling. 'I have only one interest,' she says. 'And that is sending life out into the world. New beginnings.'

We stand in silence for a few moments, until I drop my eyes. 'Would I be able to send a letter to Jack?' I ask.

'Of course,' she says, and my shoulders lower. 'Just leave the envelope on the black side table in the front hallway. Julia takes the mail to the post office on Thursdays.'

Knowing I can write to Jack makes me feel better. We walk a little further along the hall, past a long window that offers a view of the tall fir trees where I encountered the hooded figure.

'Something the matter?' Mrs Whitlock says, following my gaze.

I look away, trying to hide the fear that has crept up on me. 'It's nothing.'

She wraps an arm around her waist, propping up the hand with the cigarette. 'Oh, that's not nothing. You can tell me. I don't bite.'

'I went outside the other night,' I tell her, feeling woozy at the memory of it. 'I thought I heard a noise and so I went outside.' I look up at her to check that she's not cross at me for snooping about, but she's still smiling, her head tilted as though she's really listening to me.

'I saw something,' I say. 'Or someone. In the woods.'

'How strange,' she says. 'Do you know who it was?'

I shake my head. 'I have no idea. They looked . . . peculiar.'

She asks what I mean, and I try to describe it. The dark hood, and the long sweeping cloak made from a dark, rough fabric. How the person pursued me when I ran.

I'm doing a bad job of depicting how terrifying it was. My description sounds childish.

She sucks on her cigarette thoughtfully, tilting her chin. 'Have you told anyone else about this?'

I shake my head. 'No.'

'Good,' Mrs Whitlock says. 'Keep it that way. Understood?'

She stares down at me, but I can't meet her eyes. The hardness is still there. 'I won't tell a soul.'

Slowly, the smile slips off her face, transforming to shock. She staggers backwards, her eyes wide and fixed on me in horror.

'What's the matter?' I say, utterly alarmed.

She begins to grasp at me in panic, blood draining from her face, whimpers escaping her mouth. I glance behind me, certain that someone must be there, some dreadful thing that has caused Mrs Whitlock to shrink in terror.

But there is no one there. All the ghosts in my skin are writhing and chanting. *Hide!* they say. *Hide!*

'What happened?' Mrs Whitlock hisses at me, her eyes wide. 'Why am I here?'

I straighten, confused. The cold, straight-backed woman that I had been speaking with before seems to have been replaced by a frightened, hunched figure. Her whole manner, and the way it has shifted from one state to the next, is bewildering. She reaches for my hand like a child. 'Oh God,' she cries.

'Mrs Whitlock, what's wrong?' I say, my heart pounding.

Her eyes dart across the space behind me. 'It's happened again,' she whispers.

'What's happened again?' I'm pleading with her, and she looks as if she's about to fold over. 'Mrs Whitlock . . . ?'

She grabs me by the upper arms in a painful grip. Her eyes shine, her voice filled with warning. 'Trust no one,' she rasps.

And then she turns and stumbles down the hallway, leaving me in the dark.

Now

Pearl

Lichen Hall, Scottish Borders, September 1965

1

Another day, another missed episode of *Doctor Who*.

I know there are worse things, and I should be grateful to be here. But at the moment I'm not feeling terribly resilient. I imagine the world beyond the gates of Lichen Hall turning without me, a whirlwind of discos and drama, Sonny and Cher, new movies at the cinema. Meanwhile, I'm stuck in a mausoleum with nothing but books for company.

To be fair, the books aren't bad. Aretta and Rahmi introduced me to The Store Cupboard, the Aladdin's Cave of Lichen Hall. Oh my God: the little broom cupboard tucked away on the second floor contains an entire bookcase of novels, including – inexplicably – twelve copies of *James and the Giant Peach*. I arm myself with several Agatha Christies and Shirley Jacksons, a bright red lipstick (unused), some cute baby clothes, and a deck of cards. Aretta and Rahmi have invited me to join them for a game of cards tomorrow night, and I was too embarrassed to admit I've no idea how to play. I'll teach myself. At least I've made inroads into befriending Aretta.

I'm heading downstairs for my walk through the gardens when I hear voices at the other end of the hall. I peer down the loops of the stairwell, spotting a man and woman heading to the Wisteria room. I hear a child's voice chatting to someone, and there's a young woman, too, but she seems out of place – she's desperately thin and shabbily dressed, with a long ratty plait down her back.

I keep out of sight, trying to piece together the details of the scene to work out what's happening down there. Once again, Mrs Whitlock shuts the doors, which suggests it's a private gathering. No food is served either, which suggests it's a formal meeting – not friends coming over. The Wisteria room is the most remote room of Lichen Hall, set apart from the common areas. Whatever business is conducted in that room is secret.

I think about what Mrs Whitlock said to me when I asked about the guests. *There are certain matters of business at the house that must be kept separate.* Matters of business. My first thought is that she's meeting with prospective adoptive parents. But the young woman is the sticking point. Why is she there?

I hang around the stairwell as long as I can without being spotted, pretending to be absorbed by the paintings there. After an hour, I hear the door creaking open, and the guests begin to file out. I dare not peer down and risk getting caught. Instead, I listen hard to the voices, trying to discern what's going on. What kind of business would involve children, and the strange girl with the shabby clothes?

2

I head back along the corridor to the other side of the house, not wanting to be caught. In the kitchen, I start washing dishes that have been left on the side of the sink. About ten minutes later, I hear Mrs Whitlock's voice, and I peek outside, keen to let her know I've definitely not been snooping on her clandestine meeting, but have been innocently washing dishes the whole time.

'Ah, there you are,' Mrs Whitlock calls to me. 'Pearl, come and meet Wulfric.'

'Glad to,' I say, beaming with non-snooping virtue. Wulfric looks at me warily, as though the introduction is a punishment. I dial up the charm.

'I believe we've already met, haven't we, Wulfric?' I say brightly, a kind of 'we're-in-this-together' ploy. I extend a hand. 'Can't have too many introductions, though, can you? Pleased to meet you. Again.'

He lifts his hand to mine, obediently. 'How do you do?'

Mrs Whitlock looks at me queryingly – I can tell she hates not knowing something. 'We met briefly in the kitchen last week,' I tell her.

'Ah, good,' she says. 'You've already met. Perhaps you could commence tuition today?'

'Absolutely,' I say, nodding at Wulfric. 'Perhaps we can start with a walk? You can fill me in on what subjects you'd like help with?'

'Why don't you show Pearl your hen house?' Mrs Whitlock suggests.

He gives a reluctant nod.

'There we go,' Mrs Whitlock says rousingly, patting Wulfric on the back. 'Though not near the shepherd's hut, OK darling?'

Another nod.

'I love hens,' I say as we leave through the side door. I'm surprised to see that we're heading into the forest – I would have supposed a hen house to be in a yard, or near the gardens. He walks slowly, dragging his feet, both hands shoved deep into his pockets and his face sullen. He's a heavy-set boy, about five foot ten, a belly poking out under his shirt. I can see the beginnings of stubble on his cheeks, and that typical teenage angst emanating from his pores. Everything about him reminds me how much I hated being fourteen.

'All right, then,' I say, as we pass through the treeline. 'Tell me all about your current school, Wulfric. What subjects do you enjoy?'

It seems to be the wrong question. 'I used to go to St Columbus,' he says, his tone sullen.

He offers nothing further, so I press a little. 'What kind of school was St Columbus?' I ask lightly.

'Boarding school. It was shite.'

'Boarding school certainly isn't for everyone,' I say, thinking immediately of my brother, Charlie. My parents sent him to boarding school after he fell in with the wrong crowd, only to pull him out a year later because he had fallen in with an even worse crowd who nurtured a rather serious cocaine habit.

'I got expelled,' he says.

'Expelled?'

'I miss school dinners,' he sighs. 'Grandma doesn't let me have as many seconds here.'

'What about subjects?' I ask, keen to keep the mood light. 'What did you enjoy doing at school?'

'Nothing.'

'You didn't have a subject you were particularly good at?'

'I'm not good at anything.'

His tone stops me in my tracks. He sounds miserable, and so down on himself. 'Oh, Wulfric,' I say. 'It can't be all that bad, can it?'

He turns. 'The hens are just up here.'

We continue on, heading towards the line of trees at the edge of the forest. I hear what sounds like laughing. Squinting towards the sound, I see it – a large rectangular coop in the middle of the forest, the brown and black bodies of hens moving around inside it. I count twenty of them, all clucking away. When Wulfric approaches they all run to him, and he bends and strokes their heads through the wire.

'This is marvellous,' I tell him, admiring how sturdy the coop is, how well-fed the hens look. 'And there's you saying you're not good at anything.'

He blushes, cheering up a bit. 'This is Margaret,' he says, nodding at the white hen that's demanding a chin scratch. 'She's a bit bossy. That one's Natalie, and the black one's Anna.'

He names them all for me. They've all got human names.

'I have pets at home,' I tell him. 'Cats, though, not chickens.'

He brightens. 'I wish I had a cat. Do you miss them?'

'I do,' I say. 'Soup's the oldest. She wakes me every morning by nuzzling my cheek. Beans is the cheeky one. We found her in a box at the side of the road. She must have been a day old. She could fit in the palm of my hand and I fed her warm milk with a syringe. Toast is huge – she's fluffy and black and very playful. I think they'd like your hens.'

'Or they'd eat them.'

'Not a chance.'

'Do you want to hold one?' he asks.

'I'd love to.'

He pulls the bolt from a makeshift door, allowing the hens to file out into the forest. 'There are fox dens all over the place,' he says. 'So we have to be here when they're out. That's what the stick is for.'

There's a stick propped against the side of the coop, presumably to beat off predators. Wulfric opens a satchel tied to the other side of the coop and squats down, holding handfuls of chicken feed for the birds. He lifts one – a black bantam named Rosie – and passes her to me. I'm nervous about taking her in case she pecks me, but she sits contentedly in my arms, laying her neck along my arm placidly.

'What did you mean when you said mushrooms made you think about death?' Wulfric says.

'What?'

'That day, in the Micrarium. You said mushrooms made you think of death.'

'Oh. I suppose I did.'

He stops and wipes his nose on his sleeve, holding me in a flat stare. 'What did you mean?'

His mood has shifted. I set Rosie down. 'Well, fungus feeds off decaying matter, doesn't it? It grows on rotten wood and dead bodies.'

'Yes, but that's its job,' he says, turning to fling a stick, hard, into the depths of the woods. 'If it didn't feed on that stuff then all the dead stuff would still lie around. It breaks down the dead stuff so new things can grow.'

I flinch as the stick sends a dozen crows shrieking from a tree. 'You're quite insightful, Wulfric,' I say, trying to coach him back to his former mood.

This time, he can't hold back a goofy smile. I've touched him, and I feel pleased that we've connected, and in such a short space of time. But then, throwing another stick: 'I hate being a kid.'

'Oh, surely it's not all bad,' I say, touching my bump. 'No responsibilities. Pocket money. Trust me, you don't want to wish your life away.'

'When will it happen?' There's a sob in his voice.

I stop and look at him, startled by how upset he seems. 'When will what happen?'

He looks wistfully into the distance. 'Growing up,' he says. 'Being an adult.'

'I promise, you,' I say, as sincerely as I can, 'it will happen, Wulfric. But *enjoy* being young. It really isn't as bad as you think.'

He looks up at me, and there's a moment where I feel he's trying to believe me. Where he hopes that my words are true.

3

My lessons with Wulfric commence after our visit to the hen house. We settle in the Willow room, and I find a collection of books from the library to support our study of science. Next, I bring a pot of tea with two cups. No harm in some tea while learning, especially since we're not at school.

My own scientific education was focused on human biology, but Wulfric's interests lie in nature. He slurps his tea, which makes me shudder, but I decide not to make a fuss. I make him draw a tree stump, and we focus on characteristics of tree rings: cambium, bark, phloem, xylem. When I see his interest begin to wane, I take him back outside, and we find a tree stump.

'How old is this tree?' I ask him, and he sets about counting the rings.

'A hundred and sixty-seven,' he says eventually.

'Correct,' I tell him, and he beams, proudly. A good way to end the first lesson, I think.

He heads off for some free time. The sun has come out, and so I decide to stay outdoors to have my walk. Maybe I'll have a nap afterwards.

I head towards the gardens, past the front door. It's very grand, with a tessellated stone arch above and a brass doorknocker in the shape of a lion.

As I walk along to the far corner, I spot something in one of the windows.

A poster of some kind. It's a large white square with something written on it. Two words.

HELP ME

I stand for a moment, trying to work out why the poster is here, and what I ought to do about it. Retracing my steps from yesterday's walk, I'm certain that the note wasn't here. The writing is from a mature and steady hand.

Who could have written it, and why?

It's quite an unnerving find, and I can't exactly continue on my walk without doing something about it or telling someone. I walk briskly back to the side entrance, making my way through the long corridor towards the room where the note is installed. It occurs to me that someone is playing tricks on me, intent on scaring the wits clean out of me. But Mrs Whitlock doesn't strike me as the sort of woman who would play games. And I can't imagine Aretta or Rahmi doing something like this. Perhaps it was Mr Whitlock.

I head along the corridor, eyeing up the stairs for any signs of life. The house is quiet and still, and so I find the lower rooms at the front of the house and try the doors.

The first two are open, and I glance inside, checking the windows before moving swiftly on. The door in the middle of the corridor is locked, and I'm certain *this* is the room where the sign was placed. I knock on the door and shout, 'Hello? Is anyone in there?'

I bang the door again, then lean an ear to the wood. It's very low, but inside I can make out a sound. A moaning sound.

Perhaps it's Mr Whitlock. He wouldn't be able to reach the door if he's fallen out of his wheelchair.

I clasp the door handle and try it again, gently, then firmly, but the door is definitely locked. I'm exasperated. I'm about to call for someone, when I spot a flat metallic object on the rug in front of me. A key.

I lift it and look over the grooves, wondering if it might fit the lock on the door, then slip it inside. It turns, and I press the door gently open.

Inside, the room is quiet and still. It's a large bedroom, with floral carpet, wood-panelled walls, a four-poster bed, and wooden furniture. A pair of slippers is on the floor by the bed and I'm cautious to step inside. I don't want anyone to assume that I'm rooting around.

'Hello?' I call. 'Anyone here?'

No answer. I listen. More moaning, but this time I note the source – it's the sound of the pipes in the walls, louder now that the door is open. I must have been mistaken when I thought someone was in here. But the note . . . I step deeper into the room. I spot Mr Whitlock in bed, his mouth open and his eyes closed. He's fast asleep.

So who wrote the note?

I head quickly towards the kitchen.

Mrs Whitlock and Wulfric are nowhere to be found. Aretta and Rahmi are usually outside.

A thought occurs to me: Mr Whitlock has dementia. It's likely *he* wrote the note, then fell asleep. Yes, that's the explanation. I should have arrived at it faster, too, but I'm on edge. The effect of new surroundings, I think.

I need to relax. A walk should help. Movement for the body is soothing for the mind, Sister Clarke used to say – her rationale whenever we'd complain of having sore feet.

I head back through the side door, crossing the gravel driveway and grass bank, taking slow, even steps through the woodland. The understorey is littered with fallen branches, and slippery due to the rain we've had. The smell of old leaves fills my nostrils, acrid and earthen. The baby is due in a week's time, and my pelvis aches. Still, I press on, Sister Clarke's voice loud in my head, waddling my way through the trees until I spot a tree with beefsteak mushrooms sprouting from its trunk in the clearing.

Something moves behind the tree. I take a step back, but a branch cracks loudly under my foot. A young deer shoots off from behind the tree into bushes beyond the slope.

Suddenly, a mote of colour – a vivid, synthetic blue, not belonging to nature – catches my eye, and I move towards it. It's a small piece of cobalt blue wool tied to a tree. What is it marking? I turn and see another one further along, then another, like breadcrumbs leading me along a trail. And sure enough, once I've followed eleven of these markers, I come to the edge of the treeline and see a field with an old wooden shed in the middle of it. It's not very big, and it looks abandoned and creepy. The roof is corrugated iron, and the wood is dark with rot. Everything about it shouts *go away*. I want to turn and head straight back to Lichen Hall, but I notice the smallest piece of blue wool snagged on the wire fence, and my heart beats faster.

I clamber over the fence, ripping a massive hole in my tights, and waddle across the field. It's soaking wet and muddy, and my shoes are ruined, but I keep going. As I get close to the shed I see a metal bathtub hanging from a hook at the back, and a football outside the door.

My heart racing, I knock on the old wooden door, which is bolted and locked. *It's probably been empty for years*, I tell myself, but my instincts are screaming that it isn't empty at all.

I walk around the hut, noticing that someone has drawn in chalk across the walls. The rain has almost washed the image away, but I can still make it out – it's a stick man hanging from gallows.

The windows on the front of the shed are too high up for me to reach, but there's one on the side that's low enough, and so I cup my hands at the side of my eyes and peer inside. It's dark inside, but I can make out a sofa and something on the floor that looks like a pile of clothes. On the table is a cup.

Something flickers in the corner of my vision. At the treeline, close to where I climbed over the barbed wire fence, I see a figure. It's a man, watching me. He has followed me, I'm sure of it. My stomach is doing somersaults, and for a moment I feel completely vulnerable. He lifts a hand and waves. Astonished, I recognize him.

'Mr Whitlock?' I call, recognizing the nest of white hair. He's barefoot, wearing nothing but striped pyjamas, the top unbuttoned to the navel, revealing a scrawny white torso, his ribcage visible through fine skin. I notice him swaying, reaching out to a tree trunk to steady himself, so I quicken my pace, breaking into a run when I see him topple.

'Mr Whitlock!'

He's on the ground, conscious and pulling himself upright. He looks shaken and confused. I help him to his feet.

'I think you've forgotten your wheelchair, Mr Whitlock,' I say lightly.

'My eye,' he says in a trembling voice. 'There's something in it. Could you have a look?'

He lurches unevenly forward, and I duck away as tactfully as I can. His breath is foul. I recall our first meeting, when he asked me the same question about his eye. I realize now that there's nothing at all wrong with his eye – it's another product of dementia. Poor man. He looks rough, too, his face covered in burst veins and his hands filthy.

I stretch a smile on my face and step back, now that he seems to have steadied. 'I was just about to head back to the hall,' I say. 'Would you like to join me?'

He looks around wildly, then begins to stumble through the woods in the opposite direction. I lurch after him, worried that he'll injure himself, but he shakes my hand off his arm with surprising force.

'I need help,' he says. 'I need . . .'

He changes course, swerving down another path. His pace is quickening, though he staggers. I watch with dread, certain he's about to come crashing to the ground and snap a limb.

'Mr Whitlock!' I call after him. 'You need to take care!'

Suddenly he stops and spins around to face me.

'What are you playing at?' he thunders, as though seeing me for the first time. 'Did you do this to me?' He jerks towards me, as though unaware of his own frailty, but his ankle gives way and he crashes to the ground, landing hard.

'Mr Whitlock!' I yell, lunging towards him. But just then I see someone running through the trees: it's Mrs Whitlock, her face full of alarm. She dashes towards him, kneeling in the dirt beside him to look him over.

'Oh no,' she says. 'I think he might have broken his ankle.'

'I can help . . .' I say, but she shakes her head.

'Could you get Aretta for me, please?'

'Of course.' I lumber as fast as I can through the woods towards the hall, finding Aretta already racing out of the side door.

4

Oh God, the *guilt*. I pace the floor of my room. Despite how sore my pelvis is from so much bloody running, I cannot help but pace, my mind filled with the terrible thought that when I checked on the writer of the note I inadvertently allowed Mr Whitlock – clearly in the grip of dementia – to escape from his room. I can't remember closing the door behind me, and I'm certain I didn't lock it . . . I assumed he was fast asleep. I'm lucky he wasn't seriously hurt, or lost. I've known dementia sufferers to go missing, due to an unlocked door. He could have died.

I wonder if I ought to own up to the whole thing straight away, rather than be discovered and thought of as an interfering coward who didn't have the stomach to tell someone what she'd done. But I worry that, by owning up, I'll be told to leave. And then what?

Oh *God*.

I find Mrs Whitlock in the drawing room, arranging a vase of yellow roses on a side table. A fire is beginning to crackle in the grate, and a large stag's head glares down from the chimney breast.

'Mrs Whitlock, might I have a word?'

She turns, and on seeing me gives a bright smile. 'Oh, there you are. I wanted to check on you.'

'That's kind of you,' I say. 'How . . . is Mr Whitlock?'

'He's fine,' she says, and I let out a sigh of relief. 'He had a nasty fall, as you saw, but Aretta has bandaged up his ankle and applied some ice. He's resting now.'

'I could check him over, if you like?' I would do anything, *anything* to make up for this catastrophe.

She smiles graciously. 'Aretta and I took him back to his room. He's sleeping off his expedition after some chamomile tea.'

'I'm very sorry,' I say. 'I think . . . it was my fault that Mr Whitlock escaped.'

She raises her eyebrows. 'Oh?'

It all comes out in a tearful babble. 'I saw a sign in the window. Someone had written "help me". I went to see if the person inside that room was OK, but it was locked. I . . . I saw a key on the floor, so I . . .'

Her expression hardens. I close my eyes and take a breath. She's going to tell me to leave, I know it. I've ruined *everything*.

'My dear.' She places her hands on my shoulders and smiles, her face suddenly a portrait of sympathy. 'I assure you, it's all right.'

'It's all right?' I wipe a tear from my cheek, hating myself for crying. 'I'm ever so sorry . . . I heard a noise, you see, so I wanted to be sure . . .'

'It's not the first time this has happened,' she says. 'I keep his room locked for his own safety. You'll know what dementia can do. Sometimes he doesn't recognize any of us. And he thinks he's trapped.'

'Is there anything I can do?'

'The only thing now is to give him dignity and care,' she says, authoritatively. She rakes her eyes over me. 'I hope you didn't get a fright?'

I shake my head, though I very much did get a fright. Quickly my mind turns to the horrible hut I found in the field, and the blue bits of wool tied to the trees, as though marking the way. I remember how she urged Wulfric not to go near the shepherd's hut when he took me to the hen house. Why? What's inside that hut?

But instead, I say, 'No fright, not at all. And please – do let me know if I can help in any way. It would be a pleasure.'

She nods and smiles. 'I will.'

I head upstairs to my room, tucking my hands into the pockets of my dress like a child who has been let off the hook. I open up my book to read at the place I marked with the note Mrs Whitlock left the other day, telling me I could help myself to breakfast.

The words *help yourself*, with that exquisitely looped 'e', and the long tail on the 'p', flicked out to the left, give me pause. They're familiar.

The sign in the window, that will be forever etched into my eyeballs. The one that said 'help me', and caused me to set Mr Whitlock free.

The handwriting on that sign is identical to that on the note I hold in my hands.

The sign was written by Mrs Whitlock.

Then

Mabel

Lichen Hall, Scottish Borders, September 1959

1

Over the next six weeks, my days slide into a pattern. Mondays I'm to bake bread and cakes for the week, and I like this because I get the kitchen to myself, except when Morven comes in to cook. Tuesdays are for laundry, Wednesdays for windows and polishing, Thursdays for ironing, Fridays and Saturdays for gardening, and we rest on Sundays. In the evenings, I walk around the estate, avoiding the old woods where I saw the figure. Sometimes I sit in the meadow, cocooned by the tall reeds, or I climb one of the huge trees in the woods and watch the birds.

I never tell anyone about the weird encounter with Mrs Whitlock when she was showing me around the house. Sometimes I think I imagined it – it was so odd. I'm not sure what to make of it at all. And she never mentions it to me.

My belly begins to grow, first as though I've eaten a lot of food, then – almost overnight – into kind of a dinosaur egg, from my ribs to my hips. It's still a small bump, according to Morven, but I'm freaked out by it. I can feel the ghost baby squirming inside me, and it makes me feel sick.

At the beginning of September, it rains for three days solid and I don't go out walking in case I slip on the mud. I'm scared of the woods, too. What if someone is living there? What if they see me again?

But on the fourth day, when the sun comes out, I decide to go for a walk after dinner, carefully avoiding the part where I saw the figure. The forest is so different in the daytime – it's peaceful and makes me feel happy. I follow the road to the front gates, where a clutch of red toadstools with white spots sit neatly, the kind you find in storybooks. And behind them, a line of fat brown mushrooms, like cymbals.

I walk along the line of mushrooms, finding some buried in the leaves and others crouching under fallen logs. On the other side of the road, another line continues, the row there stretching as far as I can see. I follow it, curious at how many mushrooms have popped up overnight.

I count three hundred and forty before realizing they're leading me behind the house. A stealthy trail of them fringe the lawn and peek at me from under the rose bushes, then again at the foot of the willow tree.

After ten minutes I'm back around at the front of the house, staring at the army of mushrooms that marched all the way into the depths of the forest.

It's a fairy ring. A vast, thriving fairy ring that completely encircles Lichen Hall.

Does a fairy ring mean good luck, or bad luck?

2

In mid September Julia has her bairn, but she won't look at it. A little girl, thin and long and with a quiff of copper hair like Julia's.

'Take it away,' Julia shouts from her bedroom, over and over. None of us knows what to do. She's supposed to look after the bairn until the Whitlocks find parents for it.

Morven is meant to be preparing tonight's dinner, but she sits with Julia, trying to talk her into feeding the bairn. I've baked a fresh loaf of bread and sliced it while it was still warm. Fragrant steam curls from it in the soft morning light as I set it on the bedside table. It's cold up here on the third floor, but I've softened the butter, and the tea is steaming hot. I don't like Julia, but I feel for her. She's still crying, her wet face held defiantly away from Morven towards the window.

'It usually takes a month,' Morven tells her gently. 'Sometimes longer. You have to care for her until then.'

'I don't want to see it!' Julia shouts. 'Get it away!' She kicks out a skinny leg towards the Moses basket, toppling it. I dive for it, catching the side of the basket just before the bairn rolls out.

There's a little whimper as I tip the basket back, and as I move it safely away from Julia, the baby bursts into heart-rending sobs, shocked by the motion. Morven nods at me to comfort the bairn, so I lift her, looking over the tiny lip curled in fright, her little fists bunched under her chin. I've never held a bairn before, certainly not one so small.

Elspeth still has milk, so she feeds Julia's baby as well as her own. When she's finished, Morven makes a sling out of muslin cloth and ties Julia's baby to her back so she can look after it and continue working. It looks odd, but she says women all over the world have been doing this forever.

Julia's bairn seems content in the sling. Morven says it is because she is moving around so much and the bairn remembers being in the womb, rocked to sleep by the movement. I place a hand nervously on my tummy, worried I might feel my ghost baby move again. The thought of something living inside me still makes me feel physically sick. Even worse is the thought of it coming out of me. I'm not sure how anyone makes it through alive.

That night, I dream about the glowing mushrooms I saw in the woods, about picking one and holding it in my hand until the light dimmed. But when I pick the mushroom a small spur on the root pricks my wrist. The chalky light drains inside my skin, pouring into my bloodstream and filling my whole body until I glow.

Then, in the dream, Mrs Whitlock delivers my baby and when she hands it to me the baby is a shadow, just a dark shape, like black smoke.

The next night, I have the exact same dream, only this time the bairn is part mink, part dolphin. It has a grey dolphin face and a long, mink body. No one but me seems to notice. Jack comes into my bedroom with a huge smile on his face. He beams down at the creature in my arms and says, 'Do you love your beautiful bairn?'

And right before I wake up, I dream that the baby is a seed pod, only it's big, about the size of a melon, and a dark brown colour with a shine to it. I cradle it, and suddenly something begins to come out of the top. The whole pod shakes, and suddenly a green shoot bursts from the top, lengthening upward until a flower appears at the end of it.

But the flower is made of shadow.

Now

Pearl

Lichen Hall, Scottish Borders, September 1965

1

I'm still quite raw from my misadventures in the woods, both physically and mentally. Allowing Mr Whitlock to escape whilst in the throes of dementia was not my finest hour. I take dinner in my room, keen not to get in anyone's way, then stay up late reading Professor Llewellyn's book about mushrooms.

I keep my window open at night to help me sleep better – my bedroom gets so ridiculously warm, on account of being south-facing. Just after midnight, I smell smoke – and so I open the curtains and look out for the source of the fire.

I spy it after a few moments of scanning the trees – an orange flicker, with a long black tail rising up into the sky. I'm quite panicked, but my immediate impulse to rush to Mrs Whitlock's bedroom and hammer on her door is quelled by the thought that I might have been mistaken. After today's error, I'm more cautious than usual about causing trouble.

I watch carefully in case the fire shows signs of gathering pace. It's a damp night, so surely the rain will put it out . . . But a couple of minutes later, I see someone moving from the house into the woods. I'm pretty sure it's Rahmi, and she's carrying something. I think it's dry logs from the wood store.

Why the hell would she be building a fire in the woods at midnight?

I creep downstairs, just to be sure. I can make out the glow of the fire from here, and someone moving outside. It starts to rain, and the windows are soon slick with it, making it difficult to see. I head outside, just for a moment, to see if I can fathom why Rahmi's out there. Or if it's Rahmi at all.

I walk carefully across the gravel driveway towards the treeline. The light moves closer, and I realize that whoever has built the fire is now carrying a flaming torch. I want to shout out for them to stop – they're in a bloody forest, for God's sake, and the whole place could go up in flames – but as I squint through the trees I see Rahmi's shape, the flick of her long ponytail at her back. What *is* she doing?

My nerve begins to flag. I duck back inside the house, but continue to watch for a few moments from the safety of the side porch.

A bonfire flickering through the trees, an orange triangle that crackles in the distance. Another flame moves slowly from left to right – Rahmi making her way through the woods. I watch, mystified, as she walks in a large circle, holding the torch aloft.

2

The next morning, I go to find Rahmi. I want to ask her about last night. She's nowhere in the house, so I pull on a woolly hat and coat and head out to the woods, trying to navigate my way back to the spot where I saw her.

I smell it before I see it: the air still holds the thick stench of smoke, and I find a pile of blackened logs marking the spot where she burned her bonfire, the earth scorched. Before the pile of logs is what appears to be a grave site. It's a mound of earth, freshly cleared of leaves and branches, a small perimeter marked out by smooth round pebbles. A pet, perhaps? Surely not a human grave. I'm careful not to move them, but when I bend down low enough I can see each pebble has been painted. It's definitely a grave. I give a shiver. How macabre. Perhaps Rahmi was performing some kind of rite.

She's nowhere to be seen, and I'm too full of aches and pains to walk too much further into the gardens.

It's soon time for my second lesson with Wulfric. I decide to focus on literacy, to provide him with some variety.

I head upstairs and pull some books from the library shelves. *Romeo and Juliet* is a good text for a boy of his age, and I find some excellent grammar instruction books. At the very least, I'll soon find out what books are to his tastes.

Mrs Whitlock is waiting for me expectantly downstairs, and

I follow her to a cosy sitting room with large windows overlooking the back. The Willow room, she tells me. There is a handsome polished wooden desk with two chairs, which will be ideal for the lesson.

Wulfric joins me soon after, albeit a little sullenly. He's dressed in his usual lint-balled, handknitted turtleneck and grey trousers that are shiny at the knees, his cheeks mottled with a fresh flurry of angry red spots. Bless his heart. I ask him to take a seat at the desk, and I sit nearby.

'I enjoyed meeting your hens,' I say. 'You've put a lot of work into them.'

'Thanks,' he says, glancing over at the books. He seems a little less eager for our lesson than he was on Tuesday. I sense he doesn't like being indoors, and that he doesn't enjoy books in general. I wonder for a moment if his grandparents' teaching styles have been too restrictive, making him associate learning with punishment.

'You know, I've been thinking about what you said,' I tell him. 'About the mushrooms.'

He gives me a sideways glance. 'Fungi.'

'Ah, yes. Fungi. You said that fungi do a really important job, didn't you? That they break down all the dead stuff so new things can grow.'

Another glance. I'm getting somewhere.

'And I think you're right,' I continue. 'I was so focused on the fact that mushrooms and other types of fungi signal death. But really, they signal renewal. Which is a wonderful thing.'

'That's what my dad always said,' he says, lifting his eyes to mine. 'Even poisonous mushrooms are a good thing. And some of them are only poisonous to humans, but they can be eaten by the wildlife. So they provide food as well.'

'Exactly. They help nature to take its course.'

'Are we doing more tree rings, today?' he says.

I open up a jotter in front of him and set down a pen. 'Let's practise your handwriting, shall we?'

His face darkens. 'Why?'

'Well, good penmanship is important. If someone can't read what you've written, the communication has failed.'

Truth be told, I noticed his spelling and grammar were pretty dire during our last lesson. Handwriting is a sneaky way to practise spelling without advertising it as such. I tap a sentence in one of the grammar books. 'Shall we try this one?'

He stares down at the sentence. 'I can't read it.'

'It says, "I spied a big meat pie".'

'That makes no sense.'

'Don't worry about the meaning of the sentence,' I urge. 'It's to help your handwriting.'

'But why would I write something that makes no sense?'

'All right. What about this one. "Jill has fair hair but Jack has dark hair".'

'So stupid,' he mutters, but he picks up his pen and starts writing. I'm relieved by this, until I see what he's written. *Jill is an idiot and Jack can piss right off.*

'Your handwriting isn't too bad, actually,' I say, deflecting from the altered sentence.

'My handwriting's shit.'

'Oh, I don't think so.'

'My English teacher said so.'

'Really?'

'He said, "Your handwriting's shit, Wulfric."'

'Let's try and improve it, then. Practice makes perfect.'

He flicks the pen out of his hand and over his shoulder, sending it flying across the room behind him. I try not to let him see how shocked I am. I'm more disappointed than shocked – I had thought I was winning him round.

'You seem to have dropped your pen,' I say.

'I chucked it,' he says bluntly.

'Do you want to go pick it up?'

He fumbles in his pocket, and for a moment I think he's going to pull out another pen, but instead he produces an old-fashioned lighter, flicking it until a small yellow flame appears.

I draw a breath, reminding myself that he is, after all, a teenage boy. 'I'll take that, thank you.'

He swivels his eyes from the small flame to me. 'This was the principal's lighter. I stole it.'

'Interesting. I'm sure *that* had nothing to do with your expulsion.'

'It didn't.'

'And I'll expect your grandmother knows nothing about it. You don't want her finding out, do you?'

He snaps it shut and thumps it into my palm. I tuck it safely into the pocket of my cardigan, a little alarmed at his manner.

'Now, let's get back to work.'

He drums his fingers on the table. 'I nearly died in a car accident. Did you know that?'

'That's horrible,' I say. 'Are you better now?'

'Not really.'

I watch him for a quick moment, trying to work out if this is a line of conversation I should pursue. Perhaps I'm best keeping this session focused on his schooling. He's determined to distract me.

'I kill people,' he says.

I process that for a moment, careful not to react too much. 'Do you now? And why is that?'

He lifts his pale eyes to mine. 'Doesn't that scare you?'

'Not at all.'

'Why not?'

'Let's try and write a different sentence.'

'You don't believe me, do you?'

I tap the page with a finger. 'Try reading it aloud as you write. "The quick brown fox jumps over the . . ."'

He starts drawing on the page. A gallows, with a stick man hanging from a rope. I think of what I saw on the side of the old shepherd's hut. Wulfric must have drawn it.

I lean back in my chair with a sigh. 'OK. Why do you kill people, Wulfric?'

'Because I'm evil.'

I nod as though this is a perfectly reasonable response, though I'm growing more and more uncomfortable. 'And what makes you evil?'

He considers this. 'I don't know.'

He says these words with a ring of truth. He *is* only fourteen, I remind myself. I suspect he doesn't have any friends. Children tend to talk about their friends, even if only to gossip, but he hasn't mentioned a single one.

I think quickly back to the child I saw on my first night here. He's too young to be friends with Wulfric, most likely.

'Wulfric,' I say soothingly. 'You *know* you're not evil.'

'But I am,' he says.

'Did someone tell you that?'

He shakes his head. He doesn't stop shaking it, and suddenly I realize he's spiralling into a rage.

'Don't look at me!' he snaps, colour deepening in his cheeks, his eyes wide. 'Stop staring!'

'Wulfric, calm down . . .' I say, but he yells again, over and over, telling me not to look at him, his voice bouncing off the walls.

'Stop! Stop!'

He gets to his feet and picks up the chair, hurling it across the room. I'm suddenly afraid. I back out of the room as fast as I can, watching in horror as he starts pulling at his hair, screaming unintelligibly as he yanks out fistful after fistful.

Mrs Whitlock comes racing down the corridor towards me. 'What's happened?'

I'm trembling. She stands in the doorway and stares at the scene. I risk a glance inside.

Wulfric's mouth is red with blood, flashes of it across his white shirt. Ordinarily my medical training would take over and I'd rush in to help, but another, stronger instinct holds me in place, a hand reaching involuntarily to my bump: I'm concerned he'll hurt the baby.

She calls up the hallway. 'Rahmi? Aretta? Come quick!'

In a moment Rahmi is there, dashing towards us. Aretta follows, and I watch, stricken, as they try to grapple with Wulfric, Rahmi taking a heavy blow to the side of the face and Aretta a kick to the leg. It feels like hours, but eventually they manage to pin him to the ground, holding his limbs in place to avoid further damage to them or himself.

Wulfric's thunderous roars soften into childish sobs. Mrs Whitlock nods at Aretta and Rahmi on the ground. 'Let him go,' she says, as though she senses the storm has passed.

They do, and there's a brief moment where I'm worried he'll lash out again. Strands of his hair lie on the carpet. He curls up into a ball on the floor, weeping.

3

Wulfric's tantrum – or frenzy, I'm not quite sure what to call it – leaves me deeply troubled. The blood on his mouth, though garishly alarming, is from quite a small cut in his lip caused by his own teeth, and is quickly cleaned up. Luckily his hair is thick, so the fistfuls he managed to pull out haven't left bald patches.

Still, he is clearly distressed. Aretta rights the table and chairs in the room and Rahmi prepares supper, but I'm too perturbed to eat. Even when I hear his voice downstairs – light and playful again, laughing at japes – I can't make sense of what happened in that room. It was just him and me, and however much I replay the events, I almost wish there had been someone else with me to explain it to me, or retell it in a way that makes sense.

Why is a boy of fourteen so traumatized, so explosive?

I turn our conversation over in my head. It must have something to do with the car accident that claimed his father's life.

An extra layer of uneasiness is caused by the way Mrs Whitlock seems so unwilling to acknowledge it, laughing along with him now, asking Aretta to make Wulfric's favourite dessert. As though nothing out of the ordinary has happened.

Once he had calmed down and the sobbing had ceased, she turned to me, and I saw it happen – the naked horror that had swept across her face had been reined back in, all the cracks in the surface shifting back into a patina of perfection. She turned to me – and this was only mere minutes after Wulfric had been thrashing about the room, leaving me genuinely scared for my life – and said, 'Same time on Tuesday for the next lesson?'

I stared at her. 'Come again?'

'Or perhaps a little later in the day is best,' she said, her eyes wide and untroubled.

It has taken me the whole afternoon to process those handful of minutes.

My lesson with Wulfric resulted in him exploding into a violent fury, yelling and throwing things around the room, and she responded, not by asking me if I was all right, or whether I wished to take my leave, but by calmly arranging the next lesson for the following day.

I find myself wanting to ask her about the morgue story. There is clearly some level of truth in the rumour, given that Wulfric mentioned a car accident, and his meltdown insinuates that some trauma from the death of his father remains unhealed.

But I must be cautious how I go about discovering the truth.

4

That night, I play gin rummy with Aretta and Rahmi in Aretta's bedroom. Her room is on the second floor, one of the smaller bedrooms near the store cupboard. It's a charming room, the décor reflective of Aretta's personality – there are bright hand-woven miniature textiles on the wall, celebrating her heritage and showcasing her talent; the mantelpiece is lined with shells from the beach, and a vase on the bedside table is filled with irises from the garden. A sewing table shows some new work in progress – a bedspread, by the looks of it – and a shelf above the bed is lined with books. She's a much more interesting person than I first thought.

'You don't mind, do you?' Rahmi asks me as she holds up a cigarette.

I shake my head. 'Not at all,' and she lights up. Lucy smokes, and it feels nice to be around these women in a relaxed setting, not the stiff, busy atmosphere created by Mrs Whitlock. Aretta is wearing a long orange dress, her hair pinned up, and a gold necklace at her throat. 'What happened with Wulfric today?' Aretta asks, knocking the table. 'I saw he was bleeding after your lesson.'

'Did you smack him?' Rahmi says, a tone of hopefulness in her voice.

'Of course not,' I say. 'He got a bit worked up and hurt himself.' I look over my cards. 'Does he do that a lot?'

'God, yes,' Rahmi says. 'He gets away with murder, that boy.'

I see Aretta shoot Rahmi a look. I know that look – it's one I used to give Sebastian when he'd mention something in company that I didn't want to divulge. She's telling her to be quiet.

'The car accident with his father seems to be bothering him,' I say carefully. 'Which is understandable, really.'

'I meant to ask you,' Aretta says then. 'You were going to teach me the ways of midwifery. Given that you're about to pop, should we plan a time?'

She's changing the subject. 'Absolutely,' I say. 'My schedule is looking rather open at the moment, so name the time and place and I'll be there.'

'Tomorrow afternoon,' she says, considering her cards. She lays down a seven of spades.

'Where you both here when the car accident happened?' I ask them both.

Aretta looks up. 'What car accident?'

'The one involving Wulfric's father.' I set down a queen of hearts. 'I think it has affected him. Which is understandable.'

'That was before our time,' Rahmi says. 'We've been here just over six years.'

'So Wulfric must have been about eight when you arrived?'

Aretta pauses, calculating this. She lays down two jacks. 'I suppose so, yes.'

'Poor kid,' I say. 'Six years is a long time to spend in a place like this. No other kids around. He must be bored out of his mind.'

Rahmi smiles, then lays down three aces. 'Rummy,' she says, lighting up another cigarette in triumph.

5

I am in despair. It's three in the morning and I haven't slept a wink due to false contractions, or Braxton Hicks. We always advise women that Braxton Hicks are a sign of over-exertion or stress, and in my case it's most definitely the latter.

It's a clear night, the moon full and fat in the sky. I hear someone or something moving downstairs, the familiar creak of floorboards. Rahmi, I think, probably heading out to light one of her night fires. I forgot to ask her about it when we played gin. The thing with Wulfric put it out of my mind. God, there's never a dull moment in this place.

I throw my cardigan around my shoulders and head downstairs in search of food. Maybe a cup of tea and a stretch of my legs will help me go back to sleep.

In the kitchen, I find a teapot beside the sink, still warm to the touch. I pour the contents into a cup and drink it. Being able to drink lukewarm – or indeed stone cold – tea is a prerequisite of nursing, and at the thought of this I find tears creeping to my eyes. How I miss the ward. The noise, the drama, and the usefulness I felt there. It's stunning to me how inconsequential I feel now. And how pregnancy has devalued all my achievements. I've rescued countless people from the brink of death, cared for them in their darkest moments. But I'll never nurse again. I'm exiled in shame.

I look around for a tissue, but there's none to be found. I dab my eyes with a tea towel. The baby gives one of its huge kicks, the kind I've noticed it only does at night, a little heel rising visibly through the side of my nightdress. My belly is covered in stretch marks now, angry red gashes that look alarmingly as though my skin is splitting. My ankle bones have sunk into my flesh. I don't recognize myself. My face is puffed up, the contours of my cheekbones and jawline flattened by excess water, and my nose is *wider*, I swear to God. The reality is that my body is no longer mine at all. I'm possessed, inhabited, less a human being than a bloody hotel. I think of the word Sister Clarke used to use for babies *in utero* – parasites. I'm beginning to think she was right.

There's another creak of the floorboards in the hallway, and suddenly I'm embarrassed at the thought of Mrs Whitlock or Aretta or Rahmi finding me here feeling sorry for myself.

I give a push on the side door and venture outside to clear my head. It's not too cold, the sky shimmering with the sort of stars we never get in Edinburgh. I look towards the ocean, then the forest ahead. The latter is quite daunting, given that I've never ventured through one at night. But Rahmi must be outside, and I wonder if she's got her flaming torch again, and if she's performing her strange rite . . . Perhaps I'll join her, and ask her for the truth about that grave.

I walk slowly through the shrubs and trees. No sign of any fire, but there's plenty of wildlife – I forgot that animals would be active in the wee hours. I spot a handful of badgers, who slip away like a rainbow of black and white, and more rabbits than I can count. I stay stock still as a large hedgehog dawdles over the understorey, a spiky cortège of hoglets.

All the rustling and cheeping from the birds overhead makes me feel less afraid, despite not being able to see very much. God knows what Mrs Whitlock would say if she found me wandering about.

I squint through to the part of the woods where I found the remains of the fire. No sign of it, but then it's difficult to be sure

I'm in the right place, given how dark it is. I take the path that leads towards the river, delighting at the sight of a large heron, standing regal and silver-headed in the moonlight, before spreading his wings and lifting into the sky and across the fields, swallowed up by the dark.

I'm at the foot of the older part of the forest now, the wood that is full of ancient trees, a gnarled, warped vastation. The noises around me have ceased abruptly, no animal to be seen or heard. The ground beneath my feet has become treacherously uneven, full of old, mossy stones, and so I turn to head back.

Something catches my eye. Movement amidst the old trees – the ghost woods, as Mrs Whitlock calls them. Rahmi, I think with relief, but a second glance tells me it's something else. Something large and powerful, judging by the deep crack of the branches underfoot. Adrenalin sharpens my senses, and I hold my breath at the prospect of spying a stag – that would be quite something. I've never seen one in the wild.

Soupy moonlight falls on a surface. The hairs on the back of my neck stand up, and the baby jerks painfully, making me flinch.

I draw back behind a tree trunk and squint through the contorted branches. What I see doesn't make sense, and I find myself leaning to one side to get a better view to understand, to decipher. It *is* an animal of some sort, indicated by a plume of breath, but the shape is all wrong.

It's a *thing*, neither human nor animal, an otherworldly being about six foot tall.

Moonlight settles on a black hide, but it is viscous, like water or jam. And the creature appears to have no head. It has wide shoulders and two dog-like paws that hang, long and slender, at right angles from its chest.

Above the roaring of my heart I can hear it breathing – but the sound doesn't make sense, either. It's a sucking sound, inhaling and exhaling.

It takes another second or two to realize that the thing has sensed me, its sinister, broken form quickly moving towards me. I tear through the trees, a scream trapped in my throat, every cell in my body sparking with terror.

And then the world is upside down. My right foot hooks a tree root; one second I'm upright and the next I'm on my forearms, white-hot pain skewering from my elbow to my shoulders.

I try to pull myself up, but my foot is caught by a tangle of roots, holding me down. I hear myself yell, a raw howl that sounds like no other noise I've ever made.

Something touches the skin of my leg, just above my ankle – a cold, wet grasp, like a tentacle looping around my shin. *Oh God.*

I jerk my head back and see the creature on the ground by my feet, a confusing mass of shadow. A strange knowledge seems to slip inside me, as though the creature's touch on my skin has imparted its mood, its malice. And its thoughts.

It wants to worm its way inside my skin and wear me like a coat.

One of my hands finds its way into my cardigan pocket. My fingers meet metal. Quickly I realize that I have Wulfric's lighter, and with a trembling hand I pull it out and flick it alight. The small yellow flame is like a supernova in the thick gloom, and I hear a wild screech.

As quickly as it appeared, the creature is gone.

I don't hear it move away or run. One moment it is there, the next it is gone.

My foot slips free of the root, and I sit upright, my heart clanging and my mouth emitting sobs of its own accord. The birds are noisy now, the creepy quiet that preceded the sighting of the creature in the ancient woods replaced with raucous calls. A fox slinks by. The sheath of blackness has lifted, and the edge of the sky is iridescent, announcing dawn.

The feeling that I had before, the strange instinct that the *thing* wanted to slip inside me, has dissipated.

I look down at the lighter in my hand, feeling its weight. Gingerly I curl my fingers around the metal, clasping it tightly as a secret, before pulling myself to my feet and staggering back to the hall.

Then

Mabel

Lichen Hall, Scottish Borders, September 1959

1

'Sit still,' Morven says, and I stiffen, already certain that I'll have to turn my head a little in a moment, as holding it in the current angle feels unnatural.

Morven sits about five feet away, sketching in a notebook. She looks strange without Julia's baby strapped to her: the bairn is back at the house being fed by Elspeth. I'm sitting under a tree, and it's a Sunday, so we don't have to leap up again anytime soon to tend to the laundry or baking.

'When I first came here,' Morven says, her eyes on the page, 'the Whitlocks would make us go to church. Usually, we'd go in their car. A good thirty minutes to the church in the village. The last few months or so, they haven't been bothered. And I can't say I don't enjoy the extra free time.'

I wonder what Morven would do if she had more than one day off a week. By the end of every Sunday I can see she's growing restless, as if the lack of tasks requiring her attention sets her on edge. She always, *always* needs something to do. She says she never drew at home, but one of the girls – Nancy, from the Highlands – left behind an art set, and Morven took to it like a duck to water. She draws hastily, furiously, producing sketches that look like dreams, or memories. When I was at school I'd take for ever to do a simple watercolour; I remember the art teacher puffing and blowing with frustration as I took minutes to choose a different colour, becoming lost in the possibilities. Morven astonishes me with her decisiveness, her lack of hesitation. I want to be like that. I want to be less careful in the world.

Ten minutes later, she says 'Right', which means she's done. I wait for her to stand before rising and approaching the sketchpad.

She has drawn me in a way I've never seen myself. There's a grace to the lines that make up my face, my body, and even my hair that makes me question whether she's actually drawn me at all.

'Of course it's you,' she laughs when I ask. 'You literally saw me sitting there drawing you.'

'It looks prettier than me,' I say.

She surveys the sketch. 'But you are pretty,' she says.

I lift my eyes to hers, and she doesn't look away. 'Can I keep it?' I ask.

'Of course.'

I take the sketch upstairs and prop it up against the mirror above the dressing table. I look for a moment from my reflection to the drawing. Gradually, I can see a likeness, and I'm astonished.

It's as if I've been looking in the wrong mirror all this time.

2

Julia's bairn is three weeks old today. The adoptive parents are coming, and the whole house is tense with anticipation. Even Mr Whitlock seems on edge, though he doesn't have much to do with the babies, or us girls, at least, not as individuals. He likes to use us as an audience on occasion, rambling on about the contents of his Micrarium and his academic theories about the origins of life. I watch the new girls for their reaction when they see him for the first time in his shorts and dressing shoes. It amuses me to see the look of confusion on their faces, and occasionally one of them will burst out laughing.

Today, he's here in his shorts as usual, and they've got so baggy on him that they slip down around his hips. Mrs Whitlock is always so pristine, so put together, that I wonder what she thinks of her husband dressing like this.

Mr Whitlock watches Morven as she brings the baby downstairs, washed and dressed in clean clothes, blowing her a kiss from his fingertips.

'God speed, wee bairn,' he says. 'May you shower life wherever you go.'

Julia won't come out of her room.

'It's about bloody time,' Morven says, untying the baby sling that she has worn since Julia gave birth. She gives a big stretch, her neck making a loud crunch. Then she kisses the bairn on the head. 'It's a shame they don't remember these moments,' she says, looking down at her in her arms. 'She'll live her whole life without knowing who cared for her when she was born. Maybe it's better that way. Let's hope she doesn't ever try to find Julia.' She laughs. 'Whatever romantic notion she might have of Julia as a mother will be ill-placed.'

'Maybe Julia will have changed by then,' I say.

'Maybe. I wouldn't count on it.'

The parents arrive. An older couple with strange accents, driving a battered jeep. I overhear them mention something about an aeroplane. Morven and I hide in the kitchen, listening in. 'Mrs Whitlock prefers finding overseas parents,' Morven whispers.

'Why?' I ask her.

Morven shrugs. 'I don't know. Maybe to prevent any of us bumping into our children on the street.'

They don't stay long. Morven blows a kiss to the baby from the safety of the kitchen, and I know she's a bit sad, despite how sore her back is from carrying her.

When the parents leave, I see Julia on the stairs, crying.

3

The day after, two new girls arrive. Rahmi is from Auchtermuchty. She's short and thin, with long black hair and a bump so perfectly round it looks as if she's stuck a football up her dress. I watch carefully as she meets Mr Whitlock. Today he's wearing his hair in a small ponytail, and he's got his yellow swimming shorts on with a pair of socks, no shoes. A shirt buttoned to the neck with an orange tie. Rahmi doesn't react at all. I take a step closer, risking a hard stare to catch the slightest reaction, but she doesn't give *anything* away.

Julia does her usual thing of insisting that Rahmi divulge the details of how she became pregnant. Rahmi shrugs and says, without a hint of a smile, 'The stork came.'

'The *stork*,' Julia says, her face darkening.

'They're long-billed birds, very tall,' Rahmi says, matter-of-factly. 'Mostly from Asia and Africa. They're migratory birds, and they can live for thirty years. Did you know that?'

Julia is visibly confused. She shrinks a little, unsure of whether Rahmi is mocking her without her knowledge. She mutters a non-committal reply before slinking off to her room.

Later, Rahmi mentions to me and Morven that she fell pregnant deliberately to avoid an arranged marriage.

Aretta is the most beautiful girl I've ever seen, with the exception of Morven. She is shy, too, and doesn't quite know how to take Elspeth and Julia, so she avoids them.

A couple arrives to adopt Elspeth's baby. Elspeth seems relieved as the date of their arrival approaches; she's certainly a lot nicer to everyone, and the mood around her is lighter, like an exhale. But when the couple arrive, they seem hesitant about the baby. Mrs Whitlock asks Elspeth to take the baby out of the room for a while, and she approaches Morven and me in the kitchen, stricken.

'They're not sure they want to adopt her,' she says, handing the baby to Morven. 'What'll I do?'

She breaks down into frantic sobs, and Morven wraps an arm around her, rubbing her back. The baby is fast asleep.

'Shush, now,' Morven tells Elspeth. 'You don't want them to hear you wailing. It's a big thing, you know, adopting a baby. Maybe they just want to be sure.'

'They asked about my family's background,' Elspeth says tearfully, wiping her nose. 'They wanted to know if anyone in the baby's paternal lineage was handicapped. How the fuck am I supposed to know *that*? I didn't exactly ask.'

Morven comforts her, though I keep my distance. My tailbone still aches after she pulled the chair from behind me.

After an hour or so, the couple leaves without taking the baby. They want to 'discuss' the adoption before committing.

'What do they think she is, a car?' Morven hisses. Me, Rahmi, Aretta, and Morven are gathered at an upstairs window, watching the Whitlocks wave them off in the driveway below.

Two days later, the couple return and take the baby away while Elspeth is in the laundry room. They don't even give her a chance to say goodbye.

'They just *left?*' she says, returning to an empty crib. She seems kind of stunned. We all are. Elspeth tells her parents on the phone not to collect her for another week, and I wonder if it's because she's not sure if the baby has actually been taken.

It isn't long before Elspeth and Julia attempt to do to Aretta what they did to me. I'm carrying a bowl of vinegar and newspapers to the exterior of the east wing, and as I bend over to shred the newspaper, I spot something at the upper windows. Elspeth and Julia, holding up a bucket, ready to tip the contents over Aretta below.

'Look out!' I shout, but too late. The bucket tips, almost in slow motion – the black shine of the liquid bulging by the lip of the bucket, then a long, serpentine spill, plunging down on an unsuspecting Aretta. I drop my bowl and newspaper and race over to her as she gasps in shock. I'm expecting to be hit with the sharp smell of urine, but it's boiling hot water. She bursts into tears and falls to her knees. Painful welts rise on the skin across her shoulders.

'Come with me,' I tell her, taking her hand.

In the kitchen, I place a cold cloth on her skin while Morven goes to fetch the tub of special ointment she uses for nappy rash. She scoops up a generous amount and smears it across Aretta's skin.

'Why do they do this?' Aretta asks as Morven smears her skin with cream. 'Do they get some kind of sick pleasure out of hurting people?'

'Some of us carry our shame in our bodies,' Morven says. 'Hidden away, you know, where people can't see it. Others can't do that, and sometimes it makes them want to hurt other people.'

A ghost moves inside me, and I want to say, *Some of us have ghosts inside us*. But I don't.

Two days later, I hear the familiar creak of Aretta's bedroom door. I open mine and watch as she pads secretly downstairs, then watch from the window as she heads into the woods. I feel frantic with worry. The woods aren't safe, especially at night. I think of the figure I saw there, weeks ago. I search for Aretta among the trees, but it's too dark, and I consider going outside to check that she's safe.

After half an hour, I spot her again, moving back into the house, something held in her hands. A jar.

When footsteps tap along the hallway again, I open my door and peer out at her. She gives a jump of fright.

'You scared me,' Aretta whispers.

'What's that?' I ask, looking at the jar in her hands.

Aretta grins. 'Look closer.'

She holds it up to the light, and I squint into the glass. It's full of spiders.

I'm puzzled. She went into the woods to collect spiders?

I go to ask, but she's already padding along the corridor towards Elspeth's room. There's a horrific shriek. She continues into Julia's room, and moments later she screams, too. Aretta has tipped the spiders on to their heads.

Over the next week, whenever I remember their screams, I can't help but laugh.

4

Eight days until my baby is due to be born. I keep thinking of Julia's screams when she had her baby. Will it really be that bad?

Mr and Mrs Whitlock gather us together in the morning in the dining room. It's unusual for them to be together like this, and they're both dressed smartly. Mrs Whitlock wears a navy skirt and jacket, and Mr Whitlock wears a shirt and tie and black trousers, though he's still barefoot.

They invite us all to sit down. Julia and Elspeth take chairs on one side of the room, and Morven, Aretta, Rahmi and I sit on the other. It's clear that we're divided, and that Julia and Elspeth are outnumbered. Mr and Mrs Whitlock remain standing, and the room falls silent with anticipation of their announcement. For a moment I wonder if they're going to tell us that we all have to leave. What will I do then? The thought of going back to Ma and Richard makes me ill. I'd rather spend a night in the woods than go home.

'We have a favour to ask of you all,' Mrs Whitlock says, smiling. 'I hope it won't be too onerous. In fact, I'm hoping you'll all enjoy it.'

Morven and I glance at each other.

Mr Whitlock clears his throat to address us. He's wearing white shorts and is barefoot, yellow toenails hanging over his toes like claws. He clasps his hands behind his back and puffs out his chest, but he looks anything but authoritative.

'I'd like you to help set up a project for dear Wulfric. A hen house. As you know, he hasn't been himself for some time. We think that caring for living creatures will restore him fully. And, it will provide lovely fresh eggs for us all to eat.

'A farmhand from MacGowan Farm is dropping off some supplies. We'd like some volunteers to assemble the coop.' He eyes us all. We all look at the floor.

'In the longer term, we'd also like some help for Wolfie in maintaining the hens,' Mrs Whitlock adds. She turns to Morven, smiling. 'Morven, my dear, you've been such a help with dear Wulfric. Do you think you could assist him with their care?'

I hear Morven give a slight cough, as though she's choking. 'Yes, of course,' she says. 'Delighted to.'

I nudge her, calling out her outrageous fib. It almost makes her laugh, and she has to cough into her hand to mask it.

'So,' Mrs Whitlock says, clapping her hands together. 'Who wants to volunteer first?'

Morven raises her hand, nudging me to raise mine. The other girls follow suit, though nobody looks thrilled about it. We don't really have a choice.

'Excellent,' Mr Whitlock says. 'What a sporting bunch you all are.'

Later that afternoon, Abdul, the farmhand, delivers ten hens, as well as the 'supplies' for the coop, which turn out to be nothing more than planks of wood and chicken wire, which we're to fasten together to build a coop.

We decide to build it in the depths of the woods, mostly to keep Wulfric out of the gardens.

'Little shit's never done pulling up the potatoes,' Morven says. 'Or kicking the heads off the cauliflower. He's worse than bloody flea beetles.'

Moving the wood through the forest is back-breaking work.

Wulfric comes wandering into the forest, looking over the team of women who are putting together his project. I'm wary of him, given what Morven has said about him, but he silently passes me planks of wood as I hold them in place as Rahmi hammers in nails.

'Will your baby always be a baby?' he asks Julia.

'What do you mean?' she says, confused.

'Will it grow up to be an adult?' he says. 'Or will it stay a baby for ever?'

Julia stops hammering and looks at him. 'I should hope it'll grow up,' she says, and he wanders off then, his question answered.

'Told you,' Morven whispers to me. 'Off his bloody noodle, just like the rest of them.'

5

That night, I wake up gasping in pain. It feels as if someone has poured boiling water over my stomach. It subsides, but a few minutes later it hits again, another wave of agony, and this time there is also a stretching sensation, like a balloon expanding inside my ribs. With nauseating horror, I realize that I'm probably in labour.

I shuffle up the hallway and bang on Morven's bedroom door, but there's no answer. I open the door, but the room is empty, and right then the pain hits so badly I drop to my knees.

'Mabel?'

I look up and see Aretta standing over me with a candle in her hand. She stares at me for a few moments before she realizes what's happening.

'Stay there,' she says. 'I'll get Morven!'

'Please don't leave me,' I whisper, but she's already racing down the stairs, calling 'Morven! Come quick!'

It feels as if I'm alone for a lifetime, kneeling on the hard wooden floor, groaning like a bear. And then Aretta and Elspeth are beside me, trying to lift me.

'Morven's downstairs,' Aretta says. 'We're going to take you to her, but you need to walk.'

The pain is excruciating, and I can barely move. Aretta and Elspeth hook my arms around their shoulders and heft me down the stairs to the lower floor. Inside, Rahmi is on the bed. Morven is beside her, holding Rahmi's hand and touching her bare belly. Blood fans outward on the white sheets in terrible red blooms. Morven looks stricken. 'You've another week yet,' she says in despair when she sees me, as if I can do anything about the time the baby arrives.

I lie down on the other bed, turning on my side and cupping my hands around my stomach. 'Knickers off,' Morven says, crossing the room to me. 'I need to see how dilated your cervix is.'

I pull the side of my pants down, puffing hard as the pain trammels me again. Morven slips her gloved fingers inside me, making me jump. 'Shit. Seven centimetres.'

'Is that bad?' Aretta says.

'You're going to have to do this,' Morven tells her.

Aretta shakes her head, panicked. 'I can't do it alone.'

'I'll talk you through it,' Morven says.

'I can't . . .'

Rahmi gives a long, heart-wrenching cry that silences us all. Morven places both her hands on Rahmi's round belly and starts to manoeuvre as though she is trying to twist it.

'I can't get the baby to turn,' she says with a groan.

'What'll happen if it doesn't turn?' Rahmi whimpers.

I swallow back a cry of pain, watching Morven carefully. Suddenly she pulls off her gloves and marches towards the door.

'Where are you going?' Aretta calls after her, panicked.

'We need to call an ambulance,' Morven says. 'I've never done a footling birth. Rahmi needs a Caesarean. She needs a doctor.'

I hear Morven make a noise of shock, a little 'Oh!' Mrs Whitlock is in the doorway with a face like an ice pick.

'What's going on?' she says, glancing across us all.

'We need to call for a doctor, Miss,' Morven tells her, her voice tight.

'I thought you had this in hand,' Mrs Whitlock says icily.

'I do. I mean, I thought I did,' Morven says, tripping over her words. I've never seen Morven look so undone, so afraid.

'It's just . . . the baby's a footling. Breech. And there's two girls in labour now.'

'Aretta?' Mrs Whitlock says.

'I've never delivered a baby before, Miss,' Aretta cries. 'I can't do it.'

Rahmi gives another howl of pain, and suddenly there's a sickening gush of blood, spilling over the bed and splatting on the floor. Morven and Aretta rush to her. Rahmi loses consciousness, her hand falling limply to the side of the bed. It's a terrifying moment, and suddenly I'm certain that the same thing is about to happen to me.

'Oh God, call a doctor!' Morven screams at Mrs Whitlock.

Mrs Whitlock responds by striding towards Morven and slapping her across the face. The crack of it rings out in the room, sharp and hard. Morven staggers backward, falling to the floor. She looks up in horror at Mrs Whitlock, who stands over her.

'You seem to have forgotten yourself,' Mrs Whitlock says, staring down. 'Babies have been born since the dawn of time with less knowledge and instruments than you have between you.'

'Yes, Miss,' Morven says, scrambling to her feet.

'No doctors. No ambulance. Get on with it.'

With a last, threatening glare, Mrs Whitlock walks out of the room, her shoes clicking quickly on the tiles. It's bizarre – she was so kind the other day, almost like a different person.

I can't hold it in any longer. A yell erupts out of my mouth, everything from my waist down being pulled into the earth.

Morven is slapping Rahmi's face, begging her to wake up. I see Aretta pulling on gloves and checking between my legs. And then I can't concentrate on anything anymore, a sudden whirlwind of pain gathering me up and pulling me inside a cauldron of agony. I can feel myself trying to block out the pain, my body shutting down and my mind fleeing somewhere else.

6

I come to as Aretta is talking to me, telling me to push. I can hear myself growling and grunting. I'm back in my body again. I have no idea how much time has passed.

And then a terrific lightness sweeps over me, a beautiful spaciousness. Suddenly the pain stops.

Aretta is holding something in her arms, a bundle of something covered in blood.

Quickly she places it on my stomach, and I howl in fear. I don't want to touch it. I don't want to see it. I can feel arms and legs squirming against me.

'We did it!' Aretta says, leaning over me, oddly elated. She rubs at the thing with a towel. Why is she giving it to me? Why does she seem so happy about the creature?

She encourages me to inspect the thing on my stomach, then arranges it in my arms so I can see its stomach, its curled-up legs.

I make myself look. It doesn't look like a chimera, or a ghost, or a plant.

'He's your baby,' Aretta says gently.

Slowly the creature transforms before my eyes. There's a thick head of black curly hair, a squashed-up face, two ink blots staring up at me.

I try to repeat the words in my head, but they sound wrong.

My baby. *My baby.*

Now

Pearl

Lichen Hall, Scottish Borders, September 1965

1

I can barely walk today, after my adventures in the woods last night. When I tripped in the forest I must have fallen on my left hip, because there's an ugly black bruise there, surrounded by deep scratches. My knees are both bruised, too, my forearms badly scraped. Some cuts on my face, close to my eyes, a welt from a branch running right across my eyelid.

I could have blinded myself. I'm lucky I didn't land on my stomach. The baby is moving as normal, so it seems unharmed, and I've been watching carefully for any bleeding to indicate trauma to the womb. I may be giving up this child for adoption, but I certainly don't want any harm to come to it.

I've thought long and hard about how to explain what happened to me in the woods last night. About the tall thing with no head and a voice of mud. About how I felt it touch me, and how its will slipped into my mind, loud and clear as a bell.

That it wanted to *wear* me.

I flicked Wulfric's lighter, a last, desperate instinct to protect myself with fire, and how it worked – the creature disappeared instantly.

It makes no sense.

Did I dream it all? Or was my mind playing tricks on me? Things always seem different in the dark, *especially* a dark forest in the dead of night. Even more so an ancient wood that is full of gnarled, ghostly trees.

I lift my eyes to my reflection in the bathroom mirror. The truth is, I *want* to believe that I dreamed it all, I really do. It would be a hundred times easier than the alternative, which is that I really did encounter some terrifying thing that wanted to kill me. A ghost, and unlike any ghost I've ever seen depicted in a film, or read of in a book.

Something unspeakably evil is stalking the grounds of Lichen Hall.

2

It's Tuesday. I'm to teach Wulfric this afternoon. I rise early, watching the hands of the clock in the drawing room with trepidation. I am quite genuinely, and not irrationally, scared. I am not one for being frightened. The life of a nurse is filled with more peril than people realize. Countless times I've dealt with addicts, armed to the teeth with blades and the occasional gun, raving incoherently and threatening to do us harm. One man followed me into the toilets once and locked us both in there, intent on – as he put it – ripping me out of my uniform. A swift kick to the bollocks put paid to that, and I unlocked the door and called the police on him.

But I am not in the relative safety of the hospital. I'm in a place where, more and more, I feel afraid, both inside and outside the house.

'Pearl? Are you there?'

It's Wulfric, calling from the floor below my bedroom. I check the clock in case I've lost track of time, but it's only twelve.

'Just a minute,' I call. 'What is it?'

I peer outside and spot him through the banisters.

'It's my lighter,' he says. 'You took it. Can I have it back now?'

A device capable of burning the house to the ground is probably not best placed in Wulfric's care, but he's right – it's his lighter, albeit a stolen one. And I ought to return it. 'I'll bring it to our lesson,' I call through the door. 'One hour.'

I wait until I hear his feet move across the floor downstairs before ducking out of the bathroom and heading back upstairs to my room, where I retrieve the lighter.

Downstairs, I have lunch – leek and potato soup and bread – followed by two cups of tea to try to steady my nerves.

At one o'clock, I find Wulfric in the Willow room, standing on the windowsill and holding onto the top of the frame with his hands.

'Hello, Wulfric,' I say lightly as I enter. 'Please get down from the window.'

He jumps down with a heavy thump that causes a vase to topple from a side table. Mercifully, it doesn't smash.

'Here you are,' I say, holding the lighter towards him. He approaches and reaches for it, but I swipe it back out of reach.

'What you doing?' he says, confused.

I glance at the door, checking that no one – particularly Mrs Whitlock – is in earshot. 'I want to ask a question,' I say, holding the lighter away from his grasp. 'But I want you to swear – and I mean, *swear*, on your precious lighter – that you'll not tell anyone what I ask.'

He lifts his eyes sullenly to mine. 'What is it?'

'You have to swear,' I say. Then, in case he doesn't understand: 'And if you ever tell anyone, you have to give me your lighter for keeps.'

He nods. 'OK. I swear.'

I take a seat by the desk, and he follows, sitting in the chair opposite. 'What's this about?' he says, his interest piqued.

'You know the old wood?' I say, nodding at the trees behind the window. 'The one with all the white trees?'

'The ghost woods?'

'Was there ever any mention of something living there? An old rumour, perhaps, of a . . . ghost?'

He screws up his face. 'A ghost?'

I struggle to think of how best to put it. The creature flashes in my mind again, and I wince. 'Perhaps a dark tale of something horrible living there.'

He glances at the trees, visibly turning over my question in his mind. 'Some of the girls talked about a woman in the woods,' he says.

This sounds familiar. I remember Rahmi mentioning it.

'Did they know who she was?'

He shakes his head.

'When was this?' I press. 'Who talked about the woman in the woods? Did something happen?'

He looks suddenly afraid, and I worry I've pushed him too hard.

'I don't want to talk about it,' he says.

We study each other for a few seconds. I have an urge to ask him about the morgue story, too, but my moment seems to have passed. He glances away, but I can see colour has risen to his cheeks, and he seems disturbed by my probing. Perhaps he too has encountered the thing I saw last night. I best not press him further in case he makes a fuss and flips out again.

'Here,' I say, handing him the lighter. 'And thank you.'

He seems heartened to have it back, immediately flicking it alight.

'Be careful with that, won't you?' I ask him.

3

We proceed with the lesson. I decide to focus on mathematics, avoiding literacy in case it triggers another outburst. We review his times tables, then fractions, but I'm distracted. My mind keeps turning to what he told me.

A woman in the woods.

Is *that* why Rahmi was out there with her flaming torch? Was she trying to ward off something dangerous?

I think of the oil painting in the hallway that I spotted on my first day here, the portrait of a fairy carrying a baby.

Once our lesson is over, I head straight there to inspect it.

It *is* strange, and even more so now I look closely – the fairy is wearing a fine blue dress. She is slender of face and body, with long blonde hair, and there are wings visible at her back, so in other words she fulfils a certain archetype of feminine beauty. But her face is craven, and her open mouth is full of small, pointed teeth. Her hands are bloodied, and there is blood on the babe she carries. The child doesn't seem to be asleep, but dead.

What a bizarre painting to have in a hallway.

There's a brass plate on the frame, at the bottom, with a faint inscription.

Neachneohain.

I took Gaelic at school. It's pronounced 'Nicnevin', which rings a bell. I think I saw it in Professor Llewellyn's book about fungi.

I head upstairs to the library and sink down into a chair by the bookcases, feeling scared and sad. The mind can be so easily agitated. Perhaps it was my examining this painting that gave rise to last night's escapades. Or maybe Rahmi's comment stirred something in my subconscious, causing me to *think* I saw something in the woods.

No, I think. I really did see that thing. Part of me hopes it was a figment of my imagination. But it was real. I felt it touch me.

I pick up Professor Llewellyn's book and flick through the pages, finding a mid-section of illustrations reveals some of the mushrooms I spotted. They all have such fabulous names. Bridal Veil Stinkhorn. Amethyst Deceiver. Gassy Webcap. Bleeding Tooth.

No indication of their medicinal purposes, though I scan a lengthy chapter on the general medicinal use of fungi. Professor Llewellyn estimates there to be millions – millions! – of species, and says they are closer to animals than plants. He says they are one of the oldest organisms on earth, and without them, trees wouldn't exist. Nor would humans.

I discover that the mushrooms I saw in the herb garden aren't native to Scotland, but from all over the world. I think quickly to the family photographs mounted on the wall in the hallway, near the kitchen. Why are Skyblue Mushrooms, native to New Zealand, thriving here in Scotland?

The Whitlocks must have brought the mushrooms back from their travels. A shiver runs through me. I don't care how medicinal or aesthetically-pleasing mushrooms are – a fungal disease almost killed me, and I'm forever averse to all things mushroom.

However, I'm finding a strange understanding amidst all this fungal scrutiny. Mushrooms are chimeras, existing in the cusp between nature and the human world, a seam neither wholly botanical nor animal. It makes me think of my pregnant body, the space this baby occupies – the margin between the mortal world and that other, not-mortal place; an existential lacuna. Pregnant, I am also a chimera, nine months inhabiting the boundary between worlds. In a way, the story about the fairy and the mushroom baby makes sense – both fairies and mushrooms belong to some space outside the real world. Like pregnant mothers.

There it is – that word underneath the painting, anglicized in Professor Llewellyn's book. *Nicnevin*. A witch, he says, not a fairy. 'Scotland's Hecate'. He writes about a girl who gave birth to a baby that wasn't fully human, a kind of root creature that was part-fairy. When the girl's horrified parents killed it, Nicnevin cursed the family and the house, claiming it as 'a palace of rot and ruin'.

The house was called Lichen Hall.

II

Then

Mabel

Lichen Hall, Scottish Borders, September 1959

1

I wake up in my bedroom, sunlight streaming through the window. I'm out of my nightdress and wrapped in a clean towel, clean knickers lined with a menstrual pad. Morven is standing by the bed. She's grinning down at me, and I see that she's wearing clean clothes and her hands are no longer stained with blood. I wonder if I dreamed it all. Maybe the baby was a dream.

From somewhere in the room there's a little cry, like a kitten. Morven reaches down into the crib next to the bed and gathers a baby into her arms. She places it into my arms, wrapped up in a white blanket. I stiffen, trying not to look too much at the baby. It feels small, like a doll, and I remember Julia's baby, how lovely she was. I'd felt sorry for her when Julia wouldn't hold her, but I feel the same.

I force myself to look down at the thing in my arms. It's only a baby. A tiny baby boy, with a squashed-up face and red skin.

The baby starts to squirm inside the blanket, his mouth opening like a little beak, his toothless gums like apple slices.

'Try feeding him,' Morven says. 'He'll want feeding.'

She doesn't leave the room, and I feel stung with embarrassment. But then I remember that she must have seen me naked, given that I've been changed out of my clothes. A quick flash of my breast is nothing now. I pull the towel down a little and move the baby close.

'Tap your nipple to his nose,' Morven urges. 'That way he'll know to latch on.'

I use my free hand to lift my breast and tap my nipple on his little nose, just like Morven instructs. His mouth opens and he gives a quick shake of his head, as if he can't find the nipple. Then he clamps on and suckles. The pain is startling.

'Ah!' I gasp, and Morven laughs.

'It won't hurt for long,' she says. 'Your tits will get used to it.'

But it does hurt, and after a while it makes my tummy hurt, too, as though I'm about to give birth again. Morven says this is normal.

When the baby stops feeding, I place him back in the crib and hobble to the bathroom. The thought of peeing is terrifying, but I have to.

'Seven pounds five ounces,' Morven announces when she places the baby on the scale. 'And he's long, too. Just over twenty inches. I told you you were hiding a big 'un.' She passes him back to me carefully, then pours a cup of tea from a pot on a tray on the floor.

'How's your eye?' I ask her, noticing a dark bruise forming over the side of her face. Where Mrs Whitlock hit her.

'It's fine,' she says, straightening and passing me the tea. 'Looks worse than it is.'

'Has she ever hit you before?'

Morven shakes her head. 'She's different these days. She never used to be this way.'

She glances at the baby, who is fast asleep. 'Does he look like the father?'

'I don't know,' I say, looking down at him. 'I don't know who the father is.'

'Ah, OK.' She says it as though she's learned something new and awful about me.

'I've never slept with anyone,' I say quickly. 'I don't know how I fell pregnant.'

She studies me carefully, waiting, I think, for me to tell her I was joking. When I don't, she says. 'Maybe it's parthenogenesis.'

'Partheno-what?'

She continues wiping down the scale. 'Happens all the time in nature. Virgin births. I once heard about a shark in an aquarium that had three babies. Everyone was baffled, because she was the only shark in the tank. Turns out she made babies all by herself. The scientists call it parthenogenesis. Plants can do it, too. Most mushrooms are grown that way.'

I straighten, my mind racing. 'Can humans do it?'

She shrugs, and I can tell she isn't taking me seriously. 'Maybe you're the first.'

'How is Rahmi's baby?'

Morven's face tightens. She clears her throat. 'He didn't make it.'

I draw a sharp breath. Poor Rahmi.

A floorboard creaks in the hallway outside. Mrs Whitlock peers around the door, her face stretched in a smile. Morven flinches and stands up, anxious at her presence.

'Good day,' Mrs Whitlock says, beaming at us both. Her eyes fall on the baby in my arms. 'Oh, a little boy. Congratulations, Mabel.'

'Thank you,' I say shyly.

'How are you feeling?' she asks. Then, before I can answer: 'Morven and Aretta did a tremendous job delivering him.'

Morven keeps her eyes down as she gathers up the tray and the teapot, but I can see colour rising at her cheeks.

'She did,' I say.

'Thank you, Mrs Whitlock,' Morven says quietly. Then she leaves the room.

Mrs Whitlock checks Morven has gone before closing the door behind her. She sits on the end of the bed.

'I don't know if Morven has told you,' she says, 'but there's a little ritual I like to do when the babies are born. It's an old family tradition. Do you mind?'

'What's the tradition?' I ask cautiously. One of her hands is clasped, as though she is holding something. A gift, perhaps.

'Fairy dust,' she says, opening her hand to reveal a pinch of some kind of powder, or ash. 'A little concoction from the woods to wish the child good luck.'

I've never heard of such a thing. Maybe it's a tradition in the Scottish Borders.

'OK.'

I watch with curiosity as Mrs Whitlock takes the baby from me, chatting to him softly as she walks to the window. Then she lowers her face to his, whispering to him, saying words I can't understand. Gaelic, perhaps? As she whispers, the light from the window seems to grow stronger, putting them both in silhouette. I can't see her face. Something feels wrong, and two ghosts start pacing in my collarbones. I remember the figure I saw in the woods that night. I see the shadow of Mrs Whitlock raise her hand in the air, sprinkling the powder down on to the baby as though she's seasoning meat. He sneezes, and the light dims.

'There,' she says, passing him back. 'Now he's right as rain.'

2

Three days later, Morven tells me Rahmi is going to bury her baby.

'Where will he be buried?' I ask Morven. She's showing me how to 'top and tail' my bairn by laying him on the bed and washing his head and bum with a cloth and warm soapy water in a bowl.

'Here,' she says. 'In the grounds of the hall.'

'Shouldn't he be given a proper burial?' I ask Morven. 'You know, with a priest and everything?'

'The Whitlocks won't have it,' she says. 'They won't let us call or tell anyone about it. You know what she's like about doctors. They've become so secretive. It's not right.'

I feed the baby and lay him down to sleep in his crib. Then Morven takes me down to the birthing suite, which reeks of bleach. Morven has thoroughly washed the place, but a tiny drop of blood remains on a tile in the corner. It tugs at my memories, making my skin crawl.

Rahmi is already down there, her bairn wrapped up in a blanket on the bed she gave birth on, a small white hat and BabyGro laid out next to him.

Morven carries a bowl of hot soapy water, fresh towels draped across her wrist. She approaches Rahmi gently.

'We can help you wash him, if you like?' she says. Rahmi glances at us both and nods. In silence, we unwrap the little body from the blanket, then set about washing him delicately. He's just like a little doll.

Then we dress him, swaddle him in a blanket, and place a teddy in his arms. He's a big baby, almost nine pounds, with a full head of black hair. He has Rahmi's lips and nose, and chunky arms.

Rahmi wants to bury the baby by herself. Morven and I go back upstairs, but watch from the long windows by Mr Whitlock's Micrarium as Rahmi carries the wooden flour box into the woods. I feel uneasy, and angry. It's a beautiful day, the sunlight falling crisp and golden across the fields, the birds singing in the trees. The sun shouldn't shine when such an awful thing is happening.

'Maybe this will help Rahmi feel better,' I tell Morven, looking down at her as she carries the small coffin deep into the trees.

Morven doesn't say anything for a long time. We watch as Rahmi returns to the shed by the garden, heading back through the trees with a shovel.

'Maybe it's better this way,' she says.

'What do you mean?'

'Sometimes the babies die,' she says. 'The first time I thought it was a punishment. Now I think it's a blessing.'

'A blessing?'

'When the baby's adopted, you spend every day wondering what they're doing. How they'll grow up. You worry about them getting hurt and you not being there to make it better.' Morven bites her lip, and I can tell she's talking about herself. She looks at me, her eyes shining. 'At least if they're dead, you don't have to worry about that stuff. You know?'

Now

Pearl

Lichen Hall, Scottish Borders, September 1965

1

Had I not encountered the thing in the woods, I wouldn't give the story about the witch, Nicnevin, a second thought. But it's very difficult to cast it aside, given the fact that Lichen Hall *is* becoming a palace of rot and ruin, thanks to the fungus growing out of the walls, and the fact that I had my own run-in with something that I can't yet describe.

I need to tell someone. And at the same time, I feel embarrassed. What if they don't believe me? What if they think I'm just some halfwit who believes in folk tales?

I go out into the gardens to find Rahmi. She was the one who mentioned the woman in the woods, so she's more likely to believe me. I'm only outside a few seconds when I spot a little boy racing across the long strip of lush meadow at the side of the house. Instantly I think back to the first night I was here, when I saw a child running down the hallway in the dark. It was this child, I'm sure of it.

I call out to him and wave. 'Boy!'

He darts into the trees. I swerve quickly through the garden to the woods, ducking to see if I can catch sight of him.

The terrain of the woodland is uneven, thick roots snaking out of the ground. I tread carefully, scanning the mossy trunks for movement.

Something stirs near a clearing. I head towards it, clambering over rocks and fallen branches to get to it. The exertion feels good, the noise of the birds and the wind in the high branches sloughing the fairy story from the book from my mind, so I keep going, no longer sure who or what I'm chasing.

There. About twenty feet ahead, a little face peeking out from behind a tree. We lock eyes and he darts away, absorbed in a few seconds by the camouflage of trunks.

'I can see you,' I call out.

He responds with a bright laugh. It's a game, now.

'I'm coming to get you,' I shout. 'I'm the Scary Woodland Creature, and I eat small boys for my breakfast!'

A high shriek, followed by laughter. My heart is racing, but I quicken my pace until I'm lightly jogging, a little worried now that I'm driving the boy deeper into the woods. I keep scanning the trees for any sign of the thing I saw last night. I should probably stop in case I trigger early labour.

I follow after him until we reach a clearing. There's a huge tree in the midst of it, a dozen beefsteak mushrooms jutting out of the trunk like shelves. I sit down on a tree stump next to it to catch my breath.

'Boy!' I call. 'We should turn back now. Your parents will be looking for you.'

'What are "parents"?' a voice says, and I jump. The boy appears from behind the mushroom tree and stands right in front of me. He's wearing navy trousers that are too short, a mismatched pair of socks, and a vivid blue hand-knit jumper. I think of the bits of wool I saw snagged by the wire fence on the edge of the forest. He's wearing oversized wellies. His hands are filthy, as though he's been playing in the woods all day, but his face and curly black hair are clean. He has swarthy skin and striking round eyes the colour of horse chestnuts, the sort that you notice before anything else, and his front teeth are missing. His accent is Scottish.

'You know, "parents",' I say. 'Your mother and father. Are they nearby?'

'I don't have a father,' he says.

'Oh.' I don't know what to say to that. 'Where do you live?'

'In this tree,' he says, patting the trunk fondly. 'This is Ollie Oak Tree.' He points to the beefsteak mushrooms. 'And these are Alice, Morris, Susan, Herbert, Philip, Robin, and Jemima.' He nods at a big red toadstool by my feet. 'That's Ruby. Careful you don't step on her.'

I chuckle at his naming of mushrooms. 'Does Ruby talk?'

He looks puzzled. 'Of course not. She's a toadstool.'

'I don't think you live in a tree,' I say.

'I *do*,' he says defiantly. 'Well, I don't sleep in Ollie. But he lets me play inside him. Look.'

He shows me a large hollow at the other side of the trunk, and climbs inside to illustrate its spaciousness. 'See?'

'All right,' I say. 'You may well play here. But you don't live here. You live in Lichen Hall, don't you?'

'Sometimes.' He looks worried. 'Promise you won't tell?'

'I promise.'

'Where do *you* live?' he says from the hollow of the tree. He squats and looks closely at something in his palm, and I flinch – it's a large spider.

'I'm staying at Lichen Hall,' I say. 'Just until my baby is born.'

'You're from Edinburgh, aren't you?' he says. I raise my eyebrows. I must have more of an accent than I thought.

'I'm Pearl,' I say, holding out a hand. 'Pleased to meet you.'

'I know,' he says, ignoring my hand. 'Pearl Gorham.'

'Cripes, good guess,' I say, laughing. Mrs Whitlock must have told him about me.

'I'm Sylvan,' he says.

'Sylvan,' I say. 'What a lovely name. And how old are you, Sylvan?'

'I'm almost six.'

'Almost six! What a wonderful age. Do you have anyone to play with, out here? What about Wulfric? Do you play with him?'

He lowers the palm holding the spider to the ground, watching as it scurries off. 'Want to see what I can do?'

'Go on, then.'

He raises his hands in the air, then lowers them on the ground in a handstand and walks forward for six steps.

'Bravo!' I say, clapping. 'You must have practised that forever.'

'Just two days,' he says. 'So if someone ever cuts my legs off I'll be able to walk on my hands.'

What an odd thing to say. I step forward, but suddenly a female voice rings through the woods, and I see a young woman standing at the top of the slope.

'Sylvan!'

She makes her way quickly down the top of the slope, clearly upset that Sylvan is talking to me. She's very thin, her jawline sharp as a razor. She carries a rattan basket full of branches – for firewood, I assume – and is wearing a long grey dress with wellies. The bones of her face are visible, even from a distance, the knuckles of her hands like spikes along the basket. Her hair is a ratty brown braid down her back.

I recognize her. She's the girl I saw going into the Wisteria room the other day, when Mrs Whitlock was conducting her business meeting.

'Hi, Mum,' Sylvan says to her, brightening. 'I was being chased!'

His *mother*, I think, taking in their exchange. They must live in Lichen Hall. There are no other houses for miles.

'Who was chasing you?' the girl says, heading down the slope and glancing at me nervously.

'The Scary Woodland Creature,' he says, grinning at me.

'Hello,' I say to the girl, holding out my hand. 'I'm Pearl. I spotted your son before, inside the hall.'

She turns and glares at him, and I wonder what I've said wrong.

'What?' he says to her defensively. 'No one saw me.'

'It's clear that someone saw you,' she snaps at him. She means me.

'I won't say anything,' I say, not sure why it's such a secret. 'I didn't catch your name?'

'Her name's Mabel,' Sylvan volunteers. 'Mabel Haggith.'

The girl visibly bristles at Sylvan's divulgence. 'Sylvan!' she hisses.

I flash my best smile at her, but she won't meet my eye.

'We need to do our chores,' she mutters, holding out a hand to him. 'Come on, now.'

'Bye, Scary Woodland Creature,' Sylvan tells me, frowning.

'It was lovely to meet you both,' I call after them. 'Perhaps we can have tea some time?'

But Sylvan and his mother walk quickly up the slope, Sylvan throwing me disappointed glances until they disappear over the crest.

Then

Mabel

Lichen Hall, Scottish Borders, September–November 1959

1

The baby is a week old. When he was born, his skin was red, as though he'd been cooked. Just as Morven predicted, his colour has started to change, from that deep, slapped red to bile yellow. Today she's worried he is jaundiced. 'Mrs Whitlock doesn't let the babies go to hospital if they get jaundiced,' she says warily, sitting on the end of my bed.

I look down at the infant in my arms, his eyes like ink blots. I'm still convinced that he'll change into something else. That he isn't a proper baby. That he's a ghost.

'Why do the babies need to go to hospital?' I ask her.

'Jaundice can cause brain damage if it's not treated.'

She glances out of the window. It's growing colder, and all the trees are shedding their leaves. Julia and Elspeth both left two days ago, gone back to wherever they're from. It's as though the house is exhaling, its inner weather changing. The fields are golden, and in the mornings you can see mist lying all over the valley like a silver veil. Cloud inversions, Morven calls them. But today it's bright and sunny. 'Let's get him out into the sunlight,' Morven says.

We wrap him in a blanket and Morven slips a hat she knitted

over his head. 'He's bonny,' she says with a smile. 'Just like his mammy.'

We take him for a walk around the gardens. Morven takes him, as I'm nervous about holding him. I've never carried an infant before, not outside. He's so wobbly, unable to hold his head up, and he doesn't seem to know what his hands are for. I think there must be something wrong with him, but Morven tells me this is perfectly normal. All his muscles are brand new, she says, and he has to learn how to use them.

When the sun comes out Morven says we could sit down on the grass and take the baby out of his blanket, just for a while. 'To get the sunlight on his skin,' she says. 'It'll help the jaundice.'

'How does it help?' I ask.

She scrunches up her face. 'I don't know, exactly. Ma always made us take bairns like this into the sunshine, and they usually got better.'

We make sure to hold him in the light. He fusses and squirms, and I can tell he doesn't like the wind on his skin or the sun in his eyes. So I hold his face to mine, his cheek to my cheek, and speak to him a little. And then he quietens.

'We'll do this twice a day, until he's better,' Morven says. 'And keep feeding him as often as you can.'

I feel awkward about the breastfeeding. It hurts like mad, and now every time he cries I feel anxious, because I know it's going to hurt again.

'You could let Rahmi feed him for a bit,' Morven says when I mention this. 'Her milk will be in. And it might be a comfort for her.'

This suggestion brings relief. I don't know what to do for Rahmi. I know her sadness is like a labyrinth, all twisted and layered with confusion. She came here to have her baby adopted, and now he's dead. She doesn't speak, but often I see tears rolling down her face, and her eyes are dark and haunted. I thought she would have packed her bags and left the next day, but she's still here. I suspect Mrs Whitlock has encouraged her to stay; she's good with the hens, and they're thriving.

2

The next day I knock on Rahmi's bedroom door. She opens it, but simply stares at me without saying anything.

I glance at Morven, who waits down the hall, throwing me looks to get on with it.

'I wondered if you'd like to feed the baby,' I ask Rahmi. She stares at me for what feels like an age. She can't have washed since burying her baby; her hair is wild and tangled, still holding leaves from the forest. Without saying a word, she shuts the door in my face.

I turn to Morven.

'At least you tried,' she says.

Later, when I'm in the kitchen baking scones, I hear a floor-board creak in the hallway. Rahmi appears out of the shadows. Her hair is tied up and she's changed into a clean dress.

'I'd like to feed the baby,' she says. 'If that's still OK.'

I nod and set the dough aside, taking her quickly upstairs to my room. She seems uncomfortable, so I ask her to have a seat in the wicker chair next to the window. Then, I pick up my bairn from his crib and sit down next to her, holding him so we can both see his little face. He's still fast asleep, but my breasts tell me it's only minutes until he starts fussing, looking for a feed.

'Do you miss your son?' I ask Rahmi.

She nods. Her eyes fill with tears and she swipes them away.

'I can't stop crying,' she says.

'Me neither. Morven said all new mums do it.'

'It's like I've got a leaky tap somewhere in my body,' she says.

'I know.'

Right on schedule, the baby starts to wake up, his mouth turning to find a nipple to suckle. I hand him carefully to Rahmi, who cradles him in her arms. I see her soften as she looks down at him. 'He smells just like my baby smelled,' she says. Her voice is hoarse.

I find her a pillow to place on her lap, and she lays him there, before unbuttoning her dress. The baby feeds, not making a sound, lifting his little fists to the sides of his head as he eats. Then he lies back on the pillow and goes straight to sleep.

Rahmi feeds him like this again that night, then the next day after dinner. She likes to do it, and I know she wants to do it more, but Morven warns against it.

'Your milk will dry up,' she tells me.

I want to say that I'd like my milk to dry up. It feels weird and horrible to have milk in my body, coming out of me, sometimes staining my clothes. I can't get used to it. I wonder if all the other girls have felt OK about it, if I'm the only one to feel that it's kind of gross.

But I don't want to ask.

3

It happens four days later.

The bairn is awake, and the sun is rising, the skies streaked red, as though they're bleeding. He's lying on the bed. I take off his nappy and wipe a wet cloth along his forehead to wash him. As I turn to dab the cloth in the little bowl of water, glancing over his skin to check that the jaundice has gone, his left leg begins to shine.

I run a finger along his shin to see if it's an oil or a powder residue on his little body, but my finger comes away clean. For about a minute, he seems to shine, his skin bright as silver, just like the mushrooms I saw glowing in the woods that night.

There's a knock on the door, a rhythmic handful of raps.

'Just me,' Morven says, coming inside.

'Do you see that?' I ask her.

She looks down at the baby. 'See what?'

I'm too struck by what I saw. Did I imagine it?

She checks his belly button. The umbilical cord has left a horrible stump that has started to turn black. 'That happens to all babies,' Morven says when she notices me staring at it.

I exhale loudly, releasing all the pent-up fear. 'I don't know what I'd do if you weren't here,' I say.

'Oh, you'd manage,' she says with a smile. 'It's all new for everyone at some point. The early days are rough. But you'd manage.'

'I don't think I would,' I say, lifting my eyes to her.

She blushes and shrugs it off.

'Whoever made you feel that way about yourself?' she says.

I stare at her, and she reaches out a hand to touch my cheek. It's only a moment, but her fingers against my cheek send electric sparks shooting down my neck, into my arms and my tummy. She moves away, and I sit for a moment, wondering what on earth just happened.

'You've done a good job looking after him so far,' Morven says, unpacking the basket of BabyGros and handknitted cardigans. They've all been left behind by the other girls who have stayed here over the years to have their babies. There are even clothes for older babies: sailor dresses, leather shoes. Some of them look old-fashioned, and I wonder how long Lichen Hall has been hosting expectant mothers. At least ten years, Morven says.

She sets about separating the dresses into a different pile, putting clothes for the baby into the chest of drawers. He kicks his legs, enjoying the freedom to move, his fists bunched up against his chin. He turns his face to the window, mesmerized by it, while I put on his clean nappy. Something moves at his ribs, a small pinprick of light. I look around, trying to see where it's coming from – perhaps the sunlight has bounced off a reflective surface. But when I move my hand over it, it's clear it's not a reflection. The light is *in his skin*.

'There's something strange on his leg,' I mutter to Morven, tapping the light with my finger as it moves. 'It looks like . . . silver.'

'Sylvan?' Morven says, mishearing me. 'Is that your name for him?'

I look again. It's gone now, the silvery light I'd seen before. His skin is swarthy, not as pale as mine, which made the light stand out even more. But it looks normal now. As though the light has disappeared.

Morven comes and sits down next to me. I want to mention the light to her but it's completely gone. She lifts the talcum powder and puts a small dusting on the black stump at his navel as I pin together his clean nappy. 'There we are, baby Sylvan,' she says.

Sylvan, I think. He does look like a Sylvan.

'Did you name your baby?' I ask her.

'Edward,' she says, sadly. 'Edward McCormack, after my grandfather. Whatever his adopted parents called him, he'll always be Edward to me.'

'Do you know where he's living now?'

She shrugs. 'No idea. He could be anywhere.'

'How long do you think you'll stay here?' I ask. 'I mean, at Lichen Hall?'

She holds me with her bright, bold eyes. 'I don't want to go home. Not ever.'

'I don't want to go back to Dundee,' I say, the words seeming to come out of my mouth before I think them. I look up, half-expecting Morven to say something critical. *You should be glad to return to your home.* The thought is in Ma's voice.

'Stay here with me,' Morven says, moving closer, her face lit up with excitement. She says it like a dare, as if she's challenging me, but her eyes say something else.

'How can I just stay?' I ask her. 'Mrs Whitlock said I can only stay here until the baby's adopted . . .'

'I'll teach you,' she says, grabbing my hands. 'I'll show you how to deliver babies. How to take care of the mothers. Mrs Whitlock doesn't want doctors involved. She wants to control everything that happens at Lichen Hall.' She reaches and takes my hand, and it feels like the most natural, sure thing to feel her skin against mine. 'I bet you anything she'll have you stay. It's not like she pays me anything. But it's a roof over my head, right?'

Mrs Whitlock scares me, and I wonder for a moment if Morven feels the same way. She spoke so highly of Mrs Whitlock when I arrived. My eyes trace the mark on Morven's face from when Mrs Whitlock struck her, knocking her to the ground.

'I'm sorry she did that to you,' I say. I lift a hand to touch the bruise, not to hurt her, but to let her know how bad I feel about it. She lets me touch her face, and there's a breathless pause, my fingers at the most vulnerable part of her, volumes spoken in a momentary touch.

And suddenly the thought of never seeing her again is terrifying.

4

Aretta has her bairn at the end of October. She's two weeks overdue, and her pains start in the middle of the night. Morven wakes me to help her; she said she would teach me, so that I can help deliver babies with her. That way I can prove to the Whitlocks that it's worth letting me stay at Lichen Hall.

I debate in my head whether to bring Sylvan down to the birthing suite with us. He's fast asleep, so I decide to leave him in his cot and run back up every ten or fifteen minutes to check on him.

I feel sick when I see Aretta in labour. All I can think of is Rahmi losing her baby, and all the blood . . . I bet Morven is thinking the same thing. Her face is pale and drawn, all her sass gone. Morven's always sassy. But not tonight.

Aretta's labour progresses quickly, and within an hour she's on all fours on the floor, grunting and groaning.

'That's it,' Morven says, pulling on her gloves. 'This is her bearing down. Not long now.'

'What's all the noise about?' a voice says, and I almost jump out of my skin. Morven and I look up to see Wulfric standing in the doorway of the birthing suite. Usually he sleeps through the births, or isn't interested. Mr and Mrs Whitlock don't have much to do with them, either. But Wulfric is standing there now, gawping at Aretta on the floor with her bottoms off.

'*Bed*, Wulfric,' Morven says fiercely. 'Or there's no chocolate cake for a month.'

The threat works: he turns on his heel and thumps up the stairs.

Aretta doesn't scream, but holds on to me very tightly as Morven kneels behind her, checking for the baby's head.

'I can't do this,' Aretta says, looking up at me. There is fear on her face, and I remember how I felt, right before Sylvan was born. The pain was so intense I really believed I would die. But I didn't.

'You can,' I tell Aretta. 'You really can.'

She looks more hopeful, but she squeezes my arms tightly as the next contraction hits, her cries turning to growls.

'This stage is called transition,' Morven tells me. 'You can tell by the sound. Some countries call it the groaning, because the mother starts to sound like that.'

Morven has me check for a head. There isn't any sign, though Aretta is growling and pushing, rocking back on to her heels. With each rock, more water comes out, but no baby.

But then, I see it – the black seam of a little head.

'It's coming!' I tell Aretta, and she rears up, her face contorted in pain.

'Don't push too hard,' Morven urges her. 'You'll tear. Nice and slow.'

She makes me squat on the floor, a towel in my arms to guide the baby out. But on the next contraction, Aretta gives a huge push. The baby comes out so quickly that I have to catch it, slippery as an eel.

Morven checks over the baby in my arms.

'A little girl,' she tells Aretta proudly.

Aretta promptly bursts into tears, and I do too, as though it's my baby. I caught her. I'm watching as she takes her first breath.

'Why are *you* crying?' Morven laughs, and I shake my head and laugh at the silliness of it. I'm overwhelmed. Giving birth is something that women do every day, and yet it's still such a hugely emotional thing. A new life, here in my arms.

I pass the baby to Aretta, remembering suddenly that I've not checked on Sylvan. My whole body goes icy cold. But Aretta isn't ready to take the baby from me. Morven has to check her over, and I need to clean the baby.

'No tearing,' Morven says, peering between Aretta's legs. 'Thank God. I hate doing stitches.'

Once the placenta is delivered, we help Aretta back upstairs to her room with the new baby. As soon as she's settled into bed I race to my room, my heart in my mouth. What if Sylvan has been crying all this time? What if he has stopped breathing?

I reach the doorway of my room and gasp, noticing the inside of the crib lies in darkness, empty. I stagger forward and pull at the blankets, tears reaching my eyes.

'It's OK,' a voice says.

Rahmi's nursing Sylvan on the bed, sitting on top of the bedclothes. I sink down beside her with relief.

'I thought . . .' I begin, but I don't finish my sentence. I don't know what I thought. That he'd vanished into thin air? Sometimes I think he really is a ghost baby. That he'll slip away one moment, when I'm not looking.

Rahmi smells like smoke, and she's clearly upset. Her hair is undone, hanging in a wild tangle around her shoulders, and she's trembling.

'What happened?' I say, sitting on the bed opposite her.

'Promise me first you won't say anything,' she says.

'I promise.'

'A couple of days after I buried the baby I went out at night to be with him. I couldn't bear the thought of him out there, all alone in the cold.'

I nod.

'Two nights ago I went and sat with him for a while.' She falls silent, her trembling growing harder. 'I could see someone, or something, in the forest. I thought it was maybe you, or Aretta, coming to check on me. But it wasn't.'

With a hard swallow, I think back to the night I saw the hooded figure. 'Do you know who it was?'

She gives a small shake of her head and bites her lip, her eyes filling with fear. 'I don't even think it was a person at all. It was *evil*. I could feel it.'

She finishes feeding Sylvan and fixes her shirt. 'I was so scared. But I couldn't rest, knowing that something was out there with my son.'

She tells me she went out tonight again to be with him. This time she took a flaming torch. By the grave, she saw a terrifying shape in the gloom. She held up the torch out of instinct and it shrank away.

'I don't think it likes fire,' she says, exhaling with relief. 'It disappeared as soon as I waved the torch. I built a fire over the grave.'

'Why?' I ask.

'To protect him.'

I tell her that I saw something, too, when I first arrived. 'It was tall and thin, wearing a black cloak,' I say, feeling nauseous at the memory of it.

'What do you think it is?' she asks. 'A ghost?'

I hesitate – was that really what it was in the woods? I'm not sure. Ghosts are small things, echoes of people, and they live inside bodies. I know that.

The thing in the woods is something else.

5

It's November, or mushroom season as Morven calls it. She says it's a season all on its own, on the cusp of autumn and winter. The forest is alive with mushrooms. All sorts of them, everywhere, like an invasion. Fallen tree branches reticulated by tiny orange lanterns. Puffballs swelling amidst the leaf litter like strange new planets. The fairy ring around Lichen Hall has persisted – that first slim row of mushrooms has thickened into bold brown clusters, like an imminent reckoning. Morven swears that the ring means good luck, but I still find it strange – a fairy ring large enough to encircle the hall, a kind of garland, or perhaps a noose . . . At night, when the windows are honeyed by tungsten light against a navy sky, Lichen Hall reminds me of a votive, sitting within the hoop of mushrooms.

A bell rings through the house, a distinctive *ding dong* that I've never heard before. It must be the doorbell. I lean over Sylvan, who is lying in his cot sucking his fists and making little noises. He has grown quite a head of soft dark curls, and his eyes seem to be turning brown. Every time he sees me his face lights up and he gives me the biggest, toothless smile. My heart tugs as I lift him and spot the delight on his face.

'Come on,' I tell him, looking away. 'Your parents are here. Time to go.'

I've already packed his bag, though Morven says it's a waste of time. 'The parents don't want his old things,' she says. 'They want to forget he was ever here.' But I'll feel better, knowing he leaves with everything in order. He only has two outfits, but I packed the one he's not wearing, along with some clean terry nappies and his favourite teddy, the little frog in a waistcoat that I knitted for him.

At the bottom of the stairs, Mrs Whitlock is waiting for me. She's wearing a smart navy skirt and white blouse, her short hair combed back, a slick of coral lipstick, diamond earrings.

'Mabel, dear,' she says graciously, smiling at Sylvan. 'Come meet our guests.'

My skin crawls. I follow her into the drawing room, where a man and a woman are standing. The man is a lot older than I imagined he'd be, white haired with a bald patch, a tight brown suit. The woman has dry yellow hair to her chin, garish make-up, a salmon pink dress. There are at least thirty years between them.

'Mabel, this is Mr and Mrs Askew,' Mrs Whitlock says, and I give them a wary nod.

'Hello.'

The husband is puffing on a cigar. Pungent smoke swirls around the room, making Sylvan sneeze.

'Oh, what an adorable sound,' Mrs Askew says. She sweeps forward and plucks him straight out of my arms, stepping back into the cloud of cigar smoke. 'Isn't he adorable, Ted?'

English accents. I file this away, in case it might be useful in future. Whatever Mr Askew says is drowned out by Sylvan, who bursts into tears at being taken from me so abruptly. I want to reach out to him, but I clasp my hands together tightly and watch as Mrs Askew bounces Sylvan up and down, as though she might bounce the crying out of him.

'Give the lad to me,' Mr Askew says. He takes him, and Sylvan stops crying. He has spotted the cigar in the man's mouth, stubby as a pine cone, and reaches for it. Mr Askew lifts a hand to stop him, but somehow the cigar gets knocked from his mouth and tumbles to the floor, scorching the white carpet.

'Morven?' Mrs Whitlock shouts. 'Can you come in here at once, please?'

Morven rushes into the room. 'Yes, ma'am?' she says.

Mrs Whitlock points at the mark on the carpet. 'Clean that up.'

Morven darts out of the room to retrieve a bucket and cloth. When she returns, she flicks her eyes at me, just for a second, but I can read everything she wants to say.

'Who's a lovely boy?' Mrs Askew asks Sylvan as she takes him back and continues to bounce him up and down. She ignores Morven, who is scrubbing the carpet beneath her.

'You must have a long journey ahead,' Mrs Whitlock says, hinting at them to leave. 'London, isn't it?'

'We're staying at a friend's house in Edinburgh for a few weeks,' Mr Askew replies. Astonishingly, he lights a new cigar, without a word of apology for the damage inflicted on the carpet. 'Never been to Scotland,' he says. 'It's a whole other country, isn't it?'

'Is it?' Mrs Whitlock says. 'I thought we were part of the same kingdom. United in both geography and sovereign.'

'If you say so,' he says with a hoarse laugh. He studies Sylvan in his wife's arms. 'I can tell this boy's into cigars, just like his old man.'

Sylvan starts crying again, his face turning to me, pleading. The thought of the Askews raising him makes me want to be sick. I try to count the tassels on the nearest cushion to distract myself.

'Shall we go, then?' Mrs Askew asks her husband. She notices the bag at my feet and picks it up. She doesn't say thank you, or look at me, but simply marches out of the room with Sylvan in her arms.

My heart drops. It all happens so quickly – Sylvan looks at me from Mrs Askew's shoulder, his eyes filled with trust. And yet I've just let these people claim him as theirs, forever.

The front door closes in my face.

I race back to the window of the drawing room, watching for him. All the ghosts inside me are screaming, a chorus of longing.

Sylvan, Sylvan!

The car engine starts. I bang my fists on the glass. Behind me Morven is calling my name, but it's as though I'm underwater, fighting to reach the surface.

I watch, helpless, as they drive away.

My legs go slack, the air around me thinning. I can't believe he is gone. I can't believe I'll never see him again.

Morven helps me to the armchair, where I press my face into my hands and weep.

'Idiots,' Mrs Whitlock says under her breath, referring to the Askews. If she sees me weeping, she doesn't let on. 'Morven, move the rug so it covers that spot, will you?'

'Yes, ma'am.'

'And open a window. Bloody cigar smokers.'

'I will, ma'am.'

It feels as if my heart is shattered. As if I'll never be the same again.

Now

Pearl

Lichen Hall, Scottish Borders, September 1965

1

I run back to the hall, where I find Aretta at the top of a ladder propped against the side of the house, cleaning the gutters with a broom.

'I just saw him!' I shout up to her. 'The boy from the stairwell!'

She stares down at me, confused. 'Who?'

'Sylvan! The little boy. Does he live here?'

She climbs down the ladder and wipes her brow. 'What are you talking about?'

'That little boy I spotted on the stairs on my first night here,' I tell her, pointing in the direction of the woods where we met. 'I saw him again. Do you know him?'

She turns and looks over the woods. 'Are you sure it wasn't Wulfric?'

I laugh. As if I don't know what Wulfric looks like.

'There is no other boy here,' she says. 'I really don't know who you mean . . .'

'*And* his mother,' I say firmly, refusing to be dismissed. 'She's called Mabel. You've really no idea about her? I saw her coming into the house. She went into the Wisteria room. She was with Mrs Whitlock.'

Aretta climbs back up the ladder, shaking her head. 'Sorry, I've got work to do.'

I'm gobsmacked. She is patently lying. We've played blackjack and bloody gin rummy in her bedroom, shared laughs together, and I made her and Rahmi a meal. Why is she lying about this?

I go inside the house, determined to find Rahmi. Surely she'll tell me who Sylvan and Mabel are.

I find her in the laundry room, folding sheets.

'Who is Sylvan?' I say, cutting straight to the chase. 'And Mabel, his mother?'

She stops what she's doing and looks me directly in the eye. 'Who?'

I clap my hands to my face, wanting to scream. 'Are you kidding me? I *saw* him. He spoke to me in the woods. And his mother, Mabel – I've *seen* them both here before. In the hall.'

She gives me an innocent smile and shrugs. 'We're playing Cluedo tonight,' she says, changing the subject. 'I found it in the store cupboard. Fancy joining us?'

I give her a long, hurt look. Why lie about this? I don't even want to ask her about the woman in the woods. I don't make a habit of storming off, but this warrants it.

I thought we were friends, but clearly I was wrong.

Later, as the sun is setting, I hear a car pull up outside. I open my window and peer down, spotting a silver Rolls-Royce. I've never seen this car in all the time I've been here. I head downstairs quickly, mentally betting my life savings that this is another one of Mrs Whitlock's 'business' meetings.

I secrete myself in my usual spot at the top of the stairs, hidden by the corner of the wall. A man and a woman go into the Wisteria room, greeted by Mrs Whitlock.

And then, from the lip of the wall, I spot Sylvan skipping along the hall, heading inside the Wisteria room, followed by his mother, Mabel.

I am utterly bewildered. Who are they? What do they have to do with the people who came in the Rolls-Royce?

Why is no one prepared to admit that they exist?

2

I make a point of avoiding Rahmi and Aretta for the next two days. I stay in the library, or in my bedroom, coming out only to tutor Wulfric. It's ridiculous, lying to my face like that. They must take me for a fool, or they don't trust me enough to tell me who Sylvan and Mabel are. Either way, I find it hugely disappointing.

When I next teach Wulfric, I can't help but ask him about it.

I've brought Professor Llewellyn's book about fungi for him to look at, hoping that this will trigger some more warm memories of foraging with his father. I've selected passages to discuss in terms of meaning, tone, theme, and grammar.

'I met a boy last week,' I tell him. 'In the woods. He said his name was Sylvan. Do you know him?'

He flicks his eyes at me, wary. 'Uh . . .'

'And Mabel, his mother. Do you know her as well?'

'I'm not supposed to say.'

'Ah.' Well, at least I'm getting somewhere. This would seem to be an acknowledgement that they exist. And he's *not supposed to say*, which is telling, too. Why, though? What's the big mystery?

He falls silent, refusing to speak even when I ask him direct questions related to the schoolwork.

'Let's do a test,' I say, trying to think of ways to keep him engaged. I tear out a sheet of paper and write a sentence with gaps for him to fill in with the correct noun or verb. I give him ten minutes to do it alone, rising from my chair to give him space.

I stand by the window, staring outside in case I see the mysterious Sylvan and Mabel. After a few moments, I hear a splatting sound. Wulfric is ripping strips from the notepaper, chewing them up in his mouth, then using his ruler to thwack them against the wall.

'Please pay attention, Wulfric,' I say with a sigh.

A splat of wet paper hits the chimney breast. 'Don't want to.'

'Don't you want to be good at writing?'

He shrugs and rips another piece of paper, balling it up and shoving it in his mouth in front of me before spitting it into his palm in a soggy, salivated mess. Good grief. My stomach turns.

Splat.

I force myself to remain calm, thinking of his outburst the other week.

'Won't your grandmother punish you for ruining her wall-paper?'

He ignores me, ripping every single page from the notebook, chewing, spitting, aiming, until I resort simply to reading aloud the chosen passages from Professor Llewellyn's book to a soundtrack of splatting.

At least, I tell myself, *he isn't shrieking and throwing chairs.*

When the hour is up, Mrs Whitlock pokes her head around the door.

'Well, Wolfie?' she says with a smile. 'What did we learn today?'

'Nothing,' he says sullenly. I take a small amount of pleasure in watching Mrs Whitlock's face fall as she clocks the state of the room. Lumps of paper bombs have dried on to the navy wallpaper, and when she attempts to remove one it peels off some of the pattern with it. She abandons the task, and once more her mask clicks back into place, all irritation filed away.

'Time for some fresh air, I think,' she says, urging him out of the room. I follow, spotting Mr Whitlock in his wheelchair outside the room. He's covered in a blanket, his mouth open as he contemplates the space around him as though for the first time. I must catch his eye, because he glances up at me, a faraway look in his eyes.

'Is this the train to Perth?' he says.

I don't know what to say. It seems unkind to say that it isn't.

'Not yet,' I tell him.

He reaches inside his blanket for an imaginary wallet. 'Can I buy a return, please?'

'Now, shall we head outside for some fresh air?' Mrs Whitlock says, walking past me and removing the brake from the wheelchair.

'I wondered if I could ask a question,' I say quickly. 'I came across a little boy the other day,' I say. 'His name is Sylvan.'

She stares at me in silence, waiting for the question.

'Well, no one seems to know who he is.'

'Good,' she says, and walks off.

3

It's three in the morning, and the moon in the night sky is as full and round as my belly. I can't sleep tonight, and it's not because of the baby. I don't know who I can trust. I don't know what to think about the Sylvan thing, about the fact that Aretta, Rahmi, Wulfric, and Mrs Whitlock have all denied that they've seen him and his mother.

I asked them point blank, and they lied to my face.

Well, that's not strictly true. Wulfric said he wasn't supposed to say anything, and Mrs Whitlock avoided the question.

I try to take my mind off it all and will myself to sleep, but it doesn't work, so at around four I creep downstairs to the kitchen.

The cupboards, as usual, are sparse, but I find a bread roll and slather it with butter, devouring it by the sink. It is the single most delicious thing I've ever eaten.

As I clean up the trail of crumbs I've left, I find what looks like half a cherry sitting at the back of the work surface, along with a couple of leaves. Up close, I recognize it as one of the black fruits from the strange weed in the herb garden. The leaves are familiar, too.

How strange that someone has picked it and brought it into the kitchen. It isn't any herb that I know of, nor any fruit, and the smell is like unripe tomatoes.

Quickly I remember a lesson I had at nursing college with

an ophthalmologist, Dr Zafirakou, who mentioned a plant you might find in the garden that they used regularly on patients before eye surgery.

I'm sure it was this one. Witch's Berry, it was called, on account of helping witches to fly, apparently. Known nowadays as banewort. I can't remember the Latin name . . . And I recall we were always told to wash our hands thoroughly after handling it – Dr Zafirakou said the Scottish army in *Macbeth* used banewort to defeat the Danes by contaminating their food with it. So it is poisonous to ingest. But if this is true, why was it casually strewn on the kitchen workbench?

I think of the banewort growing in the herb garden. Maybe Mrs Whitlock doesn't realize it. It's dangerous to have such things around when people are preparing food.

But Mrs Whitlock must already know it's dangerous. That plant has been nurtured, like a mother raising a cherished child. What is she using it for?

Is she performing abortions?

The sound of footsteps along the hall makes me start. Quick, short steps, not the brisk, hard-heeled clip that usually heralds Mrs Whitlock. I listen for a moment longer, picking up murmuring, a note of distress in the voice, before heading out into the hallway.

At first, I don't recognize the woman at the foot of the stairs, dressed in an old black dressing gown and mismatching slippers. She's clutching the newel post to hold herself upright. She has dishevelled hair, as though she's just woken up, but she seems wide awake. I notice she's talking, but I can't see who she's addressing.

'Mrs Whitlock?' I call. She turns to me, wide-eyed, mid-sentence, and reaches a trembling hand out towards me. Something is wrong.

'Are you all right?' I say, approaching her. Her face is pale and drawn, and she takes my hand in a firm grasp.

'It's happened again,' she says. 'It's happened, I know it has.'

'What's happened?' I say, looking her over quickly. She looks and sounds extremely distressed. She must be sleepwalking. I glance around to see if Aretta or Rahmi might appear to help her back to bed.

'. . . I don't know how long this time,' she's saying, 'but I'm awake now, I'm back.'

'That's good,' I say. 'Shall we go back upstairs?'

'No, no,' she says, gripping me suddenly by the top of my arms. 'Pearl, isn't it?'

I nod. 'Yes. Mrs Whitlock . . . you're hurting me.'

She holds on, her eyes burning into mine. 'I need you to help me, Pearl. I don't have much time. You *need* to help me!'

I'm alarmed. *Is* she sleepwalking? I'm no longer sure.

'Mrs Whitlock. Please tell me what's wrong!'

'The phones are dead,' she says, heading towards the telephone and lifting the receiver, as though to show me. 'I've tried to call for help, but she's cut the lines again.'

'*Who* has cut the lines?'

She looks up at me. 'Maybe you can go.'

'Go where?'

'For help,' she says. Then, as though remembering. 'Did you get my note?'

I study her. Does she mean the note I spotted against the window, the one that said 'help me'? The one I suspected she'd written?

She steps close to me and takes my hands. 'We haven't got much time, so listen carefully.'

I nod, my heart pounding.

'I need you to take Joseph's car,' she says in a trembling voice. 'The key's in his bedroom, and there's only a little fuel left. You must take it and get help.'

I nod again, my mind spinning. 'Mrs Whitlock,' I say. 'Are you in danger?'

She leans closer, her eyes wide with terror. 'We all are,' she whispers.

Suddenly there's a wetness on my legs and around my bare feet. I look down and find we're both standing in a puddle.

My first thought is that Mrs Whitlock has urinated, and I look up, astounded.

But the terror on her face has faded, and she holds me in her usual cold stare, before lowering her eyes to my stomach. It's as though a switch has flicked, all the distress from before melted away.

'Your waters have broken, my dear,' she says crisply, stepping back from the puddle. Then, lifting her chin. 'Aretta? Aretta!'

This time, I feel the gush of water that comes, and there's a pulling downward from my groin. I'm too astonished to speak. In a few moments, Aretta is beside me, and Mrs Whitlock is frowning, visibly disgusted that her feet are wet.

'Take care of that, will you?' she tells Aretta, before walking off.

I glance after Mrs Whitlock, completely thrown by this sudden change. Just a moment again she was terrified, her whole stature seized with fear. She spoke in frantic whispers. Now, she's straight-backed and clear-voiced again, and there was something entirely different about her face – it's as though she's two different people.

But then, it doesn't matter, because the first contraction hits, and I'm bent double and moaning in pain.

'This is it, then,' Aretta says. 'Let's get you to the birthing suite, shall we?'

4

I had expected labour to progress slowly, as I've seen with so many mothers. It's common for waters to break long before a baby arrives, but it's clear that this baby wants to come, and fast. I try to take comfort in the fact that I've been able to give Aretta some training. But this all feels very real, and the distance between training for the real thing and experiencing it is suddenly daunting.

With my arm around her shoulders, Aretta helps me downstairs to the so-called Birthing Suite, which is nothing more than an old wine cellar that hasn't seen a mop since the Dark Ages. I'm appalled by the state of the place, but then a contraction hits and I'm too shocked by the intensity of the pain to think about much else. Aretta helps me to sit down on the bed while she rushes to the sink for water. I reach down and touch my bump. The baby isn't moving.

'I'll check the baby's heartbeat,' Aretta says, returning with a bucket of water.

God, there are no facilities. Not so much as a stethoscope. I see her start to panic.

'Put your head to my stomach.'

She does as I say. I'm leaning back on my elbows, watching the stillness of my belly with a sudden horror. My mouth is dry. This can't happen.

'Can you hear it?' I pant.

'I . . . I think so?'

'Is it steady? Click your fingers to the rhythm.'

She clicks. *One, two, three, four, five* . . . It seems steady, not too fast, but I have no idea if she's hearing the baby's heartbeat or mine. I go to ask her to check if she can see the head, but just then a contraction bites down, hard, and I give a loud, guttural yell.

I look up to see Aretta backing away, a look of fear on her face.

'Where are you going?' I say. 'No, don't go! I need you, Aretta!'

'I promise I'll be back!' she says. 'I'll get help.' And then she runs out.

With a whimper, I scan the room, trying not to give in to panic. Sister Clarke warned us about the dangers of women being left to labour alone. Things can go very wrong very, very fast. At the hospital a mother of six died this way, as did her child.

My waters have fully broken now, and I can feel the urge to push. I need to get a towel underneath my legs. I need someone to guide the baby out.

I hear footsteps. *Thank God*, I think. *Aretta's back*. But as another big contraction hits I see a different woman approach. It's the girl I saw in the woods with Sylvan. The same ratty hair and dirty clothes. His mother.

'This is Mabel,' Aretta tells me, following. 'She's going to help you.'

Aretta takes my hand. In the doorway, a small face peeks around – Sylvan, the little boy. Aretta follows my gaze, then rises to take him by the hand and lead him away.

Mabel stands at the end of the bed and presses her hands across my belly. 'The baby's head is down,' she says. 'The baby's back is against your back. You must be in a lot of pain.'

I grit my teeth, feeling the urge to push sweep across me in a powerful rush, as though I'm a loaded cannon about to fire, the flame and gases building and building inside me. I widen my knees and bury my elbows into the mattress, readying myself for the next hard push, when Mabel puts an arm on my shoulder.

'Don't push,' she says. 'I know you want to. But you'll tear if you do. I want you to breathe slowly through this one.'

She's right – this is exactly what Sister Clarke taught us, and I marvel for a moment at how fiercely my body wants to ignore everything I've been trained to do. As the contraction climbs I fight the urge to gear up for a ferocious last *push*. Everything in me wants to shove this baby out, but I listen to Mabel as she reminds me to breathe, breathe, breathe, and she's down behind me, her hands beneath me.

'You're doing really well,' she says calmly. 'I have the baby's head in my hands.'

This astonishes me so much that I try to crane my head downward to see, but she tells me to stay upright.

'Is it breathing?' I say, though I know she has no way of knowing just yet. I feel tears prick my eyes. What if the baby is dead? What if I've killed it?

'On this contraction, you're going to push a little bit. OK? Not a shove. And not until I tell you.'

The contraction is rising, rising, a tidal wave of fire. I'm clawing at the bed with my hands, and although I want so badly to push *hard*, I wring the bedclothes and yell until I hear her say, 'Now!' and then I push only half as much as I want to, and suddenly there's a cry, a little kittenish wail, and I burst into tears. The baby is all right. It's alive.

The room falls silent, and I look down to see Mabel holding a tiny baby in her hands, covered in my blood.

'You have a little girl,' Mabel says with a smile. 'Congratulations.'

Then

Mabel

Lichen Hall, Scottish Borders, December 1959

1

Fifteen days since Sylvan left.

I can't get out of bed, can't function.

Every minute without him feels as though I'm underwater, unable to surface.

In my mind, I have replayed every single moment of the Askews' visit, again and again. The pungent cigar smoke, hanging like a thundercloud in the middle of the room. The way Mrs Askew held Sylvan as if he was a rag doll instead of my precious boy. Will they take care of him? Will they love him? Will he forget me?

'You can't torture yourself like this,' Morven says. She comes into my bedroom, a tray of food in her hands. I haven't been eating, and she knows it. Two new girls arrived the day after Sylvan left, and she's been busy looking after them. And Aretta has her new baby, too. I haven't washed or spoken since Sylvan left. But I'm so deep in my grief that the sight of Morven barely stirs me.

'This will pass,' she says, sitting next to me on the bed. 'I promise, it will get better.'

I turn my head and stare out of the window. I don't want her to make me feel better. I want to suffer. Why should I feel happy when I know my son is somewhere with those awful people?

Morven sits with me in silence for a long time. After a while I realize I don't want her to leave me alone.

'How can it ever get better?' I ask her quietly.

'You find a way to live your life around the sadness.'

I stare at her, contemplating the meaning of her words. Sylvan's absence feels like a huge rock in the centre of my life, tied to me, present in every thought, every action. When I eat, the rock is there in the room with me. When I sleep, it's in the bed. When I speak, it's in every syllable. It doesn't feel like I'll ever get used to it.

'Did you feel like this when your baby went?' I ask Morven.

She takes my hand. It makes me feel a little better. 'Yes,' she says. 'I didn't admit it to anyone at the time, not even myself. But it felt like my heart had been ripped out.' She smiles sadly. 'And then, I forced myself to think of how good a life he was living without me. Growing up with parents, in a nice house. Holidays, a nice school. I could never give him that. It really does make it better.'

I nod, taking her words in, making myself imagine Sylvan with his new parents. I wish I'd never met the Askews. It would have been easier to imagine him growing up in a wonderful family. Now, I can only think of that horrible cigar smoke, and the way Mrs Askew snatched him out of my arms.

'Do you want to hear some good news?' Morven says lightly.

She waits, but I don't answer. I don't really care about anything anymore.

'I asked Mrs Whitlock if you could stay on,' she says, taking my other hand in hers. Her face is bright, her eyes shining. 'I said you'd be a good worker. I said you'd cook and clean, and in the evenings I'd train you to deliver babies.'

'What did she say?' I ask.

Morven pauses, and I know she's deliberately holding back from telling me. She's teasing me.

'Tell me,' I say again. 'What did she say?'

Morven pulls her hands from mine, folding her arms and tossing me a coquettish smile. 'Oh, I wasn't sure you'd care.'

'I do care.'

She lifts her eyes to mine, and her smile widens. 'She said that, as long as you work hard and help me deliver babies, you can stay.'

'She really said that?'

She nods, excitedly, and for the first time in days I feel there's a future ahead of me. A future I care about. Very gently, Morven lifts my hand to her lips, pressing a kiss there. It feels as though lightning has hit my skin, zipping up my arm and into my chest. She keeps her lovely eyes fixed on mine.

'You mean the world to me, Mabel,' she says.

The room seems to shift. From the dark earth of my grief, it seems something else is growing. And I realize that, for the first time in a long while, the ghosts are completely silent.

In fact, I think they've gone.

I'm free.

2

That evening, I sit in bed watching the rain funnel down from the broken gutters across my windows, turning the world outside into a watercolour. I have never, ever met anyone like Morven. She's like a bright star in the very midst of darkest night.

I'm at once grief-stricken and falling in love, and the smashing together of such huge emotions makes me feel as though I'm on a ship on high seas.

And I'm still processing what Morven has told me about asking Mrs Whitlock to let me stay here. I'm too nervous to approach her myself, in case she decides not to let me stay after all. But what if it's true? Do I really want to stay at Lichen Hall indefinitely?

I sit on the windowsill, holding my knees to my chest as I look out over the woods. I had tried to convince myself that the figure I saw in the woods that night was a figment of my imagination. But Rahmi said she saw something too. She says that fire drives it away.

But it doesn't even matter what's in the woods. I don't want to go back to Dundee. And I don't want to leave Morven.

Downstairs, I hear the doorbell. A wave of nausea washes across me as I remember the last time I heard it – the day Sylvan was adopted. I hear faint voices, then footsteps pounding up the stairs. A few moments later, there's a heavy knock on my bedroom door. I open it to find Morven, fit to burst with excitement or fear, I can't tell which.

'You need to come with me, *quick*!' she says, grabbing me by the hand.

'What is it?' I say, but she's already pulling me, and I stagger after her in my nightdress to the stairwell. Bickering voices drift up through the loops in the banisters.

'But there's something wrong with him! He's not normal!'

'I assure you, he is *perfectly* normal.'

'There are lights under his skin!'

I recognize the voice. It's Mrs Askew. She's talking about Sylvan.

My heart thuds, and I race past Morven down to the front door. I see the Askews in the doorway, pointing their fingers in Mrs Whitlock's face. She confronts them calmly, her voice low.

At her feet is a baby basket, soggy from the rain.

I rush to it and see Sylvan's face staring up, frightened by all the shouting. Then he sees me.

There's a moment where I think he doesn't know who I am. But suddenly his face folds and he bursts into loud, anguished sobs. I pick him up and dash back across the hall before anyone can stop me.

The Askews don't seem to notice. They're shouting angrily at Mrs Whitlock, demanding a refund.

'We heard about you!' Mrs Askew yells. 'You took your son's body from the morgue!'

'Is this what you do, then?' Mr Askew says, shouting over his wife. 'You pass off faulty babies to unwitting families?'

Whatever Mrs Whitlock says in reply, I don't hear. Sylvan's cry rises into a pitiful wail, as if to say, *Why did you let me go? Why did you let them take me?* His nappy is full to bursting and his eyes are sunken. He has a bruise on his forehead, and he feels lighter in weight.

'You'll be hearing from our lawyers!' Mr Askew snarls, and he and Mrs Askew turn and walk back to their car without so much as looking at Sylvan.

'Goodnight,' Mrs Whitlock says, waving. She closes the door and turns, her eyes falling on Sylvan in my arms.

'Aretta?' she calls. 'Fetch some warm milk. Mabel's baby will need feeding.'

3

All night, I watch Sylvan as he lies asleep in the bed beside me, his arms at either side of his head in surrender, his face an expression of peace. Usually he wakes two or three times during the night, but he doesn't tonight – he's worn out. I'm exhausted too, but I just want to stare at him.

The bruise on his forehead has turned yellow around the edges. What did they do to him? I'm ecstatic that he's home – but I'm terrified that he won't wake up. I tense at every noise, in case it's the Askews. What if they decide they made a mistake? What if they take him back?

I think of what I heard Mrs Askew shout about him having lights inside him.

She must have seen what I saw that time, when he was just a few days old. I'm glad she saw them. It means I didn't imagine it. And it means he's home.

In the morning, I head to the dining room, where Aretta is feeding her baby, chatting to Rahmi. I can tell Rahmi was out again last night. Her hair is tangled and she is dark-eyed. Morven rushes through, carrying a basket of bread rolls for breakfast. All the rolls are blackened. I've been baking the bread since I arrived, but I forgot this morning, now Sylvan's back.

I find Mrs Whitlock in the drawing room. I don't usually come looking for her, but today is different. I have to fight for this.

'Good morning,' she says, turning from the window. Her eyes

fall on Sylvan, but she doesn't mention him, or the Askews. 'Sleep well?'

I nod, though this is a lie. 'Very well, thank you.'

I look Mrs Whitlock over. She's starting to dress differently. Her pragmatic slacks, wellies, and slightly shabby turtlenecks have gradually been replaced by extravagant silk dresses in jewel-colours, ruby and sapphire, as though she's about to host a party. She wearing make-up these days, too, a glossy red shine to her lips and thick mascara on her eyelashes.

She walks towards me, her long dress sweeping across the floor. 'How is the baby?'

I can't disguise a grin at the mention of him. 'He's tired, I think. And he has a bruise. But otherwise he is very well.'

'Oh,' she says, surprised. 'You're glad he has been returned.'

I nod, guarded.

She raises her eyebrows. 'They said he was broken. Doesn't that concern you?'

'They didn't seem like good people. I wouldn't trust anything they say . . .' I tail off, surprised at myself for speaking so truthfully.

'Well, don't get too glad, my dear,' Mrs Whitlock says. 'I'm arranging for an alternative set of parents.'

My face falls and my knees weaken, as though I might collapse a second time.

'Are you all right?' Mrs Whitlock asks.

I go to say I'm fine, then shake my head. I'm so relieved by Sylvan's return that I can't pretend anymore. 'I don't want him to be adopted. I want to keep him.'

'But . . . the agreement was that you were to give up your child for adoption.'

'I've changed my mind.'

She rakes her eyes across me for an uncomfortable length of time. I suspect she's trying to test me. I grit my teeth and force myself to meet her eye. I mustn't falter.

'Do you take me for a fool, Miss Haggith?' she says.

I shake my head.

'Well, that does seem to be the case.'

My vision is blurring at the fringes.

'I have decided that I would like to keep him,' I say carefully. 'I think I made a mistake before. I . . . I know it isn't the done thing for an unmarried woman to raise a child . . .'

'It's obscene,' Mrs Whitlock snaps, folding her arms. 'You'd be an outcast.'

I read her mood carefully. The darkness in her eyes and voice that has become so usual is replaced by a rare reasonableness. I push a little harder.

'If you were to let me stay here and raise him, I'll work for you, as long and as hard as you like. I'll bake bread and cakes every single day. You could sell them in the village.'

She contemplates this, her eyes narrowed.

'Or keep them for yourself,' I say, stumbling over my words. 'I'll work as much as you want. I'll work *double*.'

I can sense she is calculating something. Her eyes travel to the window.

'You would have to live outside the hall,' she says. 'In one of the outbuildings. I can't have a toddler running around while I'm taking in expectant mothers. And Lord knows, they'll keep coming. In *droves*.'

I nod. 'Agreed.'

'And you will, as you say, work double. No skiving off just because you have a child. I have two extra mouths to feed, now, and that will require much work, on your part. And if I am not satisfied with both the quality and the quantity of your work, you will be required to leave immediately. Are we clear?'

I beam, unable to contain how happy she has made me. 'Very clear.'

4

We move out that afternoon, Sylvan and I. The shepherd's hut is near the part of the forest where I saw the figure in the woods that night, and I'm scared to go near it. I haven't ventured near these parts since that night.

But this is my only chance at staying at the hall, and with Sylvan and Morven. I have no choice, do I?

My heart sinks when I step inside. The hut had clearly been left to rot. The old tap has seized up, and rats run rampant in the gap beneath it. There are holes in the roof, and some of the wood is so rotten it crumbles in my hand like sawdust.

'That *bitch*,' Morven says when she sees it. 'What kind of festering boil on the backside of a plague rat calls *this* a fit place for an infant to live?'

'At least I get to stay,' I tell her. 'And Sylvan gets to stay with me.'

She touches the old rusted stove. 'We'll need to get this place fixed up quickly. You can't stay here until it's ready. I'll talk to her. We'll make sure it's OK before you move in.'

She takes a step towards me, reaching tentatively for my hand. Then she leans forward to kiss me.

'This can be our place,' she says.

I nod, and kiss her again. 'Our home,' I say.

Now

Pearl

Lichen Hall, Scottish Borders, October 1965

1

No one told me that motherhood would involve such a weird shift in how I experience time. Little One is only a couple of days old and yet it feels like a lifetime ago that I gave birth to her.

At mealtimes, Rahmi brings me food and hot tea, setting it down on the bedside table and removing the dirty plates. At first, I don't speak to her – childishly, I'm still pissed off about the lie she told me about Mabel. But after a few silent episodes, I say, 'I suppose you're still going to tell me that Mabel and Sylvan are figments of my imagination.'

She sits down on the edge of the bed and studies her hands.

'We were told not to say anything,' she says carefully. 'There were consequences if we did.'

Aretta appears in the doorway holding a set of scales. She steps inside. 'How are you feeling?' she says.

'Fine,' I say icily. Then I recall how distressed Aretta was, and I don't want her to think I'm poorly because of her. 'You did a great job, by the way. It's not an easy thing to do, delivering a baby.'

She looks down, shame writ large on her face. 'I panicked,' she says in a small voice. 'I was so worried you'd end up dying and it would be my fault.'

'Well, I didn't die, clearly. And neither did the little one. Why did you both pretend that Sylvan and Mabel don't exist?' I ask them, looking from Aretta to Rahmi.

There's a brief pause, and I catch them sharing a look. Aretta gently closes the door, presumably to avoid our whispers being overheard. 'Mabel came here to have her baby,' she says. 'Sylvan. The adoptive parents brought him back. She stayed here. We all did.'

'He's not just Mabel's son,' Rahmi says. 'He's all of ours. The four of us raised him together.'

I'm puzzled. 'The four of you?'

Rahmi looks down, and a shadow passes across Aretta's face. 'There was another girl here. Morven.'

'What happened?' I ask gently, noticing how upset she seems.

But she turns away, and when I look to Aretta for an answer, she closes up. Sylvan is an illegitimate child being raised by an unwed mother – it occurs to me that their refusal to divulge his existence was out of protection.

'I'd like to say thank you to Mabel,' I tell them. 'Am I able to see her?'

They share another glance. 'We can take you to her,' Rahmi says. 'When you're feeling well enough.'

They leave, and I lie Little One on the scales to weigh her. She doesn't like it. Her fingers splay out and her arms go wide, as though she's falling, but I keep my hands around her chest to let her know I've got her.

'There you go. Eight pounds and one ounce. That's impressive!'

I write it down to chart her progress. She's awake so much now, and she still doesn't really smile, but she seems to be taking me in, studying me as she wraps a chubby hand around my index finger. I can see her getting longer, that squashed newborn look fading into familiar features. I lower down and kiss her cheeks, which she loves, and I can tell this because she opens her mouth in an almost smile, as though to kiss me back.

I'm trying to be so careful with my feelings towards her. Sister Clarke told us about the hormones that flood a woman's body after she gives birth, making her 'soft'. 'Just part of evolution,' she sniped. 'The mother thinks she's falling in love with the child, when really she's just experiencing hormones, designed to stop her from strangling the little parasite. Without such hormones, mankind wouldn't last a single generation, I can assure you.'

Is that it? Are these vast, powerful feelings just my hormones in action? It feels cynical to believe so. Sometimes I imagine running away with her. Fleeing in the night, finding somewhere to live, raising her on my own . . . Surely that's a genuine feeling and not just evolution? But my daydreams are smashed when I remember how things *are* . . . Unmarried women do not raise children. I could never work as a nurse again, so I would have no way of supporting a child. And even if I *did* find work, I'd have to find someone to look after the baby. My parents have made it clear that they don't support anything other than adoption. And then there's the social stigma that illegitimate children face.

I remember when I was a child, Charlie and I were instructed to avoid a little girl at school. Rebecca. She was raised by her mother, an older woman with no husband, and my parents told me I wasn't to play with her. The other children had the same warning from their own parents. I can still see Rebecca in my mind, with that pained look of longing every time we played outside. Once, I handed her a flower I'd plucked from a field. It was a five-second exchange, an act of defiance against my parents. But the look of joy in her eyes has never left me.

I don't want that for Little One. I want the world for her.

I run the bath until it's three inches deep, touching the inside of my wrist against the water to check the temperature before lowering her in, my right hand cupping her tiny bottom, her head cradled in my left. She kicks her legs fervently, splashing her heels against the water as though she might swim.

I force myself to remember everything, branding it all on my memory, like a flame to stone.

2

Later that day, Wulfric comes to find me.

'Aren't we having our lesson today?' he says.

I stare at him blankly. In truth, I have no idea what day it is, nor what time. He's clutching his jotter and Professor Llewellyn's book. I notice he has combed his hair, too, and washed his face. He is wearing a clean white shirt and black trousers.

'I've just had a baby,' I say, confused.

'I know,' he says, with a grin. 'Congratulations.'

He doesn't get the hint, and I'm too foggy-headed to think of a way to let him down gently. His mood seems high; no sign of the surliness that preceded his paper-splatting episode last time we had a lesson. I glance back into my room. Little One has just had a long feed and is fast asleep.

'I suppose we could have a short lesson,' I say, and he beams. '*But* I have one condition.'

He nods. 'Anything.'

'No tantrums,' I say firmly. 'No messing about. Got it?'

Another nod. 'Got it.'

I throw on a cardigan and pick up Little One, wrapping her in a blanket before carrying her downstairs to the Willow room.

I have him draw diagrams of the fungi he's so keen on, the Cordyceps fungus. He draws an elaborate cartoon strip of an ant climbing a tree, a speech bubble filled with imperatives: *I must climb, I must climb for my species.*

'It's a zombie, you see,' he tells me. 'It's alive, but also dead, and it does whatever the fungus wants it to.'

I stifle a yawn. 'That's good.'

It's the first time since I've taught him that he achieves full marks.

3

The day after, Mrs Whitlock comes to see me and the baby. It's all very innocent, until she asks to perform a bonkers ritual.

'It's just something I like to do,' she says. 'Nothing religious.'

I feel relieved at this. My mother queried whether the baby would be baptized. I think I lost my faith when I was seven, in that horrible hospital. Fourteen children died while I was there, children I had befriended. It never sat right with me when the priest came and spoke of a 'loving' God. No loving God would allow so much suffering to befall innocent children.

Mrs Whitlock takes Little One from me and carries her to the window, and I see her whisper some words in the baby's ear, then open her palm and blow something over her. 'Just fairy dust,' she says when she sees me looking.

When she passes Little One back to me, she scatters a pinch of a powdery substance on her forehead. I blow it off as soon as her back is turned. Pagan or religious, I don't believe in rites.

When Little One falls asleep again, I head downstairs to telephone my parents. Outside, I see Wulfric pushing Mr Whitlock in his wheelchair. I wait until they're past the window – I don't want to risk Wulfric asking for another lesson, though admittedly it's a good sign that he's eager to learn.

Even so.

I reach the telephone and find that it's working – small mercies.

'Hello?'

My mother answers, and suddenly a sob creeps into my throat. It takes me a moment to find my voice. 'The baby's here,' I say. 'She's beautiful.'

Mum cries on the other end of the line; she must have been more worried than she'd let on. She asks for a brief description, and I tell her. I know she's trying to be careful. She'll never meet this child. Her first grandchild. She'll never know her name. She'll never know *her*.

'How are you feeling now?' Mum asks.

'Not too bad,' I lie. 'A little tender, but I think I'm healing well.'

'You *must* drink nettle tea,' she says. 'And eat plenty of porridge.'

'Yes, Mum,' I say. I well know the old wives' tales about nettle tea and porridge to help iron levels and milk supply.

'Also, beer.'

'Beer?'

'Yes. A couple of pints a day. It helps with your milk.'

'I'll stick to porridge.'

I can't help myself – I ask her about Sebastian. I've been hoping he would call again about our trip to the sea, but I've not heard anything from him.

'How is . . . Sebastian?' I ask gingerly.

'Oh, he's well, I should imagine,' she says. 'Not seen much of him at all. You're not still hoping you and he will . . . ?'

'Oh no,' I say, lying through my teeth. 'I just wondered if he was all right.'

'I'm sure Sebastian will *always* be fine,' she says. 'He has that knack, doesn't he? Always seems to come up trumps. But darling, you're really not still hankering after him? Because I thought . . . well, considering you were pregnant to someone else . . . ?'

I feel like someone has slapped me. How can my mother, having lived for forty-nine years on this planet, believe that just because I conceived a child with someone else, my feelings for

Sebastian have vanished? She knows I have loved him since I was eight years old. His presence in my life is a colossus, towering over every memory. It's difficult for me to think of existing in the world without Sebastian being part of that existence.

I swallow back a sob and change the subject, asking about *Top of the Pops*. She tells me about Sonny and Cher, but I'm not listening. I dig my nails into my palm, hating myself for asking about Sebastian in the first place. Love, I decide, is the most complicated, infuriating thing on the planet, and it's probably best not to bother with it ever again.

I hang up the phone and rush to the bathroom, a sudden urge to pee frightening the life out of me. I sit down on the toilet seat and pray that the pain of urinating doesn't make me scream. I really should have had stitches after the delivery. I have a vaginal tear – a third degree tear, I think – and am still yelping every time I sit down. I have packed a healthy supply of sanitary towels, but I'm almost out of them. Sister Clarke said the vagina often heals better without stitches, so perhaps I'll be all right, as long as I don't aggravate the wound. My supply of painkillers is long gone.

In hindsight, Lichen Hall was the last place I should have delivered a child. But I didn't want to cause any more worry, and I trusted my parents. I had, after all, fallen pregnant out of wedlock, and a small part of me feels I deserve to suffer for it.

Still, the strange encounter I had with Mrs Whitlock just before my waters broke won't leave me.

I replay my memories, slowing it down, trying to make sense of it all. Mrs Whitlock seemed genuinely frightened. What did she mean when she said she hadn't much time? She looked like someone being hunted; a scared, paranoid waif. In other words, not a version of Mrs Whitlock I have encountered before or since. I'd have assumed she was sleepwalking, but she was crystal clear in her instructions about Mr Whitlock's car, and where the key is located.

And she clutched my hand and asked if I'd received her note.

Every time I think of this, and the way she whispered it so urgently, I shiver. I still have the folded piece of paper with 'help me' written on it in my drawer. I *knew* it was her handwriting.

And then there was that odd shift, right as my waters broke, as though she'd switched back to her old self.

But how can anyone change so quickly, from one extreme to the other? Is it perhaps a condition that has gone undiagnosed? Might that explain Mrs Whitlock's ridiculous aversion to doctors?

Aretta tells me I'm reading too much into it. 'She *must* have been sleepwalking,' she says. 'That's the only explanation.'

I wish I could settle for that. I wish it would make the knot in my stomach go away. But it doesn't.

4

I'm mesmerized by Little One, this perfect little girl. She's two weeks old today. When I lift her, her bunched fists draw up beneath her chin and her legs fold into her belly, just as she must have curled up in my womb. Her skin is soft as velvet, and her hair is blonde, like mine.

It's sunny and warm, and Sister Clarke instructed me to ensure babies get fresh air from the day they're born. I wrap Little One in a blanket and carry her gingerly downstairs towards the side door.

Outside, old Mr Whitlock is sitting in his wheelchair, his head lifted to the sky. I see Wulfric on the grassy bank near the trees, hurling sticks into the forest. He sees me and gives a wave, then continues throwing his sticks. It's a non-lesson day; tomorrow, I'm teaching him literature.

'Good afternoon, Mr Whitlock,' I say. 'Enjoying the sunshine?'

He squints up at me, his hand waving as though he wants to tell me something.

'What is it?' I bend down to hear him.

'My eye,' he says. 'There's something wrong with it. Could you take a look?'

'Oh, bless you,' I say.

The eye again. I can't help but check to make sure, but I'm sure there's nothing the matter with his eye. Poor man. Perhaps he's recalling a time from his childhood when he realized he needed glasses. Or an accident during child's play. 'Let me have a look,' I say, humouring him by making a show of inspecting both eyes.

'Not that one,' he says when I check out his right eye. 'The other one.'

'Oh, right.' I lean close to him to inspect it yet again, and he uses a trembling hand to prise it open, revealing the bloodshot white of his eyeball in the bright light. It does look a little bulbous, now I see it in daylight. Cataracts, perhaps.

'I think you ought to see an optician,' I tell him.

He shakes his head and keeps pointing at it, mumbling something about pressure.

'An optician,' I say, louder. 'I'll mention it to Mrs Whitlock.'

I take Little One through the gardens, intent on gathering some nettles for nettle tea. I introduce her to the leaves, the flowers, the ocean in the distance.

It's so strange how, up until she was born, I was counting the days, the *hours*, until she was born, wishing I wasn't pregnant anymore, urging Time to hasten its pace. Now, I want to keep each moment like a petal trapped in the pages of a book. I'm chasing time now, begging it to slow down. We only have a few weeks together before she goes away with her parents.

I try to explain my feelings to her, and how sorry I am. I know she doesn't understand a word I say, but maybe the words are sewing themselves into the fabric of her memory, creating an image she'll understand when she's older. Memory is a funny thing. Despite all the scientific progress of recent years, we still know so little about it. I like to think we remember everything. Every moment.

'Your grandmother is called Ena,' I tell her as she lies on my lap, her eyes taking in the clouds passing above. 'She's an artist. She likes to paint abstract works, like Picasso. And your grandfather is called Sid. He's very smart, but doesn't like feelings of any kind.'

I hesitate before telling her about Bobby. Silly, I know, given that he's her father. But I don't know much about him, which is awful, given that we produced a child together.

'Your father is called Robert Sheridan,' I tell her. 'He goes by Bobby. He's twenty-three years old, and I think he was born in Livingston. He builds houses. Some would say that's a pretty impressive occupation. Houses are important, aren't they? You'll learn all about that some day, when you get to buy one of your own.'

I say no more because that's all I know about him. Maybe it doesn't matter. It's not like he'll ever meet her. He doesn't even know she exists.

I feed her while sitting on a tree stump. I'm still getting the hang of this breastfeeding thing, and it's a damn sight more awkward than I thought. About an inch from my foot there's a single white-capped mushroom, about the size of my thumb, sitting amidst the grass. It's so lovely and delicate and I'm glad I didn't trample on it. As I shuffle my foot away from it, I spot another mushroom by my other foot, then a row of them. I glance behind me, and am astonished to find that we're sitting in a perfect circle of mushrooms. A fairy ring! I've not spotted one of these for years. And how bizarre that I didn't notice it when I sat down.

I point out the mushrooms to Little One, trying to recall some of the information I've picked up in Professor Llewellyn's book.

'People used to think that fairy rings were caused by fairies dancing, or by dragons. My grandma – your great-grandma – said they marked where the Devil churns his milk. Isn't that bizarre? Scientists say that mushrooms or toadstools are just the fruiting body of a bigger underground network of fungus, and the ring appears when the fungus finds something it can decompose. Not as good a story as dragons, I'll give you that.'

Little One is asleep, her head lolling against my shoulder. As we head back to the hall, I notice that the gate to the herb garden is slightly open, and I think of the black fruit I spotted in the kitchen. Banewort.

I check that no one else is around before pushing open the gate and going inside.

I make my way past the raised beds and the strange terrariums containing mushrooms to the banewort on the back wall, spotting the purple, trumpet-shaped flowers and clusters of black berries. I lower myself to smell them, keeping Little One safely turned away. Just like unripe tomatoes. So it *was* the fruit from this plant.

My guess is Mrs Whitlock is using it for abortions. That will explain why I've seen so many people coming and going, people who appear to be clients rather than friends. Friends have a different way of making an entrance than the people I've spotted coming to Lichen Hall. No, I've not spotted any visibly pregnant girls, but that doesn't mean their parents aren't coming here to purchase a tonic for them.

Many of the women I treated after they'd visited an abortionist already had mouths to feed at home. The industry thrives on the back streets, populated by unskilled crooks whose methods are as pricey as they are barbarous. Girls will often pay two months' wages to drink a 'potion' that is nothing more than household bleach, or they'll be drugged while the abortionist inserts a coat hanger – usually unsterilized – into their uterus.

It's terrifying to think of, but that's the reality. Sister Clarke told us we were to report any women who'd attempted abortion to the police, but we never did. 'If you don't report them, the abortionists win!' she said.

I never suspected her issue was a moral one, rather a frustration at having countless women bleed to death on our watch. Girls as young as twelve. It was distressing for the nurses, too, but what could we do?

Banewort involves less violence than a knitting needle, but it takes skill. It can easily cause death, if the dosage isn't right . . .

I cradle Little One, feeling a prick of guilt at how I'd seriously considered inducing miscarriage. I stood at the top of the stairs in the hospital, staring at the bottom, preparing to hurl myself down. I suspected that I'd end up breaking a leg and not miscarrying at all. And then Lucy whispered a solution to me, when I'd told her I was pregnant. A bottle of vodka and a scorching hot bath. It had worked for her cousin Helen. I tried the hot bath a few times, but only managed half the vodka. Needless to say, it didn't work.

I've often wondered what reason lies behind Mrs Whitlock helping pregnant girls like me. Many people in her position do it as a means of buying their way into heaven – saving the souls of wretched wenches by helping them out for a bit and thereby currying favour with St Peter, or something. Mrs Whitlock doesn't strike me as that kind of person. No. She's shrewd, and downright nasty, it seems. My bet is she's doing it for the money. A place like this doubtless costs a fortune to maintain, and she's already left the east wing to ruin.

'You'll get in trouble if she finds you here.'

I give a gasp and turn around to see Aretta behind the gate.

'We're all forbidden to come in here,' she says with a wry smile.

I nod at the banewort on the wall. 'I found this in the kitchen,' I say. 'It's toxic.'

She looks it over, and her eyes tell me she's not paid it any heed until now.

'You ever see abortions carried out here?' I ask.

Aretta raises her eyebrows. 'I haven't. Though it wouldn't surprise me. She grows all sorts.'

My mind turns to Mr Whitlock. I suppose I jumped to conclusions about Mrs Whitlock rather quickly, given how cold she's turned towards me. But Mr Whitlock is the one who collects poisonous things, like the Death Cap Wulfric showed me. Mr Whitlock may have dementia, but perhaps he's still well enough to make potions.

Or maybe he's getting someone else to do it for him.

'Do you think you could take me to see Mabel?' I ask Aretta. 'I'd like to thank her in person for helping with the birth.'

Aretta smiles. 'Of course.'

We head through the woods, bright sunlight wheeling through the canopy and landing on the forest floor in honeyed rays. I feel elated at being able to walk without waddling, my rather large bump having diminished to a pot belly that wobbles over my waistband, as theatrically as it expanded. I wonder where we are going, since Aretta is taking me to see Mabel, and then I spot the old shepherd's hut in the field, the chalk pictures on the side. Is that where we're going? Surely she and Sylvan don't live *there*?

Aretta climbs over the barbed-wire fencing, holding out her hands to steady me as I manoeuvre with Little One, and then we are wading through the tall grass towards the hut. Aretta opens the door, and there they are: Sylvan and Mabel, inside what is evidently their home.

'Hello again,' Mabel says shyly.

'Hello,' I say.

I look over the hut in a mixture of awe and astonishment. It's small and cramped, but they've managed to fit a lot in – there's a small kitchenette in the far-right corner, and a table, on which I spot paper and crayons. In the left corner is a log burner, and a settee that doubles up as a bed. Tote bags filled with toys and clothing hang from hooks on the wall, and I spot other storage items under the bed. Frameless pencil sketches of Mabel and Sylvan are pinned to the walls.

Mabel rises to come see Little One, who is starting to stir.

'Oh, she's so sweet,' Mabel says. 'Have you named her?'

I shake my head, though I'm glad she asked. I almost want someone to acknowledge the strange situation I find myself in, being a mother and not a mother, a stopgap for the adoptive parents. Aretta and Rahmi must know how I feel; they came here to give birth, too.

'Is it Sienna, Mummy?' Sylvan says from the sofa. I had thought he was sleeping, but now I see he's poorly. His voice is hoarse, and his face is pale and clammy.

'Is he all right?' I ask.

'His lungs,' Mabel says. 'Sometimes he struggles to catch his breath.'

Mabel takes Little One from me as I move to sit down next to Sylvan, holding the back of my hand to his forehead. He's cold to the touch, and I can hear a worrying rattle in his chest.

'Does this happen often?' I ask.

Sylvan swivels his dark eyes to me. 'My chest gets all sticky and tight.'

'Does he see a doctor for it?' I ask Mabel.

'We have treatment,' she says, nodding at a contraption on the floor and handing Little One back to me. It looks like an old lamp from the Victoria era, a strange tin bowl at the top of it. She moves to the kitchen bench and lifts a bowl of dried leaves, that I recognize immediately as banewort leaves.

'Belladonna,' she says. 'You know it?'

Ah, yes – *that's* the other name for it. Belladonna, also known as Deadly Nightshade. The weird herb in Mrs Whitlock's garden. I know it can be used to treat respiratory problems.

I watch, intrigued and nervous, as Mabel puts some of the leaves into the tin bowl at the top of the lamp and turns it on. Soon the leaves char and smoke, and she holds the lamp close to Sylvan, allowing him to breathe in the strands of smoke unwinding from the bowl. His voice sounds better, and his colour returns a little. But I'm wary. Belladonna is extremely toxic. It is not to be meddled with.

'You feel better now, Sylvan?' Mabel asks him.

He nods and rubs his tummy. 'A little.'

'Did you do these drawings?' I ask him, nodding at the crayon pictures on the table. I can make out jungle scenes of elephants and palm trees full of monkeys.

He nods.

'What a talent!' I say. 'They're worthy of an art gallery.'

'Morven taught me how to draw,' he says weakly, and I look at Mabel for explanation. She lowers her eyes right as the name tugs at my memory – Aretta and Rahmi mentioned a girl named Morven. It's clear that Sylvan's mention of her has saddened Mabel, and I don't question any further.

Sylvan looks over at Little One. 'Can I see Sienna?'

'Sienna?' I ask.

'The baby,' he says, and smiles. 'She's so little.'

'It's not having the same effect as it used to,' Mabel says. 'He's getting this chest thing more and more. He usually only gets it in the winter.'

We've had some heavy rain recently, and I can't help but glance at the damp spots on the wooden ceiling of the hut.

'Perhaps I can help,' I say. 'There are other treatments for this sort of thing.'

'Are there?' Mabel says, straightening.

Aretta looks from Mabel to me. 'We've been wondering whether you could help him ever since we found out you're a nurse,' she says.

I nod. 'I'd be glad to help.'

Mabel looks up. And for the first time since I've laid eyes on her, she smiles.

Then

Mabel

Lichen Hall, Scottish Borders, 1960–63

1

We find the arrowhead on Sylvan's first birthday.

He has just started to walk, still wobbly on his feet but eager to be upright, and so Morven takes one little hand and I take the other, and we walk him slowly through the forest. He's wearing a pair of corduroy dungarees in navy blue with a matching bow tie and white shirt. All handmade by Aretta. It's getting colder now, so I've brought a blanket to wrap him up in once he tires. Today is sunny and warm, though, bright sunlight filtering through the trees. The swifts have long gone, but the forest is conscious with birds, ringing with their songs.

We head to the ghost woods where, on days like this, you can see the ocean, crisp and blue, the long line of the horizon making me breathe easier. The trees are beautiful in this light, white and shining. The birds don't sing in this part of the forest, though, and it makes me realize that all the ghosts in my body used to go quiet when I came here. But I've not felt the ghosts for months. They got quieter and quieter until I didn't feel them anymore. Not even now.

'Do you hear that?' I ask Morven as we sit down on a large rock.

'What?' she says.

'The silence.'

We both turn and look back into the depths of the forest, where the birdsong can still be heard in the distance. I open the lunch bag I brought and pass Sylvan a sandwich. He sits down next to us and eats it.

'You want birds?' Morven says. 'You have to throw crumbs. That's all they're singing about back there. *Feed me, humans!*'

I laugh and throw several pieces of bread a few feet away from us. But no birds come.

Sylvan sits spreadeagled on the ground, finishing off his sandwich. Then he presses both tiny hands into the ground to stand up, lifting his hips in the air, but instead of straightening upright he gives a loud cry.

'What's wrong?' I say, lifting him up. His finger is red, and when I look down on the ground I see something sharp sticking out of the soil. I pluck it out.

'Is it a plectrum?' Morven asks, looking it over.

I kiss Sylvan's fingers to soothe him, then offer him a biscuit. He quietens.

'I think it's an arrowhead,' I tell her, noticing the worn markings on the rusted metal.

'Could be worth something,' Morven says. 'We could sell it at an antiques auction, buy a big house with the money.'

'We already live in a big house,' I say, and she kisses me, laughing.

'Yeah, but our *own* big house. Wouldn't that be something?'

I take the arrowhead to Mr Whitlock. I figure that he's the expert on found objects like this. And we found it on his grounds. It's only right that he sees it.

I find him in the Rose room, the table spread out with academic journals. He plucks a magnifying glass from a drawer in the bureau and looks over the arrowhead.

'Very impressive,' he says after a long silence. He looks at me, studying my face. 'I'd say it's iron. Which means it could be from as long ago as the twelfth century.'

I raise my eyebrows. 'That long ago?'

He nods. 'We'll need an expert to assess it. Where did you find it?'

I hesitate. 'In the ghost woods.'

He removes his glasses and stares at me thoughtfully. 'Nicnevin's woodland,' he says.

'What woodland?'

'It's an old folk tale. A witch named Nicnevin. Not just any witch – the queen of witches. The queen of war and mischief. Legend has it that she was a real person. Not just myth, but a story based on truth. She's supposed to haunt these grounds.' He smiles and looks over the arrowhead, turning it over in his palm. 'I'd put it back, if I were you,' he says, handing it back to me.

'Put it back?'

'In the woods. She'll be missing it, I expect. Folk round here say she caused the wars all those years ago. She'll want her spoils.'

I'm so stunned by this comment that I almost laugh. Surely he's not serious?

But in the end, I do exactly as he says – I take the arrowhead back to the spot where we had our picnic and sink it into the earth. As I straighten and turn back for home, something shifts past my feet.

An adder, rippling across the ground.

2

'Morven?'

'Yes?'

'Why don't you want to go back to Glasgow?'

She rolls over. 'I told you why.'

'Was it the truth?'

We're in bed, in the little hut we've made into our home. Morven still sleeps some nights at Lichen Hall to keep Mrs Whitlock from asking too many questions, and often she'll wait until it's late until she creeps back out to me. If Mrs Whitlock has seen her, she's never said anything.

Sylvan is asleep in his crib nearby, the sound of his dummy squeaking as he dreams. Morven lowers her eyes. 'Why do you want to know?'

'Because I don't want there to be any secrets between us. I love you.'

She doesn't respond for a long time. Then she rolls over on to her stomach, resting her cheek against the palm of her hand.

'I never liked boys,' she says. 'But I hid it from everyone. There was this boy called Simon. More of a man than a boy. He was my brother Cameron's friend. He'd made it clear that he liked me and called me a dick tease because I wouldn't kiss him. Sometimes I'd let him touch me so no one would think anything. Then one night, Ma went out and it was just me, Cam, and Simon in the house. They were both drunk. I went downstairs for a cup of tea and Simon grabbed me by the wrist . . .' She tails off, swiping tears from her face. I hold her hand.

'I never told anyone,' she says in a small voice. 'I kept the pregnancy a secret, trying to figure out what to do. My parents found out. They went ballistic, threw me out. I had to go live with my grandparents. Everyone just assumed I'd slept around. I tried telling my sister Aileen what happened.'

'And what did she say?' I ask gently.

Her face screws up, a fresh wound opening. 'She said I must have asked for it.'

I lie down next to her, placing my hand gently on her cheek. We are both naked, and she pulls the sheet up around her. I know she does this because she feels vulnerable.

'You're safe with me,' I tell her. 'I promise.'

She takes my hand, slowly placing it between her legs. I touch her the way she likes, kissing her face. Then I guide her to move above me, enjoying the way she shudders above my mouth, my hands on her hips. She throws her head back, gasping my name.

'You've never told me the truth about how you fell pregnant,' she says afterwards.

'I did,' I say. 'I don't know how it happened. I'd never had sex.'

She gives a dark laugh. 'Nobody just becomes pregnant, Mabel.'

'You said it could have been parthenogenesis. A virgin birth.'

She gives me an outraged look. 'That's *animals*, Mabel. I was joking. I thought you just didn't want to tell me. Things are different now. Aren't they?'

'Of course they are,' I say, moving closer to her. Our noses touch, and I go to kiss her, but she pulls back.

'Then tell me,' she says. 'Tell me how you fell pregnant with Sylvan. Or is it too much of a secret to share with me?'

I open my mouth, but there's no secret to share. For a moment I feel tempted to tell her a lie. I could say I *did* sleep with Jack, just once. We were dating, after all. But that's not the truth. I can feel myself shutting down, my breaths becoming shallow.

For the first time since I fell in love with Morven I feel a ghost stir in my heart, its feet in an artery. I start to panic – I had thought the ghosts were gone for good.

'I thought there were no secrets between us,' I hear Morven say.

The bitterness in her voice cuts through me. But I can't speak, not even when she gets up and pulls on her clothes. Not even when she walks out of the hut and closes the door, louder than usual. I curl up in the warm space left by her body, breathing in her scent.

3

The next day, Morven approaches me at the hen house.

Sylvan's asleep in the sling on my back. A twig snaps fifty yards away. I see Morven, and my heart leaps. She's wearing the denim dungarees and leather sandals left behind by Rose, who went home last week after her twin boys were adopted. It's back to being just the five of us, our unusual little family – me, Morven, Sylvan, Aretta, and Rahmi.

'I'm sorry,' I say as soon as I spot her. It's true – I am sorry. I start to tell her how much I've missed her, even though it has only been one night, and how I never want her to feel like she can't trust me. That I promise to always tell her the truth, even if it doesn't make sense.

She steps forward and kisses me, long and hard, holding my face in her hands.

'I forgive you,' she says.

Her words make me feel like I'm lifting off the ground, and I wrap my arms around her. We're usually much more careful in case anyone sees, never daring to touch when we're outside the hut.

But right now, the risk is worth it. I kiss her again, and she laughs, pushing me away gently.

'We can't get caught,' she says, her eyes falling on Sylvan in his sling.

The risk extends to him, now.

A noise makes us dart apart. Through the trees, I see Aretta, then Rahmi. There's a look on their faces that tells me they saw us kiss.

I stiffen with fear. What if they tell Mrs Whitlock? She'll throw us out, or call the police. I lock eyes with Morven – I can tell she's thinking the same thing, and my fear turns to anger. How could we have been so careless? We've promised never to touch outside the safety of the hut. We swore to it.

I'm already planning how to beg Rahmi and Aretta not to say anything as they approach.

'Please don't tell,' Morven says, her voice tight. She clasps her hands together, her face drained of colour. 'Please.'

Rahmi takes Morven's hands in hers and laughs. Then she throws her arms around her.

'Our lips are sealed,' Aretta says, smiling. 'So long as you can share our secret, too.'

Rahmi lets go of Morven and glances back at Aretta. Slowly, she reaches out and laces her fingers with Aretta's. With a start, I recognize their body language, the words and promises within small gestures. They're in love, too.

Morven throws her head back and gives a loud laugh, all her terror transforming to delight. 'You have got to be kidding me,' she says.

'Not kidding at all,' Rahmi says.

Morven falls sombre, looking over Rahmi and Aretta. 'In all my years,' she says, 'I never met anyone like me. Now there's four of us, here in this little corner of the world.'

I can't quite believe it until Rahmi turns and plants a kiss on Aretta's lips. I throw my arms around the two of them, feeling closer to them than ever before. I've had nightmares about anyone finding out, and what they'd do to Morven and me. I suspect Aretta and Rahmi feel the same. Still, we have to be careful.

Sylvan stirs, reaching out to Rahmi.

'Good afternoon, handsome,' she says, lifting him out of the sling on my back. She holds him close, then looks up at me. 'Shall I feed him?'

I nod, and she takes him to a tree stump nearby, holding him to her breast. It's his ritual in the mornings and evenings. Ever since my own breast milk dried up, Rahmi has taken over, and Sylvan loves her. Aretta reads him bedtime stories, and Morven carries him everywhere when she can. She's protective of him, and she knows how much I still fear that, one day, I'll wake up and find he's been adopted. It happened to Elspeth. She went out and when she came back, her baby was gone.

'Not while I'm around,' Morven always says when I bring it up. 'They'll have to prise him off me.'

But it doesn't stop me worrying.

Now

Pearl

Lichen Hall, Scottish Borders, November 1965

1

I wake up early, before dawn, and even though the baby isn't awake I scoop her out of the cot and hold her to me, stroking her face. Poor thing. It's not her fault that she was brought into this godawful situation, and truth be told, if I could keep her, I would. I cry a little. I should have resisted my father's suggestion that I have the baby adopted.

I have treasured these last seven weeks with her. Aretta and Rahmi have been an enormous help, forbidding me from doing anything other than letting them bring me food while I feed and change Little One. Wulfric turns up at one o'clock sharp on Tuesdays and Thursdays for his lessons, which is at once endearing and irritating. I've continued to teach him, albeit with breaks to check in on Little One, and occasionally to console her when she's realized I wasn't in the room. Wulfric's mood has improved, and there have been no more outbursts. His desire for the lessons has nothing to do with learning, I realize, and more to do with the level of attention he receives. Often I wonder what will become of him when I leave Lichen Hall. His days are spent wandering the forest, either alone or pushing his grandfather in the wheelchair, and tending to his hens.

I have visited Mabel and Sylvan several more times, making him a poultice of eucalyptus oil to helped him breathe, and instructing Aretta and Rahmi to scrub the rotten parts of the hut with bleach. That should remove the mould. I had Mabel leave the windows open to create proper air flow, and told her not to hang any damp laundry indoors. It has helped him a little, but he really needs to be seen by a doctor.

The telephone is often on the blink, and after my initial phone call to my mother I've not been able to call home, or speak to Lucy. I tried her again this morning, out of desperation. I needed to hear a friendly voice from home to remind me that what I'm doing is right. It feels sickeningly *wrong*. My parents should be here, greeting their new grandchild, smiling down at her. Little One has a little dent in the end of her nose, just like my father's, and the feline eyes that characterize my mother's line. And she's so awfully good, such an absolute darling. She started smiling at two weeks and has never stopped. Her whole face brightens when she sees me in the morning. And no shrieking the house down when she wants to be fed, just a few little grunts and whines and then she latches on and is happy.

But today is The Day.

I get her washed and dressed, then I iron the blue dress that fits me, now that I no longer have a baby bump. I curl my hair, put on some thick tights, then the dress, and force myself to stop crying.

The decision has been made. Perhaps it is the right one. It feels like the wrong one, completely and utterly wrong. But what do I have to offer her? I'm single, jobless, disgraced. I have no future to speak of. I will return to my parents' home and hope that one day I might find both an employer and a prospective husband who don't mind that I once had a child out of wedlock.

I head downstairs to the Willow room. Little One is wide awake now, intrigued by the bars of light falling through the shutters on the windows. I feel like I've been split into two people;

one is resigned to today's event and determined to face it, whilst the other is scheming to run out of the front door with Little One and flee for our lives.

But, too late – a blue Austin Morris pulls up outside. Bile rises in my throat, and I have the startling urge to cry. A couple gets out of the car and heads towards the side door. Mr and Mrs Finch, though God knows if that's even their real name.

'Come on, my love,' I tell Little One, forcing the words out. 'Time to meet your parents.'

'Knock, knock,' a voice says from the doorway. Mrs Whitlock. She wears black slacks and heels, a white shirt, red lips. Business-like and glamorous. 'Ready?' she asks, tilting her head. I nod and take a deep breath.

'Ready.'

Mrs Whitlock greets the couple like long lost friends, air-kissing and cooing over the woman's pink beret. They're nervous, and younger than I expected – mid to late twenties. The husband wears black-framed glasses and a grey suit, a psychedelic tie lessening the formality of it. The glint of a gold wedding band. The wife wears a pretty pink minidress and white pumps, brown hair curled around her neck.

Little One turns to look at them, and Mrs Finch raises her hands to her mouth in astonishment. Then she turns and presses her face to her husband's shoulder for comfort. They look every bit as happy as I imagine Sebastian and I would have been, in that parallel life I should be living.

'It's all right, darling,' Mr Finch says reassuringly, though I can tell he's embarrassed by the display of emotion. He tilts his chin at me. 'Good morning. Big day, isn't it?'

Mrs Finch turns back to Little One, wiping tears from her cheeks. 'Oh, she's beautiful.'

'She is,' I say. My voice trembles. Mrs Finch looks up at me and smiles. I can see she suddenly understands how hard this is for me. Mr Finch stands behind her, his attention fully on his wife. We are all experiencing different forms of pain. We are each other's solutions. We are wary and glad of each other, united in paradox.

Mrs Whitlock watches the proceedings from the safety of the doorway, giving us enough space to negotiate the handover of Little One and watching closely to ensure I don't make a scene.

'Can I hold her?' the wife asks.

'Oh. Yes,' I say, realizing that I've been clinging to Little One as though she might suddenly take flight. I pass her over gently, and the wife holds her in an awkward grasp, as though she's a bundle of laundry.

'Take a seat, darling,' Mr Finch tells her, and she does, arranging Little One in her arms. In a moment, Little One gives a huge yawn before closing her eyes and dozing off.

'What are you thinking of calling her?' I ask.

The wife hesitates before answering. 'Sienna.'

'Sienna,' I repeat, surprised. Sylvan called her that name, I remember, when I brought Little One to Mabel's hut. How weird.

'What would you have called her?' she asks.

Evangeline, I think, though I don't say it. 'I thought that if I picked a name for her it would make it harder to pass her over.'

'Well,' Mrs Whitlock says after a few moments, breaking the silence. 'Now that the child is asleep, it might be a good time to make your escape.'

The Finches nod and rise slowly, Little One still in the wife's arms. The husband seems unsure of what to do. He steps forward, reaching out a hand. I shake it, and he nods. 'Thank you.'

And then they leave.

I watch the car pull away, my heart breaking. I sense Mrs Whitlock behind me, but she doesn't say anything. No words of comfort or reassurance. Her footsteps trail away down the corridor.

I go back to my bedroom and look down at the empty crib, at Little One's clothes filled with her smell. I sink to the floor, every ounce of strength in me suddenly wiped away. In one explosive wail, all the sobs I held back come bursting out. Without realizing it, she has formed a shape in me, a space that is now cavernous with a frightening absence.

Then

Mabel

Lichen Hall, Scottish Borders, 1963

1

Sylvan is three when Mr Whitlock falls ill.

It happens quickly, and dramatically. One day, I bring him a cup of tea and a warm scone to the Micrarium. I stop in my tracks when I realize something is different: he's not wearing shorts. A white shirt and tie hangs over two chickeny legs, the startling invertebrate of his penis visible at the shirt hem. I clear my throat and keep my eyes down as I set the tea and scone on the table before trying to escape.

'Come and look,' he says, waving his hand for me to join him. I freeze, not sure how to get out of it. Eventually I turn and take a step towards him, trying desperately not to look.

'You've been on a train, haven't you, Morven?' he says.

I don't correct him, but it's unlike him to get my name wrong. He's usually as sharp as a knife when it comes to details like that.

He nods at his latest addition: an entire miniature railway, replete with scenes of fields and villages, running the length of the room. 'It's the journey I used to take as a boy,' he says, lowering close to the tracks, a flash of his buttocks imprinted forever on my mind. 'I built it for Wulfric to show him what it looked like when we went to see my grandparents.'

I turn my head firmly away from him, taking in the left side of the Micrarium. He has marked the boxes there meticulously to organize the contents: human history, extra-terrestrial, plant, animal, insect. The insect section has several new glass boxes – more ants, and also snakes, caterpillars, and cicadas, all of them with the same strange fungus protruding from their bodies.

'Don't forget your tea, Mr Whitlock,' I say, inching away from him.

'I won't,' he says. 'Thank you, Morven.'

I'm barely halfway down the stairs when I hear a shout and the sound of a cup shattering. Racing upstairs, I find Mr Whitlock on the floor, a dark puddle of liquid beside him. For a moment I think it's blood, but it's only his tea. He isn't moving.

'Morven!' I shout. 'Morven!'

She races upstairs and takes in the sight of him on the floor beside me. I've covered his lower half with a blanket.

'What happened?' she says.

'I don't know,' I say panicked. Admittedly, my first worry is that I'll take the blame for this.

Morven checks his vitals. 'He's alive. A stroke, I think. Help me move him.'

He's light as a feather.

Morven and I carry him along the hallway to the first empty bedroom and lay him carefully on the bed.

'Keep him on his side,' Morven says. 'I'll get Mrs Whitlock. Let's see if she won't call a bloody doctor *now*.'

But Mrs Whitlock doesn't. She examines Mr Whitlock with concern, instructing Morven and me to get him some food and water.

He regains consciousness, but he doesn't leave his bed for a week. No doctor appears.

After that, he's in his Micrarium less and less, his nightly walks a thing of the past. Mrs Whitlock asks Morven and me to make up a room on the ground floor as his new bedroom. A wheelchair appears. A stairlift is installed.

I never see him walk again.

2

'Mummy? Why can birds sing but not talk?'

'That's a great question, Sylvan . . .'

'How do you make water?'

'Well, if it's hot inside, you can make steam, and then . . .'

'Morven?'

'Yes?' Morven says.

'You know jellyfish?'

'Yes?'

'Are they really made of jelly?'

'Not the sort you can eat, sweetie pie. You don't want to eat jellyfish.'

'Why? Have you eaten jellyfish?'

'*No*, my love. Absolutely not.'

'Sharks eat them. That shark has three rows of teeth!'

Morven gives me a confused look. 'A shark? Where on earth have you seen one of those, pal?'

'I can see him now,' he says. 'He thinks seals are yummy.'

His curiosity about the world knows no bounds. Four years old. How did this happen? It seems only moments ago that he was a tiny baby, and I felt completely out of my depth. This last year, he's really become a little boy, all his baby looks and ways a thing of the past. He seems to get smarter every day.

It's April, and the grounds of Lichen Hall are battered after a savage winter. Storms, blizzards, and floods have scarred the land, transforming a field into a lake and bringing down a huge horse chestnut tree across the driveway, close to the front gates of the estate.

Mrs Whitlock asks Morven, Rahmi, Aretta, and me to clear them.

'How the hell are we supposed to move this, exactly?' Morven says, her hands on her hips. We're standing on the wall that runs alongside the driveway, looking over the aftermath of the storm. The roots have come away from the soil in a flat slab, twenty feet in diameter. A hundred branches lie scattered across the road, several feet thick. The tree trunk is at least fifty foot long. It would have made sense to ask a professional to tackle the job, or a farmer, who could make good use of the wood. But I suspect Mrs Whitlock is holding me true to my promise – I said I'd work double if I could stay at Lichen Hall, and she has ensured that the promise is kept.

We decide to start by moving the smaller branches by hand to the field opposite. Sylvan helps, too, gathering up smaller twigs and stacking them in a pile, though after a while he grows bored of clearing and decides to build a tree hut.

I can see Morven is growing tired too, her movements slowing quickly. Her face is pale, and when she turns to the light, I see a fresh bruise on her forehead. A lump, too, about the size of a marble on her hairline.

'What happened?' I ask her, my fingers reaching for it. She winces at my touch.

'It's nothing,' she says.

'Did you hit your head?'

'Not that I know of. I'm fine.' She moves away from me. 'Jings, I've had worse than this in my time.'

I watch her as she struggles to shift a long branch, swearing under her breath.

The mark on her head wasn't there yesterday, I'm sure of it.

We move slowly, taking smaller bundles of broken branches

and piling them up by the side of the road. It isn't long before Sylvan is whining, telling me that he can't breathe properly. It's happening more and more.

'I can take him home,' Rahmi tells me. She opens her arms to him and he walks to her for a cuddle. 'What's wrong, wee pal?' she asks him. 'You needing a nap?'

'My chest hurts,' he tells her breathlessly, and she looks up at me. When I lower down to him I can hear it: a rattle in his chest.

'You take him home,' Rahmi tells me. 'Let him rest.'

I nod, gathering Sylvan up. He feels limp in my arms.

'Will you be all right?' I ask Morven. She waves me away with a smile, but her face is drawn.

Sylvan goes straight to sleep the minute I lay him down. I light the fire, keeping him warm, checking his chest every five minutes. Gradually, the rattle lessens. But it's scary, the way he has to gasp for air. I've never seen him like this.

It's already dark when I hear voices outside the hut. I open the door to find Aretta and Rahmi carrying Morven, her arms looped across their shoulders.

'She's all right,' Aretta says when she sees the look of horror on my face. 'She's just overdone it, that's all.'

They bring her in and lay her on the bed beside Sylvan. The two loves of my life, laid out, poorly and weak.

I hold back the words of panic that want to fly out of my mouth. 'What happened?' I ask.

'I must have fallen asleep,' Morven says groggily. She sounds drunk.

'She collapsed,' Rahmi explains. 'She was out of it for a while. We brought her straight home. Mrs Whitlock can deal with that mess herself.'

I press my palm to Morven's forehead; her temperature seems fine. Her colour is off, though – she's white as a sheet, and the circles beneath her eyes are dangerously dark. The bruise on her forehead is still there. The lump at her hairline looks bigger.

'You need to rest,' I tell her, unable to conceal the irritation in my voice. One of the things I love most about Morven is how she'll keep working, long after everyone else gives up. She does it because she loves us. She wants to take care of us all. But right now, I'm angry at her for not quitting sooner. *She's making herself ill*, I think.

'All right, all right,' she says, her words slurred. 'I'll take it easy, OK?'

3

It's Christmas Day. Since I've been at Lichen Hall, Rahmi, Aretta, Morven, and I all usually have Christmas dinner together in the kitchen, after we've served Mr and Mrs Whitlock and Wulfric in the dining room.

But this year is different. Mr Whitlock still hasn't recovered from his fall. Mrs Whitlock tells us that she'll take a light lunch with Wulfric in the Wisteria room while Mr Whitlock rests. She has been spending more and more time alone like this, and seems withdrawn. I've noticed that she's stopped smoking, and she seems thinner, rarely eating. I think she's worried about Mr Whitlock. He's never been one to rest this long, always busy outdoors in the woods, or with his Micrarium. When I see her pushing him in the wheelchair for the first time, he's unusually silent. She must be very lonely.

Morven, Sylvan and I will have Christmas dinner together, and then we'll meet Aretta and Rahmi later tonight. Not quite the majestic setting of the hall, but we've set the table and made hand-painted bunting, which Sylvan and I hang around the hut.

'This looks lovely,' Sylvan says. His voice sounds hoarse, and there's a wheeze in his chest. He's probably coming down with a cold.

'Do you think Morven will like it?' he asks.

'I think Morven will be the happiest girl *ever*.'

We set her presents on the table, waiting for her to come and celebrate.

But she doesn't show up.

Eventually, Sylvan and I wrap up warm and walk to the hall, where a small fir tree is garnished with tinsel and lights. We head to the kitchen, where Aretta and Rahmi are washing up after their meal. Sylvan runs up to Aretta and Rahmi to thank them for his gifts. Aretta crocheted him a teddy and knitted him three pairs of thick woollen socks, while Rahmi helped Morven and me build him a new log cabin in the woods. It's no more than a bundle of branches stacked in a triangle, but he adores his little nooks like this.

Aretta and Rahmi give him a hug and feign surprise at the gifts that Santa Claus brought him. We had to concoct an elaborate tale about Father Christmas squeezing himself down the narrow chimney of our stove into the hut, though Sylvan has already decided that Santa Claus doesn't exist. 'I know you have to make up the story at Christmas,' he told me. 'And I know you made the gifts.'

'Where's Morven?' Rahmi asks.

'I was going to ask you that,' I say. 'You've not seen her?'

They shake their heads. I leave Sylvan with them while I head upstairs to check Morven's bedroom, though it's unlike her to sleep past dawn. As expected, she isn't there. Her room is pristine, the bed made. She isn't in any of the rooms.

I head downstairs to the Wisteria room. Mrs Whitlock is reading a book by the fire, and Wulfric is playing a game of chess with himself, by the looks of it.

'Sorry to bother you, Mrs Whitlock,' I say. 'I don't suppose you've seen Morven?'

She looks up and removes her reading glasses. 'I'm afraid I've not seen Morven since the day before yesterday,' Mrs Whitlock says. She turns to Wulfric. 'Wolfie, have you seen Morven?'

He looks up and shakes his head.

'No problem,' I say, forcing a smile. 'Sorry to bother you.'

'Merry Christmas,' she says.

'Merry Christmas.'

'Where *is* she?' Sylvan says when I head back to the kitchen, and I know he's frustrated because he's excited for her to open his gift to her. He made me teach him how to sew so he could make her a fabric pencil case. He spent ages stitching her name to the front, too, using green thread – her favourite colour.

We check the hen house, then the gardens behind the house, taking the path right to the cliffs. I start to feel uneasy. If Morven isn't in the house or the gardens, where is she?

I think back to when she was ill earlier in the year. Maybe she's blacked out somewhere. 'Let's head back to the hut,' I tell Sylvan. 'In case she's already there waiting for us.'

My heart sinks when we don't find her there.

It's getting late, and Sylvan is pale and lethargic. I make him a plate of food but he turns away from it. I sit down opposite and watch him carefully, noticing a light travelling along his little lips. A silvery light, small as a pinhead, glowing through his skin. I've not seen this since he was a baby.

'Morven's in the ice cream place,' he says.

I stare at him. 'What ice cream place?' Sylvan has never had ice cream. 'Did you see Morven go somewhere?'

He sits upright, colour returning to his cheeks.

'Sylvan?' I press gently. 'Did you see Morven go somewhere? Did someone come for her?'

The light on his lip moves across his cheek towards his ear. I think of Morven, being kidnapped. A scene plays out in my mind – someone found out about our relationship. They punished Morven for it. I've heard about things like that happening. My stomach cartwheels. I take Sylvan's hand and squeeze, hard.

He looks up at me with wide eyes, startled by my grip. I hadn't meant to hold him so tightly, and I let go at once.

'I'm sorry,' I tell him, cupping his face with my hands. 'Please tell me what you saw.'

'I think Morven's asleep,' he says quietly. 'She's not doing anything. Just sitting there.'

I don't know what he means. I rise to my feet, my cheeks hot. I want to cry.

'It's very dark,' he says.

'What's very dark?' I ask. The light on his ear sweeps across his cheekbone, shining beneath one of his eyes, turning the iris from dark brown to a bright copper. I'm suddenly frightened that he is falling ill. Nobody has lights in their body like this. Do they?

He stares ahead, his gaze far away. 'Maybe Morven is sick.'

I nod. 'Why do you think that?'

'She looks sick,' he says, lifting his eyes to mine. 'Do you think we can go help her?'

My heart is pounding. Why is he saying this? What does he mean?

'Mummy?'

'Yes?'

He screws his face up in disgust. 'The place with the ice cream. It's smelly.'

I kneel in front of him. He's only four, I remind myself. I must be patient. 'When was this, Sylvan? When did you see Morven?'

It's Sylvan's turn to grow exasperated. 'I see her *now*.'

'Tell me what you see.'

'I told you. She's in the ice cream place.'

'What's it like?'

'I can hardly see anything.' He gives a full-body shiver and rubs his arms. 'It's so cold.'

'What else?' I say. 'Can you see Morven?'

He nods. 'She won't say anything. She only has one shoe on, Mummy.'

There's a knock at the door, and I turn to see Rahmi coming in.

'Morven still isn't here?' she says, and I shake my head. A sob rises to my throat. It all feels very confusing.

'She's still not in the house,' she says. 'Not in the gardens, either.'

'Did Morven mention anything about having ice cream with anyone?' I ask her.

She pulls a confused look. 'Ice cream? No.'

I turn back to Sylvan. The light that was moving in his face has gone now, and he slumps down as though he's tired.

'Mummy?' Sylvan says. 'What *is* ice cream?'

Now

Pearl

Lichen Hall, Scottish Borders, November 1965

1

'Are you OK?'

Aretta's feet come into view. It's Tuesday, the day after Little One was adopted. Wulfric has already approached me for a bloody lesson, but I simply stared through him until he took the hint and sloped off.

Right now I'm sitting on a blanket beneath a tree, my knees drawn up and my head in my hands. I'm quite close to where the *thing* happened with the creature that night, and I don't even care. My grief overshadows any terror, any number of fears. I feel I've regressed from a grown woman to a five-year-old. I want to hide from the enormity of my feelings. I want my mother to hold me and tell me it will all be all right. But I know that's not possible.

It will never be all right.

Aretta sits down on the ground beside me.

'How you doing?' she says.

I don't answer.

'My little girl was born on a day like today,' she tells me. 'A beautiful sunny day. She was nine pounds, a real chonk. I had her with me here for three months. She laughed all the time. At everything. The sound of her laugh made my heart sing. I was so scared she'd look like *him*, but she looked exactly like my mother. Identical. A reincarnation. I watched all the other girls here cry after their babies were taken. I promised myself I would prepare myself for it. That it wouldn't break me the way it broke them. That it was the best thing for her. But secretly I thought about running away with her. I knew I had nowhere to go.' Her voice breaks. 'And when the parents came and took her, I wanted to die. I had tried to prepare for that day for months. It was all for nothing. So I know what you're going through. I know what this feels like. It *will* pass.'

We sit together in silence for a few moments. Her words help me, just a little. When the sun comes out, I lift my face to the sky, and hope Little One is all right. That would be enough, I think. Just to know she's all right.

'Listen,' Aretta says. 'Do you think you could come and check on Sylvan? He's not doing too well today.'

I turn to her sharply. 'He's ill again?'

She nods, and I get to my feet. I had thought he was on the mend. We head quickly to the hut.

When Mabel opens the door, I can tell immediately he's grown worse. His wheezing is louder, and he lies limp on the bed, not moving. I look at the lamp on the floor.

'Is the belladonna not helping?'

Mabel shakes her head, visibly distressed. I don't think she's slept at all. 'I gave him too much. He started hallucinating.'

The room smells funny. I gather Sylvan up in my arms to help him sit upright. His pallor makes me wince.

'We need to open up his airways,' I say to Mabel, who gathers some cushions for me to prop him up. He is so weak and limp, and up close the rattle is alarming.

'Have you any strong tea?' I ask.

'I can make some,' Aretta says, and she does. We help Sylvan drink it, but it's not enough. His lips are turning blue, and I feel my stomach knot in fear.

'What is that smell?' I ask Mabel, and she glances at the fire.

'I think we must have burned some bad wood,' she says. 'It's smelled like that for days.'

'Have you seen a difference in how Sylvan has been since you began burning that wood?'

She nods, and I kneel in front of the fire, trying to work out how to fix the problem. The fire is out, and the stove is cool enough for me to open it and look inside.

'Have you a torch?' I ask Mabel. Aretta finds me one and I crane my head to peer inside the chimney. It's clogged. The smell isn't from bad wood – it's from the narrow chimney of the stove. Tiny bits of ash sometimes get trapped inside these and float around the room. It's a health hazard, particularly to someone with respiratory problems.

'We need to clean this immediately,' I tell Mabel. 'Wait here.'

I head outside and into the woods, searching for the branch of a fir tree, thickly bristled with needles. Finally I find one and bring it back to the hut, then ram it up the chimney with all my might, making sure the needles catch the smaller particles. Instantly the floor in front of the stove is covered in loosened bits of ash and soot, and Aretta helps clean it up.

'We need to keep the chimney clean,' I say. 'Every other day, give it a clean like this. And maybe try and keep him in Lichen Hall for a while, until he recovers?'

Mabel smiles, but I can tell this isn't an option. 'Thank you,' she says.

She helps Sylvan sip more tea, and despite the chill in the air we open the door to let the air circulate. The rattling dies down. Thank God.

Mabel and I share a look of relief.

'Who's Sebastian?' Sylvan says hoarsely.

'*Sebastian*?' I say, confused. Have I mentioned Sebastian to Sylvan?

'I see him,' Sylvan says. 'He's outside.'

Just then, I hear a strange noise beneath the sound of the birds in the trees and the hens chortling nearby: the drumming of a car engine. The crunch of tyres driving over the gravel in the driveway. The Finches. They've realized they made a mistake. They've brought her back.

I scramble to my feet and race out of the hut towards the house. I only make it halfway up the hill when I hear someone shouting.

'Pearl! Pearl?'

2

Someone is shouting my name. I stop, dumbfounded.

'Pearl!'

I recognize the voice, or rather my body does, my heartbeat immediately shooting through the roof. And then, another voice, answering the caller, asking him if they can help. Rahmi, or perhaps Mrs Whitlock. I keep running, spurred on by adrenalin, desperate to see if it really is him. If I've imagined him shouting for me.

I turn the corner to the front of the house. There he is. Sebastian, his bottle-green Ford parked by the front entrance. He races towards me and gathers me up in his arms, spinning me around and shouting, 'Pearl! Oh my God, I can't believe it!'

'Is something wrong?' I say when he puts me down. 'Is it my dad?'

'What?' he says, confused.

'You're here to tell me something,' I say. 'Is someone ill?'

He laughs. '*No*. Nothing's wrong. I just . . . I had to see you.'

'Oh.'

We look each other over. He is clean-shaven, smartly dressed in a black sweater and pea-green trousers, his chestnut brown hair to his collar. He smells as gorgeous as he always did – of home, and comfort.

'You look different,' he says, smiling. I flinch. I must look an absolute state. I'm still wearing the clothes I slept in, and my eyes are puffy from crying. And considering I gave birth seven weeks ago, I daresay he means I look 'different' in all the wrong ways. I draw back, embarrassed.

'I mean you look beautiful,' he says. 'I've missed you like crazy.'

I study him carefully. 'Really? Because you barely spoke a word to me when I was back home in Edinburgh.'

He looks away, as though I'm being petulant. 'Will you come out with me?'

'Where?'

'To the beach. We planned a day trip, remember?'

'We did?'

'I made us a picnic.' He walks to the boot of his car and opens it, revealing a picnic basket and a bottle of champagne in a bucket of ice.

'Good God,' I laugh. I almost forgot what being around Sebastian was like. Sixty seconds of his company and I'm already transported to a world of fun and excitement, all the pain from the last two months drifting steadily away.

'I need to tell the others that I'm popping out,' I tell him.

'Who?' he says. But I'm already racing off to tell Aretta that I'll be away for the afternoon, and that I'll check on Sylvan the minute I get back.

When I return to Sebastian twenty minutes later – my face washed, hair brushed, wearing a chunky woollen jumper and red bellbottom trousers with white Chelsea boots – he winks. 'You look ravenous,' he says, opening the car door. 'Let's go have some fucking *fun*.'

We drive with the windows down, and the movement of the car and the wind on my face is incredible.

'You heard much from anyone back home?' he asks.

'No, not at all,' I say, a sudden homesickness twisting in my gut. 'The phone doesn't work very well at Lichen Hall. I've written to Lucy loads but never heard a word back.'

'What about your folks?' he asks. 'You heard from them lately?'

'Not really,' I say. Then: 'Actually, they've pretty much ignored me since I came here.'

'Mum thinks they're having money problems,' he says.

'Money problems?' I say with a laugh. 'My parents? Why on earth would she think that?'

'She said she saw your mum at the greengrocer's being confronted by the owner. Apparently she already owed him and he wasn't going to maintain her credit.' He glances over at me and sees I'm worried. 'I thought you should know.'

I'm aghast. My first thought is that Cheryl – Sebastian's mother – misinterpreted whatever she saw. Or exaggerated it. But then, Cheryl isn't like that – she's always struck me as a very honest, shrewd person, before she started calling me a whore. I'm reminded all over again of how much I used to love Sebastian's family. It wasn't just him I lost – it was his parents, his brother, Arlo, even his bloody dog, Bentley.

'Why would my parents be having money problems?' I say.

'Maybe Sid's taken up gambling?'

'My father's never gambled in his life.'

'Ena, then.'

'Don't be ridiculous.'

He laughs. 'OK. Maybe Mum got it wrong. And anyway, it was stupid of me to spring that on you. Charlie's dating Cora, did he tell you?'

I stare at him, stunned. 'No! *Cora?*'

He gives me a look that says *Yes, that Cora.*

Cora's the girl who lives across the road from us. She's sixteen but could pass for twelve. She's the quietest thing, a little dormouse who won't look at anyone. Her parents never sent her to school because she's frightened of crowds, and people in general. My brother's the loudest, most obnoxious arsehole you ever laid eyes on, so I'm not sure how on earth they've managed to forge a relationship. Also, Charlie's twenty-one, so I'm sure her parents aren't thrilled about him courting her.

'Did you graduate?' I ask him. 'Have you started work at a law practice already?'

He doesn't answer, but stares at the road. 'What?' I say. 'You *didn't* graduate or you didn't start work as a lawyer?'

He purses his lips. 'Dad asked me to come work for him. So I dropped out.'

'But . . . you were planning to graduate in June . . .'

'Things changed,' he says simply. 'I wasn't sure law was for me anymore. This way, I get to earn good money right away. And it's secure. I can't provide for a family as a trainee.'

He looks at me meaningfully, then reaches out for my hand. I let him hold it, but I realize sharply that he hasn't asked me how I am. We've barely spoken since January. He hasn't asked about the baby, hasn't acknowledged why I'm staying at Lichen Hall. It's not like him.

We park at the beach, facing a long strip of firm sand that's clean of shells and people. White waves unfurl on the shore with a deafening crash. The sky is shining silver, like a new coin.

Sebastian and I get out of the car and walk, side by side, along the sand. We don't talk for a while, but it's not an uncomfortable silence – we've known each other since we were children, can communicate for long periods without saying a word, or even looking at each other. We used to take day trips to the beach with our families, a long time ago. For a moment I have a flash of a time when Charlie and I dug a hole in the sand and buried Sebastian up to his nose. It might have been this beach.

So much has happened since then.

We reach the tide. I remove my boots and dip my toes, relishing the coldness and the rush of the waves. They help me stay grounded in the here and now, the past and future both dissolving in the icy bite of the water. Sebastian still has his shoes on, and the tide catches him unawares, covering his brogues.

'Shit,' he says, and I laugh as he jumps back, only to trip and fall flat on his arse. The tide rushes up, soaking him. I laugh harder as I pull him to his feet. His shoes, trousers, and the bottom of his jumper are soaking wet now. 'Fuck it,' he says, scooping me up and carrying me screaming with laughter into the waves. One crashes into us; we fall over, and I feel the water rush over my head, the clap of the waves above me and my mouth filled with salty water. We both crawl, coughing, drenched, up the sand past the tideline. Then we sit and look at each other, giggling like children.

'I heard you had a little girl,' he says then. His words are like a thunderclap. For a moment I had almost forgotten everything that has happened.

'Yes,' I say. 'Seven weeks ago.'

He nods, scooping up a fistful of sand and running it through his fingers. 'Why did you sleep with him?'

'You broke up with me, Sebastian. Or had you forgotten that small detail?'

The hurt of it is so raw, all these months after. He tosses the rest of the sand over his shoulder, like salt. 'I hadn't forgotten.'

'Why did you do it? Why?'

'You know why.'

'No, I don't,' I say, and there's a sob in my voice. 'I really don't, Sebastian.'

'I thought you did.'

'Well, I *don't*,' I say. 'I never understood it. I guess you decided I wasn't good enough for you. Or you wanted someone else.'

He turns and stares at me, and there's a pained look in his eyes. 'I regretted it, you know. Breaking up with you.'

'I bet you did.' I say it bitterly, and before I've thought it through. I don't believe him. Why else would he have done it, when we were on the brink of getting married? We'd talked about it on New Year's Eve. That it was time. Sebastian knows I wasn't big on surprises, and we'd been together since we were sixteen. We talked about the future so many times, as though it was cast in stone. The two of us, together.

'Sebastian, if you'd *not* wanted to break up with me,' I say, 'you wouldn't have done it.'

He gives a long, meaningful sigh. 'I was having a bit of a crisis,' he says slowly, raking the sand with his fingers.

His words twist something inside me, pressing the wound. Why didn't he tell me this at the time? 'What kind of *crisis*?'

'It's the only way I know how to explain it,' he says. 'I spoke to Dad. I mentioned we'd talked about getting married.'

He falls silent, and I feel a chill run up my spine. 'And what did he say?'

'Well, he wasn't keen on the idea.'

'He wasn't keen on us getting married?'

He nods, and I feel nauseous. 'It was over the feud. About the tree. Remember?'

Alan and Dad fell out a couple of years ago. They'd been friends for years. And then there was an issue about the big sycamore tree in our back garden. Alan wanted Dad to have it cut down because it was creating shade in his garden. Dad said no, the tree was hundreds of years old, and he wasn't inclined to kill it because of a small patch of occasional shade. It was ridiculous. They stopped talking.

'Alan didn't want you to marry me,' I repeat slowly, trying to get my head around this, 'because of a fucking *tree*.'

'Well, it wasn't exactly that black and white . . .'

'Then what was it, Sebastian? He wanted you to marry me or he didn't?'

He looks down at the sand. For a long moment, there is only the sound of the waves, getting more and more violent as they roll towards us, clapping against the beach. 'He said it would be difficult for our families. And he said that, when we had children, it would be hard for them to understand why their grandparents didn't talk to each other.'

I want to scream.

'But that's ridiculous,' I say, my throat growing so tight that it hurts to talk, to breathe. 'All he had to do was apologize to Dad, or agree to disagree . . .'

I'm spluttering.

'I did try,' Sebastian says, holding my gaze. 'Back in March. I tried to make it right. I told him that his issue with Sid was *his* issue. And I came to find you to tell you I'd changed my mind. That I wanted us to get back together.'

'No, you didn't,' I say.

He nods. 'I knocked on your door. Your mother answered.'

My skin crawls. When was this? Why did she never tell me this?

'She brought me into the house,' he says, resting his hands in the sand behind him, looking up at the sky. 'She said you were at work. And that you were expecting a baby.'

He looks at me for a long moment, and I can't speak. My lungs feel like they've collapsed.

I can't sit a moment longer. My mother never told me *any* of this, and I want to yell at the waves, at fate, about how unfair everything is. I told Mum I was pregnant about a week after the doctor confirmed it. Regret widens in front of me like an endless chasm. Inside a year, I have lost the love of my life, my job, and my daughter. I feel like I'm being eaten alive.

I get up and start to walk briskly, wiping away the tears that come freely. Sebastian follows, easily keeping pace.

'I only slept with Bobby because you broke up with me,' I say. 'Didn't you know that?'

'No. I didn't know that. I took it that you had moved on. That you'd found someone else and were getting married. I didn't know *what* to think, to be honest.'

My throat burns. *Why* did Mum tell him that? Why?

'And then I went home and told my parents,' he says. 'Looking back, that wasn't the smartest decision.'

I stop and stare at the ocean, imagining it all. This is the thing when you know people inside out – you know exactly how they'll react in any given situation. I can see Sebastian's father glorying in the news that I was pregnant. Telling Sebastian *I told you so*. Sebastian would have been hurt, and his hurt would have made him believe every word they said – whether true or false.

'Your dad wanted you to date Mariella,' I say, recalling what Charlie told me. 'Didn't he?'

He lowers his eyes. 'He offered me a chance to work for him,' Sebastian says. 'But he made it clear that a condition of the job was that I move on from you. I'm inclined now to tell him to screw himself.'

I shake my head. 'You can't just quit your job . . .'

'Not immediately. But when I save enough money to set up my own business.' He holds my gaze. 'I want to be able to provide for a wife and family.'

There's a long silence where I take that in. Somehow, at the end of this long, hideous road we've both travelled, there might be a future. But it's a future without Little One.

'Was the baby adopted?' he says then, as though he's reading my mind.

I keep my eyes on the horizon. 'Yes.'

'Is that a relief, then?'

I shake my head vehemently, but the image of Little One shines in my mind. I crumple into tears, and he puts an arm around me, and everything I was holding together is undone, the guilt is too heavy, unspeakably heavy. I feel like I might implode with hopelessness and anger, bright, livid rage, alive as a flame.

Sebastian tries to pull me to him. 'I'm sorry. Forgive me, Pearl. I didn't think . . .'

'I shouldn't have given her up,' I say through tears. 'I wouldn't have if she'd been yours.'

We reach the car. The sun has withdrawn and I'm suddenly freezing, my teeth chattering.

'God, you're freezing,' Sebastian says. He grabs a towel from the boot and throws it around me. 'Take your clothes off,' he says, and I attempt a laugh. 'No, I mean it,' he urges. 'They're wet. I won't look.'

He turns his head and keeps the towel wrapped loosely around me as I take off my jumper and trousers, leaving me in my underwear. My bra and pants are wet, too, but I leave them on and pull the towel around me. Then he wraps me in his arms and rubs the towel into my skin to warm me up.

'Get in the car,' he says. 'Need to get warm.'

We clamber inside. Seconds later, the heavens open, drumming the windscreen. We sit in silence, me huddled under the towel, him soaking wet and visibly afraid to say the wrong thing.

'You should take off your clothes, too,' I say. 'You'll catch your death.'

I hold him in a long look. He returns it. Then he pulls his sweater over his head, and I reach out to run a finger over his bare chest. He glances at me again to read my stare, to make sure. Then, slowly, tentatively, he leans over, and kisses me.

It is like a fire has been lit inside me.

His lips against mine, his tongue in my mouth, against my neck. Suddenly I'm pulling at his belt, tugging down his boxer shorts, though it's difficult because his skin is so wet and grubby with sand, and we laugh at the awkwardness of it. We always had amazing sex, even after years of being together. I have missed it. I have missed *him*.

He kneels in front of me as I sit in the passenger seat, and we manoeuvre hastily to find a position in the tight space of the car, the seat laid back, my legs around his hips.

His lips find my breasts, but a moment later I flinch with pain.

'Sorry,' he says, pulling away as though he's touched flame. He looks down at my naked body. My breasts are full of milk, hard and round as bowling balls, and my abdomen is still livid with purple stretch marks cut deep into my skin, as though I've been set upon by tigers. 'God, Pearl.' He looks up at me with tenderness in his eyes. 'I don't want to hurt you. We can stop.'

'You won't hurt me,' I say, though the truth is my body aches. But his tongue on my neck feels good. His lips against mine, along my inner thighs, feels good. I guide him into me, assuring him it's OK, and the mix of sharp pain and the sensation of him inside me again is ecstasy, sending bright lights flashing behind my eyes.

He moves slowly and gently at first. 'Is this OK?' he says softly, and I say yes. He moves hungrily then, his lips on my shoulder, grinding his hips in urgent circles. Outside, lightning flashes across the sky, then thunder. I come loudly, shouting out from the intensity, then he does.

Afterwards, he holds me for a long time and kisses me deeply, with longing. Like he used to.

3

'When are you coming home?' he says as we head back up the driveway to Lichen Hall.

'Now, if you'll wait for me to pack my things.'

'Serious?'

I nod, then remember about Sylvan. 'Shit. I need to check on Sylvan.'

He looks at me like I'm crazy. 'Who?'

'A little lad I was tending to at the hall. I need to make sure he's all right.' I sit for a moment, transporting myself mentally back into the present. Sylvan needs proper care. Even though he seemed better earlier, I need to be sure he gets treatment. 'Give me a couple of days to say goodbye to the girls here. Then come pick me up on Friday. OK?'

'OK.'

He parks outside the hall, then reaches out and touches my cheek. 'I love you,' he says. 'Always have. Always will.'

I kiss his fingers, smelling myself on them. 'Love you, too.'

I don't watch him drive away. I keep walking, headed for the side door of Lichen Hall, where I'll gather my clothes and Little One's lock of hair. Then, once I've checked on Sylvan, I'll return to Edinburgh and begin my new life.

Then

Mabel

Lichen Hall, Scottish Borders, January 1965

1

It's New Year's Day. Morven and I were supposed to see in 1965 together. Morven sneaked a bottle of fine wine from the cellar in Lichen Hall a few weeks ago – 'it's not like the Whitlocks drink any of it', she said – and we were going to celebrate together in the hut after Sylvan went to bed. We were going to talk about the future. We've known for a while that we can't stay at Lichen Hall for ever. Morven says the world outside is changing, becoming more accepting.

But she's still missing.

I'm turned inside out with confusion. I've checked every inch of the gardens and the woods, searched every nook and cranny of Lichen Hall, including the crawl space in the roof. I feel like I'm going mad. Surely she wouldn't just leave me? Did she say something about leaving and I forgot? Did we have a fight? Did she break up with me and I shut down so hard that I blanked it out?

Aretta, Rahmi and I have traced the whole estate. Rahmi's pleaded with Mrs Whitlock to let us spend days searching instead of working. She's let us. She seems worried, too.

* * *

That night, I wake to the sound of banging. Outside the fields are thickened with white snow, fresh flakes tumbling down. I scramble to my feet, still tangled in dreams about Morven.

'Mabel! Mabel! Please, open the door!'

I stagger across the room. At the door stands Aretta, sobbing so hard I can't make out what she's saying.

'Oh God, oh God!' she wails.

'What's happened?' I say. 'Aretta, what's wrong?'

She falls into my arms, weeping and shaking. She's wearing a heavy overcoat, but her hands are icy cold. I hush her, worried that she'll wake Sylvan. 'Come with me,' she whispers. 'I need you to come.'

'Where are we going?' I say. I don't want to go anywhere in this rain.

'It's Morven,' she says finally.

'Morven?' I say, my breath catching. 'You found her?'

She nods, but then her face crumples. My stomach plummets. Something terrible has happened. I go to ask if Morven is all right, but I can't. I don't want to know if she isn't. I can't bear it.

I follow Aretta quickly across the field to the woods. She clutches my hand tightly but doesn't speak, the wind roaring in our ears. The light of her small torch bounces off the white of the forest floor.

She leads me towards Lichen Hall, and I expect to go inside. Morven will be sitting in the kitchen with Rahmi, a blanket across her shoulders and a cup of tea on the countertop in front of her. Maybe she left, as I feared, but she's home now, and that's all that matters.

But Aretta continues on past the house, her light sweeping up the gravel towards the gardens.

'Where are we going?' I ask her, my stomach dropping. She holds my hand tighter and keeps walking. 'Aretta?'

She doesn't answer. All the lights in the house are off, no sign of movement. Hail falls now, a punishing blizzard, the wind pummelling us sideways.

'There,' Aretta says finally, her torchlight resting on the old shelter that Mrs Whitlock told us to keep away from. It's nothing more than a concrete cylinder, with an old black door wedged shut that leads down some old steps to a tiny room underground. Mrs Whitlock said they used to store meat and ice down there, before the hall had electricity.

Why are we here?

'I kept thinking of what Sylvan said about "ice cream",' Aretta says, her teeth chattering. 'And tonight it made me think of this place. I realized we'd never checked it.'

I'm still not sure why we're here. I watch as she half climbs, half slides down the bank to the black door of the shelter. Her torch shows that it is open.

I climb down quickly after her, my mind spinning. Aretta's right – they used to keep ice cream down here, though I have no idea how Sylvan knows that. Suddenly I don't want to be here. I want to go back to the hut and pretend this is all a bad dream. Nothing good can be here.

Aretta pauses by the open door, nodding inside. 'In there,' she whispers.

She presses the torch into my hand. I squeeze through the door, an awful smell hitting my nostrils. The light falls on a stone wall.

Inside are two rooms, not one as I'd thought.

'Morven?' I say. I swing my light towards the adjoining room. It's freezing cold. I step forward, noticing a shape on the ground. The torch reveals a brown shoe, the laces undone. I recognize it instantly.

It's Morven's shoe.

My torchlight finds an arm, then a body.

I reel back, gasping in shock at the sight of Morven sitting on the ground, her legs outstretched, her lifeless head tilted to one side.

I drop the torch, the light skittering along the floor. For a handful of terrible seconds I'm in the dark with her.

I hear a cry, and I'm at once conscious that I'm the one making the terrible howls and whimpers and unable to stop. My hands shake as I pick up the torch, raising it to Morven.

Her hand is stiff, stone cold. Her long copper hair hangs like curtains across her face, her palms upturned and her bare legs scratched and muddied. There are pine needles in her hair and on her dress.

A tree branch is lodged deep in her head. A weapon.

She was murdered.

2

'In the *ice house*?' Mrs Whitlock says.

Aretta and I stand in the Willow room. It's early, just after eight. It seemed wrong to wake Mrs Whitlock after finding Morven, so I went back to the hut and Aretta went back to break the news to Rahmi. We are all broken, exhausted from a night without sleep, and at the same time my body vibrates with the impossible knowledge that Morven is dead. I feel like I want to shut down, make my mind go elsewhere – but I have to stay present. For Morven's sake.

'We were careful not to touch the body,' Aretta says in a low voice. 'Nor disturb the scene. We know you'll want to call the police.'

Mrs Whitlock raises her eyebrows. 'Are you sure the poor girl was dead? Not unconscious?'

'Whoever killed her left the weapon in her head,' I say. My voice is hollow. I feel the urge to shut down again and again.

'Good God.' Mrs Whitlock turns to the window, processing this terrible news. She presses a hand to her chest, her face stricken. 'It must have been such a shock, finding her there.'

'It was,' Aretta says, her voice catching.

Just then, Sylvan runs in. I had occupied him in the dining room with Wulfric's old train set, but he must have heard us talking. 'Morven's where the ice cream is,' he says loudly. 'I *told* you.'

'What?' Mrs Whitlock says, eyeing me sharply for explanation.

'The *ice cream place!*' he says again.

'Oh, you mean the ice house?' she says, bending down to him. She glances at Aretta, as though querying why on earth Aretta would tell him such a terrible detail as where we found Morven's body. Aretta says quickly, 'We never told him that.'

'Didn't you?'

'I told *them*,' Sylvan says, pointing at himself proudly. 'I said I saw Morven in the ice cream place and it was very cold.'

'Really?' Mrs Whitlock says, curious. She pauses, as though thinking over his words, trying to make them make sense. 'And how did you know she was there, Sylvan?'

He gives a simple shrug. 'I see things.'

'Well, I see things too. You must see them differently, do you?'

He gives a nod. 'I do see things differently. Don't I, Mummy?'

'Sylvan . . .'

He persists. 'I have two different eyes.' He points at them. 'This eye sees things in this room. And sometimes *this* eye sees things somewhere else.'

Mrs Whitlock gives a strange little smile. She straightens, and I can see the wheels in her head turning.

'He's just a little boy,' I say, though I'm not sure why.

'Indeed,' she says.

Now

Pearl

Lichen Hall, Scottish Borders, November 1965

1

I watch Sebastian's car pull away from Lichen Hall, and I want to do a little leap for joy. Yes, Little One is gone, and I have a sense that part of my heart will always be broken for her. But returning to Sebastian, to my old life in Edinburgh, lies ahead of me now. A chance to put things right.

A fork in the road, allowing me to step over into that parallel life.

I go straight to the shepherd's hut to check on Sylvan.

He's still weak, and his cheeks haven't as much colour as I'd like. I prop him up with pillows and tell Mabel to make sure she keeps him on his side.

'It'll help him breathe easier,' I tell her, and I promise to send her proper medication for him as soon as I get home to Edinburgh.

'It's a shame you're leaving,' she says sadly.

I give her a hug. 'I'll write to you,' I say. 'And I'll send medicine for Sylvan. I promise.'

I decide that I should tell my parents that I'm coming home on Friday, and that I've arranged for Sebastian to pick me up.

The phone has a dial tone; I dial my home number quickly.

'Hello?'

It's Mrs McQuade, our housekeeper. I ask to speak to my parents.

'Och, is that you, Pearl? So sorry my love, but neither of them is in just now. Shall I ask them to ring you?'

I tell her to pass on a message to my parents that Sebastian is bringing me home. Saying it aloud brings so much relief, and I feel butterflies in my stomach all over again at the thought of seeing him.

'I'll be sure to pass that on. You keeping OK, luvvy?'

'I am,' I say, beaming. 'I'll see you on Friday.'

2

That night, I can't sleep. The empty crib next to my bed is torturous, and I keep thinking about Little One in her new home. She's only small, and I'm told that babies adjust quickly. But I feel that I've failed her. I miss her face beaming up at me. I miss her smell.

Finally I decide to move the crib out of the room entirely. The emptiness of it is agony. I get up and open the door, and it's then that I see something on the small flight of stairs from my bathroom.

A face.

I blink.

A long shadow falls on the stairs, and when I look down I see what appears to be a set of fingers close to my feet, gripping the lip of the top step. A face glances up at me. It's an old woman, her body lying against the stairs, a hand stretched out to the top step as she pulls herself up towards me.

I stagger backwards, falling to the floor, my mouth open in a soundless scream.

With a trembling hand I pull myself up and turn on the light.

The stairs are empty. There is no old woman there, thank God.

But something *is* on the steps.

Shaking, I lower myself to see.

On the top step, directly where I saw the hand, is a long, stag-shaped mushroom poking out from a crack in the wood.

3

The next morning, I rise early, stepping nervously into the hall to check the stairs. No sign of the woman, but the mushroom is there. I bend down to survey it. A strange thing to be growing inside the house. I lift my foot and stamp on it, pressing until it is obliterated, then wipe up the mess hastily with toilet roll.

'Pearl?' a voice calls upstairs.

'Yes?'

'You've got a phone call.'

I didn't even hear it ring. I head downstairs to the phone seat. It'll be my parents, returning my call.

'So you *are* alive,' Lucy says on the other end of the line.

'Oh, *Lucy*,' I say. My heart sinks a little. As much as I'm glad to hear from Lucy, I'm eager to hear from my parents to tell them that Sebastian is picking me up.

'. . . not a single letter,' Lucy is saying. 'I thought you might have at least written.'

'What?' I say with a nervous laugh. 'I wrote loads of letters to you, Luce. Didn't you get them?'

'Nope.'

I glance at the table just a few yards away from where I stand. Mrs Whitlock instructed me to leave my letters on that table for the postman to deliver. *He comes every Thursday*, she said. I've never received a single letter, either. My anger flares. I bet she put all my letters in the fire. She probably read them, too.

I need to get out of this place.

'Anyway,' Lucy says with a sigh, and I can tell she thinks I've abandoned her, when really I've been writing to her all this time. 'Pearl, look – I need you to do something for me. I have to tell you something, and I need you to sit down for it. Don't worry, nobody's dead or ill. But I still need you to sit down.'

She's pregnant, I think. 'What is it, Luce?'

'You need to sit down, Pearl. Tell me you're sitting down.'

'All right,' I say, still standing. 'I'm sitting down.'

'It's about Sebastian,' she says with a sigh. 'He got married on Monday. To Mariella Fotheringham.'

'No, he didn't,' I say, and I start to explain about his dad and the feud and how he was pressured into courting her. 'He was with me on Monday. We went to the beach.'

'Darling, I saw them,' Lucy says.

'Saw what?'

'I saw them outside the registry office, getting photos taken. It was Mariella and Sebastian. I'm so sorry, love. I know you're still hung up on that bastard so I wanted to make sure you got it straight.'

I go to refute it, but my skin has turned ice cold. 'What day did you say they got married?'

'Monday. About two o'clock. I'd popped out on my lunch break to buy a Coke and get some fresh air. I'm walking past the Town Hall and I see Sebastian, looking very dapper. And I think, what's he up to? So I stop, and I see bloody Mariella walking up to him and she's wearing a white dress suit and carrying a bouquet of flowers, and his father's with him, also in a suit. And they start posing for photographs. It was a wedding.'

'What day is today?' I ask her quietly, my heart racing.

'Wednesday.'

On Monday, Little One was adopted. Tuesday was the day Sebastian came to see me, not Monday. We made love. It was the day after his wedding. He was a married man. He betrayed me. Again, again, and again. In my weakest moment, he deceived me.

'OK,' I say.

I hang up and sink to my knees. The air has been wrung clean out of my lungs. I can't think, can't speak. I'm drowning. I feel like I'm drowning.

'Are you all right?' a voice says.

I look up and find Rahmi standing over me. I'm on the floor, gasping for air. The room is swaying, as if there's an earthquake. My heart feels like it's going to crack my ribs open.

She holds out a hand to help me to my feet, but I can't seem to reach her, I can't lift my arm. Eventually she calls Aretta, and the two of them squat down to check my vitals. They're saying my name, asking me to respond, and I open my mouth like a fish, but nothing happens.

I'm not sure I'm in Lichen Hall anymore. I feel like I'm dying. I'm falling deep into the earth, falling and falling and falling.

4

'Rahmi told me there was a problem.'

I look up to see Mrs Whitlock standing in the doorway to my bedroom. Outside it's dark, and the moon is white and round in the window frame. My suitcases are splayed open on the bed and I'm packing them.

'No problem,' I say. 'I'm going home.'

She folds her arms, a look of confusion on her face. It's as though my body and brain are working of their own accord, and I'm somewhere else, curled up in a dark hole.

'My daughter's been adopted,' I hear myself say. 'I'm going home.'

My heart is broken.

'Rahmi said you were upset earlier,' she says. 'May I ask what happened?'

How could you, Sebastian?

Inside me, something has broken. I don't feel that I'm leaving this place as the same person who walked in. The person I loved most has broken my heart. He has made me an adulterer. He insinuated we had a future, the future he knew I wanted so desperately. He brought me the brightest hope, only to crush it in his hands.

But I won't cry in front of Mrs Whitlock.

'There was a misunderstanding,' I say, forcing myself to stretch a wide smile on my face to show her that I'm fine, totally and utterly fine. 'Thanks for your concern.'

'I see.' She doesn't believe a word I've said, and I feel a surge of anger. She stands, watching me as I fold my underwear, my slips, and set them carefully into my bags. I'm glad, now, that I took such care to clean the bedroom before I started packing. It is spotless, gleaming, and the bed made with the precision of an army recruit.

'I thought you agreed to teach Wolfie,' she says.

'I have.'

'He is still in need of your assistance.'

I grit my teeth and continue folding my dresses, putting them neatly into the suitcase, ignoring her.

'Have you informed your parents?' she says.

I don't answer. I'm irritated by her presence, by her questions.

'Are they aware of your plans?'

I look up and face her. 'Yes. As a matter of fact, they are.'

Her face is tight, though she's wearing a small smile. She steps inside my bedroom and stands on the opposite side of the bed. I stop packing and look up at her.

'You're not going anywhere,' she says.

I look up, expecting a coy addendum to that statement, perhaps a word of thanks for what I've done for her grandson. 'I've taught Wulfric twice a week for the last two months,' I say, astonished when she says nothing. 'Two days after giving birth, I was back teaching him.'

She ignores me. 'You should really put all of this back into the wardrobe.'

'Beg pardon?' I say, and she holds me in a cool stare.

'You won't be leaving Lichen Hall any time soon,' she says, stepping closer. I can see the moles on her face, the soft grey hairs on her upper lip. Her eyes are wide, filled with hate. 'You won't be leaving for a long, long time.'

I'm too astonished to speak. She holds me in a hard stare for a moment longer, until she's certain I have the message, before turning and walking out of the room.

I wait until she's gone, absolutely stricken by what has just happened. Why on earth does she want to keep me here? I pad quickly downstairs to the telephone. I need to call my parents. The dial tone is gone – of course it is.

Rahmi helps me bring my luggage downstairs. We carry it all the way to the front of the house, so that I can avoid Mrs Whitlock and scan the road for my parents' car at the same time. I give Rahmi a huge hug and thank her for what she did earlier.

'You're feeling better?' she says, and I nod. Truth be told, I'm numb. I don't know what or who to believe anymore.

'Make sure you and Aretta keep in touch,' I say, pressing a folded piece of paper into her hand. 'That's my address. Please write, or better yet, come and visit.'

She nods. 'I will.'

I wait, and I wait.

At midnight, it begins to rain. I stand, stubborn as a rock, letting it soak me, refusing to take my eyes off the road. Perhaps they had an accident. The thought chills me. I have no way of knowing, now the phone line has been cut. No way of calling for a taxi. They probably don't even come out this far. In four hours, not a single car headlight has passed by on the main road.

I hear footsteps approaching, and I stiffen.

'I told you you wouldn't leave,' Mrs Whitlock says in a low voice. She stands slightly behind me, and I refuse to turn around.

'I expect you up each morning by six o'clock. You're to clean all the skirting boards, the staircase, and the bathrooms. Aretta will show you where she keeps the mops. You'll tend to Wolfie and help him with the hens. No visitors, talking, or noise of any kind. There is no use of the telephone without permission. No venturing beyond the grounds of Lichen Hall without approval. Understood?'

I say nothing.

'The phrase we use is, "Yes, Mrs Whitlock",' she says.

I grit my teeth. Who the hell does she think she is?

'I'd check my attitude if I were you. Food and lodgings are dependent on both your service and my satisfaction.'

I close my eyes and force myself to repeat it. 'Yes, Mrs Whitlock.'

'Good. Now, get out of my sight.'

Then

Mabel

Lichen Hall, Scottish Borders, January 1965

1

A day passes. I don't bake, or sleep, or move from the windows overlooking the driveway. No laundry or cooking is done. Sylvan is breathing better, playing with his ball at the front of the house while I keep watching the driveway for the police.

But nobody comes.

The ponds are frozen over, the ground outside brittle with frost. The stillness of the hall is bewildering. I see Mrs Whitlock in the gardens with Wulfric, watching on as he builds a snowman. I want to scream. Why is no one here for Morven?

Aretta, Rahmi and I convene in the dining room, when Mrs Whitlock is well out of earshot. 'Maybe *we* should have called them,' Aretta whispers. 'The police.'

'Did you ask Mrs Whitlock if she's called them already?' Rahmi asks me.

I shake my head. I'm too afraid to ask her something so directly, and it chills me – the knowledge that, even though Morven is dead, I'm so scared of Mrs Whitlock that I can't ask her a perfectly reasonable question. I'm in shock at what happened. My thoughts run out of control, and it takes all my strength just to function.

I still have to care for Sylvan. I have to pretend nothing is wrong, for his sake.

I've been thinking about what he said about Morven being in the ice cream place. It unnerves me, the things he says sometimes. The things he talks about that he has never experienced, or even read about, and yet he knows so much about them somehow – animals in parts of the world I can barely pronounce. Famous footballers, politicians. I've been able to put a lot of these things down to overhearing Aretta or Rahmi talking, or perhaps catching some of it on the wireless, which Mrs Whitlock turns on occasionally.

But Morven's death is something else.

I ask him, gently, how and when he saw her, and he thinks about it.

'Do you remember the dog we read about in the story?' he asks. I think back. I've been reading him a bedtime story about a dog called Barnaby who has a blue eye and a brown eye.

'Barnaby,' I say, and he nods.

'Well, I think I have two different eyes. One eye sees what's here and the other sees other things.'

It gives me chills.

Even if he really did see Morven's body in the ice house, he is too young to understand what he saw.

But how *could* he have seen her? And why?

I'm not sure I can persuade myself anymore that it's a lucky guess. I have to face facts: Sylvan can see things that I can't.

And the lights beneath his skin tell me that his abilities are beyond human. That he will never be accepted outside these walls.

2

A man calls at Lichen Hall. Aretta, Rahmi, and I huddle by a curtain at a window upstairs to watch as Mrs Whitlock greets him and takes him to the gardens. He's wearing a heavy overcoat and a hat, so it's difficult to see if he's a policeman.

'He must be a detective,' Aretta whispers.

'Don't they usually come in pairs?' Rahmi says.

Aretta and I shrug. We've never met a detective before. We don't know what happens when someone dies like this.

We watch as Mrs Whitlock walks with him through the gardens to the forest. 'He'll want to interview us,' Rahmi says. 'I know that for a fact.' She looks to Aretta. 'He'll want to ask you about how you found the body.'

Aretta gives a solemn nod. Then, with a tone of fear, 'What if he thinks I murdered her?'

'He wouldn't,' Rahmi says, but her tone lacks conviction. We all share a look. We're the only girls at Lichen Hall at the moment. It feels strangely vulnerable, now it's just the three of us.

'I heard about a maid at one of the houses outside Glasgow,' Aretta says. 'One of the kids had an accident in the house while playing, broke his neck. The family accused her of it. She's in Barlinnie for murder.'

'They could blame us for what happened to Morven,' Rahmi says darkly.

We watch on, even when the man and Mrs Whitlock pass out of sight.

Later, Mrs Whitlock comes to the hen house while Sylvan and I are collecting the eggs. She's wearing a mink coat and fur-lined galoshes while Sylvan and I shiver under blankets. I expect her to say something about what the detective said about Morven. She's carrying something in a white box. A cake.

'I was thinking of you and poor Sylvan,' she says. 'I know you and Morven were . . . close.'

I avoid her gaze as she looks over me. 'Here,' she says, handing me the box. 'Wulfric and I attempted to bake this afternoon. We made this for Sylvan.'

I open it. A chocolate cake glistens inside.

'Thank you,' I say.

She folds her arms, and I can sense she's here on a mission. Then, her eyes turning to Sylvan: 'May I have a quick word?'

We move away from the hens to keep Sylvan out of earshot. 'How are you feeling?' she asks. 'Devastated, I expect?'

I nod but keep my eyes on the ground. I feel as if I might fly apart, but I don't want to tell her that. I'm still mulling over the way she said Morven and I were 'close'. Maybe I'm paranoid, but it sounds like a threat. As if she might use it against me.

She gives a heavy sigh and folds her arms. 'Poor dear. I know you and Morven were terrific friends.' There's an almost imperceptible emphasis on the word 'friends'. 'Which makes what I have to say even harder, I expect.'

My ears prick up. 'Did they find out how she died?'

'How she died?' she repeats, not understanding me.

'If it was . . . foul play?'

'Ah, yes. The detective said it's likely she slipped and banged her head. She would have lost consciousness and passed away in the ice house.' She closes her eyes. 'Dreadful.'

I don't believe she cares at all. With a shiver, I think of the branch that was lodged in Morven's head. She was murdered. I'm sure of it. Her death was not due to a mere fall.

Mrs Whitlock steps towards the hens, making a clucking noise. 'She's estranged from her family. I'm sure you already know that.'

I nod.

'I think we should bury her here,' she says, looking over at the trees. 'In the grounds of the hall. She would have wanted that, I think. And perhaps it'll be better for you and Sylvan to have a grave to visit.'

My mind lurches to the time we prepared Rahmi's baby for burial. I can't imagine doing that for Morven.

I can't imagine digging her grave.

3

Aretta, Rahmi, and I carry Morven's body out of the ice house to one of the outbuildings. We cover her with a white sheet.

Then, we go into Morven's bedroom, quickly rifling through her drawers, her wardrobe, and even her sketchpads in case there's a letter or diary that shows an address for a living relative. None of us has received letters for years. I've never heard from Jack or Ma, and I'm sure Mrs Whitlock confiscates any post that arrives for us.

We find nothing. None of us know how to locate her relatives.

Two days pass. The detective doesn't return. No interviews, no answers.

No priest is called to officiate the burial, no headstone ordered. We are still too stricken and too afraid to question such things, and too felled by her loss to do anything more than make sure she gets a proper burial.

The next day, I send Sylvan to draw quietly in the Rose room and make him promise to stay there until I come for him. Once he's settled, Aretta, Rahmi, and I take basins of clean water and towels to the birthing suite to wash Morven's body.

Rahmi sings the whole time; it's an Algerian folk song, she says, sad but not mournful. It keeps us distracted enough to finish the task. I don't understand the words she sings, but in my heart I imagine them expressing the dark feelings that keep threatening to drown me.

My love, how are you gone? How am I to continue on?

Gently we remove the leaves and twigs from her hair and wipe away the bloodstains from her hands. Her eyes are closed and appear sunken. Her skin has dulled in colour. I wash her hair with shampoo, but it still looks less vibrant than I remember. It feels as though every bit of Morven has vanished.

We try to move the branch that's protruding from her head, but it's stuck fast. Aretta resorts to cutting it close to the skull. When we remove her clothes, I see something in her chest. Another branch, shorter than the other one, lodged deep in her heart.

We stop and look down at her body in horror.

'Mrs Whitlock must have done it,' Aretta says bitterly.

'Why would she do that?'

'She's a witch,' Rahmi says quietly. 'That's what people are saying.'

'We don't know what anyone's saying,' Aretta says. 'We're not allowed to leave the grounds, remember? We have no contact with the outside world.'

'Abdul,' Rahmi says, and we look at her. 'The farmhand who came for the eggs last week. He speaks Arabic. He told me.'

'What did he say?' I ask her.

'He said both her and Mr Whitlock are evil. That they'd used their own son's body for experiments. He said that's why they picked up the body from the morgue. To carry out experiments.'

'Maybe that's why we've never found their son's grave,' Aretta says.

'Or maybe his grave is in a churchyard,' I say, looking down at Morven. 'Just like hers should be.'

I concentrate on wiping Morven's arms and legs gently, using a small toothbrush to clean her face. I remove dust and pine needles with tweezers from her eyebrows and ears. When that is done, we clothe her in one of the dresses left behind by one of the girls who came to Lichen Hall to have her baby. The dress is a fine green silk, which seems appropriate. Green was Morven's favourite colour.

We move her into a large crate that Aretta and Rahmi have jimmied together as a makeshift coffin, lined with silk scarves from the store room. We raise her up on to our shoulders like standard bearers, and carry her slowly to the resting place in the forest.

Rahmi officiates. As she speaks the words of an old Scottish blessing, I think of the day Morven drew me sitting underneath the horse chestnut tree directly opposite. I had never felt seen until that moment. I had never felt like I had a presence in the world until I met Morven.

And now she's gone.

We mark her grave with a small pile of stones. Then we sit and share memories, and hold hands and laugh. Silently, each of us knows that Morven was murdered.

Each of us knows that the murderer is still out there.

4

'Where's Morven?' Wulfric asks the next day.

I'm cleaning out the chicken coop, sweeping the droppings into a bucket and changing the hay. Sylvan follows the hens around the forest, making sure they're safe.

'She's not here,' I tell Wulfric. It takes so much concentration to keep my voice level.

'She's dead, isn't she?' he says. I glance quickly at Sylvan. I've not yet figured out a way to tell him the truth. He adores Morven. The thought of breaking his little heart is too much for me, so I've lied. I've told him she had to go away for a few weeks.

But he knows I'm lying. He says she's underground. He can see the worms, and the tree roots, and the fungus growing around her. It hurts to hear him say such things.

Wulfric knows something is up, too.

'Why don't you ask your grandmother?' I say, when he asks about Morven.

He stares at me. 'Who?'

'Or your grandfather?'

'He's dead.'

I stop what I'm doing and stare at him. 'Go away, Wulfric.'

He's sucking a lollipop. 'I know she's dead,' he says.

I turn away before he sees I'm upset. It's not just the truth of his words that cuts me – it's the coldness in his voice. I'm too raw for this.

'If you know so much,' I say, 'why can't you look after your hens? Hmm? Or did you forget that we set this up for you?'

He walks around the coop.

'Did my dad do it?' he says, peering in at me through the wire.

'Do what?' I say, trying not to sound too interested. The truth is, I've asked myself if perhaps Wulfric knows something. Nobody has questioned him, and he's always snooping around the hall, gleaning whatever information he thinks he might be able to use against someone. Mr Whitlock used to home school him, but now that he's ill, Wulfric is often in the garden attacking the shrubs, or in the forest, throwing sticks.

'What he did to me,' Wulfric says.

He's standing directly opposite me on the other side of the fence. I straighten, alert to something in his tone that tells me I should listen. 'What did he do to you, Wulfric?'

He turns and looks at Sylvan, checking he can't hear. 'Promise you won't tell?'

'I promise.'

He steps forward, his expression softening. 'He told me I'd feel different for a while. He said I might even get sick. But he said it would be OK because at least I'd survive.'

I try to work out what he's talking about. His expression is unreadable, his head twitching. I know whatever he has told me is the truth, but I don't understand it.

'Wulfric, what did your grandfather do to you?'

He takes another step forward, and suddenly he looks afraid.

'Mabel? Is that you?'

Mrs Whitlock's voice rings out through the woods. Fear streaks across Wulfric's face, and he bursts into a lumbering run in the opposite direction. I watch him disappear through the trees, his words still hanging in the air.

'Good afternoon,' Mrs Whitlock says. I try not to look at her, but it's difficult to hide my confusion at Wulfric's comment. My mind is doing cartwheels.

'I thought you and Sylvan could do with some cheering up,' Mrs Whitlock says, recoiling at the smell of the coop. 'I thought we might have some lunch. Do you want to join me inside?'

She takes us to the dining room in Lichen Hall, where Rahmi has cooked the most delicious-smelling food. I can't help but stare at the tray as she places it on the table before us, lifting the silver lids to reveal a whole cooked chicken, a plate piled high with roast potatoes, and a bowl of peas with a knob of butter melting into them. Sylvan and I have been eating nothing but boiled carrots and potatoes for weeks.

'Here you go, dear,' Mrs Whitlock says, sitting down next to us. 'There's cake for pudding.'

Sylvan and I don't look sideways until the chicken is stripped clean and the pile of potatoes reduced to a gleaming film of oil on the plate. Sylvan lifts the gravy boat, swipes his finger inside to gather up the residue, then sucks it. I don't tell him off.

'I wondered if you and I could have a little chat,' Mrs Whitlock says quietly. She glances over at Sylvan, and I realize she wants to speak to me in private. She lifts the lid on another dish and reveals a banana cake, glistening in the dim light of the chandelier.

'Would you like a slice, Sylvan?' she asks him. He nods eagerly, his head of dark curls bouncing. She lifts the cake slice and cuts slowly into the layers, placing a thick wodge on a plate. She passes it to him, and he stuffs it into his mouth without a word.

Mrs Whitlock rises from her chair and moves to the fireplace. I follow, enjoying the warmth of the fire behind me. The crackle and snap of the wood in the grate.

'How *did* Sylvan know that Morven's body was in the ice house?' she asks.

'I don't really know,' I say, cautious about why she's asking such a thing.

'It seems a remarkable coincidence. If I recall, he mentioned that he could see her in the ice cream place. Interesting, isn't it? Because that is indeed what the ice house was built for.'

I lower my eyes, too afraid to nod. I need to protect him.

'He's never had ice cream,' I say, because I don't want to agree with her.

She pauses. 'I've heard of people who can see things that others can't. Would you say that Sylvan has such a gift?'

'He's very special.'

'I have a dear friend, Gwendolyn, whose oldest son, Rafe, went missing a few years ago,' she says. 'They believe he's alive, as he seems to have upped and left the family home, but without leaving any indication of where he was going. Rafe's an adult, but nonetheless she has worried herself to the point of a breakdown about his whereabouts. She's coming over for coffee tomorrow morning. Would you be agreeable to Sylvan having a conversation with Gwen?'

So this is what she wants from me. I look over at Sylvan. He's so very young, and I am deeply wary of allowing him to participate in such a thing. And I'm not even sure if it really is a gift. Maybe it's all just lucky guessing.

'I know what you're thinking,' Mrs Whitlock says. 'You're worried about putting pressure on the little chap. You're worried he might get upset.'

I lift my eyes to hers, and her smile widens, the flicker of the fire lighting up her face in a strange grimace.

'Why don't you both stay here tonight?' she says then.

'In the hall?'

'There's quite a nip in the air tonight, don't you think? I'll have Rahmi make up a lovely warm bed. And tomorrow, *if* he's feeling up to it, perhaps Sylvan can simply meet with my friend. Just meet with her.' Her pale eyes glimmer, dangerous as knives. 'No pressure.'

The thought of staying in the warmth of the hall is a small

comfort. Our hut is cosy, but sleeping without Morven in my arms is still a nightly torture.

'All right,' I say, guarded. But ghosts are stirring in my veins, and I can't put my finger on why I feel so scared.

5

The next morning, Aretta brings Sylvan and me breakfast in bed.

'What's she up to?' she mouths at me.

I shake my head, holding her in a look. She nods, understanding that I can't tell her. Not while Sylvan is here.

'Why are we here, Mummy?' Sylvan asks, staring out at the gardens from the huge window.

'Mrs Whitlock thought we could have a sleepover.'

'What's a sleepover?'

I dip a hairbrush in a bowl of water to comb his hair, flattening his dark curls. 'Today we're meeting one of Mrs Whitlock's friends.'

'Why?' His tone is sour.

'Just to say hello.'

'Can't we go home?'

'Of course we can. But first, we'll say hello to Mrs Whitlock's friend. OK?'

'If we have to.'

We eat our breakfast at the table by the window. Not long after, a car pulls up, and I watch from the window as a woman gets out. She's wearing a wide burgundy hat with a matching coat. Mrs Whitlock greets her with a kiss on each cheek.

'It's Gwendolyn,' Sylvan says, dipping his toast soldiers in his egg. 'Isn't it?'

Mrs Whitlock calls up the stairs before I can answer. 'Mabel? Would you and Sylvan like to come and meet Gwendolyn?'

Sylvan cocks his head. 'Why does she want us to meet her?'

'She wants to ask you a few questions about her son,' I say, struggling to lie convincingly. 'She doesn't know where he is, and she thinks maybe you'll be able to see where he is.'

Surprisingly, he nods, as though this makes sense to him.

'How does she know about my funny eye?' he asks. 'The one that sees things?'

'I'm not sure,' I say. A half lie.

I wait until he has finished his breakfast before taking him downstairs. We find Mrs Whitlock in the Willow room sitting opposite the woman with the burgundy hat. Gwendolyn is around Mrs Whitlock's age, with short silver hair peeking out from beneath the hat, long earrings, and kind eyes. Her face lights up when she sees Sylvan, who eyes her warily.

Mrs Whitlock rises from her seat. She plays the part of the gracious hostess remarkably well. 'Sylvan, Mabel, allow me to introduce you both to Mrs McTiernan.'

'Call me Gwen, I insist,' the woman says, reaching out to shake my hand. She bends down to Sylvan. 'You must be Sylvan,' she says. 'How dapper you look in your little suit! And I love your hair. I used to have curls just like that.' She throws me a warm smile. 'You have a handsome little boy.'

'Thank you,' I say, warmed by her compliment. Sylvan looks nothing like me. Sometimes I wish I could see a little bit of myself in him, just to feel like he's mine.

Sylvan touches his hair, frustrated that his curls have bounced up again despite my best efforts to flatten them. Something on his hand catches my eye. A glimmer of light.

'Should we sit by the window?' Mrs Whitlock says, gesturing at the round white table in the bay window, long blue curtains held back at either side with brass hooks in the shape of willow branches. The table has already been set, a fresh pot of tea sending a feather of steam into the air, and a cake stand laden with cream scones and pastries.

I try not to stare at Sylvan as we take our seats. I try not to stare as Mrs Whitlock begins to explain to Sylvan that Gwen is an old friend, and has travelled some distance. She has a son, she says, who she misses very much.

'Is your son called Rafe?' Sylvan says then.

Gwen's face falls. She glances at Mrs Whitlock, then sits back in her chair, fanning herself. Mrs Whitlock turns to me; for a moment, there is gratitude in her eyes.

'Can you see him?' Gwen whispers to Sylvan, tears welling.

'Is there any banana cake?' Sylvan asks, poking suspiciously at the scones.

'Later,' Mrs Whitlock says briskly. 'Tell us more about Rafe, please, Sylvan. What can you see?'

He looks down at his hands, visibly disappointed by the absence of banana cake. Mrs Whitlock must spot this as well, for she corrects herself.

'If you speak with Gwen just now and tell her everything you see, I'll get you a whole banana cake just to yourself. OK?'

'A whole cake?' he exclaims.

She nods. I spot a dot of light wiggle on the side of his face. I worry in case Gwen and Mrs Whitlock see it. What will they think?

But, for now, they seem too transfixed by Sylvan's gift to notice. 'There's a beach,' he says, sitting up on his knees, getting comfortable. 'It's very hot.'

'Where? Which beach?' Gwen asks.

'I don't know,' Sylvan says with a shrug. He pokes the top of a pastry and sucks his finger, visibly enjoying the taste. 'The water's really blue,' he says, his finger in his mouth. 'There are some huts, like ours, only nicer. They're by the water. I think Rafe lives in one of them.'

Gwen claps her hands to her mouth and bursts into sobs. 'He's alive,' she says. 'Oh my God. That's all I ever wanted.'

'Is he safe, Sylvan?' Mrs Whitlock asks.

'Safe?' Sylvan queries. 'What do you mean by safe?'

I lean towards him. 'Does Rafe look happy?'

Sylvan pokes his finger in another pastry. I go to tell him not to.

'It's all right,' Mrs Whitlock says graciously. 'He can have all the pastries he likes.'

'Rafe is smiling,' Sylvan says. 'I think he likes the ocean. He takes a big table out and stands on it on the waves.'

'A table?' Mrs Whitlock says, looking to me for explanation.

'Is it a surfboard, Sylvan?' I ask.

He gives a shrug. 'It's red and pointy.'

I flick my eyes at Gwen and Mrs Whitlock to say yes, that sounds like a surfboard.

'Oh, but he needs to be careful, 'cos there are sharks in that ocean. And jellyfish. Oh, did you know that jellyfish aren't *actually* made of jelly?'

'What's he doing right now?' Gwen whispers, tears falling freely down her cheeks.

'I just told you,' Sylvan says. 'He's on the table. He's not even falling over.'

'Can you speak to him for us?' Mrs Whitlock asks. 'You know, send him a message?'

Sylvan sits back on his heels, considering this. He shakes his head.

'Does he look happy?' Gwen asks.

'I think so,' Sylvan says.

They ask more questions, trying to ascertain whereabouts Rafe lives, though it isn't long before they realize that Sylvan is only five years old. He has never been beyond the grounds of Lichen Hall.

'Oh,' he says suddenly, and we all straighten.

'What is it?' Gwen asks anxiously.

'There's a woman with a big belly. She lives in the hut with Rafe.'

'A big belly?' Mrs Whitlock asks. 'Do you mean, she's having a baby?'

Sylvan nods. 'It's a boy.'

Gwen gives a loud gasp. I can see Sylvan beginning to tire. He sinks back into the seat, his shoulders slumped. The light has gone.

'I'm sleepy,' he says through a yawn, resting his head against my shoulder. I can see Mrs Whitlock is eager to press him for more, but I lift my eyes to hers and give a small shake of my head.

'Thank you, Sylvan,' she says then, backing down. 'That has been a true gift.'

'It has,' Gwen whispers tearfully. 'It has.'

6

Later, once Gwen has left, Mrs Whitlock brings in another banana cake for Sylvan. While he eats, she sits down beside me. I can tell she wants to ask me something, and I bristle with nerves.

'Gwen is tremendously grateful,' she says. 'I can't quite put into words what she's been through. Today was huge for her. Just to know that Rafe is alive, is well . . . And the mention of the grandchild.' She shakes her head, as though words won't do the moment justice. I nod, but I feel uneasy. Part of me had hoped he wouldn't be able to see anything. That his 'gift' would prove to be nothing but a lucky guess.

'I think he could help a *lot* of people,' Mrs Whitlock says. 'Wouldn't you agree?'

I try to force myself to nod, but I can't. Yes, he has the capability of helping people like Gwen, who wish to find her son. But I don't want to put pressure on him. I'm wary of exploiting him. And I saw how tired he grew. He's too young for this.

'Let me make you an offer,' Mrs Whitlock says. 'If you and Sylvan were to remain here, and offer Sylvan's gifts to help people, I would ensure that Sylvan would receive the finest education.'

I glance over at him, lifting chunks of banana cake to his mouth with both hands.

'He wouldn't have to travel?' I ask.

She shakes her head. 'I would invite people in need of his help to come to Lichen Hall.'

My shoulders lower. Nobody wants to come to Lichen Hall. At least, nobody in the region. 'How long would we have to stay?'

'Well, we can decide that. I mean, you've been here for years already. It's not like you have anywhere to go *to*, is it?'

I look down at my hands. Of course I don't. I never want to go back home. But for the first time in many years, I feel trapped. Morven is gone, and it has been torturous, being here when she isn't.

'How many people would he have to see?' I ask, thinking back to how drained he was before.

She mulls this over. 'Once a week? I think that's fair, isn't it? An hour a week in exchange for the best education money can buy?'

I want to ask what such an education entails, but there isn't really any point. I left school at fifteen, and my schooling was poor, at best. I have nothing to compare it to.

'He gets sick sometimes,' I say then. 'His lungs. Especially when it's wet and cold. It's like he can't breathe properly.'

'I see.'

'I think he needs a doctor.'

She hesitates. 'We can look into that. Does he wheeze, at all?'

I know how much she hates doctors. She's never called one for any of the pregnant girls who have stayed at the hall, not even when they got into difficulties during labour. 'Yes. And there's a rattle in his chest, sometimes. It frightens me.'

She nods. 'I'll have Aretta set up a bedroom for him. He can sleep inside the hall, on the nights prior to a sighting. Agreed?'

I wish he could sleep inside *every* night. 'What about food?' I say, glancing at Sylvan reaching across the table towards the cake.

She raises her eyebrows. 'My dear, you ask for rather a lot in exchange for a small act of service.' My cheeks flame, and I shrink into myself. She follows my gaze to him. 'Perhaps a hot meal when he stays here. That's the best I can do. Agreed?'

I nod, and she beams. 'Good.' Then, glancing over at Sylvan: 'Another slice of cake, my love?'

7

That night, I dream of Sylvan. He's looking for Morven.

I see my son wandering through a forest at night, only he is a lantern drifting through a shadowy sea of eyes and knives. From a lampless corner of the forest, a darker shadow stirs, moving after him, curious about him.

He senses he's being followed. He can feel those hideous eyes watching him, and he starts to move faster. Perhaps, he thinks, if he finds Morven, she'll protect him from his pursuer.

The shadow wants to touch him. Perhaps it could slip inside his skin for a while.

Sylvan is lost, and he's tiring. The cold damp air of the forest is difficult for him to breathe. He wonders if maybe he's mistaken – maybe the person following him is actually Morven.

And so he turns, hoping to see her there, laughing at him, ready to pick him up for a cuddle.

But what he sees is a creature he can't describe, formless and reaching for him. And as he opens his mouth in a high-pitched scream, the lights in him burn so fiercely that the shadow shrinks away, though not before its name has drifted into Sylvan's mind.

When I wake, Sylvan isn't lying beside me. I hurry from the hut and find him trembling on the forest floor, close to where we found the arrowhead years before. He can't speak for crying, and I ache for him. I lift him and hold him close to me, too furious at myself for not waking sooner to be scared of anything that hides in the woods.

At home, he turns away from me in our small bed. I see a small light moving along his collarbone.

'You're going to kill me,' he says with a whimper. 'You want me to burn in the fire.'

His words land like blows. I look over his sweet face, at his soft brown eyes that hold no guile. Why would he say such a thing?

'Do you know why?' I whisper. The words are hard to say.

'Because of what I am.'

I reach out and take his hand in mine. 'I would never, ever hurt you,' I say gently.

A shadow falls across his face.

'But you will.'

Just five years old, filled with such terrible knowledge.

My son.

IV

Now

Pearl

Lichen Hall, Scottish Borders, November 1965

1

Sebastian doesn't come on Friday as he promised.

I don't know why I'm surprised. Perhaps I hoped he would at least turn up and explain himself. But he doesn't.

I manage to ring home. I speak to my mother. I ask her why she and Dad haven't come to pick me up. I try, and fail, not to cry.

'Your father,' she says through angry tears, 'is divorcing me.'

She tells me they're having money problems, just like Sebastian said. Mum had an affair, but then it turned sour, and the man she fell for blackmailed her. She paid the money he requested, but Dad's business was struggling – the money she used was intended to pay creditors. The result? They can't afford to support me at home. They're selling the house, and Charlie's moving to Glasgow to take up a trainee position at an architecture firm. They need me to stay at Lichen Hall while the dust settles.

They've already spoken to Mrs Whitlock, who of course agreed. They've arranged for me to work in service here for my keep.

I'm not sure which is worse – learning that my parents are penniless and set to divorce, or that I'm to stay at Lichen Hall as an unpaid servant without any consultation or warning from my parents beforehand. Coming on the heel of Sebastian's betrayal and the loss of Little One, it feels unbearable.

I suppose I could simply refuse. I could walk right out of the gates and ask Lucy if I can stay with her until I get myself sorted. But the fight is knocked clean out of me. I have nothing left to give.

I go back upstairs to my room and unpack my things slowly, trying not to cry out of sheer fury. I had expected to be sleeping in my own bed tonight. I had looked forward to seeing my cats. Instead, I'll be here, in the employment of Mrs Whitlock. I feel as stupid as I do shell-shocked by this turn of events.

I hear voices downstairs. Quickly I put down my things and poke my head outside the door, listening, hoping it's Sebastian. But it isn't. Outside the window I see a familiar car – the silver Rolls-Royce, grand and gleaming as a royal procession. I walk carefully along the corridor and glance down through the loops of the stairwell. I catch sight of Sylvan moving through the hall. So he's here again, meeting with that same couple, and the little girl. What exactly is going on?

I take off my shoes and pad lightly across the landing, taking the stairs quickly while trying to concoct a story about why I'm snooping. I'll say I was cleaning. A washcloth fell and the wind must have caught it, so I'm searching everywhere.

I'm almost at the bottom of the stairs when a door opens, and I freeze. Mabel steps outside and the door closes abruptly after her. I hear Mrs Whitlock on the other side of the door, and Sylvan's voice calling after his mother. Mabel doesn't see me. She's too upset. I watch her stand against the wall next to the door, tipping her head back with a sigh. She reaches into her pocket for a handkerchief and dabs her eyes.

'Mabel,' I whisper. She starts, and I approach her with a

finger to my lips. I nod at the side door and she follows me outside.

We're in the garden. I check behind in case anyone has followed us.

'I thought you left,' she says, drying her eyes.

'Long story,' I say with a sigh. 'Are you all right?'

She nods, then shakes her head. 'I've always sat with him, before. He hates being left alone like that. It's not a sighting, it's an interrogation.'

'*What's* an interrogation?' I say. 'And what's a *sighting*? Who are those people?'

Mabel tells me that Sylvan has a gift. He can see beyond the here and now, like a fortune teller, but without the crystal ball. She's not sure how he does it, but it seems he's always been able to perceive things about people, including those who have died, or people he has never met. Once Mrs Whitlock clued into this she started arranging for Sylvan to perform 'sightings' for people in need. Nobody from the region, of course, as they'd likely only come armed with pitchforks. Mrs Whitlock has used her connections to invite people from further afield – London, mostly, but others from Aberdeen, Edinburgh, Oxford, and often from overseas.

I'm still trying to wrap my head around the idea that a child can see into the future.

I don't believe in such things. I don't believe in an afterlife, or God, or mysticism in general. But then, I also don't believe in headless supernatural beings haunting ancient woodland, but I've seen one of those. And I remember how Sylvan knew that Little One's name was going to be Sienna, that he asked about Sebastian before I'd mentioned him.

I guess my capacity for believing in the impossible has stretched recently.

'It used to be mostly people whose loved ones had gone missing,' Mabel says. 'Most of the time, Sylvan would be able to give enough details to let them know that their loved ones were all right, or in some cases, he was able to provide enough evidence to show they'd been killed, and who had done it.'

'That sounds like he did something marvellous,' I say, and she nods.

'I understand that they're desperate,' she says. 'But it drains him. And you know how poorly he's been. He's not well enough for a sighting today, but Mrs Whitlock won't have it.'

'Of course,' I say. She's right – he should be resting.

'He got much better in January,' Mabel says. 'I really thought he was on the mend. But after the summer he's started to get ill again, just like before. Mrs Whitlock said she'd call a doctor if he gets any worse, but I'm beginning to think she's lying.'

'How long has she been saying this?' I say. 'Has Sylvan *ever* seen a doctor?'

She shakes her head, and I can tell she feels ashamed.

'She said she'd make sure he'd get a good education,' Mabel says, tears filling her eyes. 'She said doctors take a while to see patients, so I've been waiting. But it's been almost three months since he fell ill again.'

I listen carefully to the arrangements she made with Mrs Whitlock for Sylvan's services, his 'sightings'. Occasionally, he and Mabel are allowed to sleep in the hall. They are able to eat good food while at the hall, too, and, more importantly, the promise of a good education for Sylvan means that his future is assured.

Mabel well knows that the odds are stacked against a boy like Sylvan, raised as he is by an unwed mother in little more than a shack. But he turned six a few weeks ago; he should be in school by now. The thought of Mrs Whitlock reneging on this promise sends a new flash of anger through me.

'I'm assuming these people pay for Sylvan's sightings,' I say.

Mabel shrugs. 'I've never asked.'

I can't imagine Mrs Whitlock hosting sightings out of the

goodness of her heart. I think back bitterly to the strange performance she put on right when I went into labour, cowering and whimpering like a frightened child. She's like Jekyll and Hyde, but none of it genuine. She adopts whatever persona she feels will manipulate the situation for her own gain.

I tell Mabel that I spotted Sylvan when I first arrived at Lichen Hall, but everyone pretended he didn't exist.

'Why was that?' I ask. 'Was that Mrs Whitlock's doing?'

'She told me we were to stay out of sight,' Mabel says bitterly, her eyes brimming with fresh tears. She swipes one from her cheek. 'She said we weren't to speak to anyone, even the people who came for sightings. She wanted to keep Sylvan safe. That's what she said.'

Safe, my arse. Mrs Whitlock's making sure no one knows he's here. I bet his birth was never even registered.

Mabel and I take the path through the garden towards the ocean. The wind finds us, tussling our hair, and it is both torture and relief to see the horizon in front of us.

'You said it was an interrogation,' I say then. 'What are they doing to him in there?'

'That's the thing,' Mabel says. 'It used to be people who were really at their wits' end, and I could understand why Mrs Whitlock wanted Sylvan to help them. But these people, they want to know their daughter's future. Like he's a fortune teller.'

She tells me the girl's name is Violetta, the only child of Mr and Mrs Belliston from North Berwick. From the kind of questions they've been asking, it seems they want to know both good and bad events in their daughter's future, to avoid the latter and improve upon the former – as though her life is a game of chess they can rig to their advantage.

'It's confusing for Sylvan,' she says. 'He has no idea how to give them what they want, but they keep coming back, barking orders at him, insisting he tell them what lies ahead.'

We reach the chicken-wire fencing at the end of the garden, hemming us in from the edge of the cliff. Mabel is visibly worn out from grief and stress, and I notice how awful she looks, especially up close – her face blotched red with eczema, similar marks on the backs of her hands. Her brown dress is filthy, and her coat is falling apart, the hem ragged and gaping holes under both arms. Her leather shoes flap open, as though they're talking, clapping against her feet with each step. She could do with seeing a dentist, too. She looks a lot older than her twenty-three years; living in that horrible hut must be taking a hard toll on her. And on Sylvan.

'I know she's promised a good education for Sylvan,' I say carefully, 'but it sounds like you need to find work elsewhere. At a different home. I'm sure there must be other jobs you could find.'

'Jobs?' she says, and I remember – like Aretta and Rahmi she's a slave, living and toiling at Lichen Hall for nothing.

'We'd better head back,' Mabel says then. 'I don't want Sylvan to think I've left him.'

We turn and walk quickly across the garden, my mind racing. 'Sylvan isn't well enough to stay here,' I tell her. 'You know that, don't you?'

'Of course I do,' she says in a small voice.

'Has he had his vaccinations?'

She looks puzzled. 'What vaccinations?'

'To protect him against whooping cough, for example?'

She shakes her head. I draw a sharp breath.

'What about diphtheria? Tuberculosis? Polio?'

She looks deeply sad, and I feel bad for pushing her. But these are important vaccinations. Even if he manages to survive these illnesses, they can cause permanent damage.

'He needs to see a doctor,' I say gently. *And he needs to be in school*, I think, *and have friends who aren't chickens, and live in a proper house.*

'I can take care of him,' she says solemnly. 'Morven taught me.'

I bite my lip. It's clear that Mabel loves her son, and that she's worked hard to care for them both. But I wonder if she realizes what she's risking by keeping Sylvan here.

Now

Mabel

Lichen Hall, Scottish Borders, November 1965

1

Pearl and I walk back along the path towards the hall, but instead of going inside I make for the window of the Wisteria room, hiding by the drainpipe to peer inside. Pearl hides behind me.

'What can you see?' she whispers.

Sylvan is sitting on a chair near the window, but his shoulders are rounded, and I can tell he's tiring. The little girl – Violetta – sits cross-legged on the floor near Sylvan, playing with a toy. Just behind the door, I can see a table with an electric fan on it, and I freeze.

I've noticed this before, Mrs Whitlock's strange habit of setting up an electric table fan in the room where Sylvan gives his sightings. I thought it was simply to keep him cool, but even on days like today, when the air has a nip to it, she sets up that fan. A week ago, I spotted her through the crack in the door before a sighting began – she was setting a small handful of something on the table before the fan. When the couple arrived, she switched on the fan and something flew up into the air: tiny little grains, like salt. Just like when Sylvan was born, I thought – that strange ritual she'd performed.

'Do you know what year it is, Sylvan?' I hear Mrs Whitlock ask.

Sylvan gives a weak shake of his head. 'The woman is sitting in the office with a man,' he says, licking his lips. 'The woman's name is Violetta.'

'And who is the man?' someone asks.

Sylvan's head nods, as though he's falling asleep.

'Sylvan?'

He starts. 'I don't know his name.'

'Well, what are they *doing* in the office?' Mr Belliston demands, and I wince. I hate how he speaks to my son. I want to run in there and scream in his face.

Suddenly Mr Belliston marches up to Sylvan and grabs him by his shoulders. 'Are they getting married?' he shouts. 'Is she signing papers? What?'

My stomach lurches. *We have to get him out of there*, Pearl mouths at me. I want so much to get him out of there, but I know that if I interfere with the sighting we'll lose everything I've agreed with Mrs Whitlock. We'll lose Sylvan's future.

Mr Belliston lets go of Sylvan, who sits limply in the chair. 'Is this a scam?' Mr Belliston says.

'I beg your pardon?' Mrs Whitlock answers.

'Well, the boy hasn't told us anything, has he? We've paid damn good money for these "sightings", as you call them, and all we've had is some vague depictions of things that make little sense.'

Mrs Whitlock says something I can't make out, but her tone is icy, and I can imagine her telling Mr Belliston that Sylvan's reputation was well established. To a small group of privileged people, Sylvan is a saviour, or a savant. They cling on to his every word.

I'm so caught up in this train of thought that I don't notice Pearl stepping past me and marching around the corner towards the side door.

'Pearl!' I hiss after her. 'Don't!'

She ignores me. A few seconds later, I follow after, finding myself in the house heading into the room where Sylvan is giving his sighting. I creep behind her, my whole body cold with fear.

'Pearl?' I hear Mrs Whitlock say.

Through the crack in the door I see Pearl standing before Mrs Whitlock and the Bellistons, her hands clasped confidently and her shoulders squared.

'I *do* apologize, ladies and gentlemen,' she says in a loud, clear voice. 'But as Sylvan's nurse I'm afraid I must interrupt the session today due to his having viral rhinitis. This is a *highly contagious* condition, and I apologize for not warning you sooner. Come along, Sylvan. We must away until your condition improves.'

'Viral rhinitis?' I hear Mrs Belliston say. She throws a look of disgust at Mr Belliston, who wipes his hands on his suit jacket.

Sylvan follows Pearl out of the room, then she takes him by the hand, walking quickly past me and heading upstairs. I follow, all the way to Pearl's bedroom at the top.

'There they go,' Pearl says, looking out of the window at the Bellistons' car below. 'Assholes.'

Fear has knocked the wind clean out of me, and I sink down on to the bed next to Sylvan. He is pale and weak, dark circles beneath his eyes that I didn't notice before. I listen hard for the sound of Mrs Whitlock's footsteps. She won't be pleased at Pearl for cancelling the sighting so abruptly. She'll make us pay for it.

'What is viral rhinitis?' I ask Pearl.

'It's the Latin for a common cold,' she says, looking over at Sylvan. 'So I wasn't exactly lying.'

'I'm worried,' I say. 'What if she kicks us out now?'

'Oh, I don't think she'll do that,' Pearl says, but my skin is bristling with fear. Everything that I've worked so hard for could be undone because of this. All the promises Mrs Whitlock made about Sylvan's education – she could decide that I've breached my end of the bargain. The Bellistons are bullies, and they'll be furious about Pearl's intrusion. They'll have questions. They'll probably blame Mrs Whitlock for it all. And in turn, she'll want payback.

Footsteps sound on the stairs. I freeze, my stomach lurching. I'd know those footsteps anywhere.

'Mabel?' Mrs Whitlock calls in a shrill voice. 'Sylvan?'

Pearl gets to her feet and nods at me. 'Stay here, and don't make a sound,' she says firmly. Then she steps outside into the hallway and shuts the door behind her. I am turned inside out with panic.

'Mummy,' Sylvan says weakly. His voice is little more than a croak, and his lips have turned a deep purple. For a terrible moment, I think he's dying. I move towards him and take his hand. It's breathtakingly limp. I stroke his face. I don't dare breathe until I see his chest move.

Pearl comes back in and shuts the door behind her. She looks pleased with herself.

'I told her that Sylvan is very ill with a highly contagious viral infection and that as I have already been exposed to it, I will be caring for him.'

'And she was OK with it?' I say.

Pearl smiles. 'I reminded her that she'd hardly want to risk Sylvan falling ill and never being able to sight again.'

Pearl must see how distraught I am, because her face changes, softening into concern.

'Are you all right?' she says, and I nod, but tears brim in my eyes. I'm still holding Sylvan's limp hand. *He's asleep*, I tell myself. *Not dead. He isn't gone.*

He can't go.

2

Pearl acts quickly; she tells me to run a hot bath and add drops of eucalyptus oil while she turns Sylvan on his side to get air into his lungs. I carry Sylvan into the bathroom, holding him on my lap on the floor while he breathes in the steam. His chest is so raspy it frightens me. He falls asleep in my arms. After an hour, his breaths sound clearer, less wet.

'He needs to eat,' Pearl says. 'I'll go downstairs and make him some food.'

I carry Sylvan back into the bedroom and lay him on the bed. 'Are you OK, Mum?' he asks in a hoarse voice, his little face staring up at me.

'Yes, of course I am.'

'You're worried,' he says, his eyebrows knitting together. 'You're worried about Mrs Whitlock.'

I study his face. We've had the conversation so many times about what he can see. But I feel frightened. Ever since that day in the woods, when he told me I would kill him, I have feared his gift. I've never told anyone what he said. But what if he's right? What if I harm him without realizing it?

I've considered leaving Lichen Hall, letting Aretta and Rahmi raise him here. The terror of his prediction coming true makes me frantic. If I leave, the risk of the sighting coming true is removed. But I can't leave him. I can't.

'Here we are,' Pearl says, coming back into the room with a tray of food. 'Hot chicken soup, buttered bread, some cooked meats and chopped vegetables. Oh, and I got you both some nice hot tea.'

'Do you miss Sebastian?' Sylvan asks Pearl.

I can tell Pearl's interest is piqued. She sets the tray down on the bed, then sits down and smiles at Sylvan. 'Glad to see you're a little better. You've mentioned him before, I think. How do you know about Sebastian?'

Sylvan tilts his head thoughtfully. A pinhead of light swirls across his jaw.

'There's a tree in a garden that links your houses. A sycamore tree.'

Pearl nods. 'Yes. Yes, there is. But, how did you . . . ?'

'Sebastian hurt you, didn't he? He told lies.'

I watch as Pearl's face falls. She leans in, listening hard. Sylvan gives a long yawn, and the light in his jaw slips up his cheek. He gives a little shudder, as though he's cold. I wonder if he can possibly feel the light inside him, as though it's an entity, or a temperature.

'Is there anything you want to ask him?' I ask Pearl gently. 'Questions about the past, or future?'

'My little girl,' Pearl says. 'Is she happy?'

Sylvan tilts his head. 'Sienna, you mean?'

Pearl catches her breath, shocked all over again by his ability. 'Yes.'

'She likes the woman,' Sylvan says. 'The woman sings to her. She thinks about you. She wonders where you've gone.'

I see Pearl's eyes brim with tears, and she presses a hand to her cheek. 'God,' she says, shaking her head. 'I should be careful what I ask. It might break me.' She bites her lip. 'One last question. Will I ever be a nurse again?'

'A nurse?' he asks, confused by the meaning of the word.

'It's someone who helps sick people in hospital, remember?' I tell him. He's never been inside a hospital, nor outside the gates of Lichen Hall, but I've given him lessons about the world beyond, with pictures from books we found in the store cupboard. He knows what a hospital is.

Sylvan squints at something across the room. Pearl does the same thing as every other adult I've witnessed in this situation – she tries to see what he's looking at. But she won't, and never will. Nor will I. There's a skin removed from the world that only Sylvan can see. He describes it as a cloud filled with images and whispers. He just has to think about the person in front of him and the cloud shows him things. He says the images in the cloud have become clearer, faster, and sometimes they confuse him.

'You're in a hospital,' he says. 'You're walking down a corridor with a man. I think you work there.'

'Am I wearing a white cap?' she asks hopefully, describing her uniform.

He shakes his head, and Pearl looks a little deflated. 'Well,' she says after a few moments. 'At least I work there. That's all that matters.' Then, brightening: 'Maybe I'll be a doctor.'

Pearl is concerned about his physical well-being, and rightly so. But above all, it's the mind of my little boy I worry about. He saw Morven's body, but he couldn't understand that he was seeing a corpse. What happens when he does understand?

What happens when he knows he can see rape and murder?

His eyes are growing heavy, and the light moving in his fingers is duller than before.

'Perhaps it's time for supper,' I say gently. But he's already asleep.

3

'I appreciate what you did earlier,' I tell Pearl as Sylvan sleeps. 'I know I didn't show it at the time. But you handled it well.'

She gives a warm grin. 'I worried I was maybe being a Meddling Martha.'

'What's a Meddling Martha?'

'Just a name my mum used to give to people who interfered.'

'I think you're just a Passionate Pearl.'

She looks pleased. 'Nobody's ever called me passionate.'

'I find that surprising.'

'Bossy, irritating, know-it-all . . .' she says with a grin. 'Never passionate.' She glances at Sylvan. 'It's interesting, how he has this kind of glow about him during a sighting. Has he always had that?'

'I saw it when he was just born.'

'Really?' she says, fascinated. 'That must have freaked you out.'

I shake my head. 'Not really. I always knew he was special. When I saw his skin shine, it just confirmed it.'

'Does it run in the family?'

'What do you mean?'

'You know, Sylvan's gift. Did his father have the sight?'

I shake my head. 'He doesn't have a father.'

She gives me a pitiful look. 'Oh, I'm sorry. Did he die?'

'No, I mean he literally doesn't have a father.' I eye her nervously. 'He's a ghost baby.'

She looks confused. 'A *ghost* baby?'

I bite my lip, feeling a ghost squirm in my neck at the silence that seemed to stretch for ever.

'I had never had sex before I had Sylvan,' I say.

'You don't have to have full sex to fall pregnant,' she says gently. 'I treated a girl once who swore blind she was a virgin. And when we examined her, her hymen was intact. She'd managed to fall pregnant without penetration.'

'What's a hymen?'

'It's a small membrane inside your vagina,' she says, and I'm astonished that she said 'vagina' without flinching. 'Nobody really knows why it's there. Like it doesn't really do anything, it's just there. Usually, it breaks the first time you have sex, which is why it's so painful.'

Something moves in my head, and it feels like one of the ghosts has painted a picture across my mind. I'm in my bedroom back in Dundee, and it's dark. Someone is walking out of the room, and I try to open my eyes but I can only do it a little bit.

'Mabel?'

I snap back into the room. Pearl is leaning towards me, her face folded in concern. I must have shut down without realizing it.

'Sorry,' I tell her. 'I . . .'

'Do you do that a lot?'

'Do . . . do what?'

'I don't know the exact word for it,' Pearl says, moving back to her spot on the floor. 'My cousin Eliot used to do that. He'd kind of go blank sometimes. You'd see something change in his face and you knew he wasn't even in the room anymore.'

Go blank. That's exactly what I do.

I think back to the day I found out I was pregnant. I remember standing in the butcher's and going blank, all the ghosts taking over my thoughts, my body. 'I've done this for years,' I tell Pearl, and my body is suddenly trembling, as though my words are dangerous. 'I once wrote a note to our butcher, telling him my stepdad was going to kill Ma. I have no idea why . . .' I tail off, because actually, I think I *do* know why. I had just learned that I was pregnant. I was terrified. I had no control over anything. Maybe the note was a way of regaining that control. Or because Richard . . .

'I've seen a few patients do it, too,' Pearl continues gently. 'With Eliot, he had a terrible episode when he was young. He saw something and he never recovered from it. Emotionally, I mean.'

'What did he see?'

She gives a sad sigh. 'He saw his best friend drown. They went out on a fishing trip with his dad. God, he was only thirteen.'

'How did he drown?'

'I don't know. Eliot would never talk about it. He and the boy's father tried everything they could, but . . .' She doesn't finish her sentence. 'And ever since, Eliot would sometimes do what you just did. One minute he was there, the next . . .'

I look over at Sylvan, fast asleep. It chills me to think I might lose him.

'Anyway,' Pearl says. 'What were we talking about?'

'Sex,' I said. 'And hymens.'

'Oh, right. And you were saying how you had never had sex but you still conceived Sylvan.'

I can feel it happening this time. The shutting down. As though her words have triggered another room inside this one, a room only I can see, a room which only I can enter. I feel a part of me slip into it, this inner room, and I'm looking back at myself in this room.

Only, the room has changed. It's my bedroom back in the guest house in Dundee. I can hear a noise – a rhythmic *thump thump thump*. The sound of a headboard banging against the wall. I feel the ghosts curl up inside me, terrified.

Finally, the bed stops banging. I hear a door open, then close.

I open my eyes. Pearl's sitting close to me again, leaning forward, her hand on mine.

'Are you OK?'

I go to answer, but my voice has disappeared. Suddenly my jaw goes tight, and my body starts to shake. First my hands, then my arms and legs. I can't stop it.

I look at Sylvan on the bed, but suddenly I'm in that other room, the inner room. My bedroom. It's night. I'm in bed, pretending to be asleep. I can hear every sound, every knock of the bedframe against the wall.

'Excuse me,' I hear myself say, getting to my feet. 'I have to . . .'

'Mabel, I'm sorry,' Pearl says gently. 'I shouldn't have asked . . .'

I curl up on the floor, feeling my legs and arms tremble. Images flash brightly in my mind.

Richard in my bedroom.

Richard in my bed.

Richard with a hand across my mouth.

Now

Pearl

Lichen Hall, Scottish Borders, November 1965

1

God, poor Mabel. I pull a blanket across her and hold her hand. She's been through so much. I can't imagine raising a child here, with all the craziness. But we need to get him out.

I wait until I'm sure Sylvan and Mabel are fast asleep before slipping out of the room. It's two in the morning, a full moon streaking the floor of the hallway with tigerish shadows. I pad lightly on the soles of my feet towards the staircase, my ears tuned to the noises of the house.

Something has stayed with me since the night I gave birth: Mrs Whitlock's weird episode, right before my waters broke. She mentioned that Mr Whitlock had a car; she said the key was in his bedroom.

Mabel can't drive; neither can Rahmi and Aretta. But I can. Dad taught me when I was young, and I sat my test when I became a nurse.

I want to find that car, and drive us all out of this place, far, far away. Sylvan is gravely ill. We almost lost him tonight, I'm sure of it. I'm trying to keep calm so I don't alarm Mabel, but he urgently needs to go to hospital. His lungs sound like he has bronchitis, or perhaps advanced asthma. He has no business being here. He's just a child.

There are seven outbuildings in the grounds of the hall, not including Mabel's hut, and I *thought* I'd seen inside all of them. But earlier it occurred to me that the long tool shed at the back of the house has another wooden door that is bolted and locked – I suspect the door leads to another room in the outbuilding. There's an old rusted spare tyre propped up against the wall outside the outbuilding. I'll bet anything there's a car locked up in that garage.

I go downstairs to the kitchen. There's a door leading to a boot room where I've seen a key box. I head there, taking the stairs briskly and keeping to the walls to avoid creaking floorboards. So far, so good – no one seems to be awake.

In the boot room, I close the door and pull the light switch, and a few seconds later a naked lightbulb pushes a weak sulphur glow through the darkness. There must be twenty keys of various shapes and sizes hanging from wall hooks – old rusty skeleton keys that look like they've been dredged up from a shipwreck, and small silver keys that might fit a lock.

The gravel courtyard outside is noisy, even when I tiptoe, so I remove the wellies I'd put on and make the rest of the distance barefoot, though the stones hurt the soles of my feet. I see a light through the trees ahead. It's small, like a candle, or perhaps the flame of a lighter . . . I bet anything it's Wulfric, wandering around with that bloody lighter. My first instinct is to leave him to it – I don't want to go anywhere *near* those woods.

It moves, a small gold light. Oh God. I'm going to have to go out there, aren't I? Terrifying images play out in my mind of Wulfric being hunted. If something were actually to happen to him, I'd not be able to live with myself. I have to go and tell him to come inside.

I put my wellies back on and head quickly towards the light, a sudden anger at his foolishness growing in me, propelling me forward. I smell the source of the light – it's a fire, some distance away in the woods. It's a cold, dry night, and I'm worried about the fire spreading. But I'm even more worried that I might encounter that *thing* again, and when something moves in the clearing ahead, I freeze.

Darkness swamps me. I see a plume of breath suspended in the icy air. An animal, or a human. I move away from it towards a clutch of trees, but when I look around again realize I've lost my bearings.

I try to keep the light of the fire ahead of me, squinting at the trees in case I might recognize one and gauge my way. But everything is different at night, twenty times as terrifying. I try hard to keep calm, but my heart is racing, the memory of the headless creature looming large in my mind. The hairs on the back of my neck stand on end, and a sixth sense tells me I'm being followed.

I keep the fire behind me as I push forward, taking care to survey the ground in case I fall like last time. When I look up again, I see a figure standing next to a tree, someone in a hooded cloak, their head tilted down at the ground, and a scream rises in my throat.

'Pssst,' a voice says, and this time I *do* scream, spinning around to feel a hand on mine, a familiar face lit up by a flaming torch. It's Rahmi. Thank God, thank God! It takes a moment to gather myself. I spin back to the spot where I saw the figure, but it's gone.

'I . . . I saw something,' I tell Rahmi, my mouth dry. 'It was right there . . .'

'Take this,' she says, handing me the flaming torch. It's just a stick with twigs and leaves wound around the top end and set alight, but it lifts the darkness, and I feel less vulnerable holding it. 'Go back to the house,' she says, giving me a shove to my left. 'Keep the torch lit. It won't bother you.'

I nod and thank her, breathless with adrenalin. 'What do you mean by "it"?' I ask.

She hesitates. 'Nicnevin. Don't let it touch you.'

'Right.' It dawns on me a second later that she's referring to the witch I read about in Professor Llewellyn's book. I'll believe anything at this point.

I stumble off in the direction she sent me in, my heart racing and my head spinning. At the treeline I turn to check that Rahmi's OK. I see her wrapped in a shawl, heading back to the fire deep in the woods.

2

I head to the outbuilding and try every key in the box, but none of them fit. I'm almost about to give up when I notice a large white stone by the door. Since I was little, my parents have kept a spare key underneath a similar stone at our own front door. I lift the stone and move the fire to illuminate the space below – and there's a key. I lift it triumphantly and slip it inside the lock. It opens and comes loose in my hand.

Inside, there's a sudden flittering of whatever creatures have made this their home. Several large moths bat at the flame, causing me to drop the stick. I catch sight of a large object beneath tarpaulin right before the fire goes out, plunging the place into thickest dark. Leaning forward, I find the tarp with my fingers and pull it free. The shiny paintwork of a car meets my palms. I try a door handle, but it's locked, and a quick feel of the tyres tells me they're almost flat. Goddamn it.

Still, it's a start, finding it here. We can pump up the tyres.

But I need the car key.

I move lightly on my feet back inside the house along the ground floor hallway to Mr Whitlock's bedroom. Placing my hand on the handle, I turn it, slowly, to avoid making any sound. It opens. I can't quite believe I'm doing this, but suddenly I'm inside, my heart leaping with panic.

My eyes adjust to the light. There's a dressing table between two long windows, a sliver of moonlight cutting through the curtain join and falling on the four-poster bed. I listen deeply for the sound of snoring, or heavy breathing, but I hear neither. I map the rhythm of his breaths and move past the bed to the furniture along the far wall.

My fingers meet the lip of a chest of drawers, and I open the drawers carefully, one by one. Nothing but dusty bottles of cologne and shaving foam in there.

I glance at the slim mound in the bed. It must be Mr Whitlock. He's lying flat on his back. Where is his wheelchair? The car key could be anywhere in this room. It could be in a box under the bed, or deep in a cupboard in his dressing room.

I move lightly to the bedside table. There's a lamp on the table, and a cup and saucer, and as soon as I pull open one of the drawers, the cup and saucer gives a rattle.

I freeze, keeping my eyes trained on Mr Whitlock for any sign of disturbance while my hands sift through the contents of the drawer for anything key-like. An old tin cigar box, a Swiss army knife, some notebooks . . . I lift out the tin box, slowly, slowly, then open it to inspect the contents. A medal. He must have fought in the war. I close the box reverently but sweat makes my fingers slip on the tin and I drop it, oh God, the box clangs on the floor with enough noise to wake the dead. I freeze, ice cold, expecting Mr Whitlock to sit sharply upright and spy me in his room. A shout of alarm.

But he doesn't move. Why isn't he moving? There's no movement from his chest, no sound of snoring. He's deathly still.

I bend to reach the tin, but my fingers brush against something else. A key. Quickly I place it inside my pocket, then hold the tin to his nose, counting ten seconds, just to be sure. I remove it, holding it to the moonlight. There's a mist of breath there. Good. But as I place the tin box back in the drawer, I notice something on the saucer that's on the bedside table. A dark petal. With a shiver, I recognize it. It's from the belladonna flower.

'What are you doing?' a voice behind me says.

I almost jump out of my skin. I turn, frantic, and see the tall frame of Wulfric standing by the door. He tilts his head, suspicious.

'Why are you in here?' he says.

'I thought I heard a noise,' I hiss, certain he's seconds away from yelling for his grandmother and telling her I'm snooping around. 'The door was open, so I came in to make sure your grandfather was all right.'

In the dim light I can see he's frowning, considering whether my words add up.

'Let's go back to bed,' I say, walking slowly towards him. 'It's late. You need your sleep.'

'Is he OK?' Wulfric says, turning to look at his grandfather.

'Let's go back to bed,' I tell Wulfric again, eager to get us both out of the room before Mrs Whitlock is alerted.

'Not until you tell me what's wrong with him,' Wulfric says, his voice rising. I lift my hands to quieten him, but I can see he's not leaving without a fuss.

'OK. The truth is, I'm worried about him,' I say, keeping my voice low. 'He hasn't stirred.'

'Why are you worried about him?'

I relent. 'I think he's drunk something poisonous.'

'What do you mean, poisonous?' he says.

I lift the petal from the saucer. 'Belladonna. It's poisonous.'

'It's not poisonous,' he says, taking a step forward to survey the petal. 'It's to help his dementia. Aretta makes it for him.'

I take that in, realization suddenly settling in.

'How long has she been giving it to him?'

He narrows his eyes. 'Why?'

'How long?' I press.

'I don't know. It's meant to help him.'

'And does it?' I ask.

He stares at me. 'How am I supposed to know? My mum said she had to make it for him.'

'Your mum?' I say. 'You mean – your grandmother?'

He nods.

The silence brings us to a terrible mutual knowledge – she's been poisoning Mr Whitlock. Drinking belladonna tea would cause behaviour not unlike heavy inebriation. Heavier doses would cause unconsciousness, hallucinations, paralysis, death . . . I think back to the day I spotted Mr Whitlock on the edge of the field, close to Mabel's hut. He was walking, albeit like someone learning to walk, but on two legs, upright. Aretta said he'd been wheelchair-bound for several years. If he was ingesting belladonna tea, he'd be unable to walk. He'd be unable to wake up.

Wulfric goes back to bed, and I head quickly back to my room, a different fear guiding my steps. There's a violence lurking in Lichen Hall, but not the one I thought.

The one I perceive now lies hidden, coiled up like an asp in a basket of figs, waiting to strike.

Now

Mabel

Lichen Hall, Scottish Borders, November 1965

1

Sylvan seems to be on the mend, thank God. His colour has returned, and this morning he said he felt well enough to go for a walk. I thought some fresh air and sunshine would do him a bit of good, so Aretta and I are helping him walk to the hen house. He walks between us, holding our hands, and we take it slowly through the trees. Aretta has brought a bag of apples for the hens.

At the hen house, Aretta opens the door of the coop and lets him in. The hens cluck and race around him as he hangs the apples from the chains we've attached inside the coop. The hens enjoy pecking at them, and the chains keep them from rotting on the ground.

'Two eggs, Mum!' Sylvan calls back, holding them up for me to see. 'Mildred's laid *two* eggs! Good girl, Mildred!'

I watch him with a fuzziness that is partly caused by stress, and partly due to how stunned I am to realize the truth about who he is. Sylvan isn't a ghost baby. He is Richard's son.

I feel filled with ghosts, every corner of my body squirming and wriggling with them. When I fell in love with Morven they disappeared. But ever since she died, they've been coming back, one by one. Today, my whole body feels as if it might burst under the weight of them.

'Come here, William,' Sylvan says hoarsely, bending to feed the chicken who survived a fox attack. William's right leg is broken and she hobbles around, clucking painfully. No matter how deep we dig into the ground, the foxes always find a way to get in, or snap at a chicken who gets close enough. And oddly, the chickens often want to escape. Despite the terrors that lie beyond the hen house, they seem born to wander, to break free.

I know that Pearl was worried about me last night. One minute we were talking and the next I shut down, like a hermit crab pulling inside its shell. I felt as if I was having an out-of-body experience, the memories pounding me like tidal waves.

'Are you OK?' Aretta says, reading my face.

'I know who Sylvan's father is,' I say carefully, though the words were difficult to speak aloud. 'I thought I'd never had sex, but I had.'

I tell her what I remember. About Richard coming into my room at night. It must have happened for years.

Aretta listens to me as I describe it all in stuttering, incoherent sentences. I have to keep stopping and starting, the ghosts moving around in my bones. I keep focused on the wind that moves through the trees and the light falling through the branches, tiny hen feathers drifting across the understorey.

When I finish, Aretta has tears in her eyes. 'Oh, love. That's not sex.'

'It isn't?'

She shakes her head. 'It's rape.'

I fall silent, processing this word. I've always thought rape was a stranger grabbing you in a dark alley.

Richard is my stepdad. I remember feeling confused when he started coming into my room. And then I became terrified. I started having panic attacks at school for no reason. Twice on the bus home, I vomited. I learned to shut down, to hide inside my skin.

One night, I heard Ma walk past my bedroom to use the toilet. She paused outside the door, and I thought she was about to come in. She would see and she'd throw Richard on to the street. But her footsteps continued on into her bedroom. And I knew then. I had done something to deserve this.

'Are you sure?' I ask Aretta again. 'Are you really, really sure it counts as rape?'

She pulls me into a hug. 'You've gone through hell, haven't you, love?' she says, rubbing my back. She pulls back and fixes me with a stare. 'I swear *on my life* that it counts as rape.'

I can feel myself wanting to shut down again, but I think about the feel of her hands on my arms, about the words she speaks.

'It happened to you, too,' I say. 'Didn't it?'

She doesn't answer for a moment. 'Yes,' she says finally. 'I never told anyone either.'

'Why not?' I say.

'I didn't think they'd believe me.'

She laughs, and I laugh, too.

It seems the only thing to do when everything is so messed up.

2

We head towards the hut, Aretta carrying the basket of eggs with one hand, holding Sylvan's hand with the other. We keep it slow, even though he seems much better than yesterday, moving through the field towards our home.

Suddenly, Sylvan stops.

'What's wrong?' Aretta asks as he bends down to retrieve something from the ground.

'A dandelion clock,' he says. 'To make a wish.'

He takes a deep, raspy breath, then puffs hard, sending the fine silvery seeds into the air around him. We watch for a minute as the seeds scatter on the back of the wind.

It makes me think of the fan Mrs Whitlock sets up in the Wisteria room. I turn to Aretta. 'When you had your baby, did Mrs Whitlock do a ritual on her?'

She thinks for a moment. 'You mean the "fairy dust" thing?'

I nod, and she says yes. 'It was weird. Did she do that to Sylvan?'

Just then, Sylvan says: 'Mummy, you know the fan that Mrs Whitlock puts in the room when I do my sightings?'

'Yes?'

'Why does she do that, Mummy?'

'She says it's to ensure you don't get too hot.'

He pulls a face. I see a light behind one of his eyes, and his mouth falls open.

'Are you all right?' I ask.

'But this is for a wish, not to make them sick,' he says.

'Who? Make who sick?'

He sinks down into the grass, and I lower to my knees in front of him, holding his hands.

'The fan sends them into the air,' he says. 'And they make people sick. Some of them die!'

I look up at Aretta. She's as confused as I am.

'Tell me what you see,' I say.

'Liam,' he says.

'Liam?' I think back – Liam was a little boy we met last year. His parents, Mr and Mrs Delorme, had brought him to Sylvan for a sighting when he fell ill with leukaemia. The doctors had run out of options for his treatment. It was a strange sighting, because Sylvan did something he had never done before – he lied. He told the Delormes that Liam would get better. But later, he told me he saw that Liam would die. I asked him at the time why he told the Delormes a lie, but he was conflicted. He said he'd seen Liam get better, but later he saw him fall ill again.

'Liam died because of what Mrs Whitlock did in the room,' he says, breathless.

'What do you mean?' I ask. 'How could he die because of Mrs Whitlock?'

He looks up, his eyes sunken. 'Because of the spores.'

Spores?

I've spotted Mrs Whitlock placing a pinch of powder by the fan. I had no idea what it was, or how they might make someone sick. But it doesn't matter. And if Sylvan's sighting is true, we are also infected.

But Mrs Whitlock was in the room, too. If she really was placing spores before the fan to be blown up into the air, sickening everyone there, she would also be infected.

Why would she infect herself?

3

Sylvan has a sighting this afternoon, and I feel utterly torn about taking him.

Did Liam die because of the spores?

It doesn't make any sense. Why would Mrs Whitlock want to infect people?

Sylvan must be mistaken. He's only little, after all. He doesn't understand half the things he sees.

I decide I will get him washed and dressed, and insist on holding the sighting in a different room. At the very least, I'll tell Mrs Whitlock that she can't use the electric fan.

But Sylvan has made up his own mind.

'I'm not doing it,' he says, folding his arms.

'It's time,' I tell him, rubbing a piece of food from the corner of his mouth. 'I'll tell Mrs Whitlock that we're not to use the fan. OK?'

He pulls a face and shakes his head. 'Don't want to.'

'Are you feeling better?' I say, deflecting.

He nods, and I take a quiet breath of relief. His colour has returned, and that awful rasp in his lungs has faded.

'Come on,' I say, fixing his hair into place with my fingers. 'There'll be dinner afterwards.'

'Why should I?'

'You know why.'

'Mrs Whitlock is a *bitch*.'

'Don't say that.'

'I'm not doing it. I *hate* her.'

I cup his face and look deeply into his eyes. 'I'll tell her not to use the fan. Please do it. For me.'

4

I take Sylvan to the Wisteria room in Lichen Hall.

My stomach clenching, I spot the fan set up on the sideboard. Sylvan stops at the doorway, refusing to go in. I throw him a look, urging him on.

Mr Merrill stands facing the window, jangling something in his pocket in a way that suggests he's agitated. He is tall and narrow, always dressed in a crisp black suit, no matter the weather. His black hair is slicked in a side-parting, and his gaze is calculating, full of suspicion.

Last time he came I noticed how he twisted his wedding band around and around, and it struck me that he was the first client I'd come across who attended alone, without a wife. Later, as I listened in to the sighting, a story emerged: Mr Merrill's wife had left him, taking their twin daughters Emily and Aurora. His searches proved futile.

More than a year later, his wife had not filed for divorce, nor had she petitioned him for financial support. She had simply vanished. He had hired private detectives to find her to no avail. Sylvan is a last resort.

Last time Mr Merrill came, Sylvan was able to tell him that the girls were playing in a park. I have never seen a man shift so suddenly from relief to anger.

'I wonder if we might turn the fan off?' I ask Mrs Whitlock delicately, glancing at Sylvan.

She narrows her eyes, visibly calculating the reason behind my request. 'Oh, of course,' she says mildly, unplugging it. 'There we are. Happy?'

Sylvan looks up at me. 'I'm not doing it,' he says.

'Something the matter?' Mrs Whitlock asks, striding towards us. 'Don't you look lovely, Sylvan?' she says. 'Did I ever tell you that my hair was as curly as yours, once? Nowadays I have to use a curling iron to get it to look like that.'

'Shall we make a start?' Mr Merrill says, glancing at his watch. 'Come along, boy. Sit down, over here.'

Sylvan doesn't budge from the doorway. He's making a stand.

Mrs Whitlock senses that something is amiss. 'Why don't you come in this time?' she asks me. 'Just until Sylvan settles.' She glances at Mr Merrill for approval, and he gives it.

I stand in the far corner of the room, trying not to be in the way. Mrs Whitlock positions a chair in the centre of the room and invites Sylvan to sit there. He flicks his eyes at me, and I nod encouragingly. He sits down in the chair with a thud, his expression souring.

'Let's pick up from where we left off last time,' Mr Merrill says, sitting down in the armchair opposite. 'You told me you could see Emily and Aurora playing on swings. You said there was a dog, and Emily was stroking him. Maybe we could go back to that scene and get more detail. Where *is* this park?'

Usually I feel sorry for the people who come to see Sylvan, but Mr Merrill has such a bullish, aggressive manner that I wonder if his wife has taken his daughters into hiding for their own good. I turn to Sylvan, holding my breath. Perhaps he knows this, too. Perhaps he's scared. What if he tells Mr Merrill the truth? Would there be consequences if the sighting reveals something Mr Merrill doesn't want to hear?

'Sylvan,' Mr Merrill snaps when he doesn't respond. He clicks his fingers, as though drawing Sylvan out of a trance. 'The park. Where is it?'

I notice a dot of light circling Sylvan's ear. He is sighting. He keeps his gaze fixed on the rug in front of him, his jaw tight. The silence stretches in the room, as though something is about to burst.

'Sylvan, my dear?' Mrs Whitlock says from the chair to his left. Sylvan looks up, his head turned to her.

'I know who you are,' he says. 'Who you *really* are.'

She looks puzzled. 'Beg pardon?'

I watch on, trying to work out what he is doing. Why is he sighting Mrs Whitlock?

'You're Mrs Whitlock, but you're also Nicnevin,' he says.

I have to stop myself from chiding him. Nicnevin is the name of the witch of the woods – it's a slur.

'What is this?' Mr Merrill shouts. 'Stop talking nonsense and answer my bloody question. Where is the park? Where are my daughters? Where is my wife?'

Sylvan keeps his eyes on the floor, and I watch Mr Merrill step forward as though to strike him. I jump up, and his eyes blaze at me.

'What the hell are you doing?' he asks me. He nods at Sylvan. 'Make the boy answer.'

'Sylvan . . .' I urge, a note of warning in my voice. I'm on edge at how stubborn he's being. There will be consequences if he doesn't give Mr Merrill the information he wants. He lifts his head.

'No,' Sylvan snaps, folding his arms. 'I told you. I *won't*. I won't do the sighting.'

Suddenly Mr Merrill grabs Sylvan, plucking him in the air and shaking him, screaming in his face. I leap to my feet, pulling at his arms. He turns on me then, grabbing a fistful of my hair and dragging me across the room.

'Mr Merrill, *please*,' Mrs Whitlock says, rushing to him. 'This is no way to ensure the child helps you find your family.'

Her words seem to drive home reason, and he lets go in

disgust. The room spins. I stagger to a seat, clutching my head. Sylvan is right beside me, screaming.

'Mum! Mum! Are you OK, Mummy?'

'I'm fine,' I tell him weakly, but he's inconsolable. He wraps his arms around me and whimpers into my shoulder. My head throbs, and a handful of hair comes out in my hand. Mr Merrill stands by the window, his hands in his pockets, as though nothing out of the ordinary has occurred.

'Come on, boy,' he chides Sylvan. 'Your mother is fine. Let's continue.'

Sylvan clings to my arm, glaring at him. 'No,' he says firmly.

'Perhaps we might need a few moments to catch our breath,' Mrs Whitlock says.

'*No*,' Sylvan says again. 'I'm telling you *nothing*.'

'I've paid a great deal of money for our meeting today,' he says to Mrs Whitlock. I notice her eyes lifting at me, just for a second.

'Of course,' Mrs Whitlock says, nodding at Mr Merrill. 'Come along now, Sylvan. All we're asking for is a little bit more information, if you please . . .'

'I'm not telling you anything,' Sylvan says, folding his arms. His face is set. We all look at each other, not sure how to proceed. There's a painful silence, as though the room itself is holding its breath.

'Perhaps, if you return in a day or two, we might have a little more calm restored,' Mrs Whitlock tells Mr Merrill. 'And therefore, a little more information to help you become reunited with your wife and children.'

Mr Merrill flashes Sylvan a strange, cruel smile, and for a second it looks as if he's about to lunge at me again, but he pulls himself together. 'I've waited a year. What's a few more days?'

I watch him storm out of the house and drive away, so relieved and shaken that I want to cry.

Suddenly, Mrs Whitlock storms back into the room and grabs Sylvan by the arms, making him scream in pain.

'All I ask is for you to do one small sighting in return for a home here on the estate,' she snarls at him. '*One sighting.*'

Sylvan pulls free and I step in front of him, keeping him safely behind me as Mrs Whitlock rants.

'Mrs Whitlock, he's just a child,' I say. 'How dare you hurt him!'

A vein on her forehead trembles dangerously, and I brace myself. With a shout, she knocks me to the floor, my head connecting hard with the leg of a table. Shadows form at the edges of my vision.

When I come to, Mrs Whitlock has her arms around Sylvan's waist. He kicks and squirms, but she manages to carry him out of the room, marching quickly down the hall and disappearing down the narrow stairs to the birthing suite in the basement. I scramble to my feet and stagger after.

'Mrs Whitlock!' I shout. 'Stop! Let him go!'

She doesn't stop until she's in the old birthing suite. She drops Sylvan on the hard floor, a terrible thud ringing out as his head hits the tiles. She pushes past me, locking the door behind us both.

'No!' I scream, hearing the key turn. 'Let us out!'

She glares at me through the stained-glass window at the top of the door, her eyes wide and wild. 'You will stay here until Mr Merrill returns. And if Sylvan doesn't give him the information he wants, you will return here until he does. Understood?'

There is blood on Sylvan's head from where she dropped him, pooling in his hair and dripping across my hands. I scream at her to let us out, threatening and pleading. But she leaves us there in the dark, with nothing but our arms around each other to keep us warm.

Now

Pearl

Lichen Hall, Scottish Borders, November 1965

1

I sleep late the next morning – too late.

I get dressed and head to the hut, preparing a plan. I'll get Aretta and Rahmi to distract Mrs Whitlock while I take Mabel and Sylvan in the car to the hospital.

But she's not in the hut, and neither is Sylvan. I find Rahmi in the vegetable garden and tell her about Mr Whitlock's car.

She continues pulling up potatoes from the dark soil. 'Sylvan has a sighting in half an hour,' she says. 'We'll have to wait until it's over.'

I make a noise of frustration. Mabel said that sightings weaken him, and he can't afford to get any weaker.

'OK. As soon as they finish, you and Aretta tell Mrs Whitlock that she needs to see something in the gardens. That way she won't be able to see me, Mabel, and Sylvan as we drive off.'

She frowns, doubting me. 'But what about when she finds out you're gone? She'll go crazy at me and Aretta.'

I remind myself that Aretta, Rahmi, and Mabel haven't been outside the grounds of Lichen Hall in years. Sylvan has spent his whole life here.

'Look, I know this is your home . . .'

'Sylvan comes first,' she says with a tone of resolution. 'We'll do whatever it takes.'

I nod, showing her that I respect the sacrifice she's making. 'Did you know that Mrs Whitlock is poisoning her husband?'

She narrows her eyes. 'Poisoning him? How?'

I tell her about the banewort in his bedroom. About how he was unconscious. 'Wulfric said she was giving it to him.'

'To help him with his dementia,' she says, but falters. We both know by now that Mrs Whitlock isn't invested in helping *anyone*. Not even her own husband.

We find Aretta and take her to the hut to discuss the plan – when Sylvan's sighting finishes at three o'clock, Aretta and Rahmi will lead Mrs Whitlock to the gardens at the back of the house while I drive Sylvan and Mabel in the car to the hospital. Aretta would prefer to wait until it's dark, but time is of the essence – we just can't wait any longer.

But when we head to Lichen Hall just before four o'clock, the Rolls-Royce that was parked outside is gone. The Wisteria room is empty.

There is no sign of Mrs Whitlock, Mabel, or Sylvan. We check all the rooms, and the grounds. The only explanation is that whoever was driving the Rolls-Royce has taken them all.

I find Wulfric with the hens and ask him if he's seen his grandmother.

'Mr Merrill came,' he says. 'I saw him leave in his car.'

I don't ask who Mr Merrill is. 'What time was this? Did she go with him?'

Wulfric shrugs. 'I don't know.'

'What about Mabel and Sylvan? Did you see them go with him?'

'Aren't they at home?'

I tell him we can't find them, but I'm not sure if he believes me, or fully understands why I'm so anxious. Mr Whitlock's room is locked, and the house is quiet.

I head to the hall and lift the telephone receiver. There's a connection, but I hesitate. Who do I call first? The police?

I dial a number nine, but my hesitation has cost me dearly.

The connection cuts out.

2

It feels like the longest night of my life.

At first light, Aretta checks all the rooms in Lichen Hall for a second time while Rahmi and I check the outbuildings. One of them remains locked, and we bang on the door. But there's no answer. No sign of them at all.

I sink down at the top of the stairs, exhausted from searching and wracking my brains. Perhaps Mr Merrill kidnapped them. Perhaps he took Mrs Whitlock, too. I've knocked on her bedroom door, but it's locked.

It occurs to me that it's unusual for her to lock her door. I go back upstairs, treading lightly along the corridor to her room, glancing around in case I spot anyone. The corridor is empty, but I can hear something. It's coming from her room. I lean an ear to the wood of the door and hold my breath.

It's the faint chatter of a wireless.

She's inside.

I look up to see Aretta at the end of the corridor, gesturing to me. I point at the door and mouth, *She's in there!* But she waves at me to come.

'The birthing suite,' she says when I reach her. 'We think Mabel's in there.'

I think back quickly to the horrible cellar where I delivered Little One. We haven't checked there. I expected it was locked. We've had no new girls here in months.

Aretta leads me downstairs to the ground floor, then down the cold stone steps tucked discreetly behind a false wall. We take the steps, but Rahmi's already there, trying the door handle.

'It's locked,' she says, shaking her head. She stands on her tiptoes and looks down through the glass, then presses an ear to the door. 'I can't see or hear anything. I don't think they're in there.'

I tap on the door. 'Mabel? Are you in there?'

We wait. No reply. We're just about to head back upstairs when something moves underneath the door.

It's an old label from a wine bottle folded up and pushed across the threshold.

Rahmi, Aretta, and I share a wild look before I bend and pick it up. Inside the folds, a message is written in blood.

Mrs W locked us in
S hurt head
No food/water
M

Shit. How badly has Sylvan hurt his head?

I lean right down to the gap between the door and the floor, trying to see inside, but it's too dark.

'Is Sylvan breathing?' I whisper. 'Give one tap for yes, two for no.'

I wait, my heart racing. One tap. I hold my breath in case another follows. It doesn't. Good.

'We're going to get you out,' I say in a low voice. Already I can feel rage thundering in my veins at Mrs Whitlock for doing this. All this time, she's been in her fucking room, watching us as we picked the house apart, searching. She is even worse than I thought.

Aretta, Rahmi, and I head quickly back upstairs. Rahmi bangs on the door to Mrs Whitlock's bedroom, while Aretta searches the kitchen for the key to the cellar door. I take a plate of bread and a carafe of water downstairs. A glass won't fit beneath the door, but a plate does, and I keep filling it carefully, a little at a time, until the carafe runs dry.

A set of tiny fingers reaches underneath the door.

Sylvan's.

'Hello, darling,' I say, my voice catching. 'Are you OK?'

'Pearl,' he says weakly. 'Can you get us out?'

'Yes,' I tell him. 'I'm going to get you out. And I'm going to take you to hospital.'

'With all the sick people?' he says, and I laugh.

'Yes. And all the doctors. They'll make you better.'

There's a long silence. I'm worried he has fallen unconscious.

'Sylvan?'

I squeeze his hand. There's a light over his knuckle, a small white globe.

'Why are you climbing it if you don't like heights?'

'Climbing what?' I say.

'The Eiffel Tower,' he says. 'In Paris. You're afraid of heights but you want to look over Paris.'

I give a confused laugh. 'Paris? I've never been there.'

'You're *there*,' he says weakly. 'So am I. And I'm bigger.'

'Bigger?'

He nods. 'I'm a *man*,' he says with astonishment. I register this, trying to make sense of it. Why would we both be in Paris? Is this a sighting? Is he seeing something in the future? With a sinking feeling, I decide he's probably just delirious.

I hear Mabel coax him back from the door.

'He's cold,' she says. 'I'm going to hold him until he falls asleep.'

I go back upstairs and try the phone again, determined to call the police this time. But there's still no dial tone. With a scream of frustration I rip the phone from the wall and throw it across the hallway. Then I run upstairs and pound on Mrs Whitlock's door with my fists.

'I know you're in there!' I yell. 'Open this fucking door! Open it or I'll kick it down!'

No answer. Aretta and Rahmi appear at the top of the stairs. With a lunge, I kick against the wood of the door, but it doesn't budge. My foot bends painfully, and I fall to the floor, yelping in pain.

'She's not there,' Rahmi says, holding up a key. 'I've already checked.'

I feel utterly defeated. I limp down to the kitchen and fetch more bread and water, then take it down to the cellar door and slip it beneath. I can't bring myself to leave them. I curl up by the door, my hand reaching beneath.

When I wake a few hours later, I find someone has covered me with a blanket.

3

The next morning, I knock on the door to check on Mabel and Sylvan. No answer.

And I can smell something terrible. Oh God. It's smoke.

I race upstairs to try to find the cause. From the window, I see a strong plume of thick black smoke rising from the gardens, and I make for it quickly.

It's the vegetable garden. As I near it the taste of bitter smoke fills my mouth, and I see Aretta and Rahmi stooped over the raised beds, frantically trying to salvage whatever is left.

The whole garden has been destroyed. The metal garden bins in the corner seem to have been filled with wood and set alight, the ash drifts on the smoke, scattering across the vegetable beds. Even the greenhouse has been smashed, the tomatoes and runner beans have been torn away from the wall. Ashes heaped over each row of new cabbages, not a plant missed.

I approach Aretta and Rahmi. None of us speaks. I can see they're both too stricken by what has happened to even acknowledge my presence. Aretta has her arm around Rahmi, weeping listlessly. I reel at how violent, how calculated the destruction is. Who could have done this? The loss of so much produce affects us all.

'It was *her*,' Rahmi says through angry tears. 'It was Mrs Whitlock. I know it.'

'The herb garden's been destroyed too,' Aretta says, shaking her head. 'She'd never ruin her own garden.'

'Yes, she would,' Rahmi says. 'She's gone crazy. Why else would she lock Mabel and Sylvan up like that? She's lost her fucking mind.'

With a shiver, I wonder if she's intending to wipe us all out, one by one. Who would come to our aid? The telephone line is dead. She's managed to contrive such an isolated environment that a servant girl can die on her property and no one bats an eyelid, not even when the servant is buried illegally in the grounds.

And she can lock a mother and son in her own cellar knowing that no one will intervene.

4

The vegetable garden isn't the only thing that's destroyed.

Smoke spirals behind me, a long dark feather of it rising from the middle of the forest.

'Rahmi?' I say. 'Did you light one of your fires last night?'

She shakes her head, then clocks the smoke. I break into a run.

Something is scattered across the understorey, and it takes me a moment to work out what it is. When I bend down to catch one I realize it's chicken feathers, swirling amidst the leaves. I glance towards the hen house, just visible through the trees to my right.

The sight that greets me makes me fall to my knees and vomit. The hen house is blackened by flame, long strands of smoke rising up through the branches. Someone has broken in and wrung the necks of all the hens, tying their bodies high up on the wire of the pen.

I must shout for Aretta and Rahmi, because in a moment they are there beside me, taking in the terrible sight of the burned hen house.

I get to my feet and stagger away. The mindlessness of it, the poor bodies of those lovely birds . . . Sylvan will be devastated. And Wulfric. They were his hens. He knew them all by name. I glance back at the house, worried in case he's about to lumber through the trees at any moment.

But there's no sign of him.

By the time I reach Lichen Hall I'm drenched in sweat and filmed in filth and ash, with feathers stuck to my hair. I find the last pieces of bread in the kitchen and a jug of water, then head down to the cellar and knock gently on the door.

'Mabel?'

I hear shuffling on the other side of the door. 'Pearl?'

It's Mabel. I slip the pieces of bread beneath the door, then pour the water on to a plate and slide it carefully towards her. It's a painstaking process, but nothing more will fit beneath the door.

'How is Sylvan?' I ask.

She sounds as if she's crying. 'He had a bad night. He had terrible nightmares and his chest sounds bad again.'

'Can he talk?'

I stand up and peer through the stained-glass window. I see him crawling across the floor towards me, his head low. He seems too weak to stand.

'Hi, Pearl,' he says. I sink back down to the ground, stricken by how weak he seems. I can't bear the thought of how devastated he'll be when he finds out about the hen house. I can't bear the thought of his confusion. Of his innocence slipping away.

'How are you feeling?' I say through the door, holding my voice steady.

'I'm OK,' he says, though I can make out a faint rattle in his chest. 'How is Mildred? I'm worried about her.'

Oh God. Mildred is one of the hens.

'Is she OK?' he asks again. 'I saw something really bad . . .'

'I'm going to get you out of here, Sylvan,' I tell him, sidestepping the question. 'Give me an hour. Can you do that?'

'OK,' he says. 'I think so.'

I go back up to the ground floor, anger pulsing in my veins. 'Mrs Whitlock?' I shout. 'Mrs Whitlock, I need to speak with you immediately.'

Wulfric appears at the top of the stairs, dressed in his pyjamas, his hair wet from a bath. He looks me over, spotting the dirt on my face and the feathers in my hair.

'Sylvan's locked in the cellar,' I tell him bluntly. 'Your grandmother has locked him and Mabel up. I need you to tell me where she is.'

He looks astonished, and slightly afraid of me. He points up the hallway towards her bedroom.

'Are you sure?' I say, and he nods.

He whispers, 'I saw her go in there this morning.'

Her bedroom door is unlocked. Inside I find the large four-poster bed made, the dressing table and wardrobes neatly organized – but no sign of Mrs Whitlock. No sign of the wireless I heard the other day, either. I look around, determined to find some clue that might tell me where she's hiding. The large red rug on the floor is slightly rumpled against the far wall, and as I approach it I see a join in the wallpaper, almost concealed by a large painting.

It's a fake door, a small brass handle screwed into the wall, blending into the wallpaper.

I tug it, revealing a small day room, with a sofa and armchairs, side table, and a wireless. Mrs Whitlock is sitting in an armchair, reading.

'Give me the key,' I say.

She looks up mildly, as though she's been expecting me.

'Good morning, Pearl,' she says. 'A little sunnier today, isn't it?'

'Why did you do it?' I demand. 'Aretta and Rahmi worked *so hard* on that garden. It fed all of us. And now we'll struggle to eat. Why destroy it?'

She removes her eye glasses. 'What the devil are you talking about?'

'And the hen house. How cruel of you to kill them all. They were Wulfric's hens. And Sylvan loved them. Is that why you did it?'

She gives a light laugh. 'I'm afraid I'm going to have to ask you to explain yourself.'

'The cellar,' I say. 'Give me the key.'

A puzzled smile. I want to strangle her. I imagine putting my hands around her neck, just as she has done to the hens, and throttling her. But I can't. It's not in me, not even now, when fury is blistering beneath my skin. Still, I can threaten her.

'I know you've been poisoning your husband. Locking up Mabel and Sylvan is a crime, and if you don't open that door right now, I will tell *everyone*. Understood?'

She folds her arms and leans forward, unflustered. 'Well, this is quite a tale, isn't it? You seem to have everything all worked out. Marvellous.'

'Where is the key?'

She cocks her head, her eyes darkening. 'Surely you can sniff that one out, Detective Gorham? A mere door key?'

I stand firm. 'The *key*,' I say.

5

Just then, a loud clang of metal against metal rings out from downstairs, not a crash of furniture or dishes, but something else, a deliberate strike. It rings out again, and again, as though someone is battering down the door.

'Wolfie!' Mrs Whitlock cries, and she dashes past me, taking to the stairs quickly. I follow, and the clanging continues. I can hear Wulfric screaming.

Downstairs, we race towards the sound. The horrible banging sounds are coming from the cellar. My heart lurches. As I look down through the loops of the banister I see Wulfric swinging something metal at the door. A long-handled axe.

'Wolfie, stop!' Mrs Whitlock shouts, but he ignores her and swings the axe over his head again, missing her by mere inches. This last, powerful blow manages to knock the handle off, opening the door.

Quickly I push past her, ducking inside the cellar. I grab Mabel from behind the door, then scoop Sylvan up in my arms. We race quickly up the stairs to the ground floor, along the hallway, bursting through the front door. My heart is pounding, and Sylvan is so heavy, but I keep going, my legs pressing hard into the ground, propelling me forward.

We cut through the woods, not daring to look back.

By the time I reach the barbed-wire fence along the field I am soaking with sweat. One last push – I climb over it, careful to keep him hoisted over my shoulder, before making the last dash to Mabel's hut.

Inside, we lay Sylvan down on the bed, looking him over. Mabel bolts the hut door and collapses on the floor, exhausted. It's a small protection against Mrs Whitlock, but it makes us both feel a little safer. I'm a mess, my limbs trembling from running while carrying Sylvan. He is weak and cold, and his hair is horribly matted with dried blood.

Mabel sets about lighting the lamp, filling the air with the familiar scent of belladonna. He breathes it in.

A knock on the door. We both freeze. Mabel looks out of the window.

'It's Aretta and Rahmi,' she says, unbolting the door.

'Is he OK?' Rahmi says, looking down at Sylvan on the bed.

I nod, but that cut on his head worries me. His pallor is concerning, too. His body is limp, and he falls quickly asleep. Mabel says nothing, but her eyes show how afraid she is.

I find some coffee in a tin and boil a kettle, making us all something to drink. My hands won't stop shaking. The warmth of the mug feels good in my hand. We sit in a circle on the floor, too stricken to speak.

I keep watch out of the window in case Mrs Whitlock shows up. The thought crosses my mind that she'll try and burn the hut down, with all of us inside.

'You know we have to leave the hall,' I say in a low voice. They all look at me blankly.

'Sylvan's sick. This isn't going to get any better.'

I tell Mabel about the car I discovered in the old shed. That I have no idea how far we'll get, but with the phone lines down it's the only way we can leave. And we need to leave, urgently.

'I want to be clear,' I say. 'We have to leave here *for good*. Not just to take Sylvan to hospital.' I turn to Mabel. 'He can't live here anymore.'

Rahmi looks shocked. 'Where will we go?' she says.

'We can fix the vegetable patch,' Aretta says, drawing looks of confusion from Mabel. 'It'll take time. But we've had failed crops in the past . . .'

I glance at Sylvan on the bed. 'If we leave him like this there's a good chance he won't make it.'

Silence hangs in the room. We're all taking different risks: for Mabel, Aretta, and Rahmi, they'll lose their home after this. There is another risk: a doctor might see that Sylvan is malnourished, his birth not registered, and contact social services. He will possibly be taken away from Mabel and placed in foster care, which would be devastating for her. I've seen it happen, many times.

'There's nothing else I can do for him,' I say quietly. 'He needs to go to hospital.'

Aretta sobs into her hands. She stares at Rahmi, who won't look back. Finally, she reaches a hand to Aretta, who takes it. Sylvan takes a long, deep breath, and the wet, sticky sound of it makes my stomach turn.

Mabel is too weak to walk to the car. She's skin and bone, her eyes dark hollows in her face.

'OK,' I say, getting to my feet. 'I'll drive to the village. Once I'm there, I'll contact the police and get them to come back here for the rest of you.'

'I'll come too,' Rahmi says, but I tell her no. 'You and Aretta need to stay with Mabel and Sylvan,' I say. 'We don't know what Mrs Whitlock will do.'

6

I head quickly back towards the hall, jumping over the barbed wire and moving quickly through the woods.

I've only been walking a few minutes when I hear twigs snapping behind. I grit my teeth, refusing to be deterred, but the sound continues, and I feel the hairs on my neck stand on end. Someone is following me.

It is growing dark. I keep moving, adrenalin propelling me forward, and scoop up a rock from the forest floor to defend myself, if need be.

Another sound behind me, closer this time.

Birds lift off from the trees, frightened.

I zigzag through the forest, then realize with horror that I'm heading towards the old wood. The one with the twisted, white branches, like ghosts, where I encountered the headless thing.

I retrace my steps, picking out the lights from the house and keeping it in sight as I orient myself.

I breathe easier once I make it to the outbuilding. No sign of anyone around. Carefully I find the key and open the lock, then filch the car key from my pocket and open the door. I turn the key in the ignition.

Nothing happens.

I try again, and again. The engine wheezes.

'Come *on!*' I shout, thumping the steering wheel.

The engine springs into life. My heart leaps. *Success!*

Quickly I jump out of the car to prise the shed door open a little further so I can drive out, the car purring obediently behind me.

But as I shift the door with my body weight, something heavy crashes down on my head, a blinding pain shooting from my skull to my arms. My knees buckle and I hit the ground like a felled tree.

Above, a figure closing over me.

Then darkness.

Now

Mabel

Lichen Hall, Scottish Borders, November 1965

1

Sylvan is passing in and out of consciousness. I keep my eyes trained on the window, fearful of the shape of Mrs Whitlock emerging from the treeline. A few times I think I see her, and my body goes ice cold, my heart rate shooting up. And then I realize it's only an animal, or the wind rearranging the branches.

I steel myself. I can't run from her. I have to fight, for Sylvan's sake.

Aretta is sitting on the floor, her breathing laboured. Rahmi stoops down, holding her hands. 'What's wrong?' she says, pressing a hand to Aretta's forehead. She looks up at me in alarm.

'I think I did it,' Aretta says in a thin voice.

'What?' Rahmi says. 'Did what?'

Aretta lifts her face up to me. Her eyes roll back in her head slightly, and she looks as if she's going to be sick. 'I'm sorry,' she says. 'I think I killed the hens.'

Rahmi jumps to her feet, horrified. 'What are you saying?' she gasps, glaring down at Aretta. 'Why would you do that?'

Aretta wrings her hands, and I notice she's panting. 'I think I destroyed the vegetable patch too.'

Rahmi looks from me to Aretta, her horror growing. 'Will someone tell me what's going on?'

I shake my head, telling her I'm every bit as confused as she is. I bend to Aretta, pressing the back of my hand to her forehead. Her skin is clammy to the touch. Her pupils are dilated, and I think she's about to pass out. 'Aretta, you're sick,' I say. 'Have you been poisoned?'

'I think so,' she says with a drowsy nod.

Now

Pearl

Lichen Hall, Scottish Borders, November 1965

1

I hear voices. My head throbs and my eyelids feel so heavy that I wonder if they're taped down.

Slowly, I open my eyes. It's dark, but I think I'm in Lichen Hall. The room spins. I see a small sofa, and a window, and a wardrobe. Wind rattles the grate of a fireplace. I'm in something that feels metallic beneath my arms. A wheelchair.

'Are you awake now?'

My head throbs. I reach up to touch the part that hurts most and find a large bump on the right side of my skull. I remember being in the woods, then starting the car in the garage, then feeling something exploding on my head.

Wulfric stands above me, his expression full of childish concern. My God, he must have hit me.

His face is suddenly close to mine, and I give a gasp of fright. He moves back and nods at a cup of tea on the side table. He lifts it unsteadily and hands it to me.

'Here,' he says. 'It's tea. I made it for you.'

With shaking hands I take it, still not sure whether I'm dreaming. My head feels as if it's been bashed in. At the fringes of my awareness I can sense that his mood has slipped again.

'You think it's belladonna, don't you?' he says, his face falling. 'It's not. Drink up.'

'Wulfric,' I say, my voice rasping. 'Did you hit me with something?'

He nods, looking sheepish. 'I need you to help him,' he says defensively. 'And I knew you'd say no, so I had to bring you here.'

I sit up and look around, my memories of what I was supposed to do flooding quickly back – I should be in the car, driving to the village. Instead, I'm in Mr Whitlock's bedroom. What happened to the car? Wulfric must have used Mr Whitlock's bloody wheelchair to cart me in here. I can see someone sitting up in the bed, murmuring.

It's Mr Whitlock.

'I didn't hit you too hard,' Wulfric says. 'There's only a little bit of blood.'

I reach for the part of my head that hurts the most. God, it aches. I glance in horror at Wulfric, realizing he must have followed me through the forest. He attacked me.

'What's all this about?' I say weakly. 'Why did you hit me?'

'I need you to help my dad,' Wulfric says in a pained voice. 'You were right. He's been poisoned all this time. But you can fix him, Pearl. You're a nurse.'

I blink, trying to stop the room from swimming. 'Wulfric, your father passed away.'

He shakes his head, growing agitated. 'You don't understand.' He looks at the shape in the bed. 'He's not my grandfather. He's my dad.'

'Mr Whitlock is your father?' I say, turning unsteadily to stare at him. Wulfric nods. 'But . . . your father died in a car accident. Didn't he?'

Wulfric takes a step towards me.

'It was me,' he says in a low whisper. 'It was me that died.'

Now

Mabel

Lichen Hall, Scottish Borders, November 1965

1

Rahmi is on the floor beside Aretta, holding her face in her hands. Slowly, Aretta gets to her feet, holding on to the table for balance.

'Get the torch,' she says.

'You're *not* going outside!' Rahmi says, but Aretta insists.

'The torch,' she tells me firmly. I pass it to her, but she shakes her head.

'I want you to turn it on.'

I do, and she pulls up her sweater and turns around. The light from the torch falls on the bumps of her spine, then on something else close to her waist. To the left of her spine, there's a faint lump, as though something is trying to protrude through her skin. To the right, it looks as if she's been stabbed, a thick brown object piercing her. The skin around it is bruised and wet.

It looks like a tree branch.

'What is this?' Rahmi shrieks. 'Who did this to you?'

'No one,' Aretta says. She draws a breath. 'I think we've all got it.'

Now

Pearl

Lichen Hall, Scottish Borders, November 1965

1

'I don't understand,' I tell Wulfric. 'What do you mean you *died*?'

'I was in a car accident,' he says. 'About nine years ago. I was riding my bike when a car hit me. I was in a morgue.'

I can feel my senses sharpening again. I glance at the bedroom door, wondering if the car engine is still running. There was only a little bit of petrol left in the tank. Every second he talks is lessening the chances of us getting out of here.

'Do you know what Cordyceps is?' Wulfric asks then.

I lift my eyes to his, recalling the word. I saw it in Professor Llewellyn's book.

'It's a zombie fungus,' I say. 'We did a few lessons on it, I think?'

He nods. 'My dad studied it,' he says, wiping his nose on his sleeve. 'He found that the fungus kept the ants alive even after they died. It could control their brains. It could also heal them He said that he'd heard about people using it for humans. Peopl who'd been injured. Mushrooms can do all sorts of things. Thi kind brought people back to life, in a way.'

Wulfric's head twitches, a movement that strikes me as invol untary, unnerving. 'But sometimes it makes me do bad things, he whispers. 'And sometimes . . .' He lifts his shirt, revealing what looks like a twig spiking out of his abdomen.

The room sharpens. It's an actual twig, the texture of something earthy. I reach out to touch it, my mouth open in shock. He flinches.

'I hate being a kid,' he says. 'When will I be a grown up?'

I struggle to take in what he's telling me. This can't be real. Can it?

'I remember waking up,' he says, stepping back. 'My dad said he'd brought me back. He showed me what he'd given me, but it was so small it looked like nothing.' Wulfric turns his eyes to Mr Whitlock in the bed, his voice breaking. 'I think he's infected with it, too. He has convulsions. It's why Mum was giving him belladonna to drink. It made him better. But then it started to make him unconscious. And *you* said it was poison. So, I made sure he didn't drink it anymore.'

Mr Whitlock starts to murmur, his sleep disturbed by Wulfric's cries. 'Spiders,' he says, his face twisting in fright. 'I can see spiders.'

'Why's he saying that?' Wulfric says, growing upset.

I look at my reflection in the mirror. One eye is badly swollen, closed over from where Wulfric bludgeoned me. There are bloodstains on my dress. I feel nauseous, and I have to focus hard on not throwing up.

'He's hallucinating,' I tell Wulfric, breathless. 'If he was taking belladonna then he's probably withdrawing too fast.'

'You're a nurse! Help him!'

'I'll need a small quantity of belladonna,' I tell him slowly. 'And as many cold wet towels as you can find.'

'Belladonna?' he says. 'But you said it was poison.'

The truth is, I have no idea how to wean someone off belladonna. And it may well be that the hallucinations are a result of long-term use, not a withdrawal symptom.

'My eye,' Mr Whitlock says with a groan. He presses his head back into the pillow, his jaw tight with pain. 'My eye!'

He starts to cough and choke. I reach for the glass of water by the bed and bring it to his lips, but his eyes are rolling back in his head, and he grips his throat. I scan him quickly to work out how to help, but it's not a heart attack. He starts to convulse, his arms and legs lifting off the bed.

'What's happening?' Wulfric screams.

One of Mr Whitlock's eyes is bulging dangerously, the white expanding until it's visibly larger than the other. His mouth is wide open, the veins in his face thickening under the skin. Suddenly, his eye pops entirely, a gruesome shower of blood and gristle hitting the bedclothes, something pushing violently through the eye socket.

I stagger backwards against Wulfric, wondering if I'm dreaming. I have never, ever witnessed anything like this. Mr Whitlock falls back against the pillows, his limbs limp at his sides.

But the object that has protruded from his skull continues shooting upward to the ceiling, a grotesque tree branch.

Except it's not. Something plumes on the end of it, a purple, testicular-looking spore that is steadily ripening, about to burst.

The bedroom door is open, and I see Wulfric running away, yelling and crying. I lunge after him, but suddenly the door swings shut, tight.

I can't get out.

Now

Mabel

Lichen Hall, Scottish Borders, November 1965

1

I look at the thing growing out of Aretta's back. It looks like a twig, and with a shiver of fear I think of the branch we found in Morven's head.

I think of the ant in Mr Whitlock's Micrarium, with the spores protruding from its body.

I think of the powder Mrs Whitlock blows over the babies, and the people who come for sightings.

'Got what?' Rahmi shouts at Aretta. 'We've all got what?'

My mouth runs dry. I keep thinking about Morven. The strange illness that felled her.

She hadn't been herself.

I thought it was murder. The thing we'd thought was a weapon in her head.

'You have it, too,' Aretta says to Rahmi. She reaches out to touch her face, but Rahmi steps back, her eyes wide with horror.

'What are you saying?' Rahmi says.

'The growth on your leg,' Aretta says with a sob. 'It's a root.'

Rahmi staggers backwards, falling on the chair by the table. Her face crumples, and she begins to cry. Slowly, she rolls up her trouser leg to reveal a thin black stem, two inches long, poking out of her shin.

Her face twisted in horror, she looks up at me and Aretta. 'What is it?' she says with a whimper.

'It's a fungus,' I say weakly, glancing at Sylvan. 'It's a kind of parasite,' I say, thinking back to what Mr Whitlock told me all those years ago. 'It controls its host. And then it kills it.' I sink down beside Sylvan. 'The Whitlocks killed Morven,' I say. 'It was the Whitlocks.'

And then I lift my hair, showing them what I've been hiding behind my long plait for just over a year: a dark stem hanging from the base of my skull, a black bulb on the end, the size of a grape. No matter how much I've cut it, it always grows back, strange and horrifying.

'The Whitlocks have killed all of us,' I say.

Aretta's face hardens. Suddenly she lifts the torch from the table and lurches towards the door.

'Where are you going?' Rahmi calls after her.

'To have a chat with Mrs Whitlock,' Aretta says. Rahmi and I share a look. Aretta is in no state to go anywhere, let alone deal with Mrs Whitlock.

'I'll go with her,' I say.

Rahmi nods from the floor, resigned. 'I'll stay with Sylvan.'

Aretta stumbles through the long grass towards the trees, falling to her knees twice before pulling herself quickly up. I catch up with her quickly, linking my arm through hers to support her. She keeps her gaze straight ahead, a single tear running down her cheek. Neither of us says anything, but we both know what we have to do. Aretta's confession has locked together a thousand disparate pieces, forming a picture that is truly horrifying.

If what she says is true, there is no alternative.

We all know our fate now.

2

Inside the house, we head straight to Mrs Whitlock's bedroom. She's not there, not in any of the rooms on that floor. Not in the cellar.

'I'll take the top floor,' Aretta says quietly.

'I'll take the east wing,' I say.

I take the stairs to the corridor that links to the east wing, recalling vividly the first time I entered Lichen Hall: the Grecian statues lining the vestibule, the tapestries, the glimmering chandelier hanging overhead, the size of a bath. I'd been so spellbound by the grandeur, by the vast display of wealth. But the velvet curtains are filthy with mould, the windowsills dotted with mushrooms. It is turning to ruin.

I open the door quietly to the top of the staircase, covering my mouth with a hand. The smell of mould ambushes me, a choking stench of decay. The fungus has grown worse – it climbs out of the staircase, resinous and determined, like a tumour.

As I step towards the top of the stairs, a cry rings out from the vestibule below. I look down, trying to find the source. Another cry, a long howl, like a wounded animal. The mezzanine juts out over the vestibule, but I can make out something below, a flash of red on the chequered tiles. A glossy puddle of blood.

I descend the stairs carefully, stepping over blooms of fungus. The scene on the vestibule below stops me in my tracks. Mrs Whitlock is sitting on the floor close to one of the Grecian statues, sobbing over Wulfric, his arms by his sides. He is laid out on his back, his head resting on her lap as she strokes his hair. Blood pools darkly around them, a stripe of it at his neck.

He's clearly dead, his mouth open and his chest unmoving.

She lifts her head to me, alerted by the cry of alarm that slips out of my mouth. Her face is twisted in a tortured grimace.

'Help us,' she whispers, stretching out a hand. 'Help us!'

I pause on the final step, too sickened by the sight of poor Wulfric's bloodied body to go any closer. I can tell right away that the weeping, pathetic woman on the floor is the Mrs Whitlock I've encountered sporadically in the past – frightened, confused, not sure how much time has passed, or when she might be allowed to surface in her body again.

'Nicnevin,' a voice says, and I turn to see Pearl limping down the stairs towards us.

She is badly injured, one side of her face bloodied and swollen. She stands next to me, her eyes falling on Wulfric. She recoils as though struck, then lifts her eyes to Mrs Whitlock. 'Nicnevin,' she says, her voice charged with emotion. 'That's your real name, isn't it?'

Mrs Whitlock's face changes. The naked fear that was there a second ago flicks to fury, and she snatches up a bloodied knife from the floor. Pinching the blade, she reaches her arm back and flings it at us, almost catching my side. The blade wedges itself in the wood of the banister next to me.

'Why did you kill him?' I shout at her, shaking my head at the sight of Wulfric on the floor. 'Your own grandson?'

Mrs Whitlock gets to her feet and dusts down her black dress, a cruel smile on her face. 'Not my grandson,' she says in a low, hoarse voice. 'The woman's son.'

I look to Pearl, confused, but Pearl keeps her eyes on Mrs Whitlock.

'You're Nicnevin,' Pearl says to Mrs Whitlock. 'Why don't you stop hiding behind Mrs Whitlock and show yourself?'

Mrs Whitlock gives a small laugh, as though Pearl has told a childish joke. 'I think you must have taken some magic mushrooms,' she says. 'Either that or you suppose yourself smarter than you really are.'

'I know a little about the work you do,' Pearl says to Mrs Whitlock, stepping down on the floor of the vestibule and approaching her carefully. 'You exist by throwing spores into living creatures, don't you? The spores take over, causing sickness, then burst out. And the cycle starts all over. You're using human beings instead of soil.'

I think of what Aretta said. *We're all infected.*

That's what she was doing to the babies. It was the only reason she ever invited expectant mothers to stay with her. To spread the spores.

'So . . . all the babies that have been born at Lichen Hall,' I say to Mrs Whitlock. 'You infected them?'

'Infection's a terrible word,' she tuts, kicking Wulfric's arm roughly to one side. 'How do you think we've survived for forty-eight million years? If we're to continue the work that keeps the planet alive, we have to live. We have to throw our spores into the wind.'

'Or into people,' Pearl says through gritted teeth.

'Whatever it takes,' she says with a shrug. 'Which would you prefer – the planet to die? Or to continue providing life to billions of people, animals, and plant life, at the cost of a few thousand?'

Beneath the metallic stench of blood, I smell something else. Smoke.

'Mr Whitlock is dead,' Pearl says.

I watch Mrs Whitlock for a reaction, but there is none. That same, satisfied smile stays put.

'You don't think I care, do you?' Mrs Whitlock says with a shrug.

'But . . . you tried to protect Mr Whitlock, didn't you?' Pearl continues. 'That's what the belladonna was for. It kept the fungus from killing him.'

Something shifts on Mrs Whitlock's face. 'The woman did that,' she says, cocking her head. 'Not me.'

'What woman?' I ask.

'Do you mean Mrs Whitlock did that?' Pearl presses her, but Mrs Whitlock's eyes have fallen on the knife wedged in the post behind us, taking a step towards it.

I realize then what Pearl meant by referring to her as Nicnevin. Sylvan used the same name at Mr Merrill's sighting. The name of a ghost, or fairy queen, who sought revenge on humans for killing a fairy child.

Mrs Whitlock is possessed by something. Fungus, or Nicnevin, or perhaps they are the same thing – I don't know. The woman who I've encountered occasionally, begging me to help her, who looked scared and confused . . . that's Mrs Whitlock, swimming back to the surface of her body. Nicnevin is the creature who crouches inside her. The creature who has killed Wulfric, perhaps as punishment.

Nicnevin is the creature who hates fire.

A loud bang from the door above makes me jump, the smell of flame growing stronger.

'Mum!'

Upstairs, I see Sylvan emerging at the top of the staircase, Rahmi following close behind.

'I'm sorry,' she pants. 'He ran away from me.'

'Sylvan!' I shout, racing up the stairs to him and wrapping my arms around his shoulders. I try to keep his face turned away from the ghastly sight of Wulfric's body. 'You need to go,' I tell him, glancing at Rahmi, whose eyes have fallen on Wulfric at the bottom of the stairs.

Aretta rushes through the door behind Rahmi, holding two square cans – old petrol cans, I realize. In the hallway behind her I can see flame moving up the walls.

'What are you doing?' Mrs Whitlock shouts at her.

Quickly, Aretta pours the contents of one can down over the

left banister. Rahmi takes the other can, pouring the liquid down the stairs and over the right banister.

'For love,' Aretta says, taking Rahmi's hand. And then she takes a box of matches out of her pocket, and strikes one, holding it to the liquid pooling on the stairs.

'No!' Mrs Whitlock shouts.

The stairs erupt into flames. The tapestries and rugs catch fire, sweeping the fire right along the vestibule. From the corner of my eye I see Mrs Whitlock collapse beside Wulfric's body, but something else seems to rise from her – a plume of smoke, or a dark shadow, that slides across the tiled floor of the vestibule and into a side room.

Rahmi takes my hand in hers. 'We're all infected,' she says. 'You know that.' Her eyes fall on Sylvan, who has buried his face into my skirt, his arms wrapped tightly around my legs. Such tender trust. 'This is the only way,' she says sadly. 'The alternative is that.'

She nods at Mrs Whitlock, and the shocking sight of Wulfric, lying in his own blood.

I raise a hand to protect my eyes from the hot glare of the flames, my heart racing. On the floor below, I see Pearl dashing into the room that leads off to the right of the vestibule. The sound of shattering glass pierces the air. She must have broken one of the windows to escape.

But a moment later, she reappears, waving in the doorway. 'This way!' she shouts. 'You've not got long before the staircase collapses!'

I clutch Sylvan to me, my heart breaking. All I want for him is a good life. An education. Happiness. I don't want some terrible thing to control his mind, as it has Mrs Whitlock's, leading her to do horrific things.

But I have no choice. I have to kill him with me in the fire.

I nod at Rahmi, signalling to her that I've made the decision. She puts her arms around me. Aretta wraps her arms around

Rahmi, and we huddle together around Sylvan, facing the inevitable. Already the smoke is growing so dense that I can hardly breathe.

I can hear Sylvan wheezing. 'Mummy!' he coughs. 'Mummy!'

I squeeze my eyes shut, trying not to listen. *This is for the best. This is the only way.*

But abruptly my mind turns to the glowing mushrooms I encountered in the forest when I was pregnant with him.

I remember touching them.

Is that the reason behind his gift, and the travelling light? Has he been infected by *those* mushrooms?

'Sylvan,' I say, bending down to him and taking his face between my hands. 'I need you to use your good eye to tell me something.'

His eyes turn to the fire, wide with terror.

'Are you sick, like us?' I ask him.

He squeezes his eyes shut, too scared to understand me. I grasp his arms and shake him.

'Sylvan! The thing that killed Morven. Do you have it inside you, too?'

Quickly a small light zips along his jaw. He opens his eyes and shakes his head.

The fire edges closer, frighteningly hot. I think back to the day he told me I would kill him. *You'll kill me in the fire.*

I look down at Pearl in the doorway below, calling to us. She has only been here a few months. Maybe it takes longer to infect people. It took the rest of us years. Maybe Pearl has escaped it.

And I remember quickly what Sylvan said to Pearl about being in Paris together. Perhaps that was a sighting of his future.

It's just enough of a hope to spur me to act. In one quick movement, I lift Sylvan and throw him with all my might over the banister towards Pearl. It's a terrible risk, and for one hideous moment I watch him fall down, holding my breath. He could break his legs, or his back, if she misses. The fire consumes the banister on the other side, causing it to fall to the floor with a deafening crash.

Pearl lunges forward and catches him, falling backward across the floor under his weight. I shoot her one last glance, a hopeful nod, before she disappears with him into the side room.

The fire closes in around Aretta, Rahmi, and me on the staircase, orange tongues consuming Wulfric's body on the vestibule below. Black smoke swirls around us, forcing us to cower against the remaining spindles on the right side of the staircase. Aretta and Rahmi curl up around each other, their faces tight together.

Morven's face appears in front of my eyes, and I want to reach out to her and feel her hand in mine.

My love, I'm so afraid. Say you'll be there, on the other side.

The faces of the gargoyles on the architraves are set aglow by the fire, watching on. Over the crackle of the flames I can make out the sound of a car engine squealing to a start outside, the rumble of tyres on the cobblestones. My heart leaps. It must be Pearl, taking Sylvan to safety.

The three of us clasp each others' hands tightly, and I force a single thought to the forefront of my mind: that the curse has claimed enough for the forest to be satisfied. That the three of us, huddled on the stairs of the blazing east wing, will be just enough of a sacrifice for it all to end.

Now

Pearl

Lichen Hall, Scottish Borders, November 1965

1

I throw the old car into second gear and press down on the accelerator. The tyres screech as I speed away from the blaze that's spreading through the rooms of Lichen Hall. Good God – the scene in the rear-view mirror is something straight out of a war. I'm praying this bloody car doesn't conk out at any moment.

I'm shaking with adrenalin and filmed in soot. Sylvan lies on the back seat of the car, wheezing and hacking. He's breathed in so much smoke. I don't know if I got him out in time for him to survive. . . I hear him vomit, but I keep going, shouting words of encouragement to him.

'You're safe, Sylvan!' I shout. 'I'm going to take you to hospital, just hold tight!'

We make it out of the front gates, and I give a loud yell of delight. *Freedom! We made it!*

The tyres are failing, torn off their rims. I can hear them flapping on the road. I don't dare brake, taking the corners dangerously fast, the back end of the car spinning out.

We're about a mile away from the hall when I see sparks flying up alongside the window, a searing grind of metal on the tarmac.

I drive as far as Mr Whitlock's car will let me before pulling over into a layby. I lift Sylvan out of the car, laying him carefully on the ground. His eyes roll back in his head, and his chest judders a few times before falling still.

'No!' I shout. 'Sylvan, come back!'

Placing my mouth carefully over his, I breathe, gently at first, the sour taste of smoke and vomit filling my mouth. I breathe again, harder, massaging his little chest, then placing an ear over his heart to listen.

Nothing.

'Come on, Sylvan,' I say, shaking him, urging him back. 'Come *on!*'

I do it thirty times before falling forward and weeping. He is gone. His little chest was already so weak.

I've failed him. I think of Mabel, Aretta, and Rahmi. And poor Wulfric.

I've failed them all.

I sink down beside Sylvan, all the air wrung out of my lungs. It has started to rain. I feel as if the sky is falling in on top of me. I can't believe he is gone.

I tried so hard. But it wasn't enough.

In a moment a cold shower pounds down, the black soot on my hands turning to rivers that run my arms into the ground beneath. The edge of death is so close to me I can feel it brushing my skin. For a moment, it is quite beautiful, the pain of that edge. The devastating clarity of it.

Something stirs in the corner of my eye.

Sylvan's lips. I glance over and watch him carefully, pressing my fingers to his pulse. It's very faint, but I feel it.

Quickly I roll over and press my mouth to his, pushing air into his lungs. I sit upright.

'Come on,' I say. 'Breathe!'

I cup my hands to his cheeks. He gives a small cough. Oh God, keep going!

I turn him over, laying him carefully on to his stomach, making it easier for him to breathe, chatting to him, begging him to take a breath. He gives another little cough, and I repeat the process.

His little life hangs by a thread, fragile as a dandelion seed. It's as though the door to that other world is opening right next to us on the wet grass, throwing its hideous shadow over us. Well, *fuck* that. I'm not letting Sylvan go.

I'm not letting Mabel, Rahmi and Aretta's sacrifice mean nothing.

I scoop him up and cradle him in my arms, my heart dropping at his pallor.

'Stay with me,' I whisper as I carry him back to the car. 'Please, Sylvan. Just a little longer.'

Six Years Later

Now

Pearl

Edinburgh, May 1972

Oh, what a glorious day. I'm walking down Princes Street, blood rushing through my veins after an hour-long interview at the University of Edinburgh. It was gruelling, and I was certain I'd failed – but at the end of it the man stood up and shook my hand.

'Congratulations, Miss Gorham,' he said. 'You're accepted on to our medical degree, commencing September.'

A *medical degree!* Me, a doctor! In five years' time, of course, and subject to passing all my exams, but this is all mere frippery compared to the *greatness* that is being admitted to medical school. I might just send a copy of my graduation certificate to Sister Clarke, and to Nurse Haddon, for inspiring me all those years ago.

I'm so happy I think I'll skip.

I'm still skipping like a maniac when I realize I've reached the café where Lucy, her girlfriend Emma, and Sylvan are waiting for me. Emma's a nurse, too, and she and Lucy have just moved back to Edinburgh, where they'll both be working at our old hospital.

'It went well, did it?' Lucy says, having spotted me skipping from the café window.

I feign disappointment. 'No, actually. It didn't.'

Her face falls. 'Oh, Pearl. God, I'm so sorry.'

Sylvan grins up at me. 'You got it, didn't you?'

'Fooled you!' I tell Lucy, who rolls her eyes before pulling me into a hug.

'Congratulations,' she says, planting a kiss on my cheek.

We walk with Lucy and Emma towards their flat on Rose Street. I'm thrilled for Lucy that she's found someone she loves enough to move in with. Emma is every bit as sarcastic and blunt as Lucy, which is perfect – and they look like each other, both blondes with square black glasses. It makes their living arrangements easy to pass off. People simply assume they're sisters.

'Well, Sylvan,' Lucy says, as we reach their flat. 'I guess this means you and I will be seeing a lot more of each other, won't we?'

Sylvan looks at her, confused. 'Lucy's going to look after you while I'm studying,' I tell him.

'And me,' Emma says. When I told Lucy about my plans to apply for a medical degree, she said she'd help out with Sylvan. She and Emma are going to fit their shifts around him, and my mother will help, too.

Secretly, I've been harbouring what Sylvan told me years ago at Lichen Hall. That he saw me working in a hospital. It kept me going all these years, even after Sister Clarke refused to take me back on as a nurse. I'm glad she refused me, now, because it made me more determined than ever to do what I really dreamed of. And that was becoming a doctor.

'Don't forget this,' Lucy says, and passes me the picnic basket I packed before the interview. I'm taking Sylvan for a lunch date up on Arthur's Seat, the ancient volcano that sleeps at the end of the Royal Mile, with amazing views of the city. We hug Lucy and Emma goodbye before boarding the next tram at the street corner.

'And one for your son?' the tram driver says when I hand him the fare, glancing at Sylvan behind me in the queue.

'Yes,' I say, with a smile. 'My son.'

I have been a parent now for almost seven years, after

wrenching Sylvan from the blaze and taking him to hospital, where he received life-saving oxygen and treatment for his lungs.

'Your son?' they said, and I nodded.

How the hell was I to explain it otherwise?

As Sylvan's birth was never registered, he has no birth certificate. After a lot of research, I discovered that we could appeal to the register general to issue a birth certificate in retrospect. They obliged, but stated that an investigation would be carried out to prove that he was my son . . . So, I asked Sebastian for a favour – to say he fathered Sylvan with me when we were both in our teens.

A lie, yes, but for a good cause.

We would claim that Sylvan was born and raised at Lichen Hall, and we decided to bring him home when we were older. Right before the fire razed it to the ground.

Surprisingly, Sebastian agreed, so long as I didn't petition for financial support, or involve his new wife in any form. I suspect he was worried I would tell Mariella of his infidelity if he didn't comply. Or maybe he felt guilty for what he'd done to me.

A chat with the registrar general and a signature later, and it was done – our son, Sylvan Gorham, reborn into his new life in Edinburgh. A strange shift for me into my parallel life, or perhaps a better one than I could have imagined. Sebastian and his wife have twin girls, now. Occasionally I spot them visiting Sebastian's parents. He looks miserable.

Sylvan and I take the tram to the foot of the volcano, sitting quietly together as the cityscape changes to hills and trees. I ask him about his homework, and his plans for the weekend. He wants to have his friend Stewart over for tea, if that's all right, and I tell him of course it is. Stewart's a nice boy, quiet, like Sylvan. They play in the rugby team together. Sylvan and I live with my mother in a terraced house in Slateford.

Ever since I brought him home I've thought about the infection that killed the Whitlocks. About the terrible events I witnessed in the hall, and the fire – I have mourned the women I met there.

Aretta, Rahmi, and Mabel. And poor, tortured Wulfric. He didn't deserve what happened to him.

And yes, I have mourned Mrs Whitlock. I never knew her. I only ever knew the thing that lived inside her. She was a victim as much as the others. A grieving mother, trying to restore her son to life, and protect her husband from the thing that was growing inside him.

According to the police, the Whitlocks went mad, killed their son and three maids, before burning their estate to the ground. All the rumours that had gone before tallied with this narrative, the stories of Mr Whitlock bringing his son back to life with a zombie fungus, only to become infected himself. The folk tale of a witch cursing Lichen Hall.

I still worry that Sylvan and I are infected with the Cordyceps fungus. I am haunted by what I witnessed in Mr Whitlock's bedroom, and any bruise or bump on Sylvan's skin has me watching it like a hawk in case it manifests into something more – spore-like. This is part of the driver in my decision to become a doctor. Perhaps medicine can save us.

But secretly, I take heart in what Sylvan told me, many years ago. A passing comment that I cling to like a ship's mast in a tempest.

He said he saw us both in Paris, on the Eiffel Tower, and that he was a grown-up.

Someday, I will take him there. But I'm putting it off for as long as I can, as though I can buy us time.

'Come on, Pearl,' Sylvan calls from the top of the hill. 'Let's set up the picnic.'

'I'm coming,' I say, wheezing. 'I don't play rugby every weekend like you do. It's an unfair advantage you have in terms of fitness.'

He chuckles. 'But your legs are longer than mine.'

Not for much longer, I think. He's growing at a rate of knots, the weakness in his chest hindering him not a jot from racing all over the place. He's as tall as I am, his dark hair enviably thick and curly. He likes the Beatles, though his passions are Bob Dylan, rugby, photography, and the cinema, a hobby he shares with my father. Dad must have taken Sylvan to see *Willy Wonka and the Chocolate Factory* nine times.

I climb up the hill and try not to gasp too much for air, then set out the picnic blanket. He sits down opposite me, opening the flask and pouring a mug of tea. He hands it to me, then pours one for himself.

'Congratulations,' he says, 'Dr Gorham.'

I notice a light travelling up his index finger, zipping across his hand beneath the cuff of his top. 'Shush,' I say, smiling. 'Don't tell me.'

'You're sure?' he says. 'It's good.'

'Nope,' I say. 'I like surprises. But Dr Gorham *does* have a nice ring to it, doesn't it?'

He grins. Occasionally I'll see this light under his skin, or his expression will change and I know he's sighting. We have never told anyone about his gift, and we don't often speak of it. But sometimes, he looks sad. When I ask what he can see, he shakes his head. Other times, he mentions something nice. Like Lucy and Emma – he says they'll get married one day. This fills me with unspeakable joy; the mere possibility of it.

We eat our picnic in silence, looking over the view below. From up here you can see the whole bustling city, lives in the making and unmaking, people going about trying to make the most of their lives.

On the hillside, a blossoming cherry tree showers the ground with small white petals. Under our feet, a vast web of fungus unknits the material of dead things, making them useful again, helping life to continue on this planet, for better or worse.

If I look hard enough, I can see it, forty-eight million years of evolution: tiny spores hooked to the wind, landing wherever they can find purchase for their wild new lives to begin.

And who can blame them?

Author's Note

The idea for *The Ghost Woods* stems (or spores?) in part from a photograph I came across by Igor Siwanowicz, in which perfectly domed mushrooms bloom from an old copy of *Alice's Adventures in Wonderland*. It's a satisfying image, rich with whimsy and symbolic meaning – the weirdness of the story is made manifest, the mushrooms of Wonderland having nosed out of the pages of the book into the real world. One can't help but wish that the photograph isn't staged – that the mushrooms formed of their own accord. As it happens, Siwanowicz was a neurobiologist as well as a photographer, and injected the book with *Psilocybe cubensis*, producing the mushrooms; but this knowledge doesn't vanquish the magic of the image.

This photograph stayed with me long after I came across it, gently peeling apart my interest in boundaries, margins, liminality. I am drawn to things that loiter in the cusp between the real and imagined, could live – like Alice – very happily in the spaces *in between* the existential binaries that organize reality. I imagine most outsiders will know what I'm talking about; those of us who have never felt like we fully *fit in* feel a connection to things that resist definition, where weirdness is joyously, exuberantly alive.

To me, motherhood is an experience characterized by marginality. In this book, I wanted to re-explore the experience of pregnancy in terms of the ways in which it positions the expectant mother in between, in the margins of profound physical and emotional transitions, and perhaps in terms of her identity, too.

Most of us have sadly heard about the atrocities of the Magdalene Laundries in Tuam, Ireland, and I had believed that such institutions existed only in Ireland. With a great deal of sadness, in my research I learned that mother and baby homes proliferated in their thousands across the UK, Europe, and North America, with the last home closing in the UK in 1990, which feels far too recent.

These twentieth century institutions furthered the work of female repression and control, accommodating pregnant women who were not married until they gave birth, and facilitating the adoption of the illegitimate children by married heterosexual couples. Often, adoptions were not conducted legally or with the full consent of the biological mothers. Generations of women and children were brutalized in these homes, not receiving proper care, and subjected to degrading and inhumane treatment.

Although I was not born in such a home, my mother was seventeen when she had me, and I have learned of the mistreatment she experienced during her pregnancy, and during my birth. With my oldest child now almost the same age my mother was when she had me, this chapter of women's history has taken on new meaning; as I watch my daughters grow and plan their lives, I am ever aware that, just a generation ago, their lives would have been extremely different, shaped by laws and institutions hellbent on controlling their bodies.

Until 1974 contraception in the UK was available only to married couples, and abortion was illegal until 1967 (or 2019 in Northern Ireland). So, without access to contraception or safe abortion, women in the mid-twentieth century had their lives mapped out by a long list of fierce social restrictions. If they had sex outside wedlock, it was likely without contraception. If they fell pregnant, they were disgraced, and often thrown out of the family home. They would almost certainly lose their jobs, like both Pearl and Mabel in *The Ghost Woods*. Without financial support or childcare (and with many losing their jobs and/or being paid much less than men), raising a child was virtually impossible.

These social constraints are astonishing and maddening to learn about; but I wanted to go deeper, to study the human within the snare. The woman who was pregnant at this time, perhaps without consent, and certainly without options – how did *she* experience pregnancy and birth? Certainly she would have sat outside the typical media depiction of the radiantly glowing mother-to-be, the joyous new mother. But surely tenderness existed there, too, and deep love for the baby. And perhaps, alongside these feelings, revulsion and fear. I wanted to write about these experiences without endorsing the binaries that motherhood is often reduced to. I felt I would do an injustice to the women who passed through the mother and baby homes if I did not imagine their experiences as complex and mosaic.

Of course, the history of policing women's bodies coincides with the policing of sexuality. It is harrowing to read about the criminalization of queer folk in the twentieth century, and indeed in the twenty-first century. It is difficult to capture the scale of atrocities committed against members of the LGBTQIA+ community, and often I found myself having to double check the timeline of gay rights due to the sheer recency of some legal amendments; for instance, Section 28 – legislation that prohibited the 'promotion of homosexuality' by schools and councils – was only repealed in England and Wales in 2003. Equal or 'same-sex' marriage only became legal in Northern Ireland in 2020. While it has never been illegal to be lesbian, I wanted to address the criminalization and rights violations faced by lesbians and bisexual women, and to imagine motherhood in this context. In *The Ghost Woods*, I address this symbolically. My intention, particularly in imagining the fates of Mabel, Morven, Aretta, and Rahmi, was to reflect what history tells us about the treatment of queer folk: the stigma, brutalities, and injustices they have experienced, and continue to experience.

Sylvan's perception in 1973 of a future in which women like Lucy and Emma can enjoy the same legal freedoms to marry was a last-minute revelation prompted by my editor, Katie Lumsden, a small celebration of the progress we are making in some parts of the world, and a quiet evocation of the brilliance of in-between spaces, and their promise.

The Ghost Woods is, first and foremost, a gothic novel, the last instalment of a thematic trio that considers our relationship with nature, motherhood, memory, and trauma (the previous two instalments are *The Nesting* and *The Lighthouse Witches*). I suppose the question could legitimately be asked whether motherhood, gay rights, reproductive rights, and gender inequality have any place in a gothic novel. For me, the gothic is *exactly* the space to explore darkness of any kind, and the practice of othering is one of the darkest corners of human history.

To those who have walked in that shadow, who have never belonged in the mainstream or the status quo, or who have simply felt at home in the strange – this book is for you.

Acknowledgements

I'd like to thank my superstar editor, Katie Lumsden, for her superb midwifery of the literary kind, and for taking so much care in the reading of drafts and helping me sculpt them into the book she knew I wanted them to become. Huge thanks as ever to the powerhouse that is Kimberley Young, with whom I've worked now for six years – thank you so very much for your wisdom and unfailing dedication to getting my books out into the world. At HarperCollins, thanks to the sales team, and to Emma Pickard, Amy Winchester, and Emily Goulding for working wonders and being so lovely. To the HarperCollins Canada team, my deepest thanks for growing my career in Canada – we need to celebrate in person!

A big thank-you-with-fireworks to Luke Speed and Anna Weguelin, for working genuine magic in securing TV options – this last year has been incredible, and I definitely owe you both a drink or several.

I'm incredibly lucky to have my excellent agent Alice Lutyens in my corner, and my fabulous US agent, Deborah Schneider. I'm so very grateful for your wisdom, advice, and for how hard you both work on my behalf – I cannot wait to have lunch with you again! You are both so lovely. At Curtis Brown, my sincere thanks to Liz Dennis, Caoimhe White, and Sophia Macaskill for all you do. You're just brilliant.

To my US publishing team, a massive thank you to Miranda Hall, Loren D Jaggers, and Jessica Plummer for being genuine publishing rock stars. I had such fun meeting you all in New

York! Thank you for growing my career and getting my books into the hands of readers in the US.

I was very fortunate to have a third book cover created by the publishing world's Michelangelo, Andrew Davis. It's as though Andrew sees inside my mind and plucks out exactly the kind of images I thought of when writing the book, before weaving them into a spellbinding cover. Thank you, Andrew, and please never stop designing my covers. Thanks also to Gilly Stern for reading and commenting on an early draft, and to Charlotte Webb for excellent copyediting.

To my colleagues at the University of Glasgow: Elizabeth Reeder, Zoë Strachan, Sophie Collins, Colin Herd, and Louise Welsh – thank you all once again for your support and friendship. Thanks also to my students – I hope I've followed my own incessant harping on about making space for the reader here.

To my international publishers, booksellers, book bloggers, book buyers, audio actors, librarians, and readers who shout good things about my books on social media – you have no idea the difference you make to the literature world, and to me. Thank you so much.

I started writing novels when my oldest child, Melody, was two, and Phoenix, was one, and now they are gigantic teenagers, joined by younger siblings, Summer and Willow. Thank you all for being quiet when Mummy has a Zoom interview, and for tolerating me being constantly on my laptop – please all read more books and write down all your ideas. Also, brush your teeth.

Thanks as always to my husband, Jared Jess-Cooke, for his unwavering encouragement and support, for letting me bounce ideas off him, and for making me laugh when I needed it most. I love you.

If you loved *The Ghost Woods*, make sure you pick up the new gothic thriller from C.J. Cooke...

1901. Nicky Duthie awakes on a whaling ship, the *Ormen*, held against her will. The ship's crew are all owed something only she can give them.

1973. Decades later, the *Ormen* is found, but with just one body left on board, his face and feet mutilated, his cabin locked from the inside.

Now, as urban explorer Dominique travels to the northernmost tip of Iceland, to the final resting place of the *Ormen*'s wreck, she's determined to uncover the ship's secrets.

But she's not alone. Something is here with her. And it's seeking revenge...

Available autumn 2023